Rider's Revenge

ALESSANDRA CLARKE

BOOKS BY ALESSANDRA CLARKE

The Rider's Revenge Trilogy

Rider's Revenge

Rider's Rescue

Rider's Resolve

RIDER'S

BOOK I OF THE RIDER'S REVENGE TRILOGY

REVENGE

ALESSANDRA CLARKE

DEDICATION

This book is dedicated to my mother. Without her support and encouragement the last few years, this book wouldn't have been possible.

And to my father. He always wanted to be a writer but put being a loving husband and father first so never had the chance to achieve his dream.

A NOTE ON PRONUNCIATION

Members of the tribes have names that use an apostrophe after the initial consonant. For example, K'lrsa and G'van.

To pronounce these names, substitute an i or e for the apostrophe. For example, K'lrsa = Killrisa.

This is a full listing of the tribal names used in the book:

B'nin = Benin
D'lan = Dilan
F'lia = Filia
G'la = Gila
G'van = Givan
K'lrsa = Killrisa
K'var = Kivar
L'dia = Lidia
L'ral = Liral
M'lara = Milara
V'na = Vina

1

K'lrsa wiped the sweat from her brow and pushed a strand of black hair away from her face. She tucked it into the long braid that ran down the center of her back as she rolled her shoulders, feeling the way the baru-hide vest clung to her skin, already stiff from a morning of riding across the arid plains.

The sun beat down upon her, merciless in his bright regard, as he baked her already tanned skin.

Fallion, her beautiful golden horse, shone like a jewel in the late day sun as he pranced sideways with impatience. He wasn't one for stillness. An *Amalanee* horse, he loved to run free and wild across the plains, the wind flowing through his thick mane as he raced across the barren landscape, his golden hooves barely touching the ground.

So did K'lrsa. There was nothing better than a day spent with Fallion, just the two of them, riding as far and as fast as they could.

Fallion shook his head and snorted.

"Shhh, *micora*." K'lrsa stroked his neck as she studied the herd of baru ahead of them.

About thirty of the fleet-footed creatures nibbled on an area of dry sage grass, seemingly at ease. Their slender forms blended into the desert in the distance—beige on beige—as they crowded together, looking in all directions for predators. The black and white stripes that ran from their delicate horns to the tips of their noses were the only parts of them visible in the late afternoon light. Their horns lay close to their skulls, sweeping backward a handspan past short tufted ears that twitched at the slightest sound.

She'd been tracking the herd off and on for days, rising each morning before the sun was up, sneaking out of camp before her mother could stop her, and only stumbling back home when the sun kissed the horizon goodnight.

She wished she could just stay with them, but her mother would never allow it.

The first night she didn't return to camp would be the last. Her mother would send her brother, D'lan, to drag her back like some child, shaming her in front of everyone.

She was a Rider now. Sixteen summers old. She could take care of herself. Too bad her mother and brother refused to acknowledge that.

Well, she'd show them.

And everyone else.

Show them that the faith her father had in her was valid— that she deserved their respect.

She wasn't a child anymore.

And today was the day they'd all see what a great hunter she was.

Maybe then her mother would finally quit talking about marriage and babies and realize that K'lrsa's true future was as a Rider—protector and hunter for the tribe—not as the wife of some arrogant fool like G'van. The man never listened; she'd refused him so many times she'd lost count.

Fallion pawed at the ground, bringing K'lrsa back to the moment. The baru were restless, the wind had shifted and now carried her scent towards them. Their black noses twitched and they tensed, no longer grazing as they scanned the plains for threat.

They were nervous beasts, quick to flight.

At the slightest hint of danger, the herd would flee to the desert sands where no predator dare follow. Nothing could match the speed of baru on desert sands. They seemed to glide across the surface while horses and desert cats sank into the soft surface, floundering in their wake.

It was now or never.

"Ready, *micora*?" she whispered in Fallion's ear. He nodded his head, body thrumming with anticipation.

"Now."

Fallion burst forward, his hooves kicking up a fine layer of dust as he raced towards the herd. K'lrsa's heart soared as she and Fallion moved as one, perfectly in sync like a beautiful deadly dance as they bore down on the herd.

The baru fled towards the desert sands, leaping across the dry, cracked ground.

K'lrsa leaned over Fallion's side, one hand tangled in his mane as she chose her target—a young male on the edge of the herd that leaped ahead of them, all grace and light. He tried to flee back into the center of the herd, but she maneuvered Fallion to cut him away from the others.

The swift air of their passage cooled the sweat on K'lrsa's brow even as the sharp scents of crushed sage grass and dust filled her nose. "Steady now, *micora*," she whispered as much to herself as Fallion as she released her hold on his mane to draw her bow and nock an arrow to it. Her gaze never left her target.

It was risky to let go of his mane, and she'd never try it with any other horse, but she knew Fallion, knew she was in no danger of falling with him beneath her.

K'lrsa took a deep breath and found the hunter's version of the Core—that heightened state of awareness where everything slowed down and came into focus. Time seemed to stop as she pulled the arrow taut, the bow string vibrating under her fingers, begging for release.

She held there, pausing, savoring the moment as she aimed for the soft spot on the baru's back.

Finally, she released and heard the twang of the bow string as the arrow sped towards its target, wobbling left before straightening out again.

The arrow spun through the air, each rotation visible to her mind's eye, each breath taking an eternity as they thundered forward, the herd racing ahead of them, her target glancing back at her in wide-eyed fear.

K'lrsa felt a thrill of triumph as the arrow raced towards the baru.

She was going to do it.

After months of being told it wasn't possible, and days of trying and failing, she was going to be the first Rider to kill a baru from horseback.

Her. K'lrsa. A "mere girl."

She was going to do it.

The baru leapt to the side at the last moment; the arrow buried itself in the dry ground by a large cactus.

K'lrsa cursed and felt Fallion slow beneath her as he responded to her unspoken command.

No.

No. She was not going to quit this time. She was not going to fail again.

She *had* to succeed before her father returned to camp.

She had to.

She was hot and tired and sore, her clothes sticking to her body and chafing her skin, but this was her last chance and she refused to quit. Not when she was so close. Fallion wasn't even winded, even after a day of hard riding.

She urged him forward until it felt like they really were flying like the *Amalanee* horses of legend. The wind of their passage whipped strands of hair and dust into her eyes, but she ignored them.

She would not fail.

Not again.

She leaned forward, her gaze focused on her escaping prey. She no longer saw the sweeping plains around her, no longer felt the hot sun beating down upon her back. She didn't even smell the approach of the desert as they came alongside the stumbling baru.

K'lrsa steadied herself to take another shot.

Fallion stumbled and only then did K'lrsa realize how close the desert was. A hundred more steps and the baru would reach safety.

"Steady, *micora*." She nocked another arrow and urged Fallion to a final burst of speed until they were practically on top of the young baru, his horns easily within reach.

K'lrsa leaned to the side, almost slipping from her saddle as she focused on the one spot on the baru's back where an arrow might strike and kill.

She took a steadying breath.

She could do this.

She could.

No matter what anyone else said.

She loosed the arrow, sending a prayer to the Great Father Sun and the Lady Moon to guide its path.

Time slowed as the arrow spun through the air.

Closer.

Closer.

There!

It struck true, burrowing into the soft flesh of the baru's back. The gentle beast stumbled; it tripped and collapsed forward as the rest of the herd raced onward to the safety of the desert.

Fallion narrowly missed colliding with the baru as it fell; he leapt over its bulk at the last possible moment and carried forward a few steps. His hooves sank into the soft sand of the true desert and he lurched to a stop.

K'lrsa jumped to the ground and ended the baru's suffering with one quick stroke of her knife, sending a prayer of thanks as she did so.

She knelt there, breathing heavily, as the sounds and sensations of the world rushed back to her awareness.

The sun burned her skin, its bright light harsh as it flashed into her eyes. The musty scent of the baru and the iron tang of its blood filled the air. That and the stench of her own sweat were almost enough to make her gag.

She shook, barely able to keep a grip on her knife.

She'd done it. She'd finally done it!

No.

They'd done it.

She and Fallion.

She scratched Fallion's ears as he nuzzled at her. She didn't know what she'd do without him. He was the best gift her father could've given her. A real, live *Amalanee* horse, so rare she'd never seen another one.

Fallion chuffed her hair and K'lrsa buried her face against his sweet-smelling neck. "We did it, *micora*. We did it."

She marveled how Fallion's golden coat was still flawlessly clean after a full day's hunting.

If only she could say the same for herself. She was dirty and sweaty and soon to be covered in blood.

Her mother would be horrified, but K'lrsa didn't care. Not in the slightest. She was a Rider.

She kissed the small white teardrop-shaped mark in the middle of Fallion's forehead.

Fallion nickered softly and K'lrsa glanced towards the distant horizon. The sun was low, coloring the clouds over the distant mountains a brilliant red and orange like the entire sky was on fire.

She'd be hard-pressed to field dress the baru and make it home before the sun set.

"It's okay, *micora*. We're not in the true desert. The Trickster can't hurt us here. But you're right. We should hurry."

If she didn't make it back before dark, today's triumph would mean nothing. All her mother would see was her reckless, irresponsible daughter who refused to grow up and put aside her childish obsession with being a Rider.

K'lrsa quickly gutted the baru. She ignored the grel that lowered their heavy bodies to the ground, drawn by the scent of blood and death. Their beady red eyes watched her every movement.

She hated the things. They stunk like a rotted corpse, their grey feathers coated with the blood of the animals they consumed. They'd eat anything, preferably dead, but alive worked, too. She'd seen them devour a wounded desert cat once—the sight and sounds of that day were something she'd never forget.

The grel waddled towards her, hissing and cawing at each other as they crowded ever closer, each one vying for position.

"Back." She waved her arms at them, but they didn't retreat, just slowed their approach.

If it were up to her, she'd drive them far away and give them nothing. But her father said it was always better to give death its due rather than wait for it to collect what you didn't want to give, so she flung the entrails at them.

The grel pounced on the bloody feast, tearing and ripping at the glistening mass as they fought amongst themselves for the choicest bits.

K'lrsa used their distraction to load the rest of the meat on Fallion's back. She swallowed heavily at the stench as they crept closer, demanding more.

She ignored them and mounted Fallion. "Let's go."

Fallion didn't need any more encouragement than that. He stormed through the mass of scavenger birds. They scattered to the side, cawing their displeasure.

When the grel were finally far behind her and it was just K'lrsa and Fallion riding alone across the darkening plain, K'lrsa allowed herself to smile.

She'd done it. She'd really done it. Normally it would take four hunters to bring down a baru—two to drive the herd and two to lie in wait hoping for a lucky shot as they thundered past. But she'd killed one all by herself.

Her. K'lrsa dan V'na of the White Horse Tribe. She'd done what no one else ever had.

She threw her arms wide and her head back and shouted in joy.

This was the best day of her life.

<u>2</u>

By the time K'lrsa reached camp, the sun had fully disappeared behind the mountains and the air carried the chill of an early fall night. Soon they'd have to move closer to the desert, chasing its heat as the nights grew colder.

The sweat on K'lrsa's skin had long since dried, leaving only salt and dirt behind. The rush of the hunt had faded, too. She now found herself shivering as she longed for a thickly-woven horse hair blanket around her shoulders and a fire to warm her hands.

Torches formed a perimeter around camp, casting as much shadow as light on the gathering of over a hundred tents clustered together in smaller family units. Families sat around cook fires, eating their evening meal and talking softly, their voices and the delicious scent of their meals carrying into the darkness where K'lrsa sat.

Most would be eating hare or the small desert birds that were so common in this area, if they had any meat at all. None would have baru meat; it had been too long since the Riders had mounted a hunt. They were too busy looking for raiders and worrying about attacks that would likely never come.

The tribes had been at peace for hundreds of years. Life in the desert was too difficult for the tribes to war with one another and the outside world didn't care enough to pay them any attention.

But the rumors of night attacks on the other tribes couldn't be ignored. Not when men, women, and children had gone missing. So now the Riders mounted patrols and looked for danger in every direction, turning away from their primary role as hunters.

K'lrsa was a Rider, but she wasn't allowed to patrol with the rest. She should be. She'd spent a week alone in the desert and killed a baru during a hunt just like the rest had.

It wasn't enough, though. It never was. Her father said she was too young. That if there really were raiders prowling somewhere in the night they might harm her.

All she wanted was for someone to acknowledge that she was just as strong and capable as anyone else. She wasn't a child anymore. She was a Rider.

Well, now they'd all see. Because, thanks to her, tomorrow the tribe would have baru meat once more.

They'd hear her story of her hunt and finally understand that she was a grown woman and as capable as any Rider. She couldn't wait to see their eyes when she told everyone how she and Fallion had accomplished the impossible.

That was tomorrow, though.

First she had to face her mother.

Her family tents were on the other end of camp, and normally K'lrsa would ride along the perimeter to sneak home as quietly as possible.

But not tonight. Tonight she wanted everyone to see her and know what she'd accomplished.

She and Fallion had barely emerged from the smoke of the torches when her older brother, D'lan, stepped forward to grab Fallion's harness. "Where have you been? What were you doing out after dark?" he demanded.

Fallion bared his teeth and D'lan jumped back as if burned. He still blocked their path, his arms crossed tight against his chest, a frown creasing his brow.

Nothing new there. D'lan was always unhappy. K'lrsa was just glad he'd finally married and moved away to his own set of tents so she didn't have to see his frown at every single meal.

She forced a smile onto her face. "I was hunting. See?" She gestured at the baru slung behind her.

D'lan barely glanced at the dead animal. "I see." His voice was flat, his eyes black and angry in the shifting light of the torches.

"D'lan, I killed a baru. *By myself.*" She leaned forward, looking for the slightest hint he was impressed.

He shrugged. "And what good would that do if the Trickster took you? Or raiders?"

K'lrsa rolled her eyes. There was no winning with him. Never had been. "Well, I wasn't, was I? I'm right here. With a baru. That I killed myself. Aren't you going to at least acknowledge that?"

This wasn't going at all how she'd thought it would. Of course, she should've known this was exactly how things would go. Her father was the only one who took pride in her.

D'lan glared at her. "Congratulations on being impulsive and irresponsible, K'lrsa. Way to risk your life and the life of your horse. Now give me the baru. Mom has a guest and she won't appreciate you showing up with a carcass slung over your shoulder."

K'lrsa thought about refusing, but she really couldn't. While her father was gone, D'lan was leader of the Riders and had the right to order her to do anything. She was just lucky it had never occurred to him to specifically order her to stay in camp.

"Fine."

As she untied the baru and let it slide to the ground, she muttered. "You know I did have my moon stone, D'lan. I would've been safe even if I had been caught in the desert at night."

D'lan threw the baru over his shoulders and stared at her for a long moment. "There are other threats than the shifting sands, K'lrsa."

He turned and walked away before she could say anything else.

K'lrsa rode Fallion around the perimeter of the camp, no longer wanting anyone to see her. All the joy and excitement from earlier in the day was gone, fled along with the warmth of the sun.

She knew what kind of guest her mother would have. Some boy who wanted to impress her, maybe even convince her to marry him at this year's annual gathering.

She grimaced at the blood caked to her skin and clothes. The knees of her pants were so dirty they were almost gray and a white line of sweat followed the neckline of her vest. She took a surreptitious sniff under her arm and winced.

When was the last time she'd taken a sweat bath? A week ago? Longer?

She tried to shove the pieces of hair around her face back into her braid, but it was hopeless, the braid snarled and tangled beyond any chance of redemption.

She shrugged.

What did she care anyway? Not like it would be someone who interested her. She'd long since given up on that. When you were faster, a better shot, and smarter than all the boys you knew, it was hard to muster much interest in yet another eager but unsatisfactory prospect.

If she could ever find a man like her father, she'd happily marry, but so far none were even close.

She wouldn't give up the life of a Rider for anyone, but she did want to find someone. A true equal. Who wouldn't?

Unfortunately, given her choices, that wasn't likely to happen. About as likely as Fallion suddenly taking off in flight. She patted his neck as she chuckled at the ridiculous image.

She knew it wasn't worth trying any more. Too bad her mother didn't.

3

K'lrsa took as much time as she could currying Fallion's coat, but there really wasn't all that much to do; even at his worst Fallion was far more presentable than she was at her best.

At last, when she couldn't delay any longer, K'lrsa trudged towards her family tents, walking as slowly as she could without making it too obvious.

Her four family tents, each dyed blue at the top and patterned with blue stars, surrounded a merry fire at the far edge of the camp. A pot hung over the flames; the delicious smell made her stomach grumble and reminded her that she hadn't eaten since morning.

Three people sat around the fire, silent. K'lrsa's mother, still beautiful with her high cheekbones, pointed chin, and generous lips, stared into the fire, her jaw clenched in fury. Time and temperament had etched wrinkles around her eyes and forehead.

Across from her sat M'lara—at eight summers old she was long and leggy and overflowing with energy. K'lrsa smiled as she noticed how hard M'lara was struggling to remain seated and quiet. She was a late-life surprise for K'lrsa's parents, but their pride and joy. K'lrsa's too. Already she was beautiful with her long black hair and eyes the color of dusk.

For a moment K'lrsa hoped that the man silhouetted on the far side of the fire was her father, finally back from his trip to the Tall Bluff Tribe.

But no. Her mother would never be so tense if he'd returned. The two were still like newlyweds, holding hands and staring longingly into one another's eyes whenever they had a chance. K'lrsa's mother always seemed to glow when he was around.

K'lrsa paused in the shadows. She didn't want this. Not tonight. She'd pretend she'd never run into D'lan and go find her best friend, F'lia, instead. Let this man, whoever he was, leave before she crept home.

"K'lrsa, don't be a fool. We know you're there," her mother called as she started to turn away.

K'lrsa stepped forward into the firelight. M'lara ran to greet her. "K'lrsa! You're back. I was so worried about you. Mom said maybe the desert had taken you. Or a big desert cat. Or raiders."

K'lrsa met her mother's eyes across the fire. "Have you no faith in me at all?"

Her mother shrugged. "It's a dangerous world out there, K'lrsa."

"Well I'm just fine, thanks." Before she could say more, their visitor stood to greet her.

G'van of the Black Horse Tribe. The last man she wanted to see. Ever.

He was beautiful, no doubt about it, with his bronze-colored skin and green eyes. And tall and muscular and a first son and...

And no doubt that he knew just how beautiful he was.

He ran his hand through the long black hair that he wore down like a musician instead of tied back like the Rider he supposedly was. Probably expected her to swoon at his feet. Arrogant, vain fool. How he'd ever passed the Rider's Challenge, she didn't know. He probably couldn't survive a day in the desert, let alone a week.

She fought the urge to step back from the cloying scent of flowers that wafted her way as he approached. What kind of a man scented himself with flowers?

"Your mother was about to send me out to rescue you." He smiled down at her, standing far too close.

"Like you'd be any help." She dropped her saddle by her tent and stepped around him.

"K'lrsa," her mother hissed.

K'lrsa served herself a heaping bowl of stew and sat down next to M'lara. "Well, as you can both see, I managed just fine myself, thank you."

She wanted to take off the sweaty, bloody vest, but she didn't dare with G'van there watching her. If it had just been family around the cook fire she would've thought nothing about stripping off the vest until she'd finished eating, but she didn't need G'van eyeing her like a prized mare he wanted to mount; no more than he already was.

Most men of the tribes ignored a woman's nakedness, but G'van had picked up bad habits from his friends in the neighboring Daliphate. The way he stared at her sometimes made her decidedly uncomfortable.

The bowl of millet with rabbit meat and sour greens smelled delicious. Her stomach grumbled loudly into the silence. K'lrsa could feel everyone's eyes on her, but she ignored them.

She shoved a spoonful of stew into her mouth and immediately spat it back out. "What did you put in this?" She scraped at her tongue to remove the bitter, awful taste.

"Salt." G'van sat down across from her. "I brought it for you. As a gift."

He nodded towards a small pile of items arrayed on a cloth near her mother. K'lrsa could see a bolt of green silk displayed proudly on top. What did she need with silk? She was a warrior not some spoiled woman of the Daliphate.

"Ugh. Why?" She didn't really expect or want an answer.

"Salt is precious." G'van stared at her like she was simple. "It's one of the most in-demand trade goods in the Daliphate. Men pay gold for it. Lots of it."

"Really? Why?" K'lrsa took a long drink of water from her waterskin and swished it around her mouth, trying to remove the taste of the vile substance. It almost worked.

"K'lrsa..." Her mother's tone was a warning.

14

"Well, honestly, mother. He brings all these…things…to impress me and he clearly doesn't know the first thing about me. Silk? Salt?" She turned to G'van. "You want to win my affection, bring me a bow. Bring me hunting leathers. Or sugar cubes for my horse." She turned back to her mother. "Is this really who you'd have me marry?"

G'van lurched to his feet. "I brought you gifts any *real* woman would treasure. But you can't see that, can you? You think you're better than everyone. Well, you're not."

He glared down at her, his hands clenched in fists. "You should be flattered I'd even think of marrying you. You'd be lucky to have me. Who else wants a stinky, dirty girl more interested in riding her horse than a man?"

K'lrsa leapt to her feet and slapped him.

G'van clutched at his face, his eyes flat black as he glared down at her. "You're going to end up old and alone if you aren't careful, K'lrsa."

"I'd rather end up old and alone than with someone like you." She stood toe to toe with him, glaring into those angry black eyes, her hands clenched into fists at her side, daring him to attack her.

He stepped away, shaking his head in disgust as he grabbed his saddle bags. "You'll beg me to take you one day. You'll see. I'm going to rule the tribes and then you'll come crawling on your belly to me, offering me anything just to look at you."

K'lrsa laughed. "In your dreams, G'van. No man rules the tribes."

He stared at her for a long moment before replying with complete sincerity. "I will someday. Times are changing. The tribes need a strong man to show them the path to the future."

She shivered. He really believed it.

She shook her head. "The only place you'd lead the tribes is to ruin and destruction. My father would never let that happen."

"Is that so?" G'van stared at her for a long moment, a sneer curling his lip. The shadows cast by the fire made him look like a demon. "You think your father's going to stop me?" He laughed and shook his head.

K'lrsa felt a chill down her spine as G'van disappeared into the darkness.

4

The rest of dinner was an awkward painful experience with K'lrsa's mother glaring across the fire at her and K'lrsa focusing all her effort on choking down the over-salted bowl of food.

How hard was it for a man to actually *see* her? To see who she was and what she wanted instead of assuming that she wanted what every girl must want?

She glared over at the pile of silks and trinkets. F'lia would love everything there.

But K'lrsa wasn't F'lia.

F'lia was a healer and an artist. She loved pretty things and was soft and kind.

K'lrsa was a hunter. A warrior. She loved her horse and the thrill of the hunt and the good, honest sweat of pushing herself to her physical limits.

Just once, she wanted a man who could see that.

After she managed to choke down enough food to calm her hunger, K'lrsa went to bed. It was still early, but there was no point in sitting across the fire from her mother for another moment.

She dreamed that night, a dream unlike any she'd ever experienced before. It was so real, so vivid, everything more intense than the world she knew. The colors were sharper, the scents stronger; the wind felt like a hand actually caressing her skin.

She found herself in the deep, deep desert. She'd never been there before, but she recognized it nonetheless.

It was the darkest time before dawn, but she could somehow see every detail. The Lady Moon shone bright and full in the sky above, surrounded by so many stars they almost filled the sky.

K'lrsa walked barefoot across the soft sand as it shifted and slid beneath her, as if alive.

A great city rose before her. Empty, desolate. It waited, watching her.

Nothing lived here. No animal. No plant. She knew this without looking.

This place was like an empty vessel, waiting to be filled.

She jumped when she heard the sound of another behind her. His soft steps boomed like thunder in the silence as he made his way to her side.

He studied her as she studied him. His shirt was the most brilliant blue she'd ever seen, like someone had taken the sky of a midsummer day and captured it in cloth. It matched his eyes. His pants were striped in more colors than she'd ever seen in one place at one time—red, orange, yellow, black, white, green, and blue.

He was young, like her, his skin a beautiful golden brown, his hair as black as the blackest night.

He smiled at her and raised an eyebrow. She blushed as she glanced down to see that she wore the garments of the Moon Dance—long, flowing strips of cloth that moved as if blown by a soft breeze.

They didn't speak, but she knew in that moment that this man was the one she'd sought.

An equal. A man who would challenge but respect her. Who could love her softness but support her strength.

He held out his hand and she took it. That first touch sent fire coursing through her skin.

They walked towards the distant city, but with each step it seemed to grow more and more distant.

And then he was gone and so was the city.

A woman stood before K'lrsa, so bright and beautiful K'lrsa couldn't look directly at her.

"One day perhaps, my child. But not yet." The woman's voice was soft, loving, the embodiment of motherhood.

"When?" K'lrsa stared into the distance where the city had stood.

The woman's laughter was refreshing and cool, like water trickling over rocks. "Don't you want to know the path you'd have to take, first? Perhaps it's a path you would choose not to tread."

K'lrsa raised her chin and tried to look the Lady Moon in the face, but had to squint her eyes against the woman's shining presence. "I'm a Rider. I can walk any path. I can overcome any obstacle."

For just the briefest moment, K'lrsa saw sad eyes watching her with irises as deep and vast as the night sky. "I have no doubt you can, my child. But there's a difference between being *able* to face any challenge and *wanting* to face it."

"So tell me of this path, then, if you think it would be so challenging."

The woman laughed again. "So fierce, so proud." She glanced towards the horizon. "Unfortunately, my husband rises soon and I must leave. You and your mate will meet here again another night."

As she started to fade away with the rising sun, the Lady Moon added, "Take what joy you can while you can K'lrsa dan V'na of the White Horse Tribe. The storm gathers."

K'lrsa awoke to the memory of thunder and the quiet of her tent. She stared at the point in the ceiling where baru hides intersected to form a peak and stroked the moon stone around her neck, feeling its lingering warmth as it faded from a brilliant blue back to its usual dull gray.

She'd proven herself yesterday, and now the Lady Moon had come to her.

To her, K'lrsa dan V'na of the White Horse Tribe.

She smiled in the darkness as she waited for dawn so she could find her father. He'd know what she should do next.

5

K'lrsa left camp immediately after breakfast. Her father was already two days late returning from a visit to the Tall Bluff Tribe, but she wasn't worried about him. He was too smart and strong for anything to ever happen to him.

She rode throughout the day, enjoying the time alone with Fallion. It was a cooler day, the sun hidden behind clouds for most of it.

The path she followed wove through a small grove of trees—such a rarity she slowed Fallion down, running her hand along the rough bark of each skinny trunk, marveling that anything could stand taller than her on horseback.

Once they were past the trees and under the wide open sky, she let Fallion gallop, laughing as they sped across the wide open plains, the wind whipping her hair from her face as a small flock of birds took flight ahead.

When she finally saw her father in the distance, she paused. He rode slowly, his shoulders slumped, staring at the spot between his horse's ears. For a moment, she thought it wasn't her father, that someone had stolen his horse. The man she saw wasn't the powerful, confident man she knew.

But it was her father. Up close she saw that the changes ran deeper. His face had always been creased with wrinkles from long years of living under the desert sun, but they'd always been lines of happiness. Now faint worry lines creased his forehead and pulled at the edges of his eyes.

He'd aged ten years in ten days.

"What happened? Didn't they listen to you?" She reined Fallion around to fall into place at his side.

He shook his head, staring off into the distance. "I didn't even try. How could I?"

She reached out and forced him to stop. "What are you talking about?"

He stared into her eyes for a moment and she saw such sorrow and despair that she almost cried. "They were just as bad, K'lrsa. Just like the cursed Black Horse Tribe. The first night I was there, they passed around a clear liquid, fire ice they called it. It burned the throat and altered the senses. Men who drank it passed out at the fire, unable to stumble to their tents. And the ones that weren't drinking were lost in the haze of smokeweed. And the things they talked about…"

He shook his head and urged his horse forward, hands clenched tight to his reins.

K'lrsa trailed along behind him. "But…you could still try, couldn't you?"

Sunlight shone off the gray streaks in his dark hair. When had her father grown old?

"With another tribe, perhaps. There have to be some that are untainted." He ran a hand through his hair. "I have to keep trying. If we allow this corruption to spread, the tribes will die. And then who will protect the Hidden City?"

He shook his head and stared ahead, lost somewhere she couldn't see. "We've grown soft, K'lrsa. We forget what the desert is really like. You can never let down your guard. Never assume you're safe."

He turned his attention to the distant mountains as if he could see the foreign men who lived there. "It's their fault, but ours, too. The men of the Daliphate may have brought this corruption to us, but we embraced it."

They rode for a long time in silence as her father clenched and unclenched his jaw. Finally, he shook his head and forced a smile.

"Enough of these troubles. What of you? What have you been up to while I was gone? Did your mother manage to marry you off yet?"

K'lrsa grimaced. "She tried. G'van of the Black Horse Tribe came again last night offering me silks and salt."

Her father laughed. "That arrogant little fool doesn't know the first thing about wooing my desert cat, does he?"

The sound of his laugh was like sunshine peeking out from behind clouds. K'lrsa couldn't help but smile back at him. "No, he doesn't. And, well…" She blushed. "I kind of told him as much."

Her father nodded. "Good. You can do better than him."

K'lrsa wanted to tell her father what G'van had said about ruling the tribes one day, but she didn't want to see his face cloud over again, so instead she told him about the baru.

Her father stopped his horse and pulled her close for a fierce hug. "Well done, K'lrsa. I'm so proud of you."

All her disappointment from the night before melted away when she saw the love shining in his eyes.

They spent the rest of the day talking about the hunt. Her father wanted to know every single detail. He made her go back and repeat everything two or even three times, nodding his head in approval. Once more he was the man she knew—confident, intelligent, and certain of the future.

When they finally stopped for the night, he grasped her hand in the Rider's clasp. "I'm proud of you, K'lrsa. You're a true Rider. Never let anyone question that or take that away from you."

Her cheeks hurt from the smile that spread across her cheeks. She knew this was a serious moment and a Rider should be reserved at such times, but she didn't care. She sprang forward and hugged him. "Thank you, Dad."

He always knew just what to say. She didn't know what she'd do if she ever lost him.

6

As K'lrsa and her father sat by the fire, eating roasted hare and enjoying the stillness of a night alone on the plains, her father sank back into brooding, his gaze fixed on the leaping flames. The distant sound of a night bird hunting and the crackle of the fire were the only sounds.

The moon rode high in the sky, but she was just a fraction of herself. Soon she'd retreat for a few nights to spend time with her husband, Father Sun, before returning and growing towards fullness once more.

K'lrsa smelled a thunderstorm on the breeze and watched as lightning lit up the far horizon, followed a few moments later by the sound of thunder. She touched her moon stone, wondering if the storm would reach them and they'd be wet and miserable for the rest of the night, but no, the storm would pass them by.

Finally, her father spoke into the silence. "They've betrayed us, K'lrsa."

"Who?"

He took a long swallow from the skin of fermented mare's milk at his side. He hardly ever drank, but tonight he'd had enough to slur his words and make him sway slightly. "The Black Horse Tribe." He stared at her. "Do you know what they've done?"

K'lrsa didn't dare speak; she just shook her head.

"They led traders across the desert."

K'lrsa gasped. No. No one of the tribes would do that. Would they? Protecting the desert was core to who the tribes were.

"For four hundred years we've protected the desert and they just throw it away. And for what? Gold? Silk?" He spat to the side, the most deadly insult she knew.

"Are you sure?"

He stared into the flames for a long time before continuing. "Do you want to know what's worse?"

What was worse than leading strangers across the desert? She licked her lips, waiting for him to continue.

"They're trading in slaves."

Her father was normally a gentle man. A capable warrior, yes, but one who sought peace and compromise first. Not tonight.

He snarled as he said, "It's not enough to censure them. We have to cut them out. Remove the infection before it destroys us all. We have to expel them." He took another long drink and glared at the fire.

K'lrsa grabbed his arm. "No, father. It can't be as bad as that. If you cut them out of the tribes, they'll be lost. The Black Horse Tribe doesn't have any plains land left. All they have is desert. If you expel them, they'll be forever lost in the shifting sands. No one deserves that."

He stared at her for a long moment. "We have to, K'lrsa. It's our only hope. We have to expel the Black Horse Tribe and cut off all ties with the Daliphate before they ruin us all."

She shivered. She wouldn't wish expulsion on anyone. Not even G'van.

"What of the innocents? Surely not everyone in the tribe is corrupt."

Her father gave her a long look as if he'd dispute her claim, but then he shrugged and looked away. "Let them join other tribes then. Or let them run to the Daliph and beg him for shelter. He's the cause of this poison after all. Him and his need for trade."

"Dad..."

He shook off her hold. "Enough. I won't be swayed. This is what must happen."

Her father stalked away into the night, leaving K'lrsa alone with the dying embers of the fire. She shivered as she watched him disappear into the darkness.

G'van was right. Times were changing.

7

Two weeks later, K'lrsa ate her breakfast in silence as her parents talked about the annual gathering. It had taken her father days to convince the other leaders of the tribe to agree to his plan, but finally they'd voted to recommend expulsion of the Black Horse Tribe at the next annual gathering.

He was still trying to convince them to cut ties with the Daliphate, but that wasn't likely to happen. No one wanted to sacrifice the luxuries that eased their daily lives.

The light and gaiety her parents normally shared was gone, replaced with a lingering sense of dread. Even though no one was nearby, they spoke in tense whispers, glancing around as if they expected enemies to jump from behind a tent at any moment.

Their fears were justified.

Two nights before, the camp had been attacked. L'ral, F'lia's intended, had surprised the attackers in the middle of the night as he made his way to the privy area, so they hadn't done as much damage as they could have, but everyone was on edge knowing how close they'd been.

It was men from the Daliphate. L'ral had managed to take a scrap of green and blue striped cloth from one of the men. He'd waved it around as he described how he'd struggled with the men, desperately trying to save as many horses as he could, but finally been felled by a shallow sword slice to the ribs and a knock to the head.

Ten horses had been stolen that night. Almost a fifth of the horses in camp.

At least no one had been killed, but it was only a matter of time. She could see that thought lurking in her parents' eyes as they watched her.

How would the tribes, used to hundreds of years of peace, defend themselves against the men of the Daliphate with their gleaming swords and violent ways?

Her father had sent a party of Riders, led by D'lan, after them, but the Riders had yet to return. They should have by now.

K'lrsa had wanted to go, but her father refused. He said he wouldn't risk both of his children at once.

That's what he said, but she knew the truth. He didn't really believe in her.

She ate her meal in sullen silence and chafed at the fact that she was no longer allowed to leave camp. Fallion was just as restless as she was. He strained against his tether when she visited him each day.

She was trying to figure out how to convince her father to let her go for a ride when L'ral ran up to their fire, gasping for breath.

"What is it?" Her father set aside the bowl of grains he hadn't really been eating.

"Men. To the east. At least ten of them. More of the Daliph's men."

Her father exchanged a worried glance with her mother. "Gather the remaining Riders," he said to L'ral.

L'ral nodded and ran away.

"Oh, B'nin. Is this wise? Do you have enough Riders to fight them if you catch them?"

He pulled her close and buried his face in her hair. "I'd rather meet them in the desert than have them attack you, V'na. Don't worry. I'll come back to you."

K'lrsa looked away. She wished someday she'd find the love and passion her parents shared, but until then seeing them together just reminded her of everything she didn't have in her own life.

Well, at least not outside her dreams. She'd dreamt of the young man twice more since that first dream. They couldn't talk, but they didn't need to. More words than they could exchange in a lifetime passed between them with each glance or touch.

As L'ral's voice rose in the high ki-ki-ki of the Rider's call, K'lrsa stood. "I just need to get my bow and then I'll meet you at the horse lines."

Her father stared at her for a long moment, frozen.

"B'nin…" Her mother grabbed at his hand.

He clasped her hand in his. "I know, V'na." He took a deep breath. "K'lrsa…"

K'lrsa knew that look.

She backed away, shaking her head. "No. No, Dad. You can't do this to me. Not again. I'm a Rider. Let me come with you!"

He stood and held his hands out as if she was a skittish horse. "Calm down, K'lrsa. I need you to listen to me. You have to stay here. What happens if the raiders get past us? I need someone I trust to protect your mother and sister and all the others who aren't fighters."

K'lrsa scoffed. "Oh, please. The only reason I'm the best shot of all the Riders is because mom quit when she married you. She doesn't need me to protect her. And neither do most of the women in the tribe."

Her father smiled slightly. "Your mother is a pretty good shot. But what about M'lara? Or F'lia? Who will protect them?"

She crossed her arms across her chest and glared at him. "Someone else. Anyone else. Have L'ral stay behind. He's going to marry F'lia, let him protect her."

Her father shook his head and grabbed her shoulders. He stared deep into her eyes. "Please, K'lrsa. You're the only one I trust to do this. Please. Do this for me."

When she still wouldn't answer, he continued, "These are dangerous times, K'lrsa. I need my Riders to obey my orders without hesitation. Now, are you a Rider? Will you obey your leader? Or are you a child who must have her own way no matter what's best?"

K'lrsa pulled away. "Fine. I'll stay." She couldn't stop the tear that rolled down her cheek.

Her father pulled her into a fierce embrace and kissed her on the forehead. "I love you."

"I love you, too," she mumbled.

She pulled away and disappeared into her tent without looking at him again.

She threw herself down on her sleeping roll and closed her eyes, covering her ears to the sound of the real Riders leaving camp.

8

K'lrsa paced to the edge of camp and stared into the distance, looking for any sign of the Riders returning. They'd been gone a full day now.

Her stomach rumbled, but she couldn't bring herself to eat.

They should be back by now. They should've been back the day before.

She sat down in front of her tent and started to mend her oldest hunting vest, but then sprang to her feet again a moment later to once more look for the Riders.

"Enough, K'lrsa. Sit down," her mother said.

K'lrsa clutched the moon stone around her neck. It felt almost hot. Her sense of urgency increased as she held it. "Don't you feel it, Mom? Something is wrong. I have to go find them."

Her mother frowned, her lips pursed together as she glanced to the side where M'lara watched them, her arms wrapped tight around her legs. "No, K'lrsa. You need to stay here and protect me and your sister. That was what your father ordered you to do."

K'lrsa paced in front of the tent. As a Rider she should obey his orders without question.

But something was wrong. She just knew it.

Her mother continued to pick at the seams of an old dress.

K'lrsa shook her head as she stared at the empty horizon once more. "No. I have to go. You'll be fine."

"And what of F'lia? Would you see your best friend murdered because you couldn't follow your father's orders?"

K'lrsa glanced towards F'lia's tents, picturing her bright and gentle friend trying to defend herself from attackers. She didn't want something to happen to her.

But *something was wrong*. She *knew* it.

"They should've been back by now, Mom."

Her mother shrugged, but it didn't hide the tension in her shoulders. "Maybe the raiders fled and they gave chase."

"Or maybe the raiders chased them and they're hiding somewhere right now, fighting for their lives, and I could find them and save them."

M'lara buried her face in her knees, her small shoulders shaking.

K'lrsa's mother dropped her hands into her lap. "Oh, K'lrsa, enough. You aren't the Moon Maiden reborn. You're just a young girl like I was. Good with a bow and a solid member of the tribe, but not some legendary hero. You aren't going to save anyone. Sit down and wait like the rest of us."

K'lrsa stared at her mother as tears filled her eyes.

She stared down at the ground and tried to master herself. She was a Rider and Riders didn't cry. Crying just proved her mother right.

No one else might believe it, but she knew in her heart that she could help.

Better than sitting here in camp waiting for them to finally return.

If they ever did…

"Sit, K'lrsa."

She shook her head. No. She couldn't wait another moment. It might already be too late. She grabbed her gear and strode away toward Fallion.

"K'lrsa, you get back here right now," her mother called. K'lrsa kept walking.

Something was wrong. She had to find the Riders before it was too late.

She'd deal with her mother when everyone was safely back at camp.

9

Following their path across the plains was easy. Even on dusty ground, ten horses riding at full speed left enough of a trail for even a young child to see.

She urged Fallion to go as fast as possible, the feeling that something was wrong drove her forward. In her gut she knew she was already too late, that whatever evil had befallen them had already happened.

But she had to try. She had to keep going until she knew for sure.

When they reached the desert, the trail disappeared, victim of the shifting sands that kept the desert's secrets. Legend called the shifting sands a blessing from the Lady Moon—a gift to the tribes in exchange for their vow to protect the Hidden City. But that time was long lost in the shadow of history. All she or any other tribe member knew was that even though there was never a breeze—at least none that a rider on horseback could feel—if a man stopped for a drink he could watch his footsteps slowly disappear as if he'd never existed.

Many a stranger had been lost in the desert, with no idea which may to turn, their bones buried under the shifting sands.

She clutched her moon stone, confident in its protection. As a first daughter of a first daughter going back to the beginning, she was protected, safe as long as she kept her moon stone.

She rode forward, looking in every direction, but saw nothing except empty desert.

The sun beat down and reflected off the sands until she felt like a pot fired in a clay oven, all moisture drained from her body.

She and Fallion rode throughout the day, looking and searching, but saw nothing. No men and no signs of their passage.

As the sun lowered towards the horizon, Fallion stumbled as his head dipped yet again. She gave him some of the water from her last water skin, wishing she'd taken the time to prepare better, to remember that she was riding into the desert where a man could die in the space of a candlemark if he wasn't careful.

She turned Fallion in a circle. Sand and azure sky in every direction, not even a desert hawk visible. Heat waves blurred the mountains on the far horizon.

The Riders were gone as if they'd never existed.

In despair, she reached for the moon stone around her neck. "Lady Moon, Protector, Mother, Shelter. Show me where my father is. Please, I beg of you, guide me to his side through the harsh land of your husband and away from the mischief of your son."

She'd expected the pendant to glow with a cool blue light like it did when she sought shelter in the desert, but instead it pulsed the color of dried blood and a compulsion like a physical presence pushed her north.

Fallion started forward without prompting, stumbling as fast as he could through his exhaustion.

K'lrsa tried to slow him, to turn away from the path the moon stone demanded, but her body wouldn't obey her. Each time she tried, she found herself urging Fallion to go faster instead.

As the sun painted the distant horizon with blood, they raced onward.

10

As they crested yet another nondescript sand dune, the sun dipped below the distant mountains and the sky darkened towards night.

K'lrsa prayed they were close. Not only did she fear that something truly awful had happened to her father and the other Riders, but she knew that she couldn't continue through the twilight hours between when the sun set and the moon rose.

Those hours belonged to the Trickster. Anyone wandering the desert during the between time was best off staying in the spot they'd been in when darkness fell. Men had been known to try to push through to their destination only to find themselves leagues from where they'd been when darkness fell and nowhere nearer their destination. Even torches couldn't protect men when the Trickster wandered the sands.

As they plodded forward, Fallion so exhausted his head hung down to the ground, a grel cried out and lumbered into the air, heavy with food. She saw at least three more clustered around a shape on the ground.

Part of her wanted to stop, to turn away and go home. But Fallion continued his slow but relentless pace and she found herself whispering in his ear, urging him forward.

"Almost there, *micora*." She was so numb she couldn't even cry as she saw that the shape was a body dressed in White Horse colors.

She dropped to the ground, steadying herself against Fallion's side as her legs threatened to collapse under her. She had to see. She had to know who it was.

The grel raised their heads to glare at her, their sharp beaks coated in fresh red blood.

"Go! Leave!" She stumbled towards them. They screamed at her, the stench of death wafting through the air, but they backed away, moving on to another shape almost buried under the desert sand. A horse from what she could see.

She clutched the pendant at her throat and felt its pulsing warmth as she closed the distance to the body. She prayed it wasn't her father even though she knew it would be someone she loved.

She collapsed in relief and despair when she saw L'ral's face.

He was still wearing the bracelet F'lia had made to celebrate their engagement. The bright red, green, and yellow threads had cost her a small fortune. She'd had to trade five of her most-prized pots for just those three small strands of silk. But she'd done so happily and woven into each knot her love of the man she planned to marry.

Clutched in his hand was a small piece of fabric, striped the brilliant green and blue of the Daliphate.

K'lrsa ran her fingers along the smooth strings of his bracelet as she tried not to stare at the destruction the grel had wrought on his body.

She clutched her stomach, fighting the urge to heave up the small breakfast she'd eaten that morning.

People died in the tribes all the time—it was a hard life—but not like this. Not murdered and left for scavengers.

One of the grel sidled its way back towards L'ral, one eye on K'lrsa as it drew closer.

"Go," she screamed, jumping to her feet. "Go. Go."

She ran at all of the grel, waving her arms, screaming and crying out as they watched her with their baleful red eyes.

They rose slowly, cawing their anger, as she forced them to abandon their feast.

Two circled above her, swooping down lazily to declare their displeasure, but another one disappeared over the rise of the next sand dune.

A moment later, it took flight again with a startled cry.

Was someone still alive? The pendant at her throat pulsed brightly as K'lrsa raced up the side of the dune. The sand shifted underfoot until she was almost crawling, but she refused to stop.

She had to see. She had to know.

As she crested the top of the dune, she saw a body below her, spread-eagled, hands and feet staked to the ground, belly sliced open, eyes blackened sockets.

She collapsed, all energy pouring from her like an unstoppered waterskin.

No.

It couldn't be.

But it was.

She recognized the hawk-like nose, the proud forehead. And the necklace around his throat. The one her mother had spent hours weaving charms of love and protection into.

Not that it had done any good.

Her father. Her father before her, dead.

And they'd given him the worst death possible—tethered his spirit to the desert sands to prevent him from completing his journey to the Promised Plains, opened his belly so that the fire ants could tear apart his anima until nothing remained to complete the journey, taken his eyes so he wouldn't be able to see the path to the Lady Moon's side.

She screamed, clutching at her chest, rocking back and forth as agony consumed her.

A grel landed next to the body, cawing in pleasure as it side-stepped towards his face. Before K'lrsa could chase it away, her father's head twitched and the bird flew away.

He was alive.

Her father was still alive.

K'lrsa ran down the hill to his side, slipping and stumbling on the loose sand.

11

K'lrsa fell to the ground by his side. Tears poured down her face, tracing their way through the dust that clung to her sweat-soaked skin.

She didn't know what to do.

His skin was dark red, burned from hours of exposure. The blood around the wound in his belly was already black and crusted as were the pits where his eyes had once been.

He turned towards her and she had to bite her fist to keep from sobbing as she stared at the ruin of his face.

"Oh, Father. I'm so sorry." She wiped at the fire ants crawling on his skin, oblivious to the pain of their sting. There were too many. For each one she wiped away, five replaced it.

His tongue was so swollen he could barely speak. "K'lrsa?" His brow creased and he struggled feebly against the stakes in his hands, crying out when his wounds tore open once more.

"I'm here, Dad. I'm here." She fumbled for her waterskin, pouring the last of her water into his mouth.

He turned his head away and the water splashed across his skin. "Too late. Don't waste it..." he whispered.

"No. No, we can save you. We can..."

He turned back towards her and she felt the weight of his gaze even though he no longer had the eyes to look at her.

She hung her head, fighting to stay positive, to tell him she could save him, but she couldn't deny the truth. He'd taught her to always see the reality of any situation.

And the reality was, he was already dead. He might still be breathing, but nothing could return his eyes to him or close the gaping wound in his belly.

"At least I can free your spirit." She reached for the metal stake in his right hand and pulled upward with all her strength, flinching as his flesh tore away with the stake and he gasped in agony.

"I'm so sorry, Dad." Tears streamed down her face—a waste of water, and not fitting for a Rider—but she couldn't stop them. She moved around his body and pulled the other three stakes, wincing at the strangled sounds her father made with the removal of each one, and the blood that flowed freely from all four wounds.

She tried not to smell the stench of his dying, but it filled her senses, dark and ugly and disturbingly familiar.

He gripped her arm, his face clenched tight as he tried to raise his head to look at her. "Your mother?" he demanded.

"She's fine." K'lrsa smoothed the hair back from his forehead as he lowered his head back onto the sands. "Everyone at camp is fine."

She bit her lip before continuing, knowing he'd be mad at her. "I had to leave, Dad. I had to find you. I just knew something was wrong. What happened?"

He tried to lick his chapped lips, but his mouth was too dry and tongue too swollen.

He forced each word out, slowly, wincing as his lips cracked and bled. "Ambush. Betrayal. L'ral…"

She jumped in, eager to share the small bit of news she could. "L'ral's dead. I found him on the other side of that dune. But I didn't see any of the others. Maybe they got away."

He clutched at her arm, but the effort of even those few words had exhausted him. He seemed to sink into the sands as if they were slowly consuming his body.

The night darkened further, the light of the sun almost completely gone.

She felt a ball of pure hate coil inside her belly as she studied her father's ruined face.

39

The tribes had been at peace for hundreds of years until the men of the Toreem Daliphate turned their attention their way, demanding trade, bringing change and corruption.

They'd killed her father. They would destroy the tribes.

Someone had to stop them.

She stroked her father's arm. "The Daliph and his men can't get away with this. I'll kill him. I swear it."

"No." The word was as much a moan as speech. He shook his head slowly side to side, as if in search of something he couldn't quite find.

"Yes. The Daliph must pay for what was done to you. The only way to kill a snake is to cut off its head."

"No," he said, the word stronger this time. "Promise me…not the Daliph…"

K'lrsa stared at her father. Maybe the desert heat had boiled his mind.

Or he didn't have faith in her.

Still.

"I can do this, Dad. I'm strong enough."

He moved his head just the slightest bit from side to side, clearly exhausted. "No," he sighed. "Swear it."

K'lrsa glared at him, arms crossed tight across her chest.

He reached out, floundering to find her. "Swear it," he said, his voice stronger. "Swear it."

He collapsed back into the sands, spent by even that small effort.

K'lrsa bowed her head. He was dying. And she could help ease his passage. But the Daliph had to pay for what he'd done. He had to be stopped.

She thought about it for a long moment as the sky darkened.

At last, she sighed. She owed this to him.

"Fine." She took his hand in hers and spoke the words she knew he needed to hear. "I, K'lrsa dan V'na of the White Horse Tribe do swear in the name of the Great Father, Bringer of Light, Bringer of Life, Scourge, and Destroyer, that I will not kill the Daliph of the Toreem Daliphate."

The tension left her father's body and he sank further into the sands.

Silently, K'lrsa completed the oath. "Today. I will not kill the Daliph today."

<u>12</u>

K'lrsa leaned in to give her father one last kiss on the forehead and he grabbed her arm. K'lrsa cried out in surprise, startled at his strength after all he'd been through.

His fingers dug into her skin. "Kill me."

"No." She shook her head and tried to pull away from him.

How could she kill him? The man who'd loved her and supported her her entire life. The one who'd always believed in her and encouraged her to be whoever she wanted to be. He'd been the one who taught her how to ride, the one who brought her Fallion and encouraged her to be a Rider. He was everything to her.

She couldn't kill him.

"Already dead. Kill me." His fingernails cut little half-moons in her skin.

He turned his face towards hers and she almost drowned in the dark depths where his eyes had once been. The sun was gone, the Trickster wandered the sands looking for victims.

She couldn't leave him here, defenseless and vulnerable.

But to kill her father, even as an act of mercy...

She shook her head.

It was too much to ask. She knew he was dying. But to be the one to actually deal the final blow?

No. She couldn't do it.

"Please." His voice cracked and his hand shook with the force of his emotions.

That broke her. Her father never asked for help. He never begged. He was always so sure, so confident, so strong.

She grasped the moon stone around her neck, desperate for guidance, and felt an answering pulse. *Mercy.*

Her father deserved a quick warrior's death, not the prolonged suffering the Daliph's men had chosen for him.

"Please," he sighed and fell back to the sands. His hand let go of her arm.

She closed her eyes and sent a silent plea to the Lady Moon as she reached for her knife.

The blade shone bright, reflecting the first rays of the newly-risen moon. K'lrsa swallowed.

Her hand trembled as she moved the tattered remnants of his shirt away from his dry, cracked skin.

She shuddered as her fingers brushed the hard edge of the wound in his belly.

She positioned the tip of the blade just under his rib cage.

She hesitated. She didn't want to do this.

She silently wished he'd breathe his last breath and she could bury him without having to kill him, but his chest kept rising and falling. Her strong, powerful father was unable to surrender, even now.

She bit her lip and, before she could change her mind, before she could think about what she was doing, thrust the blade upward.

He arched and cried out as the blade plunged into his heart, and then fell back, dead.

K'lrsa stumbled away from his body and collapsed to the sand, sobbing. She curled into a ball of agony and loss, rocking back and forth.

Fallion nuzzled her shoulder and she buried her face in his mane, holding tight as she cried, grateful for his steady presence.

<u>13</u>

K'lrsa wasn't sure how long she cried. Long enough for the Lady Moon to rise high into the sky.

She shivered as she stepped back to her father's body and pulled the blade from his chest.

She stared down at his face, now so calm and peaceful in the gentle silver light.

Three grel watched from nearby, their eyes glowing red in the darkness.

"Go." She ran at them and they slowly lumbered into the sky, cawing their displeasure at her.

K'lrsa wiped the last of the tears from her face. The time for crying was past.

She was a Rider and she had a mission to accomplish.

She stood over her father's body, a chill breeze pebbling her skin, and sliced open her palm with the knife, mingling her blood with her father's. She let the blood drip onto his body and then onto the desert sands as she held her head high and shouted into the night, "I, K'lrsa dan V'na of the White Horse Tribe do swear in the name of the Great Father, Bringer of Light, Bringer of Life, Scourge, and Destroyer, and on my father's everlasting soul, that I will avenge him. I will kill the man responsible for his death and I will destroy the Toreem Daliphate."

She took a deep breath. "This I swear, by my own blood. I forsake all other vows. I forsake all other ties."

She was no longer a Rider. No longer a member of her tribe. Now she was just the woman who would avenge her father.

As K'lrsa wiped the knife clean on her pants, the desert sands swallowed her father's body, leaving no sign he'd ever been there.

The desert had heard her vow and accepted it.

"Come, Fallion. Let's find shelter for the night."

14

She followed the guidance of her moon stone to a small stone shelter, hidden amongst the desert sands. It wasn't much, just enough room for her and Fallion to shelter in the case of a storm, but she didn't need much more than that.

She fell asleep immediately, curled on the hard-packed dirt floor of the shelter with her pack as a pillow.

She dreamt she was once more in the middle of the desert, the Hidden City rising before her. The young man with blue eyes wasn't there, but the Lady Moon was.

A flowing robe like the night sky wrapped her womanly curves and blew in a breeze all its own. K'lrsa could see her face this time. She had an ageless beauty, her visage seamlessly shifting from young mother to matron to crone and back again.

They walked side-by-side for a long time, neither one speaking. The air was cool, but not cold. The smell of a storm hung in the air even though the sky was clear.

"You don't have to walk this path," the Lady Moon finally said, her voice vast and deep but as intimate as an embrace.

K'lrsa felt the peace of the night and the goddess's gentle presence coaxing her to put aside her hatred, to remember those that still lived and needed her.

She clenched her hands.

She didn't *want* to lose her anger. She didn't *want* to let go of her pain.

If she did, she'd collapse.

K'lrsa glared ahead. Her teeth ground together as she held all the fears and doubts inside. She focused her mind on her last memory of her father, his belly sliced open, his eyes vacant holes as he begged her to kill him.

"Yes, I do."

The Lady Moon sighed. "You don't know what you're sacrificing, my child." She waved her hand and K'lrsa saw an image of herself with a little girl dancing at her feet as F'lia played the windpipes. K'lrsa was happy, content. She had a husband she loved and a child she cherished.

She shook her head and looked away only to see another image of herself as an old woman, this time surrounded by her children and grandchildren. A little boy sat on her lap as she taught him to make a rabbit snare.

That woman, that older version of herself, was loved, safe, a vital member of her tribe who guided and cared for the young ones.

K'lrsa closed her eyes. "Stop it. I've made my choice."

She clung to her anger, refusing to let it go. She nurtured it like a newborn child. Someday it would grow strong enough to destroy the entire Toreem Daliphate.

That would be her legacy. Her future. Not these pretty, hollow moon dreams.

"It's not too late to choose a different path, K'lrsa dan V'na of the White Horse Tribe."

K'lrsa turned to the Lady Moon. "Yes. It is. And that life? That was never the life for me. Never the life I wanted. To sit around a campfire with babies and grandbabies at my feet?" She laughed, soft and low, refusing to cry once more, to acknowledge the subtle appeal of those promises of peace and love.

She would never be the woman in those images, even if she did turn back now.

And what would she go back to?

Her father, the only one who had truly loved and believed in her, was gone. If she went back, her mother and brother

47

would call her a fool and a child. They'd insist she marry and give up Fallion and her dreams of being a Rider.

She couldn't do it.

She couldn't watch the light go out of F'lia's eyes when she learned of L'ral's death. Or watch her mother walk through each day all stoic and proud, only allowing herself to cry in the privacy of her tent in the middle of the night.

No. K'lrsa couldn't go back to that. She wouldn't.

She shook her head, shoulders tight with anger. "I've chosen my path. I made a vow to your husband. I intend to keep it."

The Lady Moon glided along the desert sands while K'lrsa's feet sank deeper with each step. "You would choose the path of revenge? Of hatred? You would swear to kill another you've never even met?"

K'lrsa refused to meet the Lady Moon's fathomless eyes. "Yes. For my father. And for the tribes."

The Lady Moon was silent for a long moment before she replied. "And what if you're wrong, K'lrsa dan V'na? What if the one you seek to kill isn't the one responsible?"

K'lrsa did meet her eyes then. She felt so small, so alone against the vastness she saw there, but she shook the feeling away. "It doesn't matter. My father was right. The Daliphate is destroying us. We become weak, unable to fulfill our sacred duty. The Daliphate must be destroyed before it destroys us."

The Lady Moon sighed, embodying in that moment every disappointed gaze K'lrsa's mother had ever given her. "Very well. It's your choice, child. Your path will be long and hard and not what you expect." She touched K'lrsa's cheek, her face once more that of a loving young mother. "Remember, it is never too late to turn aside. The desert will always be here waiting for you if you choose to return."

She faded away, leaving K'lrsa alone, her only company the long-dead city.

As K'lrsa walked forward, she wondered if there was any place in the real world where the sky was so full of stars and the air so still, as if the world was holding its breath, waiting.

As she watched, the scene shifted to midday. The heat of the full summer sun beat upon her skin, its heat so intense she felt blisters forming.

She tried to shield herself, but she still wore the flowing robes of the Moon Dance, slim strips of fabric that hardly covered anything.

The Hidden City disappeared. Sand dunes stretched to the horizon in every direction. Waves of heat rose from the ground.

"So, you want revenge." A man approached from behind her. His voice boomed like thunder.

He was a warrior, lean and tight and deadly. He stood before her, bare-chested with only a thin strip of fabric wrapped around his hips. Everywhere she looked he was covered in scars, the marks of countless battles tattooed upon his skin.

He had the tan skin and dark hair of the tribes, but his eyes burned like banked coals.

Father Sun.

The Scourge and Destroyer.

She forced herself to meet his gaze. "Yes."

He nodded and stepped to her side. "Then find this caravan. Let them capture you. Let them take you as a slave."

She turned to see a line of men, horses, and wagons crawling across the sand. In the lead was a man with skin as dark as burnt wood. He had a scar running from the inner corner of his right eye to the top of his left lip, like someone had slashed him across the face with a sword long ago.

It gave him a permanent sneer, but that was nothing to the blackness of his eyes. He was a man who cared for no one, who'd kill without thought or hesitation.

She shivered at the thought of giving a man like that power over her.

Behind him were three wagons, pulled by sturdy desert ponies, each one on a set of skids that allowed them to slide along the surface of the sand. They were followed by two camels walking side-by-side with a fabric contraption strung between them that bumped and swayed with each step.

And behind that…

Were slaves. A hundred or more dirty, tired humans stumbled through the sand, struggling for each step as men rode alongside them, lashing out with whips and cruel words when the slaves faltered.

The slaves never looked up, never tried to run. Most had their eyes closed to mere slits as they trudged along in a ragged line, the dust from the passage of the wagons hazing the air.

As she watched, a slave fell, too tired to continue. One of the men on horseback watched the slave for a long moment. He waited to be sure the slave wouldn't rise again and then rode on, leaving the man to die under the hot desert sun.

K'lrsa turned away.

"There has to be another way. I'm a Rider. I could never be a slave. I could never let anyone treat me like…like…that."

Father Sun shrugged. "Then go home to your mother. Revenge isn't the path for everyone."

K'lrsa stared at him. Didn't he care about her father and the tribes? Didn't he want to see the men who'd done this punished?

"I'm a Rider. I can't just let men…"

His eyes flashed red, the banked coals inside suddenly sparking to life. "No. You aren't. You forswore all vows." He stepped closer and the heat from his flesh burned her. "You can find that caravan, let them take you as a slave, and follow the path of revenge to the heart of the Daliphate. Or you can go home." He turned away from her, watching the caravan once more. "My wife is fond of you. I'll release you from your vow for her sake."

K'lrsa watched the caravan as it made its slow way across the sands. Another slave fell and one of the men on horseback struck him with a whip.

The man's scream echoed in her mind long after he'd struggled back to his feet and continued onward.

"Is this my only choice?"

"Yes."

Could she do this? Could she allow herself to be taken? To be chained and whipped?

Could she hold herself back if someone lashed out at her? Could she bow her head and trudge along, obeying whatever command they gave her?

Was avenging her father worth that?

Father Sun stepped closer, his voice almost gentle. "Not everyone can tread the path you've chosen, K'lrsa dan V'na of the White Horse Tribe. There's no shame in knowing your limits."

"I can." K'lrsa glared at the caravan, arms crossed tight across her chest, shivering at the thought of what was to come.

"Can you, truly, child?"

She nodded, afraid to speak again.

"Then follow your moon stone to the caravan."

"What then?" she asked, but Father Sun was gone. So was the caravan.

She was once again alone in the midst of dead and barren sands.

She shuddered, suddenly cold even with the midday sun beating down upon her.

<u>15</u>

K'lrsa stroked Fallion's nose as they watched the large cloud of dust on the horizon come closer. It had taken most of the day and they were well into Black Horse lands by the time she'd found the caravan.

She still couldn't see the actual caravan, but from the dust and the gentle pull of her moon stone, she assumed she'd found her target.

She rubbed the smooth stone between her fingers as she watched the caravan come closer.

She could still turn back. It wasn't too late.

No one had seen her. No one would blame her for changing her mind, for returning to her family. No one even needed to know.

But she didn't want to turn back. She refused to quit even though she felt ill thinking of what was to come. To allow herself to be taken by those men...

She shook her head, chasing the images away.

She'd left a message in the shelter before she left—a rough set of Rider's marks letting whoever came through next know that L'ral and her father were dead, swallowed by the desert sands, betrayed by the Daliph's men. She hadn't said where she was going, just that she was fine and not to follow her.

She hoped they'd listen. Not that they'd know where to find her. No one would think that she'd ride into Black Horse lands. Or let herself be taken as a slave.

No. Once she was captured, she was on her own. No going back. No rescue.

She'd considered stumbling upon the caravan as if by accident and letting them capture her that way, but that would never work. Fallion could beat any horse they might have and they'd know immediately that she was letting them capture her.

Maybe they wouldn't care, but if they did, she'd fail before she'd begun.

She had to let them find her. And she had to make them believe that she'd had no choice but to let them capture her.

K'lrsa shivered as she buried her face in Fallion's mane, fighting back the urge to cry. She didn't want to do this.

But she had to. She didn't have a choice.

Fallion was her other half. He was all she had now. She didn't want to lose him. But if she was going to take her revenge, she had to sacrifice everything, even him.

Maybe if she'd had more time she could have thought of another plan, but she had to act before the caravan passed by. (Or she gave in to her fear and ran back home.)

K'lrsa dismounted and gave Fallion one last kiss on his nose, scratching behind his ears. "I'm sorry, *micora*. You'll be okay, you will. I promise. It'll just hurt a bit."

She bit her lip as she drew an arrow from her quiver. She ran her thumb along the sharp edge of the arrowhead as she stepped to his side, running a hand along his back. He nuzzled her ear, blowing a strand of hair against her cheek with his breath and she rested her cheek against his face for a long moment, closing her eyes and wishing she were anywhere but here.

Fallion trusted her so much and now she was going to destroy that. She was going to use the bond they had to hurt him.

She hated herself, but she had to do it. She had to avenge her father.

And save the tribes.

What was her life, or Fallion's, compared to that?

K'lrsa broke off the fletched end of the arrow to remove the distinct markings of her tribe and then, before she could second-guess herself, she plunged the metal arrowhead into the meaty part of Fallion's back, careful to avoid any vital organs or muscles.

Fallion bucked and screamed.

K'lrsa fell to her knees. "I'm so sorry, *micora*. I'm so sorry."

He fled, racing away in the direction of the caravan.

K'lrsa closed her eyes for a moment, praying that it was just a flesh wound and that he'd run straight to the caravan where he could find help. She took a slow, steadying breath. If he did run to the caravan, then they'd find her soon.

She didn't have much time.

She removed her knife from its sheath, squinting as it reflected the late afternoon sunlight. She took a deep breath, and, quickly, before she could change her mind, drove the knife into her left shoulder, just below the collar bone.

She bit back a scream as the metal punctured her skin.

She closed her eyes against the pain and forced herself to take deep, steadying breaths. The tangy scent of her own blood filled her nostrils as she struggled to master the pain.

She knelt on the sand for a moment, swaying slightly as she tried to find the Core to take her away from the pain. It took longer than it should have, but finally, at last, she managed to float there, aware of the injury but in a place where it couldn't touch her.

With a sharp jerk, she pulled the knife free. Blood flowed down her breast as she bound the wound with strips she'd cut from her shirt. She rolled in the desert sand, hoping it would look like she'd fallen from her horse.

Blood seeped around the edges of the bandage, dripping down her arm and into the sand. She'd cut too deep. It shouldn't be bleeding this much.

She prayed to Father Sun that the caravan would find her soon. But what if they didn't?

She struggled to her feet, unable to move her left arm, and stumbled in the direction of the caravan calling Fallion's name.

The sound should reach the caravan, but she didn't know if it would. The desert was fickle that way. In some places you could hear a sound for leagues; in others you couldn't hear the Rider next to you.

As she made her slow, painful way across the sands, the sun dropped below the horizon behind her.

Blood soaked the bandage and dripped into the sand with each step she took. The world blurred and shifted as dusk fell. The Trickster's time was upon her and still the caravan hadn't found her.

She continued forward, hoping to find the caravan over the next rise, or the one after that, but she saw nothing, heard nothing.

Had she walked in the wrong direction?

Had the Trickster led her astray?

She was so dizzy, she didn't even know which direction she was walking anymore. It was too dark to see the distant mountains staining the horizon.

She tried to shout, but no sound came out; her throat was too dry from trudging through the sand.

She'd lost her pack, including her waterskin. When had that happened?

K'lrsa resisted the urge to continue. The caravan should be straight ahead. But she knew better than to keep walking during that deadly time between when Father Sun departed and the Lady Moon arrived. The Trickster was far too fond of his pranks.

She had to find them, though.

If she didn't find them before full dark, she might just disappear into the desert sands like so many before her, never to be seen again.

The Great Father wouldn't let her come so far only to fail. Would he?

She thought back to the cruel warrior who'd shown her this path and to the stories of the gods. No doubt they were real, but they were also capricious, mysterious, and not very inclined to save men from their foolish choices.

She knew the truth then.

If she failed, Father Sun wouldn't save her. Nor would the Lady Moon.

K'lrsa stumbled forward in the deepening dark, her good arm stretched before her as if it would somehow help her see better.

She slipped and fell, landing heavily on her injured arm. The pain was so intense she blacked out.

When she awoke it was even darker, the sands cold under her body. She struggled to stand once more, but couldn't. The world spun around her and she lay back, defeated.

She laughed and cried as the movement tugged at her injured shoulder.

Her mother had been right. She was just a foolish girl, unaware of the dangers she faced.

Well, now she knew.

Too bad it was too late for her to do anything about it.

She willed herself to rise, but couldn't even sit up, let alone stand.

She sank back into the sands, exhausted. Later, maybe.

When, if, the Lady Moon rose, she'd try again.

But she knew, deep down, that it was already too late. She'd never rise again.

"Fallion," she whispered, "I'm so sorry, *micora*. Please forgive me."

<u>16</u>

K'lrsa awoke in the dark of early morning. She expected to be cold, but wasn't. Maybe she'd already passed on to the Promised Plains?

No. There was a large, warm body pressed against hers.

She turned her head, blocking away the pain that shot through her at the slightest movement.

It was Fallion. He'd returned to her! And now he lay with his body curled around hers, his soft breaths ruffling her hair.

"Oh, thank you, thank you, thank you." She fought the urge to cry as a wave of sheer relief passed through her.

She stroked his nose with her good hand and he snuffled her hair with a soft whinny of affection.

"I don't deserve you, *micora*."

K'lrsa's injury throbbed with pain, the bandage now dry and crusted with blood. She didn't dare move her arm and risk tearing it open again; not in the middle of the night when she could barely see her own hand.

In the morning she'd use Fallion to help her stand and they'd go in search of the caravan. She just prayed the Trickster hadn't led her astray.

If he had...

She didn't know what she'd do. She was too weak to make it back to her tribe, especially since she wouldn't ask Fallion to carry her, not with a wounded shoulder.

Maybe this had all been one great joke played on her by the Trickster. The dreams of the Hidden City and the boy with the bright blue eyes, her conversations with the Lady Moon and Father Sun. Maybe it had all been the Trickster seeing just how stupid she really was.

It would be just like him to lead a would-be hero to an ignoble death by her own hand. The tales were full of stories of how he'd used someone's pride against them, laughing the whole time as he watched them destroy themselves.

"You haven't won yet, you sneaky little imp," she whispered as sleep took her once more.

K'lrsa awoke to a boot kicking her leg.

"Forget the girl for now. Can you save the horse?" a man asked from somewhere nearby. He spoke in trader speech and K'lrsa felt a moment's excitement. The caravan had found her.

Fallion was still curled behind her. He should've risen when the men arrived.

Oh, Fallion, she thought as she heard the man moving around to Fallion's other side and as Fallion continued to lie still against her back, the only sign he was alive his labored breathing.

It was all her fault. All her stupid, arrogant fault. What had Fallion ever done to deserve this? Poor boy.

She smiled when Fallion turned his head to snap at the man. At least he still had some spirit left.

"Hiya. No call for that, you mangy cur." The man backed away. "I say leave 'em both. Neither one's worth the effort it'd take to stitch 'em up."

K'lrsa tensed at his words. She'd come too far to fail now, but she had no choice but to wait and hope the other man wanted to help them.

"What do you know of horse flesh, Reginald? That's one of the finest horses I've ever seen. If I didn't know better, I'd say it was an *Amalanee* horse. See the white mark on its forehead?"

He walked closer until he was standing just behind Fallion. "Legend has it the things can fly."

The first man, Reginald, spit. K'lrsa flinched at the foolish waste of water as he said, "I'm not a fool, Barkley. It's just a ratty horse and horses don't fly. I say we leave 'em both."

Barkley walked around until he was standing in front of K'lrsa. All she could see were his scuffed leather boots, well-worn but carefully tended. "No. Wings or not, that horse is worth money. And I'm not leaving the girl either. "

He leaned down, staring at her with soft gray eyes that belied the cruelty of his words. "Scrub the dirt and blood off and this one'll at least be good for a night or two. If she makes it as far as Crossroads, we can sell her off there. The brothels are always looking for new meat." He reached out to grab her braid and K'lrsa flinched back. "With this long black hair and pale brown skin, I know at least one man who'll pay for a night with her."

"Ah, aye. That bastard would, wouldn't he? Just have to keep him away from her until Crossroads or she won't make it that far."

White-hot anger flared inside K'lrsa; the moon stone at her neck burned with an answering light. She'd kill them. No man of the tribes would take a woman against her will. Never. If he did he'd find himself castrated and left to wander the sands until he died.

She stumbled to her feet and reached for her knife.

"Oho, what do we have here? Seems like she had a little more life than we thought." Barkley stood an arm's length away and studied her. "Good."

He was so tall K'lrsa had to crane her neck to meet his gaze, but he wasn't looking at her anymore, he'd turned his attention to Fallion.

Reginald came around on her left, moving like a copperhead snake—silent until the moment it strikes. K'lrsa turned to keep him within sight, fighting against the dizziness that threatened to overwhelm her.

He smiled, revealing a mouth of broken and blackened teeth. "Maybe we should break her in before we take her to camp. Whatdya think Barkley?"

Barkley didn't even look at them. "Nah. Not my type."

"Never are," Reginald muttered, glaring at him. "Well, I guess she's all mine, then." He rushed her, arms spread wide to tackle her. K'lrsa barely managed to react in time, dropping low and kicking out at his knee in Crouching Cricket.

Reginald screamed in pain as her foot connected, but it was only a glancing blow. What should've shattered his knee cap and bent his leg backward had just pushed it to the side, probably tearing something vital, but not permanently crippling him like she'd intended.

"You bitch. You tribal trash. I'll gut you for that." He came for her again.

K'lrsa braced herself to fight him, blinking against the wooziness that threatened to disable her.

Barkley grabbed Reginald's collar and threw him to the side like a child's doll. "Enough, Reginald. Leave her alone until Harley has a chance to see her."

K'lrsa collapsed to the sands, her vision blurring as the momentary burst of energy drained away.

What had she gotten herself into?

<u>17</u>

K'lrsa awoke a short time later to the sound of more horses and men arriving.

"Hiya. What do we have here?" a new voice called.

K'lrsa forced herself to sit up. One of the newcomers was the man from her vision, the scar across his face even more sinister in real life. He rode a beige desert pony and wore baru hide pants and a shirt woven of some lightweight fabric she'd never seen before; he was imposing, clearly the leader even though he was small and stocky.

Behind him, long black hair blowing in the breeze, shirt half-open exposing his skin to the harsh sunlight, and riding a black stallion completely unsuited to the desert, was G'van.

K'lrsa felt a moment of hope. G'van would save her. She wouldn't need to be taken as a slave, wouldn't be used by these men for their "entertainment."

"G'van," she croaked, waving her good arm to catch his attention. "I'm so happy to see you..."

Her words trailed off as G'van stared down at her, a sneer on his face like she was a piece of manure he'd found on his perfectly polished and absolutely impractical black boots.

The other man turned to him. "You know this girl?"

"I do." G'van smiled at her and K'lrsa suddenly felt more in danger than she had with the two brutes that had found her.

"And?"

He shrugged. "She's no one. Desert trash. I'll take her until we reach Crossroads and can sell her off at the nearest brothel. You can have the profit."

Barkley snorted. "Like she'll make it to Crossroads if you take her."

G'van glared at the man, but Barkley ignored him, focusing his attention on the leader. "Harley, she has one of those stones around her neck. And look at her horse. That's the finest horse I've ever seen. The gadja bastard's lying to you. As usual."

Harley jumped off his horse and came to kneel in front of K'lrsa, staring intently at her moon stone. "What's your name, girl?"

She was still shaking from the thought that G'van would sell her to a brothel. He was supposed to be a leader of his tribe and instead he was a vain, malicious…

"I said, what is your name?" he asked again through gritted teeth.

K'lrsa blinked, bringing herself back to the moment. What should she tell him? She didn't see how it would matter one way or another who she was, so she answered with the truth. "K'lrsa dan V'na of the White Horse Tribe."

Harley's eyes narrowed and he looked at G'van once more. "White Horse Tribe? Is that so?"

"Yes." She noticed the look, but was so tired she didn't care. She just wanted to lay down and maybe sleep for a week or two.

"And what is this, K'lrsa dan V'na of the White Horse Tribe?" He reached for her moon stone, but it glowed red and he snatched his hand back before touching it.

She shook her head, trying to stay awake. "It's my moon stone."

"They're rare, aren't they? They mean something in the tribes?"

She shrugged and glanced at G'van. How much had he told these outsiders? How much could she hide from them? She settled for the truth, but a very simple version of it. "I'm a first daughter of a first daughter going back to the founding of the tribes. All first daughters have one. As all first sons have sun stones." She yawned and leaned against Fallion, closing her eyes.

G'van was a first son, but he no longer wore his sun stone. Maybe now she knew why—because he was so far from being a member of the tribes that it would burn his cursed skin.

Either that or it interfered with his vanity. A little stone disc was too boring for a man like G'van. He needed gaudy stones and silks.

She smiled slightly as her head lolled to the side.

Harley grabbed her chin and examined her face, turning her head to each side. "She'll look good once she's cleaned up. Kilgore knows, at this point almost anyone would look better than that northern princess we bought. We'll be lucky if that one survives until Crossroads."

K'lrsa forced herself to open her eyes and watch as Harley rubbed at his face, nodding quietly to himself. "What do you think, Barkley? Can we create a desert princess out of this one?"

K'lrsa laughed softly and mumbled, "There are no princesses in the desert."

Harley glared at her, his black eyes as sharp as a knife. "Would you rather be G'van's plaything? Or be passed around the men guarding my slaves?"

She flinched away from the cruelty in his eyes. "No."

"Then if I say you're a desert princess, you'll be a desert princess. And you will proclaim to anyone and everyone who wants to hear it that you are a first daughter of a first daughter of a first daughter and that this makes you special and valuable. Is that understood?" His voice lashed her like a whip.

"Yes." She curled back against Fallion, wishing she'd never left camp to find her father.

"Good." Harley stood. "Bring her and the horse back to camp. And hands off until I say otherwise." He stared at Reginald until the man nodded and lowered his head. He then turned his attention to G'van who met his stare, his face as flat as stone.

Harley held G'van's gaze for a long, tense moment and then shook his head and mounted his horse, riding off without looking back. G'van and Reginald trailed along behind him.

Barkley walked over to her.

"You can ride with me." He picked her up as if she weighed nothing and threw her over his horse's back. K'lrsa bit back a cry of pain as the movement jarred her wound. Fresh blood seeped through the bandage and ran down her arm.

Fallion struggled to his feet and followed along behind them as Barkley led his horse after the others.

"Where are we going?" K'lrsa asked as the horse made its slow way up the nearest sand dune, its feet digging into the soft sands as the sun moved higher into the sky.

Barkley walked along effortlessly as if the sun wasn't beating down upon them like a hammer. "Crossroads. We'll sell off most of the slaves there and then continue on to wherever Harley deems best."

"How far away is that?"

He shrugged. "A week or so. Depends on how many slaves he's willing to lose on the way. Faster we go, more we lose. Slower we go, more supplies it takes, less time we have to make another run before winter sets in."

K'lrsa shivered at the memory of the slave in her vision who had fallen and never risen again. She couldn't imagine anyone thinking that even one life was an acceptable loss, but it seemed these men did.

And she was now their captive.

What a fool she was.

"Is Crossroads where the Daliph is?" she asked as they made their slow way down the other side of the dune.

Barkley laughed, a rich, warm baritone at odds with his size. "Crossroads? No. The only things you'll find in Crossroads are slaves, taverns, and whorehouses."

She glanced towards the distant mountains. "So where is the Daliph?"

Barkley shook his head. "Don't you know anything, girl? He's in Toreem." He glanced at her and added, "That's two weeks' ride past Crossroads."

Three weeks then.

She could do that. She could survive with these men long enough to reach Toreem.

As if reading her mind, Barkley added, "The likes of us don't go to Toreem. We do our trek across the desert, get our slaves, bring 'em back, sell 'em, blow our money on beer and women, and do it all over again." He laughed even though K'lrsa didn't see how what he'd said was that funny.

As she watched Fallion stumbling along beside her, limping slightly, she wondered what she'd done.

Why hadn't she just gone back to camp? Why hadn't she followed the Lady Moon's advice? She'd be safe and whole and so would Fallion. They could hunt together, riding across the plains, the wind streaming through their hair...

She shook her head at her own foolishness.

That was just a dream, a memory of a day she'd never know again.

Up ahead, Harley and G'van were in the midst of a heated discussion, both gesturing angrily as they almost shouted back and forth.

Reginald rode back to them, a wicked grin on his face.

"What's going to happen to me?" K'lrsa asked, not actually expecting an answer.

Barkley shrugged. "Not sure. Harley thought he'd bought a northern princess on this trip—skin as pale as milk, hair the color of the sun. He was going to take her to Boradol and sell her to a specialty place that pays a premium for unique women. But she didn't handle the desert sun well. Now she's all scarred and ugly. Will be even if she survives. So, now?" He shrugged again. "Maybe Harley will take you to Boradol instead."

"As a whore?" she asked, shocked.

Reginald laughed, the sound low and mean, as he pulled up beside them. "Girl, it doesn't matter where you go from here. Crossroads or Boradol, you're going to be spreading your legs to make someone money sooner or later. Only difference is that in Boradol the men bathe more often."

"At least in Boradol she won't have G'van as a customer," Barkley growled, glaring ahead to where Harley and G'van rode, still arguing.

Reginald spat to the side and nodded. "There is that."

She wanted to ask what they meant, but didn't dare. She was already scared enough.

Instead, she spent the rest of the ride trying to calm herself and ignore the images that flashed through her mind.

She'd chosen this path knowing it wouldn't be easy.

She had to ride it no matter the outcome.

18

As they crested the third sand dune, the trading caravan came into view. It sprawled below them in a wide space between dunes tall enough to cast shade for the men and horses.

The slaves huddled together at the left end of camp, so close together they looked like one giant creature composed of hundreds of moving arms and legs. Two men guarded them, but were more focused on their card game than their human cargo. Probably figured the intense midday heat and threat of the desert would keep the slaves from trying to run, and they were right. None of the miserable human beings huddled together in that small patch of shade showed the slightest interest in anything.

Next to the slaves a series of tents formed a rough circle around one larger tent, the fabric of each so gray and weathered they blended into the desert. They were old, but sturdy, with few patches. To the far right of the camp, in the deepest shadows, two more tents stood by themselves. Resting on the ground next to one of the tents was the cloth contraption she'd seen strung between the camels in her vision—bright red and yellow, the only color in the entire camp.

Two women sat in front of the other tent. One watched them approach with narrowed eyes and a sour expression. She was old, her lips stained red from chewing bitter root; she had the dark hair and eyes and the light brown skin of a woman of the tribes. She sat on a small stool, a cookpot simmering on the fire before her.

As they came closer, K'lrsa saw that her ear was cut at the top, marking her as a slave. She wore loose pants and a long-sleeved top—trader clothing.

The girl next to her was so thin she looked like she'd break from a glance. Most of her skin was covered with lightweight bandages; the few patches of skin visible around them were a bright red that looked painful even at this distance. Her hair was a pale yellow, almost white. It hung across her face in matted clumps.

K'lrsa couldn't help but stare—she'd never seen anyone like her. As Harley and G'van approached, the girl curled into herself, hugging her knees tight to her chest.

The old woman gestured and the girl fled to the other tent.

"Lodie." Harley stared down at the old woman from horseback, his jaw clenched tight.

"Harley." She almost smiled as she spit bitter root at the feet of his horse, the red fluid dribbling down her chin like blood. K'lrsa remembered the grel feasting on L'ral's body, their beaks dipped in blood, and shivered.

"Tend the girl and the horse. They're injured."

K'lrsa squirmed as the woman studied her, wanting anything but to have that woman's cold gaze weigh and assess her.

Lodie nodded, but she didn't move from where she sat. "That it?"

Harley's horse danced under him and he grimaced. "Check to see if the girl is pure. G'van thinks she may be. If so, we'll get a higher price for her."

Lodie spat again, the liquid landing at the feet of G'van's horse this time. "Betraying your own now, are you? How am I not surprised."

"Shut up, slave." G'van rode his horse closer and raised his hand as if to slap her.

Instead of flinching away like K'lrsa expected, the woman stood slowly, her gaze never leaving G'van's. She was tall, taller than any woman K'lrsa had ever met. She grinned at G'van, her teeth stained red from the bitter root. "Turned you down, did she?" She turned her back on G'van. "Smart girl."

Before G'van could go after her, Harley grabbed the reins of his horse and pulled him back. "Leave off, G'van."

Barkley pulled K'lrsa off the horse without even asking and dropped her by the fire. Before she could say anything, Lodie was at her side, poking at her bandage.

K'lrsa scrambled away. "I'm fine. Please, look at Fallion first."

Lodie turned to Harley, one eyebrow raised in question.

He shook his head. "Desert fools are all alike. Fine. Tend to the horse first, but don't let the girl die." He turned his horse away. "G'van. With me."

G'van rode his horse forward another step towards Lodie, but Barkley stepped between them and stared him down, arms crossed.

"G'van!" Harley called. G'van reined his horse around, pulling too hard so the horse cried out and reared up slightly.

Lodie shook her head and muttered something K'lrsa couldn't hear as she watched him leave. When Harley and G'van were far enough away, she turned to Barkley. "You can go now."

He hesitated. "Are you sure?"

"Yes, I'm sure, you big lug. The girl and I can protect ourselves from one primped up fool. And you don't need to be here to confirm she's pure. Bunch of foolishness that is. Girl's been riding a horse her entire life." She shook her head and spat to the side. "Foolish men and their idiot beliefs. Go."

"Call if you need me." Barkley led his horse away, glancing back at them a few times as he made his way to the main camp.

"He's a good boy, that one," Lodie said as she watched him leave. "You can trust him."

Before K'lrsa could respond, Lodie shambled over to her and poked at her wound.

"Ow!" K'lrsa jerked away. "I said to look at Fallion first."

The old woman shrugged as she reached for K'lrsa's arm. "He's fine. *Amalanee* horses practically heal themselves." She tugged on the bandages on K'lrsa's arm and K'lrsa bit back another cry. "Unlike humans."

The baru hide K'lrsa had used to bind the wound stuck; Lodie used a large, curved hunting knife she pulled from her waistband to cut it free, deftly sliding the cool metal between the bandage and K'lrsa's skin. The wound underneath was red and swollen.

Lodie held the tip of the knife in the fire. "You have the looks of the White Horse Tribe."

K'lrsa didn't respond. She didn't know this woman. And she didn't need to tell her anything.

Lodie cleaned her teeth with her tongue, making loud sucking noises that made K'lrsa squirm, as she waited for the metal to heat.

Finally, she nodded to herself and, before K'lrsa could react, sliced the wound with her knife. K'lrsa screamed as the hot metal touched her skin, swaying as her vision turned black.

The smell was horrible as blood and pus ran down her arm and dropped into the desert sands.

"Hmm." Lodie dug her finger into the wound and K'lrsa's vision flashed white from the intensity of the pain.

She tried to pull away, but Lodie held her arm with a surprisingly strong grip, her skeletal fingers digging into the flesh of K'lrsa's arm as she studied the wound. When the cruel old woman was finally done poking and prodding at her tender flesh, K'lrsa curled into a ball, watching the woman with increasing distrust.

Lodie stared at K'lrsa for a long moment, a slight frown on her face, before standing and walking away.

"Please, Fallion…"

The woman waved her off and ducked into her tent. She returned a moment later with a handful of items.

Lodie sat down on a stool next to K'lrsa and shoved a stick wrapped in baru hide into her hands.

"Bite it."

K'lrsa ran her thumb along the teeth marks the woman's other victims had already made in the soft hide. It was a little too late to be handing her the stick now.

Lodie shrugged. "Fine. Have it your way." She held her blade back in the flames.

K'lrsa shoved the stick into her mouth and bit down hard as Lodie scraped away the sand and dried blood from the wound. Tears streamed down her cheeks; she'd never imagined anything could hurt so much.

"Good girl." Lodie patted her on the cheek like she was a small child.

As Lodie cleaned and sewed the wound, K'lrsa struggled to stay upright. She was so tired and the pain so intense, a few times she almost fainted, but she refused to show weakness in front of this woman, whoever she was. So she gritted her teeth until it felt like they'd crack and clenched her fists until her nails dug into the palms of her hands and forced herself to bear the agony.

When she faltered, she looked up to see Fallion standing there calmly with his wounded shoulder, his beautiful brown eyes shining with love. She deserved this for what she'd done to him. She deserved every moment of suffering this bitter old crone could throw at her.

Finally, when K'lrsa didn't think she could last another moment, Lodie finished cleaning and sewing the wound. K'lrsa collapsed forward, sighing in relief.

"Here. Chew this." Lodie shoved a pinch of dried green fungus at her. It was sleepweed. A little bit would take away the pain. A little bit more would make her sleep.

Too much would kill her.

"Not yet. Tend to Fallion first."

Lodie frowned at her, but turned her attention to the horse. He backed away as she approached, baring his teeth.

"Pzah. Foolish horse. I can't fix you if you won't let me see the wound." She stood before him, hands on hips, not the least bit scared even though she had to know that one kick of his hooves could kill her.

K'lrsa called, "Fallion, *azah.*" He froze, obeying her command to be absolutely still, but his eyes rolled around in panic. "Best hurry. He won't stay that way for long."

Lodie stepped forward and stroked his muzzle, whispering to him in a soft sing-song. As soon as she touched him, Fallion calmed and nuzzled at her hand.

"How did you do that?" K'lrsa asked, amazed.

Lodie shrugged as she stepped around to look at his wound. "I have a talent with animals. Requires physical contact, though, so not much use most of the time." She scratched Fallion's jaw and he nuzzled at her face.

Lodie explored Fallion's wound with her fingers. "So, what happened to you?

"We were attacked. Fallion was shot. I was stabbed. We escaped, but we got lost. Fortunately, those men found us this morning."

Lodie glared at her, eyes narrowed.

"What really happened to you?" She asked the question in the pidgin speech of a Rider.

How did this woman know Rider-speech? Had she been married to a Rider once? K'lrsa refused to think that maybe this woman had once been a Rider. It wasn't possible. No Rider would allow themselves to be taken as a slave. They'd die before they'd let that happen.

Except, isn't that exactly what K'lrsa had done?

No. What K'lrsa was doing was different. They weren't the same. She had nothing in common with this bitter-root-addicted crone.

"I told you. We were attacked."

"Were you now?" Lodie cleaned Fallion's wound with a rag soaked in hot water. He didn't even move although he flinched at each stroke.

"Yes."

"Where? And how did you get here?" Lodie waited for her answer.

"I'm not sure." K'lrsa tried and failed to meet the woman's steady gaze. "We didn't know where we were. We just ran and ended up here."

Lodie finished sewing up Fallion's wound in silence, chewing on a new pinch of bitter root as she worked. Finally, she sat down next to K'lrsa once more and nodded to the sleepweed. "You'll be wanting that, sooner rather than later."

She was right. K'lrsa's arm was throbbing. K'lrsa chewed on the small pinch of sleepweed. It spread through her body, numbing her senses as it went.

Lodie leaned forward. "Harley may be a fool. G'van certainly is. Well, foolish or greedy. Usually end with the same result. But I am not. So what really happened to you?"

K'lrsa swayed, trying to stay upright as the sleepweed spread. "I told you."

Lodie laughed, a harsh, bitter sound like rocks grating against one another. "No, you lied to me just like you lied to them. That horse wasn't shot with an arrow. If I had a guess, I'd say you shoved an arrow into his shoulder. And that stab wound of yours? Gave it to yourself, didn't you?"

Lodie stared into K'lrsa's eyes. "So tell me, girl. Why are you really here? Why would you hurt your horse and yourself to fall in with this lot?"

K'lrsa's stomach clenched. She had to leave.

She tried to stand, but her body wouldn't obey her.

The last thing she felt as she descended into sleep was Lodie's fingers digging into the soft flesh of her good arm.

<u>19</u>

When K'lrsa awoke, she was in a tent and it was night, the air cool against her face; a small sliver of moonlight shone through a gap in the top of the tent. Lodie snored on a pallet across from her, blocking the path to the exit. The space smelled of bitter root and healing plants. She could make out the faint outline of desert bluebells hanging from the peak of the tent and other bundled herbs beyond those.

She lay there in the darkness for a moment, wondering what to do.

Lodie knew she'd lied. Would she tell Harley? She obviously hadn't yet or K'lrsa wouldn't be sleeping comfortably in a tent.

But she still could in the morning.

If so, now was K'lrsa's only chance to escape.

Her shoulder ached abominably when she sat up. She rubbed at a spot just above the wound, wondering just how serious the injury was. She flexed her arm a bit to test it. Stiff, but nothing more.

She hoped the same was true of Fallion's wound.

She rubbed at her face, feeling the grit of the desert caked on her skin.

She'd made such a mess of things so far...

Maybe she should go home. Run back to her tribe while she still had the chance. Who was she to think that she could find the Daliph and kill him? Just a foolish young Rider who'd almost killed herself and her horse, that's who.

She buried her face in her hands, wishing for her father. He'd know what she should do. He'd tell her how strong she was and how much he believed in her.

She hugged herself, fighting back the tears. No point in crying. It wouldn't bring him back.

She dashed a tear away as it crawled down her cheek. She wanted her father to tell her what to do.

But he was gone. Forever.

She was alone now. No one was going to support her or help her. It was up to her to decide. To see this through, or admit defeat and slink back to her tribe like a whipped dog, tail between her legs, crying not to be beat.

She shook her head, dispelling the fear that weighed her down.

Her father wasn't with her, but she knew what he'd say. He'd tell her she could do this, that she could accomplish anything she put her mind to. She was strong and capable.

She pulled her thin blanket closer and nodded to herself.

She could do this. She had to. She had to avenge him. If she didn't, no one else would.

She moved towards the tent flap. She needed to be outside in the fresh night air, to stare up at the moon and check on Fallion. She needed to feel Fallion's comforting weight as he snuffled at her hair.

But Lodie was now awake, sitting cross-legged as she silently watched her.

"What do you want?" K'lrsa asked. She knew she sounded surly, but she didn't care. How long had the woman been watching her? Her grief was her own and she didn't like the thought that this old crone had watched her cry.

"The truth." Lodie's hands rested comfortably on her knees. K'lrsa didn't know exactly how old she was, but certainly old enough to hurt sitting like that. She wasn't, though. Here in the privacy of the tent she moved with the lithe grace of a young woman.

"Are you a Rider?" K'lrsa leaned forward to study Lodie more carefully.

"Pzah. I'm a slave with some skill for healing."

"But you were?"

Lodie shrugged. "I've been many things in my life."

"Including a Rider?"

Lodie waved the question away. "We're not talking about me, child. We're talking about you. Why are you here?"

When K'lrsa didn't answer, Lodie shook her head and dug around until she found a cloth-wrapped bundle. She tossed it to K'lrsa. "Eat."

K'lrsa unwrapped the small square of cloth to reveal a flat disc of bread and strips of dried meat. She took a bite of the meat and grimaced.

"Salt. It takes some getting used to." Lodie put a plug of bitter root in her mouth and sucked on it as K'lrsa ate the food in silence.

"I'm not going to tell Harley. Or G'van." She spat into a small cup and mumbled an insult so extreme that K'lrsa had only ever heard it used once before.

K'lrsa stared at her, shocked.

Lodie laughed, suddenly looking ten or even twenty years younger. "Ah, to be young again…Trust me, child. Live long enough you'll find reason to use that word yourself. Especially if you find yourself in the Daliphate. The men there are not like the men you know."

"How so?"

Lodie stared at the wall as if she could actually see the Daliphate, her brow furrowed and lips pressed tight.

After a long moment, she shook her head. "No. I won't speak of that. Not tonight. It was enough to live it." She turned her attention back to K'lrsa and demanded, "Why are you here, child?"

K'lrsa bit her lip. She had no reason to trust this woman.

But she was scared and lonely and didn't know what she'd committed herself to. She needed help. She couldn't do this alone.

And Lodie had been to the Daliphate and was once a member of the tribes.

Lodie moved closer until the smell of bitter root stung K'lrsa's nose. She leaned forward and touched K'lrsa's moon stone. The stone answered her touch with a soft blue glow of welcome and acceptance.

"I had a pendant like that once." Lodie spoke softly, her lips twitching into a sad half-smile.

No one would willingly give up their moon stone or sun stone. K'lrsa had never been without hers since the day she was born, except for the few times when she'd needed to change the cording.

"What happened to it?"

Lodie let out a little grunt of sound. "I followed its advice. And lost it."

K'lrsa leaned forward, eager to hear more. Most saw the moon and sun stones as symbols, nothing more. Some could use them to find shelter, but most dismissed even that skill as luck. Only a rare few believed their stones were capable of anything else.

When she was younger, K'lrsa had told her mother that her moon stone spoke to her sometimes, not in words but in sensations. Her mother had shook her head and told K'lrsa to get over her childish fantasies.

"What did it tell you to do?" K'lrsa asked.

Lodie stared at K'lrsa for a long while, a sad little smile tugging at the corner of her lips. "It didn't tell me to do anything. I told it what I wanted to do and it showed me how I could achieve it."

"Then how did you lose it?"

Lodie spit a gob of bitter root juice into the cup. "I journeyed to the Daliphate. Our gods have no power there. The stone was taken from me on the day I was made a slave."

K'lrsa clutched at her moon stone. She couldn't imagine losing that gentle presence. Without it she'd be blind in the desert, vulnerable to the Trickster and the shifting sands.

Lodie smiled a soft, sad smile. "Don't worry. Harley won't take it from you. He isn't smart enough to do so."

"Then why did he take yours?"

Lodie stared at her and K'lrsa felt like a hare caught by a hawk's gaze. She froze, suddenly scared.

"Harley didn't take it. And he didn't make me a slave. The one who took mine knew exactly what it was and what it could do."

"Who?"

Lodie licked her lips and looked away, the moonlight slashing across her face like a wound. "My sister."

Lodie spit into the cup again, the red juice of the bitter root running down her chin.

"Your sister took your moon stone from you?" K'lrsa couldn't imagine anyone of the tribes doing something like that. "But why?"

Lodie took the now-empty cloth from K'lrsa and folded it into smaller and smaller pieces. She shook her head as if trying to shake off a bothersome sand fly. "It doesn't matter. It was long ago. That's the least of the injuries my sister inflicted on me."

She looked at K'lrsa. "Now, are you going to tell me what you're doing here? Or will you force me to guess?"

K'lrsa wanted to tell her, but she couldn't bring herself to talk about it just yet.

Lodie set the cloth aside. She laced her fingers together and rested her chin on them as she studied K'lrsa. "Fine. I'll guess. Something happened. You swore revenge. When you did, the Lady Moon came to visit you. She showed you what your life could be like if you turned back. A vision of your child, perhaps? Or your husband? Did she let you see yourself as a grandmother holding his hand, surrounded by your children and grandchildren?"

K'lrsa didn't dare answer, she just nodded.

Lodie picked the cloth back up and started to refold it once more. "Me too."

She smoothed the fabric across her lap and met K'lrsa's stare. "I believe those images were real. She showed me what my life would've been."

"I don't." K'lrsa crossed her arms tight across her chest.

Lodie raised an eyebrow at the vehemence in her tone. "Why not?"

K'lrsa shook her head. "Because there's no man in the tribes I want to marry. Not even close. How can I have that beautiful dancing child she showed me when I can't find a man I want to spend more than a meal with?"

Lodie laughed. "Ah, so young."

When K'lrsa glared at her, Lodie patted her knee. "Child, it only takes one. You can be bored or disinterested in all the rest, but if the Lady Moon said there was a man out there for you, there was. Unless you're a...?"

K'lrsa shook her head. "No. I want a man. I just never found one." She scratched at a patch of mud caked to the knee of her pants.

"Well, you would have if you'd stayed. The Lady Moon doesn't send false dreams."

K'lrsa glared at her. "But the Trickster does."

Lodie shook her head. "Even he's not fool enough to pretend to be the Lady Moon. Or Father Sun. That's who showed you the path, isn't it? After you refused to turn back?"

K'lrsa nodded, not daring to speak. How could she know so much?

Lodie pulled her knees up to her chest and rested her chin on them. "He showed me my path, too."

She said it with such regret that K'lrsa blurted out, "Did he mislead you?"

Lodie laughed, a loud bark of sound. "No. The path he showed me led to exactly where I wanted to be. And I accomplished what I set out to do."

"Then why not go back to your tribe?"

Lodie's face went blank, all emotion hidden somewhere deep under the surface. "It was too late for that."

"Because you were a slave? You could escape. You're healthy, strong."

Lodie glared at her. "And then what? Where would I go? My husband's dead. Our child is dead. I'm an old woman. What tribe would take me?" She shook her head. "No. There's nothing left for me."

K'lrsa leaned forward. "That can't be true. There must be somewhere for you to go."

"No. Not anymore." Lodie stood in one fluid movement and stared down at her, the moonlight striking her face so that it turned the space where her eyes should be as black as the night. "If you continue down this path, child, you won't be able to go back either. You'll be forever changed. Forever alone."

She turned away. "Just like I am."

Lodie ducked out into the darkness of the night, leaving K'lrsa sitting alone in silence, trying to absorb her words.

K'lrsa shook her head.

She wouldn't be alone. She had no intention of living past the moment she stabbed her knife into the heart of the man responsible for her father's death.

20

She dreamed again. Not of the Lady Moon or Father Sun.

She dreamed of the young man with blue eyes and skin the color of the desert sands as the sun touched them at dawn. He held out his hand, smiling softly. When she took it, she felt comforted, safe, like she'd found the one place in the world where she belonged.

He pulled her hand to his lips and kissed the back of it; the brush of his lips against her skin sent fire through her blood.

She turned away from him, shaking her head.

What cruelty was this?

She'd chosen her path. Why would the Lady Moon send her visions of what could never be?

She left him behind, walking all night through the soft sands of the desert, stumbling and falling, until dawn came and she awoke once more in Lodie's tent, shivering in the cold of pre-dawn.

She squeezed her eyes shut, forcing herself to remember how her father had looked in his last minutes. The hollows where his eyes had once been, the blackened wound in his stomach, the torn flesh of his hands.

It wasn't quite enough to drive away the image of the young man from her dreams, but it was enough to keep her moving forward, intent on her goal.

She would avenge him.

No matter what, or who, it cost her.

21

Harley found K'lrsa and Lodie later that morning as they ate fried desert flowers and baru meat in front of Lodie's tent. The bandaged woman was there, too. She hunched in on herself when he approached and Lodie rested a hand on her knee to calm her. The woman had yet to utter a single word; she just ghosted between her tent and Lodie's fire, flinching whenever anyone came too close.

"Can she ride?" Harley asked, looming over them, his hands on his hips as he glared between K'lrsa and Lodie.

K'lrsa studied him as she waited for Lodie to answer. If Lodie were to stand, she'd be at least three handspans taller than the man. It fascinated K'lrsa that such a short, ugly man could lead anyone, let alone this group of men, each one meaner and nastier than the last.

Lodie finished her bite of food before answering. "We can leave tomorrow. But it's not the girl that's holding us back. The horse needs another day before we can move on."

Harley glared at Fallion, eyes narrowed.

"Oh, don't be a fool, Harley. It's an *Amalanee* horse. Do you know how rare they are? That horse is worth more than that whole lot of slaves you just dragged across the desert."

As he chewed on the inside of his lip and studied Fallion, K'lrsa held her breath. He wouldn't leave Fallion behind would he?

Finally, he nodded. "Fine. Tomorrow."

Before he could turn away, Lodie added. "The horse won't be able to carry a rider for another three or four days after that. And we'll need to take more frequent breaks until he's fully healed."

Harley shook his head and stormed away, cussing softly.

He came back a short while later and stared between K'lrsa and the bandaged woman, once more chewing on the inside of his cheek as he studied them.

Lodie was gone, tending to the slaves, and K'lrsa didn't feel inclined to speak, so the silence stretched until K'lrsa could feel the tension like someone was squeezing the back of her neck.

Finally, Harley nodded to himself as if he'd made a decision. He pointed to K'lrsa. "You. Get up."

She stood as tall as she could, trying to hide how scared she was. Lodie hadn't betrayed her yet, but she worried that G'van might say something or Harley would decide to give her to one of his men.

Harley snarled as he looked up at her—she wasn't as tall as Lodie, but tall enough that he only reached her shoulder. He stalked away without another word, obviously expecting her to follow.

K'lrsa trailed along behind him until he stopped at the cloth contraption from her vision, its bright colors in stark contrast to the weathered tents and wagons of the rest of the camp. "You'll ride in this tomorrow."

He whistled and two men came running. He issued quick instructions to them and they raced away again. "I want you to try it now so you don't delay us further in the morning."

K'lrsa laughed. "You want me to ride in that? No. I'm a Rider. Give me a horse."

Harley turned on her, his hand raised to slap her, but stopped himself at the last moment. "Desert Princess, indeed," he drawled, his eyes as cold as the deepest desert night. He stepped forward until she felt the spit from each word landing on her skin. "Do you see a bunch of spare horses lying around, *Princess*?"

She backed up but he stepped even closer, his scarred lip twisting upward as he spoke, the stench of his breath as awful as the look in his eyes. "You have two choices. Walk with the slaves. Or ride in this."

K'lrsa was about to say that she'd prefer to walk when he leaned close to her ear and whispered, "Keep in mind, Princess, that if you choose to walk, then you choose to be the lowest of my slaves, a piece of trash I'll sell at the first chance. You ride, you're a rare commodity. Worth protecting. You walk, you're nothing."

He stepped back. "Your choice, Princess. Choose wisely." He started to walk away and then turned back to her. "Oh. And if you choose to walk and one of my men decides to take a special interest in you before we reach Crossroads, well…" He shrugged. "What do I care?"

She thought of the comments the men had made about G'van and of the way he'd wanted to take her for himself the day before and shivered.

He wasn't courting her now. Who knew what he might do.

As Harley walked away, K'lrsa called, "And what of the person who was riding in it before?"

He shrugged. "I only have room for one princess. The northern girl can walk with the slaves tomorrow. Fat lot of good she'll do me with all those burns anyway."

———

K'lrsa sat at Lodie's fire and studied the bandaged girl who shivered slightly even though the day was already warm. Her skin, where it was actually visible, glistened with the sweat of fever. Sun sickness.

It was amazing the girl wasn't already dead. Surely she'd die within a day if she had to walk.

Then again, she might die no matter what.

And by then it would be too late for K'lrsa. She'd just be one of the many slaves stumbling along in the dust of the desert, trying not to die.

If K'lrsa wanted her revenge, she had to take the girl's place.

She rubbed her arms. Could she do that? Could she really make this choice knowing the girl would likely die because of it?

It was easy to say she'd sacrifice her own life to avenge her father. But could she sacrifice a stranger's?

22

As they ate dinner over a bowl of millet and sour greens, K'lrsa told Lodie about Harley's visit.

"It's not an easy road." Lodie took another bite of food, staring into the fire.

"What isn't?"

"Revenge. Oh, it's easy if you can strike back right away. A man kills your child, you kill him, it's over in a moment. But a revenge like yours? Or mine? One that takes time? That's harder." She set aside her half-eaten bowl of food, still staring into the fire as if she could see a whole world hidden there. "It's like cradling a torch to your breast. You have to nurture the fire every moment of every day. You have to let it consume everything else—your family, your friends, your future."

She finally looked at K'lrsa, her eyes black in the gathering dark of night. "It's not for everyone."

"You did it." K'lrsa forced herself to take another bite. She wasn't hungry, but she needed to keep up her strength.

Lodie nodded. "I did. But I almost turned back more than once."

"What kept you going?"

Lodie snorted. "I'd already sacrificed too much to quit. At some point, revenge became all that was left to me. It was either turn back and have everything be for naught or continue and at least succeed in what I'd set out to do." She put a plug of bitter root in her mouth. "Even if victory was meaningless by the end."

"What do you mean?"

Lodie spat to the side. "Pzah, girl. You ask too many questions. Can't an old woman eat in peace?"

They sat there for a long time in silence as the last light of day leached from the sky and the moon made her appearance on the far horizon.

K'lrsa couldn't hold her questions back anymore. "Would you do it again if given the choice?"

Lodie shook her head and stood. "Don't ask that question. Never ask that question. Down that road lies madness. There's only the life you've chosen to live. You can go forward on the path you're on or you can choose a new one. But you can never go back. Don't look behind. It's too late for that." She stormed away into the darkness, shaking her head, her shoulders tense with anger.

K'lrsa waited for her to return. She watched the fire sputter and die, deprived of the fuel it needed to keep going.

She thought about what Lodie had said. Already she felt the initial anger at her father's death growing cold. Her rage was a slow simmer now instead of the all-consuming fire it had been the day she found him.

How long until it sputtered away and died into nothing?

Could she sustain it long enough to avenge him?

Another week? Yes. Another month? Maybe. Another year? Or two? Or ten? She didn't know.

What could she use to keep it alive? Who or what would she have to sacrifice before she reached her goal?

And would it be worth it in the end? What if she failed?

Worse yet, what if she succeeded and it meant nothing to her by then?

She pulled her knees to her chest and hugged them tight to her body as she stared at the bandaged girl's tent.

23

She didn't sleep at all that night. She was too scared to dream.

She didn't want to see the young man again and be reminded of what she was sacrificing if she continued down this path.

She didn't want to see the Lady Moon again.

She filled her mind with the image of her father in his final moments, dwelling on every single detail over and over again until it was etched into her memory like a branding iron. His eyes, his hands, the wound in his belly. The last words he'd uttered to her, begging for her to kill him.

Over and over again she heard him, saw him, until the tears streamed down her face and sobs choked her.

She had to avenge him. She had to stop the Daliphate.

When Harley came to find her in the morning and said, "So, Princess. What's it to be? Ride or walk?" she met his eyes without flinching.

"Ride."

She forced herself to watch as they led the young woman away to join the other slaves. The girl had grown even more frail in just the two days K'lrsa had been in camp. She limped along at Harley's side, her eyes focused on the ground as he led her to the huddled mass of slaves on the other side of camp.

K'lrsa felt nothing.
She couldn't. Not anymore.
She'd chosen her path and she wouldn't turn back.
Not now.
Not ever.

By midday, K'lrsa almost regretted the decision to ride. The cloth contraption captured and focused all the heat of the desert, baking her like a spit-roasted hare. With each step, the entire thing swayed dangerously from side to side, threatening to collapse at any moment. She tried to adjust to the lurching movement, but each new step threw her in a different direction as her mounts traversed the sand dunes with their uneven gait.

She opened the curtains to get some fresh air, but all that did was let in the dust of the caravan's passage.

Up ahead, Harley rode side-by-side with G'van, who was laughing at something Harley had just said. Behind them were the four large wagons. According to Lodie, each one held expensive spices and fabrics worth more than K'lrsa's entire tribe had ever seen. Lodie rode on the front of the lead wagon, Fallion walking along beside her. He still limped slightly, but much less than the day before.

K'lrsa rode behind the wagons. And behind her were the slaves, straggling along in a long line, the caravan guards riding the perimeter like a swarm of locusts.

The slaves shuffled forward, their eyes closed against the dust of the caravan's passage. Most looked young, but they were so skinny and so dirty it was hard to tell. All were men.

Except for the blonde girl.

She stumbled along at the very end, barely able to keep up with the others, her mouth set in a firm line as she put one step in front of the other. At any moment K'lrsa expected her to fall, never to recover, but she didn't. She kept going, step after step.

K'lrsa watched her through the rest of the day, amazed by the woman's resilience. More than once she tripped on the soft sand, but each time she recovered and kept going. Her expression never changed, her pace never slackened.

Just like when Harley had taken her away. She hadn't cried out or cussed or screamed or collapsed. She'd just kept going.

Step after step.

K'lrsa let the curtain fall and curled into a ball, wondering if she'd made the right decision.

She grasped her moon stone and prayed for the Lady Moon's guidance, but the stone was cold against her skin.

Had her gods already abandoned her?

She squeezed her eyes shut against the fears and doubts that crept into her mind.

She was a Rider. No one could take that from her. Look at the blonde woman. If *she* could be that strong, so could K'lrsa. She'd do what that woman was doing, continue forward one step at a time.

24

They stopped that night in the midst of a large flat area that had once been fertile plains but was now just more desert. The Black Horse Tribe had no plains lands left. Five generations back they'd adopted city ways, trying to force the land in a direction it wouldn't go, and destroyed it as a result.

No wonder they'd turned to trading with the men of the Daliphate. What other choice had they had?

The sky over the distant mountains was a dark orange and purple, like a bruise, as they made camp. The men worked in silence while Harley walked among them shouting unnecessary orders and cuffing those who moved too slow.

K'lrsa hid behind Fallion's comforting bulk, watching Lodie as she checked on his wound.

Lodie shook her head. "Don't mind Harley. He's just angry at the delay. We stopped far more than normal today so we didn't reach our usual campground. This area is barren—no wood or fuel of any sort for leagues. It'll be cold rations and cold beds tonight."

Fallion's wound was almost completely healed—the only sign he'd been injured was a slight puckering of the skin around Lodie's stitches. Even after the day's riding it looked ten times better than it had that morning. She sent a quick thank-you to the Lady Moon.

"We could go faster tomorrow, couldn't we? Fallion's almost fully healed now." K'lrsa scratched his nose and laughed as he nuzzled her ear.

Lodie gave her a long, searching look. "And what of the other slaves? The ones who have to walk every day? How will they do if we go faster?"

K'lrsa glanced across the camp to where the bandaged girl lay. She'd collapsed as soon as they called a halt, curling into a small ball on the edge of the camp. She hadn't even tried to get food or water.

"That's why we kept stopping today. It wasn't for Fallion. You did it for her."

"I did it for all of them."

Lodie grabbed her medicine bag and headed towards the slaves.

K'lrsa thought about following and offering to help, but she turned away instead. She couldn't bear to see their suffering up close. She didn't want to see the dirt-covered faces and dead eyes.

One small twist of fate and she would be one of them.

She crept into her tent—a tent that had once belonged to the bandaged girl—and sat cross-legged in the center.

She blanked her mind, repeating the Pattern over and over until she lost herself in the Core, floating in a place outside of time and emotion.

She couldn't let that girl, or anyone's, suffering affect her. She had to stay focused on her goal. It was all that mattered.

She refused to think. Refused to feel.

She couldn't.

It would destroy her.

The moon was directly above camp when K'lrsa finally emerged from her tent, hunger pangs cramping her belly.

Lodie sat in front of her own tent, the blonde girl asleep on the ground next to her. There was no fire, but the moon was bright enough to cast everything in a soft silver light.

K'lrsa glanced towards the main camp. The men were still awake—talking and drinking, some standing in line outside the main tent. Inside that tent was the only other woman in the camp. A slave girl Harley had brought along to keep the men amused. K'lrsa blocked her ears to the sounds that came from the tent, not wanting to think about how easily that could've been her.

Or the bandaged girl who slept at Lodie's feet in that careless way that only children can. In sleep she had the same soft innocence as M'lara.

M'lara who K'lrsa had abandoned without a thought. M'lara who slept alone tonight, her father dead, her sister gone without a word.

What had K'lrsa done? And all so she could kill some man she'd never met?

K'lrsa took the toughened piece of meat Lodie offered and sat down to eat in silence. The girl whimpered suddenly, curling in on herself and Lodie reached down to stroke her forehead until she once more relaxed into peaceful slumber.

At K'lrsa's questioning look, Lodie shrugged. "My skill works on children, too."

Lightning struck on the horizon and K'lrsa grabbed her moon stone to see if the storm would make it as far as their camp, but the stone was cool to her touch, devoid of its usual comforting presence.

She let it go. She'd never realized what a silent source of support it was until it was gone.

Lodie took another bite of her own meal. "I told you. The Daliphate is no place for our gods. The sun is weak there. The moon hidden in haze."

"But we're not even in the Daliphate yet. Are we?"

Lodie shook her head. "No. But the Black Horse Tribe long ago abandoned our gods. It might as well be the Daliphate for all the gods care."

K'lrsa continued to eat in silence, her teeth grinding the hard meat into smaller and smaller pieces as she stared at the sleeping young girl.

"You made the only choice you could, child." Lodie's voice was soft, almost kind.

"Did I?"

The girl whimpered again and Lodie reached down to stroke her hair back from her face. "Once the sun claimed her, she was never going to be Harley's northern princess. He could never sell her where he wanted."

Lodie's lips twitched into a small smile. "Do you know that she killed six men the night they took her from her family? She's as strong as a desert cat." Her voice was full of pride.

She soothed the girl's whimpering once more. "If she survives to Crossroads they'll either kill her or break her. Perhaps it's best that she dies before then. On her own terms, fighting until the end."

"Best that they never captured her."

Lodie met K'lrsa's gaze and shook her head slightly. "I told you. You can never go back. None of us can. She's just like the rest of us. She can only move forward from today."

K'lrsa remembered the girl walking across the desert, one step after the other, moving forward with silent determination. "She survived today. She kept going."

"Yes."

"And she'll do the same tomorrow."

"Yes."

"And the next and the next until we reach Crossroads."

"Yes." Lodie's answer was so soft it was almost a whisper.

"And then they'll break her or kill her. Because of me."

Lodie shrugged. "Her path is hers. Yours is yours."

"But I made her path harder."

Lodie spat a gob of bitter root onto the ground between them. "Quit looking backward. You did what you had to. It's done. All you can do now is make sure it was worth it."

"It was." K'lrsa would succeed. Failure was not an option.

Lodie laughed, a sound like two grel fighting. "Oh, child. Such certainty…" She stood, still laughing to herself, and disappeared into her tent.

K'lrsa glared after the woman.

"You can laugh all you want, old hag, but I will succeed," she whispered, tearing off another piece of dried meat and grinding it between her teeth.

25

Three mornings later, K'lrsa watched as Lodie removed Fallion's bandage to show Harley the fully-healed wound. All that remained was a thin white line against his golden coat. She could barely tell he'd been injured.

She knew Lodie had been hoping to slow their progress one more day, but Harley was too shrewd. He'd watched Fallion the day before, circling back throughout the day to study Fallion as he walked across the hard-packed dirt. And this morning he'd demanded to inspect the wound himself.

"He's healed. We'll double our pace today."

Lodie crumpled the bandage between her hands. "He needs one more day of slow travel just to be sure."

"Don't lie to me, woman. He's fine now."

Lodie glared down at Harley. "Who's the healer, Harley? You or me?"

He glared right back at her. "Who's the slave, Lodie? You or me?"

They stood like that, glaring at each other, both taut as a bowstring ready for release until K'lrsa was ready to scream. Finally, Lodie looked away.

K'lrsa was surprised the woman would back down from anyone, but Harley nodded to himself with satisfaction. "Finish packing up. We ride hard today. I want out of this cursed place before the sun sets."

The day before, they'd crossed out of desert and into a dried-out wasteland—the dirt cracked and barren, no animals or plants visible anywhere. The skids on the wagons had been changed out and replaced with wheels before they continued. It was a miserable day of travel, dirty and hot, everyone choking on the dust kicked up by the never-ending wind.

Lodie said they usually crossed the space in one day and had never had to camp there before, but the area seemed like it would never end.

They'd stopped in the middle of nowhere, the distant mountains not even visible through the dusty haze that coated everything.

K'lrsa's sleep had been full of nightmares where her father chased her, screaming and wailing that she'd betrayed her vow to him, that she'd abandoned her people and forsaken her duty as a Rider. She'd tried to explain to him, but there was no reasoning with the wraith that pursued her. In the end she'd just fled, running and running until she finally awoke, cold and scared in the darkest part of the night.

From the looks of it, she wasn't the only one who'd had a haunted night.

Lodie slapped her arm, bringing her back to the present. "Saddle up. You might as well ride him."

K'lrsa glanced at Fallion, so beautiful and golden, even in the dull gray light of dawn. She shook her head. "No. I shouldn't. I…I don't want to hurt him."

"Too late for that." She never had told Lodie the truth, but the woman seemed to know anyway.

"I don't want to hurt him more. And…I'm going to lose him. It's too painful to ride him knowing that he's going to be taken away from me."

Not only did she love Fallion with her whole heart, but he'd been given to her by her father. She hated the thought of some stranger riding him. Or worse, not riding him, but just parading him around like some show pony.

Lodie glared at her, hands on hips. "Listen, child. I won't tell you what to do. But if it were me and I had a horse as fine as that one and only a few days left to spend with him, you wouldn't be able to get me out of his saddle, even to sleep. I'd store up every memory I could of how it feels to be free while I still was."

"I'm not free." K'lrsa glanced around the camp at the sullen men taking down tents and rousing the slaves.

Lodie snorted. "No? Child, you have no idea how free you are, even now. Just wait."

K'lrsa stroked Fallion's back and he turned to nuzzle at her ear, blowing her hair back from her face.

Her hair was dull and greasy after so many days of riding and no chance to use a comb or take a sweat bath. She knew she smelled rank, too, but she didn't really care. The way some of the men looked at her, she wished she was even more filthy and smelly, although she suspected there was no amount of dirt and grime that would deter them.

She shuddered. At least they left her alone.

She'd seen some of the men grabbing at the bandaged girl, pawing at her flesh as she passed by. Yesterday, Reginald had taken the girl up on his horse for the last little portion of the day. At first, K'lrsa had thought it was kind of him—until she'd seen the way his hands disappeared underneath the girl's clothes and the blank look on the girl's face as she stared ahead trying to ignore what he was doing to her.

They'd started taking her into the tent at night, too, chaining her next to the other slave girl and using her for their entertainment. Harley hadn't said a word when G'van dragged her to the tent the night before. He'd just looked past the tent and met K'lrsa's eyes for a long moment before turning back to his men and issuing some order or another.

It was all K'lrsa's fault. The girl would still be protected if K'lrsa hadn't taken her place.

K'lrsa spent the long days imaging what she'd do to repay the men for each little cruelty they inflicted on the slaves—each slap, each kick.

She could take any of them, given the chance. She was a trained warrior who knew a hundred and five different ways to kill a man.

Poke his eyes out.

Smash his nose into his skull.

Knife his kidneys.

But she couldn't act.

She couldn't risk failing at her true mission.

So she saved her anger for the Daliph, imagining all the ways she would kill *him* when they were finally face to face. *He* was the reason these men were trading slaves. *He* was the source of the corruption slowly poisoning her people.

All she had to do was look at G'van to know what the Daliphate had done to her people. He was the first in line to visit the tent each night, so drunk his words slurred, the scent of smokeweed clinging to his skin.

Her father had been right. The Black Horse Tribe no longer deserved to be part of the tribes. They had to be cut away like gangrenous flesh before their sickness spread and killed all of the tribes.

She was almost done saddling Fallion when she heard G'van's voice. "What do you think you're doing?"

He stared down at her from the back of his black stallion. The sun shining on his face made him even more beautiful than normal, but all she saw was the hideous man who'd betrayed everything his people stood for.

She ignored him as she finished cinching Fallion's saddle.

G'van grabbed her injured arm, his fingers digging into her flesh as he pulled her towards him. "Don't ignore me."

She didn't even think, she just acted, twisting out of his grip and grabbing the front of his shirt to pull him out of the saddle. She yanked downward and he fell in a pile at her feet, crying out in pain.

She planted her foot on his neck, wanting to stomp down and crush his windpipe, but holding back. "Don't touch me. Ever."

Before G'van could react, Harley rode up and backhanded her, sending K'lrsa flying into the dirt.

She held a hand to her cheek as she stumbled to her feet. "What was that for?"

"What was that for? You're a *slave*, Princess. You are my property. And my property does not attack one of my men. Ever. For any reason."

She backed away as he rode his horse closer to her, his face distorted in anger.

"I'm sorry." She held her hands in front of her, to keep him back. "I didn't think. He grabbed me and I just…reacted."

Fallion started towards them, but K'lrsa called out to him. "*Azah*, Fallion. It's fine."

Harley rode so close K'lrsa could see the individual hairs in his horse's coat and smell the earthy stench of him. She flinched, waiting for him to hit her again, but he turned aside. "G'van. What were you doing over here?"

G'van glared past Harley at K'lrsa, his hands clenched into fists. "She was saddling up her horse. I came to investigate."

"She's none of your business. I told you I don't want you anywhere near her. Now go."

G'van gave her one last menacing glare before he painfully mounted his horse and rode off towards the slaves, moving so fast that men had to jump out of his way.

Harley turned his attention back to her. "Why were you saddling the horse?"

"He's healed. Lodie said I could ride him."

As she answered, Barkley rode up to join Harley, but he remained silent as Harley said, "Princesses don't ride horses."

"Desert princesses do." She stood her ground, looking up at him, but she was trembling inside, waiting for another blow.

Harley laughed. "You told me there's no such thing as a princess in the desert. And now you're telling me that there are and they ride horses?"

"You said I'm a desert princess. Well, I ride horses." She had to force herself not to take a step back as he glared down at her.

Barkley nudged his horse over to Fallion's side. "You know, Harley. She may have a point. Let her ride the *Amalanee* horse in the Daliphate and word will spread like wildfire. Not like anyone would believe a woman of the desert rides in one of those palanquins anyway."

Harley thought about it for a moment, looking back and forth between K'lrsa and Fallion. Finally, he looked at Lodie. "What do you think, old woman?"

Lodie shrugged. "Barkley's right. No woman of the tribes would ride in something like that."

K'lrsa could hear the unspoken words in Lodie's response—that Harley was a fool for trying to pass K'lrsa off as some desert princess—but Harley obviously didn't.

"Fine. She can ride."

K'lrsa reached for Fallion's reins.

"But, Barkley, you take the reins. We don't want to risk losing our prize when we're so close to selling her off."

<u>26</u>

"How close are we to Crossroads?" K'lrsa asked Barkley as they rode side-by-side behind Harley and G'van. The two men weren't laughing and joking today—they hadn't spoken a word to one another since breaking camp.

"Should be there tomorrow." Barkley pointed off in the distance. "Look, the first signs of civilization."

K'lrsa stared at the object he pointed to. It squatted in the distance, square and taller than anything she'd ever seen before. It clearly wasn't part of nature with its straight lines and bright white coloring.

She squinted, trying to figure out what it was made of. "What is that?"

Barkley laughed. "A barn. It's used to protect animals or food."

"It's so big. How do they move it?"

Barkley stared at her, one eyebrow quirked in surprise. "They don't."

"But don't the people move with the seasons? How do they feed themselves if they don't migrate with the animals?"

He shook his head. "Oh, Princess. You have a lot to learn."

He spent the rest of the day explaining to her concepts like farming and raising animals for meat as he pointed out the various buildings they passed and explained their purpose. At first it was just one or two barns in the distance, then an isolated farmhouse and a barn, and then clusters of buildings grouped together where people lived side-by-side, permanently.

She'd never seen so much wood in one place. To think that trees could grow so tall they were used to build entire buildings. And that people lived in those buildings all the time; they never moved, never traveled with the seasons. They just lived in one single place.

Forever.

She forgot everything else as she listened to Barkley and studied the fields and buildings they passed. It seemed the traders who visited their tribe hadn't just been telling stories to entertain an impressionable young girl.

"Does this mean there really are bodies of water so large that a man can travel across them for days?" she asked at one point.

Barkley nodded. "Yes. Oceans. I've never traveled on one myself, but I've seen one in the north, on the other side of the Great Desert."

K'lrsa felt a small thrill as she imagined how big and varied the world really must be. She'd never known, never realized that people could lead lives so different from her own.

When they made camp that night, she immediately went to find the bandaged girl. The girl still hadn't spoken in all the days K'lrsa had been in camp, but K'lrsa was determined to get her to speak. She wanted to know about the northern lands. To hear about oceans and frozen water—Barkley had tried to describe for her how water actually froze and fell from the sky, but she just couldn't believe him.

Unfortunately, G'van reached the girl before K'lrsa could. She watched, helpless, as he dragged the girl towards the main tent where a few of the men were already waiting.

But she didn't have to be helpless, did she?

She ran forward, blocking G'van's way. "Let her go, G'van. You have the other girl. Leave this one alone."

"Get out of my way." He pushed her aside. "The other girl's dead."

"What? How?"

He shrugged as he kept walking, dragging the bandaged girl behind him. "Not everyone survives the desert."

K'lrsa ran back to Lodie's camp. "What happened to the slave girl? The one in the tent?"

Lodie spat to the side, the red bitter root juice dribbling down her chin. "She didn't make it."

"What do you mean?"

Lodie stared at her for a long moment, an almost sad expression on her face. "You didn't even notice, did you?"

"Notice what?"

"When we struck camp this morning, she was too weak to keep up. She tried, but after the third time she fell, she didn't get back up."

K'lrsa felt a chill down her spine. She hadn't noticed, too intent on Fallion and G'van. "No one helped her?"

Lodie shrugged. "The bandaged one tried to, but they wouldn't let her. I tried, too, but Harley said to leave her."

"So she's just back there somewhere, dying?" She clenched her fists, looking back the way they'd come, picturing the young girl lying on the ground, alone.

"Dead by now." Lodie spat again. "It's for the best. Tomorrow we'll reach Crossroads and the men can just go to a brothel or find a willing woman in a tavern. Harley was probably going to kill her off in the morning anyway."

"How can you say that? As if it's nothing?" K'lrsa shifted, moving away from Lodie as if the woman had a disease.

Lodie laughed. "Says the girl who didn't even notice what had happened."

K'lrsa didn't know how to respond, but Lodie continued anyway. "It isn't nothing. What they did to that girl is horrible and I did what I could to help her. But the world is far worse than that. What I've seen..." Lodie shook her head. "At least they let the girl die."

Lodie stared at K'lrsa, her eyes full of such sorrow and loss that it felt like she were reaching into K'lrsa's chest and squeezing her heart in a clenched fist. "Trust me, child. She's better off now."

K'lrsa reached out to touch Lodie's knee. "What happened to you, Lodie? You were a Rider once weren't you? What changed you?"

Lodie's eyes flashed with anger and she pulled away from K'lrsa's touch. "You should go home."

"What?" K'lrsa sat back, surprised.

"Leave. Now. Before it's too late."

"But I don't want to go home."

Lodie shook her head. "Go home, child, before the world breaks you. The land of the Daliphate isn't the land of the tribes. Go home before you find out just how different they are."

Before K'lrsa could say anything else, Lodie grabbed her medical bag and left.

K'lrsa watched her weave her way through the men's tents, tall and proud as she walked by them on her way to tend to the slaves. None even bothered to look at Lodie, but a few cast glances in K'lrsa's direction. She turned away, ignoring them.

Maybe Lodie was right. She didn't know enough about the Daliphate to succeed.

From what Barkley had said today, it was larger than anything she could imagine. He'd described cities with so many people and houses that you couldn't even count them. Cities where you could walk for an entire day and never reach the other side.

She'd thought the Daliphate was like the tribes—small clusters of families traveling together—and that all she'd need to do was find Toreem, demand an audience with the Daliph, and kill him before he had a chance to react.

But she was finally starting to understand how vastly different the Daliphate was from the tribes. Could she possibly succeed? Or was she just the impulsive, reckless girl her mother had always said she was?

Maybe she should go home now. Her mother and sister probably needed her. And F'lia.

With K'lrsa's father gone, who would speak out against the Black Horse Tribe at the annual gathering? Who would tell everyone about slaves left to die on the desert sands?

Someone had to stop them before they dragged her people into poverty and degradation. She should go back to where she could actually accomplish something.

But she wasn't the type to walk away just because something was hard.

Look at the baru she'd killed. How many days had she followed that herd? How many times had she chased them, choking on their dust as they left her far behind and fled into the desert? How many times had she shot at a baru only to see it leap away in the last instant?

But she'd succeeded in the end. She'd kept trying and she'd finally accomplished her goal.

Because she hadn't quit.

She hadn't turned aside when everyone said it was impossible.

She'd kept going.

And she knew that no matter how hard this was, she could do it.

She could.

She just had to have faith in herself.

27

They reached Crossroads at the end of the next day. The land was still mostly flat, but it had been steadily rising for a while when they suddenly came to the top of a rise and saw the town sprawled below. The distant mountains that had always shadowed the far horizon were now distinct, rising up one by one in the distance behind the town.

K'lrsa reined Fallion to a stop, her mouth hanging open in surprise. So many buildings. And people everywhere. She counted at least thirty separate structures, aligned on either side of two roads that met to form an x. The roads between the buildings teemed with people—more than she'd ever seen anywhere outside of the annual tribal gathering.

Trading caravans like their own were camped in a rough circle around the buildings, forming a large barricade of people and animals. The steady hum of so many people in one place reached them even at this distance.

Barkley stopped beside her and she turned to him, eyes wide. "It's so big."

He laughed. "Crossroads? It's nothing. Just a place where slaves are sold and men can spend the coin on wine and women. Hardly more than its name implies, really. You should see Boradol."

She trailed along behind him to a large barren area on the outskirts of the town. The men quickly made camp, eager to be off to drink some alcohol and eat a real meal. Harley had made it clear to K'lrsa that she wasn't to go with them. Not that she'd wanted to.

The thought of so many strangers in one place made her skin crawl. Every time she thought she understood the challenges she faced, she realized how wrong she really was.

After watching most of the men race away towards town, she sat down in front of Lodie's fire. Lodie mended a pile of the men's clothing as she waited for dinner to finish cooking.

K'lrsa's stomach growled at the smell of the earthy grains and pungent greens even though she was tired of eating the same thing night after night. There hadn't been good hunting for the last few days with all the people and farms everywhere and the caravan was almost out of supplies other than the millet grains Lodie used for every single meal.

After a long silence, Lodie said, "You can't heal the pain with hurt. I've tried."

K'lrsa shook off the annoying comment. "What do you mean?"

Lodie set aside her sewing and stirred the pot of food. "I don't know what brought you here, child. But I know someone you love had to be hurt. It's the only thing that would drive a Rider to be as stupid as this."

K'lrsa glared at the fire, clenching her jaw tight as Lodie continued, "You forget, child. I was once like you. And I can tell you that, even if you succeed, the pain of your loss won't end. It won't go away. You will always carry that hollow place around inside you no matter how many people you punish. The hurt you give won't heal the pain you've received."

K'lrsa shrugged. "At least my father's death will mean something. He won't have died staked out in the middle of the desert for nothing. He'll have died so I can bring down the Daliph."

Lodie laughed, the sound rolling out of her in gusts of sound that she couldn't control as she clutched at her stomach.

When she'd finally regained control of herself, she asked, "The Daliph? That's your goal? To kill the Daliph?"

"Yes. He's killing us. Look what he's done to the Black Horse Tribe. He has to be stopped."

Lodie continued to chuckle softly as she shook her head. "You're wrong, child. The Daliph isn't responsible for men like G'van. And killing him won't change things. Time only runs in one direction. You can't stop what's already begun."

K'lrsa gritted her teeth. "I'm not a child. And I can stop this. I just have to cut off the head of the snake."

"That easy is it? You just ride into Toreem, find the Daliph, kill him, and life is all perfect sunshine every day after?"

K'lrsa bit her lip. Phrased like that it did sound foolish.

"I felt the same, you know." Lodie poured soup into a bowl and handed it to her. "That's what I thought when I set out to rescue my sister. I'd go there, I'd find the man who'd taken her, I'd kill him, and we'd both come back home, safe and happy, and everything would go back to the way it was before."

"What happened?" K'lrsa took a bite, savoring the delicate taste of the spices Lodie had added—spices K'lrsa had never tasted before this journey.

Lodie shrugged. "I made it to Toreem just fine. But it took me twenty-five years to actually kill the man I'd come to kill. By then my sister wasn't who'd she'd been when she was taken. Neither was I."

K'lrsa choked on her soup. "Twenty-five years?"

Lodie nodded. "Twenty-five years. Twenty-five years of…" She shook her head, grimacing at whatever memory she refused to speak of. She took another bite of food before continuing. "When I did kill the man at last, do you know what my sister did?"

Lodie didn't wait for an actual answer. "She sold me. I was already a slave, but she could've kept me by her side and treated me as if I were free. She didn't. She sold me to Harley." Lodie laughed softly. "I killed the man who held her captive for twenty-five years and she sold me off like any other piece of property. The very next day." She glared at K'lrsa. "I hope she chokes on the profit."

"Why would she do that?"

Lodie shrugged. "She had her reasons. But it doesn't change what she did."

Lodie leaned forward, staring into K'lrsa's eyes. "Know this, *child*, whatever you think you're going to do, you're wrong. Wherever you think your path is leading, it isn't. You have no idea what is coming."

"Then tell me."

Lodie laughed. "I can't tell you anymore than I can describe a sunset to a blind man. Some things just have to be experienced to be understood." She set her bowl down and stood. "Go home, child, before you find that you have no home to go back to. Tonight's your last chance. While most of the men are away getting drunk, saddle up that beautiful horse of yours, and flee. Once Harley sells you, it'll be too late."

Lodie walked away, leaving K'lrsa alone with her bowl of congealed grains and sour greens. K'lrsa shoved at the food, no longer hungry.

She watched the bandaged girl stumble her way across the camp. Every step was a struggle, her feet left a bloody trail behind her, but the girl kept going. Somehow, day after day, she'd kept going, never stopping.

The girl flinched as she passed one of the guards, but he didn't even notice her. What would become of the girl tomorrow? She must've been beautiful once, but now she was scarred all over from her burns, her skin red and shiny.

Would anyone want her?

And if no one did...What would Harley do?

That could've been K'lrsa.

It still could be. Tomorrow or the next day. Harley could change his mind in an instant. One misstep, one change in the wind, and K'lrsa could be the one in the center tent each night. The one sold off to the lowest whorehouse.

Or killed and tossed aside like so much trash.

Each day she traveled with Harley and his men, she risked failure. But she couldn't survive without them. She knew enough by now to know that she'd never make it as far as Toreem without someone to take her there.

So it was stay and risk death or betrayal, or go home.

As the bandaged girl reached her fire, K'lrsa held the bowl of millet and greens out to her. The girl took the bowl with a slight nod and sat down to eat, shoveling the food into her mouth in great gulps.

K'lrsa watched the girl in silence. It would be easy to flee back to her tribe, but no. She had to continue.

Before she did, though, she'd do what she could for the bandaged girl. She owed her that much.

28

When Lodie returned to their fire, the sky was dark, the moon not yet risen. The bandaged girl slept on the far side of the fire, curled in on herself, brow creased as she twitched and whimpered at whatever she saw in her dreams.

Lodie made her way towards her tent without stopping, but K'lrsa reached out and grabbed her leg. "Wait. Please. I'd speak with you."

Lodie came back and sat beside her, silent, waiting.

K'lrsa stroked her moon stone with her thumb. It was cold and empty like it had been for the last few days.

"Lodie, did your moon stone ever work in the Daliphate?"

"No. I told you. Our gods are desert gods. They have no place in the Daliphate."

K'lrsa nodded. She'd known already, but she'd needed to hear it. To confirm that there really was no point in holding on to her past any longer. She didn't intend to return from this journey, so why take the stone with her?

With a deep sigh, K'lrsa removed the moon stone from her neck and cradled it in her palm. She felt one brief flare of warmth from the stone and then it once more sat there as cold and empty as any pebble found on the ground.

She leaned forward until she was almost touching Lodie. The fire distorted the old woman's wrinkled face until she seemed like a creature from nightmare. "Lodie. If I give you my moon stone, will you take the girl to safety?"

"Safety?" Lodie snorted. "And where would that be?"

"My tribe. They'll protect you. Both of you."

"Will they?" Lodie's response was half-laugh, half-query as if she thought K'lrsa naïve to even consider that a possibility.

But K'lrsa knew her mother, knew her well enough to know that she wouldn't turn them away. Not if they came with word of K'lrsa. "Yes."

Lodie was silent a long time. "Why? Why should I do this? What is there for me in your tribe? Here, they treat me well. I'm a slave, but I have my own tent, my own food. What will I be to your tribe but some old woman with no family to shelter her?"

It was true. Resources in the tribes were limited, held close, shared only with those who could contribute. And Lodie was old. She knew herb lore but so did many members of the tribes. And the girl—so pale and different—who would want her for a mate? And what could she actually do?

But K'lrsa had already thought it through and she knew the one thing that would make the tribe accept Lodie and, through her, the girl.

"My family will shelter you."

"Why would they do that?" Lodie picked up the sewing she'd abandoned earlier and started picking at the seam of a shirt K'lrsa could swear she'd sewn earlier that day.

"Because you're family."

Lodie froze. She didn't look at K'lrsa, didn't react.

K'lrsa took her knife out of its sheath. The knife she'd used to kill her father and to swear her vow of revenge.

She let the blade catch the firelight. It shone bright in the darkness that hovered between them.

Lodie slowly set the shirt on the ground and looked at K'lrsa, her face still carefully blank.

K'lrsa sliced her own palm with the knife and waited for the blood to pool and swell. She placed the moon stone in the center of her palm and, as the stone sucked up her blood, held the knife out to Lodie.

Lodie trembled as she turned her palm faced upward and held it before K'lrsa. The first glint of the moon shone silver on her weathered skin as K'lrsa sliced the knife across Lodie's palm.

K'lrsa swallowed back the tears that filled her eyes at the naked hope in the older woman's gaze.

She grasped Lodie's cut hand with her own, feeling the strength of the older woman as their blood mingled around the moon stone.

"I, K'lrsa dan V'na of the White Horse Tribe do swear..." K'lrsa paused, wrinkling her brow in thought. She knew Lodie was of the tribes, but which one? And what was her actual tribal name?

Lodie watched her, but didn't speak, so K'lrsa finally had to ask, "What is your tribal name, Lodie?"

Lodie looked away.

The moments slid by as their combined blood started to seep between their hands and drip onto the hard ground. Lodie tried to pull her hand away, but K'lrsa tightened her grip.

"Lodie?"

Lodie took a deep breath and turned back to K'lrsa, her head held high, her shoulders thrown back as she sat up straight. "I am L'dia dan G'la of the Summer Spring Tribe."

K'lrsa gasped. The Summer Spring Tribe had once been the most prosperous tribe of all. Small, yes. But they'd been the keepers of the secrets, the ones most devoted to protecting the shifting sands and the Hidden City. The ones who remembered when all others had forgotten.

"The Summer Spring Tribe disappeared. Before I was born. No one knows what happened to them. Some say they were swallowed by the sands, taken by the Lady Moon."

Lodie snorted, the sound like a last gasp before dying. "They didn't disappear. The Daliph slaughtered them—every man, woman, and child."

K'lrsa stared at Lodie. "Why?"

Lodie shrugged. "I guess he didn't appreciate my sister's repeated attempts to kill him."

As K'lrsa continued to stare at her, Lodie squeezed her hand. "Come on, girl. Get on with it. We're going to bleed to death at this rate."

K'lrsa swallowed heavily before she continued. "I, K'lrsa dan V'na of the White Horse Tribe do swear before the Lady Moon that from this day forward L'dia dan G'la of the Summer Spring Tribe is a sister of my blood. She is my family. All who are my family are hers and all who are her family are mine. Let all know this by the moon stone I give her."

Lodie's hand spasmed around K'lrsa's before she let go. She turned away, but K'lrsa saw the tears that ran silently down her cheeks.

K'lrsa took the pendant—it was clean, the blood absorbed into the stone and the cut on her hand nothing more than a shallow mark that was quickly fading away—and bound it around Lodie's neck.

Lodie clutched the pendant, her head bent down. K'lrsa rested her hands on Lodie's shoulders and whispered, "Sister of my blood, will you help me save this girl? Will you help me balance the scales?"

Lodie nodded, the silvery light of the moon shining down on her hair like a crown. "Yes."

She shook K'lrsa's hands off. "But if we're going to do this, we need to act now."

29

"You should take Fallion." K'lrsa crossed her arms tight across her chest, hurting at the thought of being so far away from him. In the last few days he'd been all that had sustained her.

Lodie shook her head. "No. Harley would send men after us if we took that horse."

"But you could outrun him. It wouldn't matter."

"No. You'll need the horse if you make it to Toreem. If the current Daliph is who I think he is, he has far more appreciation for horse flesh than women. Don't get me wrong, he likes women very much. But they're easy to come by. Horses like that one are not."

K'lrsa remembered the day her father gave her Fallion. He'd been so happy, almost hopping with excitement as he held the reins out to her, his smile brighter than the sun.

"For me?" She'd stroked Fallion's neck, marveling at how soft he felt. He'd been so much bigger than her then she'd had to stretch onto tippy toes to scratch his ears.

"For you. My next Rider." Her father had never told them where he'd found the horse. He'd been gone for months and Fallion was all he'd brought back after all that time.

Her mother, of course, had been livid, accusing her father of encouraging K'lrsa to chase foolish dreams that would never get her anywhere. But her father had simply shook his head and said, "Enough."

It wasn't often that K'lrsa's mother was silent, but at the tone in his voice, she'd closed her mouth and walked away.

K'lrsa hadn't even noticed, so enamored of her new horse and so full of pride that her father thought her worthy of such a prize.

She shook away the memory. She couldn't afford to reminisce. Not right now.

"You still need a horse, Lodie. The girl won't make it anywhere on foot. And neither will you if Harley sends men after you."

Lodie nodded in agreement and they turned their attention to the horse line. Most of the horses were sturdy little desert ponies. Good for traveling long distances, but not at all swift. And not up to carrying two passengers at once.

Most of the guards had taken their horses with them into town.

Which left only one horse—G'van's black stallion. The horse stamped its feet and shook its mane when it noticed their attention. Not an ideal choice. Too restive and poorly suited for the desert.

But it had survived the journey to Crossroads. And it would move fast the first few days as they made their way back across the farmland and the flat, dry wasteland beyond. The horse was almost unmanageable, even for G'van, but with Lodie's special talent for animals, it should be fine.

"Where's G'van?" K'lrsa looked around camp, but only saw one guard making his rounds.

Lodie frowned as if she'd tasted something bitter. "He was the first into town. There's an establishment there that keeps women to his liking."

K'lrsa studied Lodie, trying to decipher the undercurrent to Lodie's words. "He has a type? Really. Because he's been the first in the tent each night since I've been here."

Lodie snorted. "That he has. Seems the sight of you spurred him on more than usual, but those girls were a pale comparison to what he really wanted." She turned to face K'lrsa, holding her gaze. "G'van's type is a tall, lean, woman with honey-colored skin, long black hair, and green eyes."

K'lrsa tilted her head to the side, trying to understand. "Like me?"

Lodie shook her head. "So young..." She leaned forward. "Yes. Exactly like you. I never understood why until I saw you."

K'lrsa leaned back. "What do you mean?"

"G'van likes his whores to look like you. Worse yet, he likes to hurt them." Lodie spat on the ground. She wasn't chewing bitter root, so she meant it as an insult. The worst one a member of the tribes could give another.

"Hurt them?" K'lrsa shuddered, suddenly feeling the chill of the night air. What had she ever done to G'van that he would hurt women just because they looked like her?

Lodie responded as if K'lrsa had actually asked the question. "For some men, there's no reason why they hurt women. They just like to. But with G'van I suspect it's because he hates your independence. He can't stand the thought of a woman who is strong enough that she doesn't need him."

"That makes no sense. Why should he even care? Women throw themselves at him all the time."

"He doesn't want them. He wants you. And you don't want him. If you were weak, maybe you'd admire him. Maybe you'd see him as worthy. Instead you look past his pretty face and beautiful body to the useless man inside." She shrugged. "You're all he could ever want and you see the flaw at his core. Some men would change to be worthy of you. But men like G'van will try to tear you down instead. Or if they can't reach you, they turn on others like you."

K'lrsa rubbed her arms, trying to warm herself. She shook her head. "I never...Why? I never did anything to him. I just didn't want to be with him."

Lodie shrugged. "He's not the only one like that in the world, child. And some places...well, they seem to breed men like that."

K'lrsa shook away the thought. She didn't want to know. "So he's gone, then?" she asked.

"Yes. Until morning."

"And he won't be back for the horse before then?"

"Right. He lost a horse last year when he did a little too much damage. Now he takes just enough to pay for a girl, his booze, and some smokeweed."

K'lrsa grimaced at the image, but she didn't have time to dwell on it. "Good. I'll get the horse. You get ready to leave."

K'lrsa walked through the dark and silent camp. She glanced upward at the stars that danced in the sky. There were fewer here than in the desert, but they still filled the sky. So beautiful, so peaceful.

So far above the muck of human existence.

She wished she could be there amongst them, away from this world and the terrible things she'd learned.

Her yearning for her family was like a physical pain, clutching at her stomach and stealing her breath. She wanted so much to go with Lodie and the girl—to just ride away to safety and leave G'van, Harley, and the Daliphate far behind.

But it was too late.

Even if she did go back, she couldn't unsee what she'd seen or forget what she'd learned.

The home she longed for was gone. Forever.

30

K'lrsa led G'van's horse along the edge of the camp, away from the one guard on patrol. There had been two, but the other was curled up asleep, his snoring audible through the entire camp. Guess they weren't too worried about the slaves escaping so close to Crossroads.

She was almost back to Lodie's tent when a man stumbled out of the darkness, weaving side to side as he approached her.

"Heya, what're ya doin' wit G'van's horse?" He stumbled to a stop in front of her, the stench of smokeweed and alcohol enough to make K'lrsa choke.

She froze.

"What? Ain't ya got a tongue girl?" He stepped forward, a leering grin on his face. "Open up. Let me see."

Lodie appeared and slapped him upside the head. "Leave it, Grayson. She's not for you and you know it. I asked her to bring me the fool's horse. Got a rock in its foot and the man can't be bothered to tend it himself."

Grayson blinked his eyes a few times as he swayed dangerously forward. "S'rry." He shook his head as he walked away mumbling about how only a fool would treat a horse so poorly. Or a woman for that matter.

They returned to the fire where the blonde girl sat, a small bag in her lap, her shoulders tensed. She jumped at every little sound.

As K'lrsa loaded the saddlebags, Lodie nodded towards the one guard who was still awake. "We need to take care of him."

K'lrsa nodded. She'd never killed a man before, but they didn't have a choice. She finished saddling the horse and reached for her knife, but the blonde girl grabbed her wrist and shook her head.

The girl riffled through Lodie's herbs until she found what she was looking for—a small packet of dried leaves. She measured out two pinches of herbs, looking to Lodie for confirmation.

Lodie shrugged. "Should be enough to last until morning. A little more and he's dead."

The girl shook her head as she placed the leaves in a cup and poured hot water over them. K'lrsa was surprised. If it were her, she'd have added that little bit more, no matter whether the man had harmed her or not. Every man who had stood aside and allowed this girl and the other one to be harmed, who had willingly brought slaves across the desert, who had watched them die when they were too weak to continue—they all deserved to die.

The girl took the steaming cup of tea to the man's side and held it out to him. K'lrsa pretended not to watch as the man drank from the cup and then pulled the girl close.

She turned away as the man started touching the girl, but she couldn't block out the sounds they made as he took more than the cup of tea from her.

K'lrsa shook her head, admiring the girl while feeling horrified at the same time.

The girl was like a river tree—bending and flowing with the changing water so that she never broke. K'lrsa was more like the giant world tree, so firmly rooted to the ground that nothing could move her aside and the current had to break and go around her if it wanted to pass.

Before long, the girl returned. K'lrsa glanced back to the see the man lying on his side, his chest barely rising and falling.

"So this is it."

Lodie nodded.

She gave Lodie a fierce hug. The woman could have betrayed her, but she hadn't. She could've kept quiet, let K'lrsa walk blindly into her future, but she'd shared her story instead even though it cost her to do so. "Sister of my blood. May you fly across the sands, may your aim be true, and may your heart be pure."

Lodie snorted at that last, but she grasped K'lrsa's hands in hers, her fingers like twigs, so thin the bones of each one poked into K'lrsa's soft flesh. She pressed her lips firmly together as she studied K'lrsa. At last, she said, "I wish you luck in your quest. The path of revenge isn't easy, but some must walk it so others may thrive. Just..."

Lodie shook her head. "Remember. It's never too late to turn back or change your mind."

K'lrsa pulled away. She wouldn't change her mind.

Lodie paused when she reached the horse, one hand on the saddle, staring away into the dark night. "Beware the one now named Herin. She's the one who sold me into slavery and she's no friend of yours or anyone else's." She shook herself before continuing, "But she may be the only one who can save you. If you must, use my name."

She mounted the horse and turned to face K'lrsa. "Perhaps she thought this life she sentenced me to was more welcome than the death I'd chosen for myself. If so, she may yet help you. But whatever you do, do not tell her your purpose."

She pulled the blonde girl up behind her and reined the horse around. K'lrsa watched them disappear into the inky blackness.

31

That night she dreamt of the young man again. He was so beautiful, more beautiful than any man she'd ever seen. His eyes were a color of blue that couldn't be real. His skin so perfectly brown and smooth that she couldn't help running her hand along the flesh of his arm, a slight smile on her face.

They were alone in the desert, a full moon shining down upon them.

She wore the loose robes of the Moon Dance—strips of cloth that floated with each movement of her limbs.

The Moon Dance was sacred. It was the dance a woman danced for the moon to show her love and appreciation.

Or the dance she danced for her lover, alone, under the gentle light of the moon, before they came together as one.

K'lrsa felt the music fill her, soft and slow and sensual. She moved to its rhythm, her feet floating across the soft sands. The young man joined her, his body in synch with hers. They flowed together as if they were one.

So perfect...

She awoke to G'van dragging her out of her tent by her braid, his face contorted in rage, spit flying from his lips, eyes so bloodshot they were almost completely red. "You deceitful whore."

He threw her to the ground. "Horse thief." He spat. The liquid landed in a glistening gob directly before her eyes. "You should die. The penalty for theft is death."

She laughed as she sat up. "In the tribes it is. But you're no more a member of the tribes than that goat I saw yesterday."

He backhanded her, the blow so hard she felt the world go black for a moment. She held her cheek, shocked. How dare he.

He raised his hand to strike her again and K'lrsa lashed out with her foot, striking his knee as hard as she could. The knee made a loud popping sound as it bent backwards on itself.

G'van collapsed to the ground, screaming in pain.

K'lrsa followed the kick with a strike to his face, breaking his nose. Blood streamed down his face as he called her every vile name he could think of.

She stood and stomped down between his legs as hard as she could and smiled as he curled forward, no longer able to speak. "That," she said, "is for all the women who couldn't defend themselves from you."

"What in Kilgore's blasted lands is going on here?" Harley shouted.

K'lrsa froze at the rage in his voice. Only then did she realize that most of the men had gathered and were watching them.

None looked too concerned about G'van as he struggled to his feet. He bent forward, barely able to put any weight on his right leg. He pointed an accusing finger at her. "My horse is gone. So are Lodie and the northern princess. Grayson said he saw this gadja whore with my horse last night. She did it. I demand compensation. I want her. She's mine."

"No." Harley didn't even raise his voice.

"She stole my horse." Spit flew from G'van's mouth.

Harley shrugged. "You shouldn't have left it behind." He turned his back on G'van, missing the look of pure hatred G'van directed at him. "Barkley. Any chance of catching them?"

Barkley stepped forward. He was the only one of the men that didn't look like he'd had a full night of debauchery. He was clean-cut as always, his clothes neat, his eyes clear and bright. "Not easily. Probably take a couple days and we'd have to use the golden horse to do it, which means that many more days until we can sell it off." He looked at the men, not stating the obvious—that most were in no condition for any sort of hard riding—before he continued.

"Why bother? The girl was almost worthless, the old woman can easily be replaced. And the horse, well..." He smiled.

G'van stumbled forward, demanding Harley's attention. "We have to go after them. They stole my horse."

"We don't have to do anything, *boy*."

"Yes, you do. If you ever want me to guide you across the sands again, you will get me my horse. Or you'll give me hers."

Harley laughed. "No." He started to walk away.

G'van grabbed his arm. "You owe me."

Harley shook him off. "I owe you nothing." He raised his voice as he added, "Show's over. Pack it up. Get the slaves ready."

As Harley walked away, G'van shouted after him, "I can ruin you, you fool, and you know it. You aren't the only trader who wants to cross the Great Desert."

Harley came back, standing so close to G'van that their noses almost touched. "You really think I need you, you vain little shit? I let you tag along because it's convenient, but I don't need you. Not anymore. So don't you threaten me."

G'van licked his lips as he darted a look at the men who had turned back to watch the confrontation. "I know things, Harley. I know more than you think I do. Lodie? I know that..."

He never had a chance to finish his sentence.

Before anyone could react, Harley plunged a knife into his gut and up into his heart. G'van fell to the ground at Harley's feet, dead.

The men cheered, nodding to one another in satisfaction.

K'lrsa stumbled backward. She felt sick. She hadn't liked G'van, but to see him killed so coldly...

"Show's over. Get back to work." Harley cleaned his knife on G'van's tunic before turning to K'lrsa.

He didn't put the knife away. Instead he held it before her eyes, his own eyes so flat and black they were like a never-ending chasm that would consume her if she looked into them too long. "Don't ever cross me again, Princess."

He put the blade away and leaned closer until she could smell the unwashed stench of him and feel the moisture of his breath on her cheek. "The only reason you aren't bleeding out on the ground next to G'van is because you're more valuable to me alive than dead. If you so much as think of running away, I'll hurt you so badly you'll beg me to kill you."

He stepped back and K'lrsa let out the breath she hadn't even known she was holding. But he wasn't done. He grabbed her arm and twisted until she cried out in pain, holding the knife to the base of her thumb. "And if you do manage to escape? I will track you down and strip the skin from your flesh as you watch. I will cut your fingers and toes off one by one. And then I will leave you there, on the side of the road, for the animals to finish off. Do you understand me?"

"Yes," she whispered, wishing more than anything that she'd fled with Lodie the night before.

"Good. Pack up."

She collapsed to the ground, shivering as she watched him walk away.

The scariest thing about Harley's speech was the absolute calm in which he'd delivered it.

If he'd screamed in her face like G'van, she could've believed it was just bluster. But listening to his words, looking into his dead black eyes, she'd believed every word.

He spoke from experience. He'd done it before.

Barkley dragged her to her feet, his hands surprisingly gentle as he pushed her towards her tent. "Harley said to get packed up. Best do what he says."

She stumbled away, numb.

32

K'lrsa tried to ignore the shouts of strangers as they rode through Crossroads on the way to the auction block at the far end of the town.

"Harley, who's the girl on the horse? She up for sale today?" one man shouted as they rode by.

"That's some fine flesh you have there, Harley. The girl, I mean. Not the horse." This from a man missing one eye and part of a hand who looked like he hadn't cleaned himself in years.

His comment was followed by laughter from a group of rough men who made a few disgusting suggestions about what the man might like to do with a fine piece of horseflesh since he'd never get his hands on a willing woman.

Barkley rode his horse in between her and the men. Fallion bared his teeth at Barkley's horse, but settled down at a slight nudge from K'lrsa's knee. "Don't worry," Barkley said. "Harley isn't going to sell you off here. He decided last night that he can get enough for you and the horse to justify traveling as far as Boradol."

She stared straight ahead, trying not to notice all the men crowding around her. Any one of them would buy or sell her without a thought. And that only if they didn't decide to keep her for their own entertainment.

She shuddered at the thought, missing the tribes where men and women were equal and a man would never look at her the way these men did, let alone say some of the things they were saying.

"How close is Boradol to Toreem?" she asked.

Barkley kicked at a man who came too close, the movement so casual it took K'lrsa a moment to realize he'd broken the man's nose with the kick. "Half a day's ride? But might as well be on the other side of the Daliphate as far as any of us are concerned."

"Why do you say that?"

Harley signaled for them to stop outside an ugly one-story building with a sagging roof, its wooden front aged and gray and rotting in places. It looked like it might collapse at any moment.

Barkley urged K'lrsa to the side. "Stay mounted. This won't take long and I'd rather not have to fend off interested parties on the ground."

Harley's men led the slaves into the building. They were all chained together now, some barely able to shuffle along at the pace of the others, others so skinny the manacles around their ankles almost slipped off with each step.

"Barkley, what do you mean about Toreem? You said it might as well be on the other side of the world as far as we're concerned. Why?"

Reginald lounged against the wall of the building, studying the crowd with an unpleasant sneer.

Barkley turned his horse so he could keep a better eye on the crowd. "Toreem is the home of the Daliph."

"Yes. You've told me that before. But what does that matter?"

"Well, not just anyone is allowed in Toreem. It's a city, but it's also a fortress. The whole town is devoted to the Daliph and his interests. Most trade is done in Boradol and only a select few are allowed to travel on to Toreem."

"So how do I get there?"

He laughed. "You don't. You won't."

"There has to be a way." Her stomach clenched.

Barkley stared at her. "Do you still think you're on some great adventure? That you're just off to see exotic places and meet important people?" Barkley shook his head. "This doesn't end well for you, Princess. Even if Harley takes you all the way to Boradol."

He glanced over to where Harley was just emerging, handing out small stacks of coins to each of his men, and said softly, "You should've run when you had the chance, Princess. I tried to help you. I sent all the men into town except the most lazy and irresponsible ones. But instead you helped an old woman and a dying girl escape and you stayed."

He shook his head and raised his voice as he said, "Come on. Harley's ready."

She trailed along behind Barkley, too surprised to speak. He'd wanted her to escape? He'd set it up for her? Why? And why hadn't he told her?

By the time they left Crossroads, they were down to just Harley, Reginald, Barkley, two guards, and a handful of slaves that Harley had purchased.

These slaves were completely different from the ones he'd sold. None were marked in any way. They were clean and proud, allowed to ride in one of the two wagons that Harley had kept and fed alongside Harley and his men.

They camped on the side of the road that night in a large field that Harley paid a farmer to use. The farmer watched K'lrsa the entire time he was negotiating with Harley. At one point, he said something and nodded in her direction. Harley raised a hand to hit the man, but stopped himself just in time.

When Harley came back to the camp, he looked K'lrsa up and down. "Figures he thought you were for rent what with the clothing you're wearing. Or not wearing, I should say."

K'lrsa glanced at the two female slaves Harley had bought. Both wore simple loose dresses that covered them from neck to wrist to ankle. The only skin visible on their entire bodies were their faces and even those were surrounded by lengths of cloth.

She realized that every woman she'd seen since they entered the Daliphate was dressed in a similar fashion. She hadn't thought about it since women in the tribes wore whatever suited the occasion. A long loose dress in camp or nothing at all if working clay or butchering meat.

K'lrsa still wore the hunting gear she'd been wearing on the day she was captured—the baru-hide pants tight against her skin, her hunting vest fitted to allow her arms the freedom to move. She'd scraped the worst of the blood from them, but she knew they needed more care. She just hadn't been willing to do so in front of the men of the caravan.

"Barkley."

"Yes, Harley."

"She can't ride through the Daliphate looking like this. Find some spare clothes to cover her. We'll have Katie fix her up as a proper princess when we reach Lareen, but until then let's stop the rumors that she's for sale to anyone who has the coin."

"Yes, Harley." He gestured for K'lrsa to follow him. "Come on."

As K'lrsa followed Barkley over to the men's tents she wondered just exactly what a proper princess was supposed to look like. She hoped it was something more practical than the formless dresses the women she'd seen so far wore.

33

K'lrsa tripped as she left her tent, trying to walk in a too-big pair of pants from Barkley. She wore a dreadful assortment of castoffs from the men. Two shirts—one had been too tight, but the other had been too loose, so they'd settled for layering the loose one over the tight one—a pair of pants held up with a rope tied twice around her waist, cloth strips wrapped around her usually bare feet, and another cloth wrapped around her head.

The clothes itched terribly and the one wrapped around her head smelled so strongly of horse that she kept wrinkling her nose. Barkley had promised her she'd get used to it soon enough.

Harley looked at her and nodded. "It'll do."

She glared back at him, thinking that the men of the Daliphate were the biggest idiots she'd ever met if they couldn't see a woman's flesh without automatically thinking she was for sale or wanted to have sex with them.

"Have something to say, Princess?" Harley asked, his black eyes sparking.

She shook her head and turned away. She couldn't afford to anger him, but her own anger and frustration were building inside her like a covered pot kept too long over the fire.

Barkley lifted her onto Fallion's back before she could figure out how to mount the horse without the pants getting in the way. He'd warned her the night before that Harley was in a dangerous mood—he'd invested most of his money in the bandaged girl, planning to sell her for a small fortune in Boradol and was now desperate to make his money back on K'lrsa. One misstep, one hint that K'lrsa wouldn't be the prize he wanted her to be, and Harley might just cut his losses and turn back to the desert before his creditors discovered he'd returned.

As she sat in the saddle, K'lrsa tugged at the pants, rolling them so they didn't hang between her feet and the stirrups.

"Don't do that." Barkley tugged the fabric back down.

"How am I supposed to ride a horse if I can't even put my feet in the stirrups?"

Barkley glanced over at Harley. "You really shouldn't be."

"What do you mean?" She was so tired of not knowing things.

"Women in the Daliphate don't ride."

"Ever? How do they get anywhere?"

He shrugged. "They walk. Or they ride in carriages or wagons. But they definitely don't ride."

K'lrsa rolled her eyes.

"And they don't roll their eyes like that either."

K'lrsa bit back the comment she wanted to make. "Is there anything I am allowed to do?"

Barkley's lips quirked upward in a slight smile. "Honestly?"

She nodded.

"No."

She thought he was joking, but she soon saw that he wasn't.

34

Riding through the Daliphate was like riding through a completely different world. Everything was strange to K'lrsa.

First it was the roads. On the plains there were no permanent roads. Maybe a game trail that was traveled often enough to be semi-permanent, but those changed with the seasons, washed away with each spring flood.

Over the course of the week they traveled from Crossroads into the Daliphate, the roads changed from bare patches of dust weaving between farmed lands into broad, dirt-packed paths that moved straight as an arrow into the distance. And then, as they journeyed deeper and deeper into the Daliphate, the dirt roads gave way to broad roads covered with paving stones that cut straight through hills instead of skirting around them.

K'lrsa tried to imagine the number of people who would have to work to create something like that. The number of days they'd have to spend on thwarting nature. And then to maintain it, to keep those paving stones free of cracks and weeds...

She couldn't imagine it even though she saw the evidence beneath Fallion's hooves.

If that wasn't enough, there were the animals. Cows and pigs kept in pens for the convenience of their owners, ready to provide the next meal. Each of the tribes kept a few chickens around, but they ran loose through camp, never the property of one person or family. And never enough to provide a steady source of food.

She stopped the third day to stare at a fenced area full of baru, grazing on soft green grass. When she rode Fallion closer, one of the baru came right up to the fence and nuzzled at her hand as if looking for a treat.

She laughed. All those days she'd tracked the baru herd hoping to kill one single baru and here were too many to count, just waiting to be slaughtered.

It was too strange.

And the food. On the fourth day they rode through rolling green hills covered with fruit trees. She couldn't imagine what it must be like to walk outside your door and be able to pluck an apple—all round and golden yellow—from a tree whenever you pleased.

Not that she'd ever had a fresh apple before. Not until they stopped for a rest and a young girl ran up to her, eyes wide with awe, and offered her an apple straight from the tree. K'lrsa bit into its hard, crispy flesh and smiled, the sweet juice dribbling down her chin.

She finally understood in that moment why all the traders who'd visited them in the desert complained about the tasteless food.

And of course there were the people.

Before K'lrsa could thank the girl for the fruit, her father screamed at her to get away from the devil spawn on a horse. He beat the girl about the shoulders as he chased her back inside, screaming and cursing the whole way.

K'lrsa grabbed her reins, ready to go to the girl's rescue, but Barkley stopped her. "Leave it."

K'lrsa bit her lip as she heard the girl cry out. Why had the man reacted so strongly? She was just a woman on a horse. What was the harm in that?

But Barkley had been right. No women rode horses in the Daliphate. Most didn't even travel.

Almost everyone they passed on the road was a man. The few women she did see rode in the backs of wagons or walked along the side of the road, eyes downcast. Not once did a woman meet her eyes.

And, after the first day or two of seeing what was in the eyes of the men she passed, K'lrsa found herself looking away, too. She refused to look down—she was a Rider of the tribes and she wouldn't cast her eyes to the ground for anyone—but she did focus her gaze on the horizon as she shut out the men's comments and whispers.

Day by day she felt the poison of the Daliphate spreading through her mind and soul, changing her. She felt disconnected from the land, abandoned by her gods, shamed for who she was. She was scared and frightened and with each day her goal seemed that much farther away.

At night she dreamed of the young man with the blue eyes. He was her only refuge. Him and the desert where they met. They danced beneath a full moon each night, held in the Lady Moon's embrace, moving together, touching and kissing, their connection so powerful it felt more real than this twisted world she journeyed through by day.

Those dreams tempted her away from her true path, so each morning before she rose, she pictured her father. Pictured his last moments—the empty eyes, the torn hands, the wound in his belly.

Each morning she reminded herself why she was doing this. Why she was riding farther and farther into such a corrupt and ugly place and farther and farther away from the world of her dreams.

The sooner she found the Daliph and killed him, the better.

35

On the seventh day, they approached a large city sprawled between the banks of two giant rivers. K'lrsa stared at the water raging through the narrow banks as it frothed and foamed, white-peaked and so deep she couldn't see the bottom.

So much water in one place...

The traders had mentioned rivers, but she'd never understood until now.

"Move it, Princess." Reginald slapped Fallion's rump.

Fallion bit at him, but missed. Too bad. The man made her skin crawl with the way he was always watching her, fiddling with his sharp little knife, eyes narrowed. He rarely said anything. He didn't have to.

As she rode Fallion across the bridge into the city, she stared at the water rushing beneath them and felt an odd urge to jump.

Barkley rode his horse between her and the edge of the bridge. "Easy there, Princess. You jump, Harley'd make me go in after you. And I'm not much of a swimmer."

"A swimmer?"

He shook his head as they continued across the bridge. "I forget how little you know. Yes. A swimmer. When water is deep enough, people sink beneath the surface and they die. You have to swim to stay on the surface."

"You can die from too much water?"

Barkley laughed. "You can die from many things, Princess. Don't worry. The water is probably the least of your worries."

As they reached the end of the bridge, he urged his horse forward. K'lrsa stared past him to the city. She'd been a fool to think Crossroads was big. It was a speck of dust next to this place.

More buildings than she could possibly count crawled their way up the hillside. The stench was overwhelming—like a giant privy pit. She covered her mouth and resisted the urge to gag. Even the horse smell from her head wrap was preferable to the odor of so many people packed so close together.

The first houses they passed were made of wood and raised on stilts so that their entrances were above K'lrsa's head. Barkley rode back to show her the water line—it was almost to the top of the stilts—where the rivers flooded each spring.

The buildings they passed were gray with dirt and age, sagging and heavy. So were the people who trudged in from the fields outside the city.

Their group rode up the hill until they reached a wall of stones twice the height of Fallion with men standing across the road holding long metal weapons.

"Everyone off your horses." The man on the right approached Harley as the rest of the party dismounted. The man on the left started poking at the wagons.

K'lrsa stepped to the side and ran her hand along the stone wall, fascinated by how they had managed to stack so many stones so high without having them fall over.

Barkley came to stand beside her. "Secret is in the grout."

"The what?"

"The grout. See this white substance spread between the stones? When they build the wall, the grout's wet. As it dries, it sticks to the stones and keeps them together. A wall like this, if built right, can last ten generations or more."

She stared up at him. "How do you know this?"

"My father is a stone mason. He builds walls like this." He turned away, his face shadowed.

"Why aren't you one then? Isn't that how it works normally?"

Barkley crossed his arms tight across his chest. "Not possible."

"Why not?"

"My father didn't want me around."

She reached a hand to his shoulder. "Why?"

Barkley was her only friend, the only one who'd shown her any compassion since Crossroads. He was honest and hard-working. How could his own father not want him around?

"He just didn't." He walked away, his shoulders stiff with suppressed emotion.

K'lrsa watched him go, her brow furrowed with concern. There was so much she didn't understand about this world. How was she possibly going to succeed?

She didn't know, but she'd come too far to turn back.

She had no choice but to continue forward.

36

Harley led them through a series of twisty streets, the shops and houses so close together that they walked in shadow even though the sun was still shining somewhere above them. She shivered, imagining a life where you never saw the sun, never felt its warmth caress your skin.

The people they passed were dressed in such a variety of clothing that K'lrsa couldn't help but stare. Some wore black from head to toe, the women even wearing veils across their faces so that only their eyes showed. Others wore clothing with bright yellow, red, and blue stripes, the colors so bold and bright they were almost painful to look at. And others wore plain brown clothes, not a trace of color anywhere in their wardrobe.

She'd never seen so many people in one place, and they all seemed to know what they were doing and where they were going, shoving past their small group without even noticing them.

When K'lrsa asked about the clothes, Barkley shrugged. "This far from Toreem people wear what they want. Some flaunt it. Some don't."

Before K'lrsa could ask what he meant, she was distracted by a skinny little girl dressed in the tattered remnants of others' clothing—a too-big black shirt, too-short bright yellow and red striped pants, and brown cloth wrapped around her feet.

The girl held out her hand as people passed, but they all ignored her, keeping a careful distance as they passed by on their way to whatever important destination awaited them. "Just a penny. That's all I ask, you pompous prats," the girl shouted.

As people momentarily paused to stare at her, a young boy made his way through the crowd, quickly grabbing a loaf of bread from one man's bag, an apple from another, and a coin purse from a third.

The man with the missing coin purse shouted and chased after the boy while the girl disappeared down a narrow alley.

"Where are their parents?" K'lrsa asked, thinking that no one in the tribes would act that way or steal from others like that.

Barkley stepped between her and a man who reached out to touch her. "Probably don't have any."

"Then their relatives. They have to have family of some sort."

"Don't want the extra mouths to feed or don't exist."

She looked behind, but the children had long since disappeared. "So those kids are just on their own? No one to help them?"

Barkley nodded. "Yeah. That's the way it is. Your family dies or doesn't want you, you make your own way." He looked as if he would say more, but didn't.

K'lrsa cringed. She watched the indifferent people shoving past one another on the dirty streets and realized that none of them cared about any of the others. Up ahead she saw a man trip and fall. Instead of helping, people just stepped over him. One even stepped on the bag of food the man had dropped.

"How do all these people eat?"

"What do you mean?"

"There are so many people here. How do they eat every day? Our annual gathering is much smaller than this and only lasts for five days. All the tribes have to bring their own provisions with them because there isn't enough hunting to feed that many people. But these people live here. How do they eat every day?"

Barkley pushed a man in tattered rags out of the way. "Traders. They bring food into the city every day. You didn't think those farmers we passed ate all of that food themselves, did you?"

She turned away as the man Barkley had shoved aside held out a hand, begging for money, his right eye oozing pus. "I guess I didn't think about it."

There was so much she hadn't known about the world. So much she didn't want to know about the world. The tightness in her chest grew as they pressed farther into the city.

There were too many people, not enough sunlight, no fresh air. And no grass anywhere. Nothing green. The desert was dry and barren, but it was different. Natural. Life hid under the surface or lurked in small corners. This city was just dead, every plant or animal gone.

Even Fallion was restless, shaking his head and snorting as people brushed against him in the press of the crowds. She stroked his nose. "I know, *micora*. I'm so sorry. I wish I'd never brought you here."

37

Harley stopped in front of a large building, its white exterior spotless and shining against the darkness of the rest of the city. Above the door, a wooden carving of a busty woman with a tankard of beer leered down at them. K'lrsa marveled that they could so casually use wood here and that there could be a tree so big that a person could carve a whole sign out of it.

They followed Harley around the back of the building to a large courtyard with horse stalls at one end. This too was spotlessly clean. The horses she could see were happily munching on fresh hay—a meal finer than anything Fallion had ever had before.

"We're staying here tonight." Harley handed his reins to a young boy with a mop of dark black hair who appeared as if out of nowhere.

K'lrsa stared around the space. "Here?" She glanced at Barkley. "Where will we put the tents?" The ground was covered in stones joined together with grout, the surface entirely smooth.

Reginald laughed as he passed them. "We're sleeping inside, Princess." He turned to Barkley. "Does Harley really think we're going to pass this piece of tribal trash off as a princess? I doubt she's ever even slept indoors before." He shook his head as he followed Harley, calling back, "Should've sold her off in Crossroads and cut our losses."

"Ignore him." Barkley led her inside and up four flights of stairs. She stumbled on the first few, but quickly got the hang of it. K'lrsa trembled as they climbed higher and higher, catching glimpses out the window with each level. She'd never been so high above things before.

Finally, they walked through a small room to another room dominated by a large wooden frame covered in what looked like a gigantic seat cushion. She walked to the narrow window and looked out.

They were at the top of the hillside, the city scattered down the hill below them. The road they'd ridden that morning was just a narrow strip of paleness against the distant farms, the rivers that had seemed so frightening up close now just narrow silver lines at the base of the hill.

"You'll sleep here. Reginald and I will sleep in the outer room."

K'lrsa glanced around; there was no room for her sleeping roll anywhere. The wooden frame almost touched both of the walls and the small space to the right of the door was filled by a wooden pedestal with a bowl and pitcher on it and a stool that had a wooden back on it.

Reginald shoved into the room, a nasty smile on his face. "This is a *bed*, Princess. And this is a *mattress*. You sleep on it. And this is a *chair*—you do know what a chair is, don't you? Not everyone spends their life sitting on the ground, you know."

He talked to her like she was a young child. She glared at him, hating the way he laughed at her, but she was secretly grateful because she hadn't known what they were. At home they slept on furs and pillows and used small stools that were easy to transport from camp to camp; with the caravan she'd slept in a tent each night on a densely-woven cloth sleeping mat. She'd never slept indoors before.

"Leave it, Reginald." Barkley shoved him back outside. "We'll be in the next room. Harley's orders. He doesn't want you to escape."

She almost laughed. Like she could find her way back through that labyrinth of people.

"You should probably wash up a bit." He gestured at the table in the corner with the bowl and pitcher before closing the door.

K'lrsa stared at the items on the table. She was used to sweat baths—a small enclosed space that was so hot it made everyone sweat so they could scrape the dirt from their skin with a carved baru bone. What was she supposed to do with an empty bowl and a pitcher of warm water?

She paced the room, feeling trapped for the first time since she'd been captured. Even though she'd been a slave for weeks now, she'd never actually felt like one. She'd always had Fallion and the sky above her. Even as the moon and sun became more distant and weak, she knew they were still there.

But now, locked in this tiny space, in the middle of a city with so many people and buildings between her and freedom...

Her breaths came in shallow gasps. She wiped her sweaty palms on her dirty pants, but it didn't help.

She had to get out.

She had to leave.

Now.

She paced faster, the walls closing in on her.

She wanted to go home.

She wanted to go anywhere but here.

The stench of so many people.

The sound they made seeped through the walls.

She just wanted to ride Fallion, to flee into the deep desert, go somewhere where they could ride for an entire day without seeing anyone or anything else.

Her chest felt tight, like someone was squeezing the air out of her.

She threw the chair on the bed and sat cross-legged on the floor, wedging herself into the space by the table. Desperate, she started the Pattern—the series of deep, slow breaths and repeated phrases that would take her to the Core. She needed to go somewhere other than this dirty, crowded city.

She found it, eventually as her breaths finally slowed down and her mind drifted.

She stayed there long past when she should've returned, hovering in that place that wasn't a place, free for just a little while until Harley burst into the room and thrust her back into the real world. "Up. It's time you looked the part."

K'lrsa stood, flexing muscles stiff from sitting in one position for too long. "Where are we going?"

"A dressmaker friend of mine. She ought to be able to do something with you." The way he said it it was clear he doubted it would be enough.

K'lrsa scratched at her hair as she trailed along behind him. Nothing would make her look the part. She'd never been one of those girls.

F'lia? Oh, she'd be perfect as a desert princess, spinning around in layers of silks, smiling like the sun. But K'lrsa? She was a warrior, a fighter. No amount of clothing would change that.

She was smart enough not to say anything to Harley, though. No need to make him angry.

She might not like it, but as long as he was taking her closer to her goal, she'd let him dress her in whatever he wanted.

38

They walked a few blocks through the crowded streets to a shop with colorful dresses displayed in the window. Each one was brighter than the last, the fabric so voluminous K'lrsa wondered if anyone would be able to tell a woman was wearing them.

A woman certainly wouldn't be able to do anything in them. She shook her head. She didn't understand these people.

Harley knocked on the door and entered, smiling at the woman sitting behind the counter sewing a pile of turquoise silks together.

"Mistress Hawthorne, I'd like you to meet K'lrsa dan V'na of the White Horse Tribe. She's a desert princess I captured on my trip. We're bound for Boradol."

The woman set down her silks and made her way around the counter. She was short and wide, her hair graying around the edges, and she wore a simple fitted dress that somehow covered every inch of her skin while managing to accentuate her ample bosom.

"A desert princess? Oh, Harley. What are you into now?"

"Katie, can you help me or not? She needs to make a good first impression."

Mistress Hawthorne crossed her arms, accentuating her considerable bust even more, and looked up at Harley. "Now Harley Redcliffe, I may not know much about the tribes folk, but I know this filthy dirty excuse for a girl is no princess.

Look at her." The woman reached out and plucked something from K'lrsa's hair. "She has bugs in her hair, Harley. Bugs. What princess would walk around with bugs in her hair?"

K'lrsa expected Harley to get angry, but he didn't. Instead he rested his hands on Mistress Hawthorne's shoulders and lowered his voice to a soft whisper. "It's been a long journey, Katie. Will you do what you can? I need this." He stroked her arm and she blushed. "Please."

Mistress Hawthorne let out a deep sigh and turned away. She pulled at various bundles of fabric as she talked. "Boradol? You know the restrictions there. It's going to make this ten times harder than it needs to be. Sure you can't just sell her off here?"

He shook his head.

"Fine. I'll see what I can do. Maybe I can make her something like that one." She pointed to one of the dresses in the window. It had so many layers it took up half the space, crowding the other two dresses into the corners.

"No." The word was out of K'lrsa's mouth before she could stop it.

She bit her lip as Harley glared at her. "Did I ask your opinion?"

She was fortunate Mistress Hawthorne was watching them, because Harley's words were far more kind than the blinding anger that flashed in his eyes.

K'lrsa took a deep breath. She couldn't let them burden her with that cloth monstrosity. She'd never be able to walk wearing that, let alone kill a man. "I need to ride Fallion. I can't do that in an outfit like that one."

"Oh, Harley, you're not letting her ride a horse are you? Have you completely lost your mind?"

"She's supposed to be a desert princess, Katie. They're different there. And the horse…well, it's the only way I'm going to sell this to anyone."

K'lrsa stepped forward. "Then put me in something I can wear on horseback."

"She needs to look the part, Harley."

K'lrsa laughed. "A woman of my tribe would never wear something like that. She'd wear this."

K'lrsa pulled off the baggy shirt she'd been given to reveal her hunting vest. It was a little worn—the leather ties that kept it closed were fraying at the edge causing the topmost portion to gape open a little more than normal and the weeks of travel without a proper cleaning had caused it to shrink a bit, tightening around her chest.

Mistress Hawthorne gasped and threw a large bolt of dark fabric around K'lrsa's shoulders. "This is a respectable establishment, Harley. What are you thinking? Not even a whore would dress like that."

K'lrsa stepped back. "This is what I wear to hunt. It covers what it needs to and doesn't get in the way. This is what a 'Desert Princess' wears."

Mistress Hawthorne shook her head. "You dress like that you get what you deserve. And no man would think it had to cost him a thing."

K'lrsa drew her knife. "Any man who tried to take what I wasn't willing to give would lose the hand that tried to take it."

Harley stepped between them. "Ladies. Please."

"I'd heard they were savages, Harley, but I'd never realized before..." Mistress Hawthorne shook her head. "You can't take this...*thing* to Boradol. No one will buy her."

"Katie." He took her hands in his and kissed them. "I can do this, but only if you help me. Will you do it? Can you make her presentable but exotic?"

Mistress Hawthorne glanced over at K'lrsa, her expression showing how impossible she thought the task was. "I'm not touching her until she's had a good bath." When Harley started to object, she waved him to silence. "She can do it here, don't worry. Go. I'll do what I can."

Harley kissed her cheek and Mistress Hawthorne blushed. "Can you finish by tomorrow?" he asked.

"Tomorrow? Are you addled, Harley?"

He stared down at his hands. "We're staying at the Lovely Lady. I can't afford more than two nights there."

"You could've stayed with me, you know." Mistress Hawthorne glanced sideways at K'lrsa as she spoke softly.

"I know. But I wouldn't want to impugn on your honor that way." He stepped back. "I need this, Katie. It's my only hope of redeeming this whole trip. And then, maybe, we could..." He glanced at K'lrsa. "Talk about where I'll stay when I'm not traveling."

Mistress Hawthorne shook her head. "I'd find myself a backup plan if I were you. This girl's not going to fool anyone."

"She has to."

Mistress Hawthorne pushed him towards the door. "I'll do my best, Harley. But no amount of pretty fabric is going to change things. A pig in a dress is still a pig."

39

Before K'lrsa could fully register the fact that Mistress Hawthorne had just compared her to a pig, the woman had grabbed K'lrsa by the ear and dragged her to a small shed behind the shop.

"Take a bath. There's the pump, there's the tub, there's the soap. I want you spotless before you come back inside my shop."

K'lrsa stared at the implements in the shed, not sure where to begin.

"Well get on with it, girl."

"I don't know what to do. I've never taken a bath before."

"What? I knew you were a savage, but are you telling me you people never clean yourselves? Ever?"

K'lrsa clenched her teeth. "We do clean ourselves, just not like this. We use sweat baths."

Mistress Hawthorne's mouth gaped open. "You sweat to get clean?"

"Yes."

The woman looked as if she was going to faint. She shook her head as she bustled around the shed, priming the pump and moving it up and down until water started to pour into the tub. "I love that man, but he's a right fool sometimes."

When the tub was full, she gestured at it. "Get in."

K'lrsa shook her head. "It's too deep. I don't know how to swim."

Mistress Hawthorne laughed, the sound filling the small space. She kept laughing until she cried, wiping away the tears that fell down her round cheeks. "Oh, child. You won't drown. It isn't that deep. Now strip and get in."

The bath was one of the most miserable experiences of K'lrsa's life. Mistress Hawthorne scoured her skin with a gritty bar of soap until every inch of her body burned. She wasn't gentle about it in the least, either, muttering the whole time about foolish men and their even more foolish ideas.

And just when K'lrsa thought it couldn't get any worse, Mistress Hawthorne drew a new bath and started in on K'lrsa's hair.

"What's this?" she demanded holding the desiccated shell of a bug before K'lrsa's eyes.

"A sand beetle?"

"Oh, a sand beetle. Oh, okay." Mistress Hawthorne scrubbed her fingers against K'lrsa's scalp as K'lrsa tried to squirm away. "When was the last time you washed your hair?"

"Like this?"

"Yes."

"Never."

At that point Mistress Hawthorne devolved into mumbling under her breath and shaking her head as she scratched so hard at K'lrsa's scalp K'lrsa swore she must be bleeding. Then the woman took a comb and yanked it through K'lrsa's hair— starting at the bottom fortunately—until it was completely straight.

It took forever.

But at last Mistress Hawthorne finished and let K'lrsa dry herself.

"Alright. Stand up. Let me see what I'm working with."

K'lrsa stood in front of the woman, arms crossed under her breasts, and waited for more insults.

"Huh. Not bad." She slapped K'lrsa's hip as she walked around her. "Under all that grime, turns out you're actually quite attractive. A little too much muscle." She pinched K'lrsa's arm. "But I can hide that."

K'lrsa stepped back. "Why do you have to hide my body? Why can't I just be presented as I am?"

Mistress Hawthorne laughed. "Oh, child. That would never work. A woman dresses in the way she wants men to treat her. You cover yourself to show men that you're like their wives and daughters, to be treated with care and respect. If you insist on dressing like a savage, they'll treat you like one."

"That's ridiculous."

"That's the world."

K'lrsa shook her head. "How can you love a man like Harley knowing that he'd sell a woman? Or hurt a woman? Did you know there was a girl who traveled with us whose sole use was to entertain the men?"

Mistress Hawthorne tsked as if K'lrsa didn't understand anything. "A slave no doubt. Meant for that purpose. Harley would never treat someone like me that way."

"In the tribes men treat *all* women with respect. There is no right way to dress or act. We do what makes the most sense."

"Well, you're not in the tribes anymore, are you? Learn to act the right way or pay the consequences."

Before K'lrsa could argue further, Mistress Hawthorne threw a loose dress at her and turned away. "Put that on and follow me inside. Time to work a miracle."

40

The next morning, Harley had Melinda, one of the slave women he'd bought in Crossroads, help K'lrsa to dress. She felt like a child's doll, standing in the middle of the small room Barkley and Reginald had slept in the night before, turning this way and that so Melinda could burden her in layer after layer of fabric.

It took the woman half a candlemark to dress K'lrsa in the ridiculous costume Mistress Hawthorne had put together. At least the entire outfit consisted of sensible shades of brown that would travel well instead of the garish colors in the store window. And K'lrsa had managed to convince Mistress Hawthorne to make the bottom-most layer a split skirt that would still allow her to ride Fallion in comfort.

(That after a shouting match when K'lrsa asked for pants as the bottom layer and Mistress Hawthorne lectured her on how inappropriate it was for a woman to ever ride a horse and K'lrsa retorted that at least in the tribes women actually had a use and Mistress Hawthorne grew so angry she couldn't form words.)

K'lrsa stumbled as she stepped out of the room, the voluminous skirts of the dress tangling her feet. She didn't know how she was going to manage four flights of stairs without falling and breaking her neck. She was gathering the fabric in her hands to try, when the men arrived.

"Don't." Harley slapped at her hand. "Defeats the purpose if you go around showing off your ankles like a lowly street walker."

He walked around her twice, nodding his head. "It'll do. It'll do. Nice touch." He pointed to the headband Mistress Hawthorne had made her with a giant everen feather sticking out the back. Everens hadn't been seen in tribal lands for at least five generations—not that anyone in the tribes had ever worn a headband with a bird feather in it—but no one seemed to care much for accuracy.

Or even plausibility. If she did manage to stay seated on Fallion, there was no way she'd be able to draw her bow with this many layers hampering every movement.

K'lrsa met Barkley's eyes and saw him shake his head slightly, warning her against saying anything.

This was all so ridiculous. Did the people of the Toreem Daliphate really know nothing of the tribes? But Barkley was right. It would do her no good to say anything now.

So she swallowed her concerns and didn't even object when Barkley had to physically carry her down the stairs and plop her on Fallion's back like a sack of grain.

As long as they were continuing towards Toreem, that's all that mattered.

41

The next few days of travel were uneventful. They passed more and more people as they continued on towards the now not-so-distant mountains. Each group gawked at her, whispering to one another in shock.

A woman on a horse. And one in such a unique outfit. Look at the feather.

Harley told every person who'd listen that she was a desert princess he was taking to Boradol for sale to the highest bidder.

K'lrsa eventually learned to ignore everyone, staring over their heads and pretending she was somewhere else.

She spent most of each day thinking about one of two things: the young man she continued to see in her moon dreams, and her father.

She couldn't speak to the young man in her dreams, but their bodies spoke for them as they came together in the Moon Dance each night.

She'd experimented here or there with the boys in the tribe—a stolen kiss or touch behind one of the tents when no one was looking, sharing a fire and some affection on a hunting trip—but nothing had made her feel the way she did with him.

It was like every touch and kiss drove her to want another and another and another until she could barely see straight for wanting him. She spent each day in a haze, longing for another night so she could see him again.

She refused to let it go further than the dance and a stolen kiss or two. Which just left her aching for that final release she wouldn't allow herself.

And then, out of guilt and a desperate desire to keep focused on what she was doing and why, she'd awaken and force herself to think about her father. To picture those last moments with him, reliving over and over again the moment he'd begged her to kill him. Feeling once more the knife in her hand as she plunged it into his chest.

For every moment she thought of the young man in her dreams, she spent another picturing the ways she would kill the Daliph. The young man was just a dream to distract her mind. Killing the Daliph was her destiny.

––––––––––––––––––

The night before they reached Boradol, she found herself alone with Barkley. Yet again, Harley had paid for a set of rooms for her and ordered Barkley and Reginald to stay in the outer room so she couldn't escape.

The room assigned to her was narrow, the ceiling low enough that it almost touched her head. She tried to sleep but couldn't. She felt as if the whole world were closing in around her.

Eventually, she opened the door to the outer room, hoping that Reginald wouldn't be there to mock her yet again. Fortunately, he was still downstairs, gambling like he did most nights.

Barkley sat at the small table in the middle of the room, polishing his boots. There were no beds in the room, so the men would have to use their sleeping pallets. K'lrsa envied them. She dreaded the thought of another night buried in a fluffy mattress.

"Join me." Barkley gestured at the other chair and K'lrsa sank into it, still not quite used to sitting on something so stiff and high off the ground. She missed the baru hide stools of home, but that was so far behind her it almost seemed like a dream.

Barkley set aside his boot. "We'll reach Boradol tomorrow."

She'd spent the entire trip trying not to think about what would happen once they reached Boradol, but now she had no choice.

"What happens then?"

He fiddled with one of the laces on the boot, not looking at her. "Harley tries to sell you off."

"Tries?" It had never occurred to her he might not be able to. "Could he fail?"

"No. He'll find someone to buy you. There are enough places in Boradol. One has to take you." He shook his head. "I just..."

"Just what?"

He sighed. "I hope he gets enough for you. He took a big risk with all of this." He bit his lip and leaned forward before continuing. "But I also hope he fails. You deserve more than this. They all do. All the slaves."

She studied him for a long moment. "Why do you do it, Barkley? You're different from the others. So why do this?"

He sat back in his chair, crossing his arms across his chest. "It's my only option."

"That can't be true. We've passed so many people coming here. I can't believe you couldn't do what those people do."

"It isn't that simple, K'lrsa. What I am...It's not welcome. Anywhere. I have to keep moving so no one knows."

"What you are?" She stared at him, confused.

He shook his head. "Forget it. It doesn't matter." He leaned forward. "Tell me something. Why didn't you run when you could've? All those days we crossed the desert, that last night outside of Crossroads. Why didn't you run?"

"Because I need to reach the Daliph, so I can kill him." She knew she should keep the secret to herself, but she was tired and scared and needed someone to talk to. She no longer had her gods or her moon stone or even Lodie.

Barkley blinked slowly. "You want to kill the Daliph?"

"Yes."

"The Daliph? The grand leader of every single man, woman, and child that we've passed on our way here?"

"Yes."

He laughed. "Impossible."

"No, it isn't. I'm going to do it." She glared at him.

Barkley stared at her for a long moment and then shrugged. "Well, you wouldn't be the first."

"What do you mean?" She leaned forward.

"The old Daliph was killed by one of his servants two years ago."

"Really? How?"

"Poisoned." Barkley took a coin from his pocket and handed it to her. It was flat and square, made of a heavy metal she'd never seen before. On one side the number five was stamped. On the other was a man's face, the eyes and jaw heavy, skin sagging. He looked like a giant bullfrog, but the eyes were those of a desert cat. The image was somehow revolting and compelling at once. She shivered as she studied it.

Barkley nodded at the coin. "That's him. Heard his grandson is Daliph now."

Finally, she knew what her enemy looked like. Younger than the man on the coin, of course, but likely equally as vile.

She handed the coin back to Barkley. "If someone was able to get close enough to poison him, I can get close enough to the grandson to kill him." She'd never thought of poison before, but if a direct attack was impossible, it might be an option.

Barkley smirked. He picked the boot back up and started to polish it once more. "Only took her twenty-five years."

"Twenty-five years?" K'lrsa's throat clenched. That long? Could she hold out for that long if that's what it took?

He smiled. "Yep. So the story goes. Worked her way up the ranks to be his taster—the one who checks his food for poison. And then she poisoned herself at a great feast so she could poison him, too. Hundreds witnessed them choking to death side by side. Good riddance." He took a long swig from a flagon of beer. "Too bad it didn't happen about twenty years earlier."

"Why do you say that?"

He scratched at a spot on the table. "The old Daliph he, uh…he took my aunt. She was a young mother, with two little girls. He didn't care. He came through town, saw her, wanted her, and took her. We never saw her again."

He finished off the beer and stood. "Of course, most people love him. He brought the Toreem Daliphate out of the gutter when he established those trade routes with the tribes. Now it's someone else's turn to provide slaves for the rest of the Daliphana."

"What about the current Daliph?"

"I don't know. This is the first time we've gone past Crossroads since the assassination." He stared into the bottom of his empty flagon. "You really want to kill him?"

"Yes."

He nodded, scrunching his lips up as he thought about it. "Alright. I can't make any promises, but let me see what I can do to get you to Toreem."

Before she could say anything further, he left, closing the door firmly behind him.

She stared at the door for a long time after he'd left, trying not to feel hope. She'd come so far, telling herself every day that it would happen, that she'd find a way to keep her vow. But secretly she'd wondered if she could do it. If she'd ever even have the chance to kill him, let alone succeed if she did.

She'd spent the last week wondering if she'd sacrificed everything—the man of her dreams, her mother, her sister, Fallion—for nothing.

But now, thanks to Barkley, she felt a small twinge of hope.

Maybe, just maybe, she would have her chance.

42

The road they followed throughout the next day slowly climbed until they reached the top of a ridge to gaze down upon Boradol where it spread across the plain below them. The buildings were all made of dun-colored stone that blended in with the barren fields behind the city, the only spots of color the elaborately tiled roofs of each building. They shone in the late day sunlight—the blues, reds, and yellows mingling and clashing together.

At the far edge of the plain, barely visible, another city rose, jagged mountains loomed behind it.

"That's Toreem." Barkley nodded at the distant city. "It's one of the most secure cities in all of the Daliphana. The mountains are almost impenetrable and the ground for half a day's ride on all sides is kept clear so they can see any threat long before it arrives."

K'lrsa frowned. "How do they eat?"

Barkley laughed. "You and food, princess."

"If you'd ever lived in the desert, you'd understand. Water is essential—without it you die almost immediately. But food, food is what you spend most of your time and energy finding."

He nodded. "They have enough food stored at any point in time to feed the residents of the city for at least three months. Not that anyone wants to eat the food they have stored, of course. That's all dried meats and grains. No. Traders flow in and out of Toreem every day bringing delicacies from all over the world. There's a greater variety of food available in Toreem than anywhere else in the Daliphate."

"How do you know this?"

"That's where I grew up. My father was stone mason for the old Daliph." Before she could ask more, he urged his horse forward to ride next to Harley.

As she followed after, K'lrsa studied the mountains that now loomed on the far side of the valley, covering half the sky. They'd always stood there on the horizon, a distant smudge on the background of her life, but now, as the sun set, they cast a shadow halfway across the valley as if reaching for her.

She shivered as she watched the shadow come closer and closer.

"Princess." Harley waved her forward and K'lrsa joined him, fingering the cold stone he'd bought her to replace the moon stone she'd given Lodie. (Like anyone who knew the tribes would be fooled by the lifeless lump hanging from a plain brown cord.)

"What do you think of your new home?" Harley waved his hand through the air like a street entertainer introducing a new trick.

She glanced at Barkley, but he was staring straight ahead, ignoring them. "It's very nice?"

Harley laughed. "Not like you'll be seeing much of it once I get you sold off to the Exquisite Garden."

"The Exquisite Garden?" K'lrsa swayed in her saddle, feeling faint. So Barkley hadn't been able to arrange anything.

"Yes, they specialize in providing something unique and different to a discerning clientele." He smiled at her, looking almost happy. The sight of Harley happy was so disconcerting she almost forgot that he was going to sell her to the highest bidder the next day.

She stared towards Toreem. Somehow she'd find a way to bridge that distance and get her revenge.

That night, K'lrsa paced her small room, unable to sleep. Barkley had sent a letter to a friend, telling him Harley had a young, beautiful, and exotic desert warrior for sale.

It was the best he could do.

At least if Barkley's friend bought her she'd be in Toreem instead of Boradol.

And one step closer was one step closer.

But Barkley hadn't heard back yet, and it was possible he never would.

She couldn't bear the thought of being sold off like nothing more than a pretty necklace or fine horse.

She had to escape. She didn't know where she'd go—a woman alone in the streets would draw all eyes, and the only clothing she had was the ridiculous get-up Harley thought made her a desert princess (he'd burned her Rider's clothing after the little incident with Mistress Hawthorne)—but she couldn't sit in her room and wait for life to happen to her.

She had to act. Now. Before it was too late.

She wrenched open the door to her room and found Reginald seated in a chair, leaning back against the wall, arms crossed, smokeweed stuck in his teeth as he leered at her. "Going somewhere, Princess?"

She wondered briefly if she could kill him, but decided against it. He *was* smaller than her, but he had a wiry speed that belied his normal casual slouch and a viciousness that would be deadly in a fight.

He settled his chair on the floor and leaned towards her. "You know, the Exquisite Garden is a little steep for the likes of me, but I'm thinking I might just splurge this once. Not every day a man can have himself a princess." He winked at her. "Whatdya think? I could be your first customer."

He stood and swaggered towards her. "Hell, maybe we can get started tonight. Barkley's gonna be gone a while and..."

She wanted nothing more than to shatter the teeth in his mouth, forever destroying that sickly grin. Instead, she slammed the door in his face and blocked it with the heavy wooden bar attached to the frame.

K'lrsa sank down to the floor, her back pressed against the dark wood.

What had she thought she was going to do anyway?

She wouldn't leave without Fallion. And there was no way a lone woman was going to be able to just ride a horse out of the city and across the valley to Toreem. And not like she could sneak up to the Toreem city gates.

And even if she could do all of that, what then? Just walk up to the palace and demand an audience with the Daliph? Barkley said the man was always surrounded by at least ten guards—the fiercest, biggest, meanest men he could find.

It was impossible.

She stared around the little room and felt the walls closing in on her. There wasn't even a window—no chance for her to stare up at the sky and pretend she was anywhere other than a crowded, smelly city so far from the world she knew that she could barely remember what it had felt like to race across the plains, wind whipping through her hair.

She refused to sleep. She didn't want to dream. Not tonight.

She longed to lose herself once more in the Moon Dance with the beautiful young man with the blue eyes, but she couldn't. It was just a dream. One she could never have in real life.

She stripped out of her clothes, pushed the furniture out of the way, and seated herself cross-legged in the middle of the room.

She started the Pattern. With each breath and repeated phrase her awareness sank deeper, her muscles relaxed, the tension in her body flowed away. But each time she was on the verge of reaching the Core, of separating herself from the world and floating in that timeless twilight, she lost focus.

The Core slipped through her fingers like water, impossible to hold.

First it was thoughts of the young man—his blue eyes and golden skin calling to her. Then it was her father—his dying words echoing in her mind.

He'd made her swear she wouldn't avenge him.

Had he known how impossible it would be? How unwelcoming this world would be to someone like her?

Maybe it hadn't been a lack of faith in her, but a better understanding of what the world was like.

And yet she'd charged ahead, as foolish and headstrong as her mother had always believed her to be. She'd thought doing this would prove how wrong everyone was about her. Instead she'd proven them right.

She was a fool.

She gave up on finding the Core.

Peace eluded her, so she turned to violence.

She spent the rest of the night working her way through the hundred and five attacks, imagining with each kick or thrust of her hand that she was killing the Daliph, picturing his froggy eyes bulging in surprise as she killed him over and over again.

At last she collapsed onto the bed, sweaty and exhausted, and fell into a dreamless sleep.

43

Her salvation came at breakfast. She was in the tiny anteroom, sharing a meal with Barkley, Reginald, and Harley when the messenger arrived—a young boy, dressed in the non-descript brown clothes everyone seemed to wear in Boradol.

He burst into the room, skin flushed from running up the stairs. "Master Harley?"

"Yes." Harley set aside his fork and knife.

"I've a message for you. From Toreem." The boy held a piece of paper out to Harley, his hand shaking.

Harley grunted, but he took the message. The boy continued to stand there until Barkley slipped him a small coin and sent him on his way.

They all sat in silence as Harley read the note and then read it again. He whooped in joy after the second reading, patting K'lrsa so hard on the back that she almost choked on her bite of food. "Well, see now, you were right Barkley. Letting her ride that horse and parading her along the road paid off. Word's spread as far as Toreem."

"Oh?" Barkley took another bite of sausage, appearing barely interested in the conversation.

"This letter is from the Gilded Lily. The owner's heard I have a beautiful, unique bed slave and wants to buy her from me sight unseen. He says he'll give me a hundred fifty golden hawlers for her!" He laughed. "Can you imagine, Barkley? Best we were going to get here was fifty."

Reginald grinned as he shoved a bite of eggs into his mouth, but Barkley set his silverware down carefully and looked across at Harley. "Are you sure it's worth it, Harley?"

K'lrsa tried to hide her surprise. Barkley had arranged this, hadn't he? What was he doing?

Harley pursed his lips. "Why wouldn't it be?"

"The old woman. Seems to me she wanted us to leave and never come back. She was quite explicit about the whole thing."

"Ah, she's probably dead by now the old hag. And even if she isn't, we'll get in and get out before she even knows we've been there. You'll see."

Barkley gave him a long stare, but eventually nodded. "If you say so."

"I do. Don't ruin my enjoyment of this moment, Barkley." Harley laughed again, happier than K'lrsa had ever seen him. "A hundred fifty golden hawlers." He shook his head, smiling. "We'll be able to pay our debts and still come out ahead."

K'lrsa stared at her plate, trying not to show her own excitement even though all she wanted was to dance around the room.

Harley ruffled her hair, the gesture so unexpected, K'lrsa couldn't help but gawp at him.

"And maybe after we've sold you off, little lady, I'll go back and make an honest woman of Mistress Hawthorne. Couldn't'a done it without her now, could we?" He winked.

K'lrsa didn't know what to say. How could he talk about selling her as a whore in the same breath he talked about marrying the woman he loved? Didn't he see how ridiculous that was?

But no. It seemed he didn't. Like all the men of the Daliphate, he couldn't see how hypocritical everything he did really was. Sheltering and protecting some women while abusing and demeaning others when the only difference was in how they dressed and where the man had met them.

So be it. She'd sworn to destroy the Daliphate and now she would and they could all take their foolish, backwards, hateful ways and choke on them for all she cared.

She was going to Toreem.

44

As Harley, Reginald, Barkley, and K'lrsa rode toward Boradol, Harley whistled a charming little tune that K'lrsa imagined was great for dancing. He'd sold off the other slaves in the morning—at lower prices than he should've according to Barkley and Reginald, who'd both muttered their objections—and dismissed the remainder of the guards. Now it was just the four of them who rode towards Toreem.

Fast and quick. In and out, according to Harley. At least for the men.

As the day progressed, the city rose above them, its buildings climbing higher and higher into the sky until it seemed they would touch the clouds. And at the top, the largest building K'lrsa had ever seen, the Daliph's palace.

It dominated the skyline, stretching the entire length of the city. It stood at least six stories high. Every inch of the palace was decorated in bright colors—greens, reds, blues, yellows, oranges, black, white—all interwoven to form mesmerizing patterns on every surface.

The rest of the city was subdued in comparison, the same dun-colored stone buildings they'd seen in Boradol with roofs of one color each. Together they blended to complement the palace looming above, but individually they were dull and forgettable.

As they rode through the barren grassland outside the city, a giant wall became visible. It surrounded the city and held all the buildings close to the mountainside.

K'lrsa stopped her horse and stared. The Daliph was up there, somewhere, in that palace, surrounded by guards. But where?

She heard the sound of hooves thundering towards her and turned to see a black stallion charging towards them at full gallop, his rider pressed against his neck as they practically flew across the plain. The man's long black hair streamed behind him as he maneuvered his horse through a series of intricate forms. The two moved so perfectly together they might as well be one.

In the center of the horse's forehead was a white teardrop mark, just like Fallion's. It was an *Amalanee* horse, the only other one she'd ever seen.

She stared in awe as the man and horse approached.

Behind them, just visible in the distance, a woman in black rode a dark brown horse towards them, her shouts audible but unintelligible at this distance. She was clearly chasing after the man, but the distance between the two only grew as the man thundered down upon them. Even farther behind her, K'lrsa could just make out a larger group of riders, some in white, some in brown, all riding towards them.

"Kilgore's bloody balls. No." Harley fought to control his horse.

Barkley looked ill, but he didn't say anything.

K'lrsa rode Fallion forward as man and horse slid to an abrupt halt before them. She wanted a closer look at the magnificent horse. It was the first time in days she'd seen someone who actually knew how to ride properly, and on such a beautiful creature. (Second only to Fallion, of course.)

She glanced at the man and froze.

It was him.

It was the young man from her dreams—his eyes that impossible blue color she hadn't believed could be real, his skin even more golden brown than she'd remembered.

He smiled, his face alight with joy. He was breathing heavily, still recovering from the race across the plain.

"Beautiful," he said.

K'lrsa shivered, her body answering the call of his voice, remembering all those nights they'd come together in the

Moon Dance, bodies pressed close as they moved across the desert sands.

She didn't know what to say. She hadn't really believed he was real; now here he was.

But who was he? What did this mean?

She didn't know what to do, so she focused on his horse instead, urging Fallion forward. "Is your horse an *Amalanee* like my Fallion?"

The man nodded, turning his horse so he continued to face her. "Yes. Figures the woman of my dreams would also have an *Amalanee* horse. Did you know they're supposed to be able to fly?"

She laughed, unable to suppress the thrill she felt at being so close to him. "Well, I don't know about yours..." She pretended to look for wings on his horse. "But Fallion certainly doesn't."

The man answered her laughter with his own. "Neither does my Midnight. But I keep hoping. He is the fastest horse I've ever seen."

"Not faster than Fallion."

The young man grinned at her, riding his horse even closer. "Care to see?"

"Absolutely." K'lrsa gathered Fallion's reins in her hand, but the woman who'd been chasing after the young man joined them and he sat back, a chagrined grin on his face.

"Badru, pzah! Don't you dare ride away from me like that again."

The woman was old, her face lined with wrinkles, but still tall and proud. She had the coloring of the tribes, making K'lrsa wonder just how many tribeswomen lived in the Daliphate. She'd never known of any woman who'd left the tribes.

"What were you thinking? You can't just ride off like that." She cuffed him lightly. Her lips squeezed together like she'd been sucking on bitter root for the past decade.

"Grandmother, it's fine. Midnight needed the run. And you know no one else can keep up with him when he has his full head. But look! Another *Amalanee* horse."

The woman turned her attention to K'lrsa, her shrewd gaze stopping on the everen feather in K'lrsa's hair, the stone around her neck, and the quiver of arrows strapped to her back. (Harley had insisted on the latter even though there was no way K'lrsa could reach them. "To complete the look," he'd said. Idiot.)

"Hm. Is that so?" She slowly rode her horse around Fallion, and then reached out to rub at the mark on his forehead as if it would come off on her thumb. "Well, at least the horse is real."

K'lrsa stared at the woman's hands. The top joint of each thumb and each finger were missing. That couldn't be an accident.

What had this woman done for someone to maim her so?

K'lrsa backed Fallion up. "Don't."

The woman raised one eyebrow at her, but didn't speak.

K'lrsa glanced at Harley, wondering why he hadn't ridden forward to proclaim her a desert princess like he had with every other person they'd passed for the last week, but he was frozen in his saddle, mopping at his sweating brow as he watched the woman.

Barkley too looked like he'd rather be anywhere but where he was.

Reginald, however, wasn't affected by whatever had frozen the other two men. "My apologies, grandmother." He bowed from the saddle. "These desert savages don't have any manners. This girl here is a desert princess, brought from the far tribal lands." He turned his smile on Badru. "We'll be selling her off to the Gilded Lily today if you care to drop in and have a taste."

Badru stared at Reginald with wide eyes. K'lrsa didn't have time to think about why, because the old woman snorted. "A desert princess, huh? Is that so?"

Once more she slowly looked K'lrsa up and down, this time with a slight sneer on her face. "Harley, what manner of foolishness is this? Did you honestly expect to pass this girl off as something she isn't?"

Harley licked his lips as he ran his horse's reins through his hands over and over again. "Omala, please. She...she *is* a desert princess. As much as they have princesses in the desert."

"Is that so?" The woman glanced at K'lrsa. "I doubt she's even a member of the tribes. Probably just the unwanted bastard child of a tribesman."

"How dare you!" K'lrsa rode Fallion forward, forcing the woman to acknowledge her. "I'm K'lrsa dan V'na of the White Horse Tribe and I'm a Rider. Who are you?"

The woman smirked at her. "One smart enough not to be trying to pawn myself off as a princess. If you're a Rider, prove it. Draw an arrow. I'll give you a target."

K'lrsa glared at her, but didn't move.

"I said draw an arrow, girl." Her voice lashed at K'lrsa.

K'lrsa raised her chin. "I can't. You know as well as I do that it would be impossible in this outfit."

The old woman nodded with a slight smirk on her face. "Exactly."

Harley rode forward and clutched at the woman's arm. "Omala, please. It wasn't a lie. We just dressed her up a bit, to help those who wouldn't recognize what she is otherwise." He gestured at K'lrsa. "She's first daughter of a first daughter going back to the founding of the tribes. See her stone?"

The woman threw her head back and laughed, the sound like rocks grating together. She turned on K'lrsa. "So you lied to him? Is that what happened?" She rode closer and flicked the cold, dead stone around K'lrsa's neck. "Let me guess. He captured you and you didn't want to be sold like a common slave, so you told him a lie about being a first daughter of a first daughter?"

She looked back at Harley, shaking her head. "The girl lied to you, Harley. She's nothing. No one. Now leave Toreem before I have you killed."

She turned her horse towards the group of riders who had almost reached them. "Come, Badru. Time to return."

She rode away, not looking back.

With one glance at K'lrsa, Badru followed.

45

"Let's go." Harley turned his horse and started back towards Boradol. Barkley was right on his heels.

K'lrsa and Reginald stared at one another, actually on the same side for once. Why turn back just because one old woman told them to?

"Now." Harley snarled back at them.

Reginald shrugged and reached for Fallion's reins, but K'lrsa jerked away from him.

No. It couldn't end like this. Not when she was within reach of the city walls.

She rode after the old woman and Badru. "Wait. Take me with you."

The old woman reined her horse around. "You really are a fool, aren't you? You lie to Harley, you trick him into bringing you to the one place he should've never returned to, and now, what? You think that you can use your looks to beguile Badru?" She shook her head. "No. I won't allow it."

Badru rode his horse back to them. "This is the one I've dreamt of grandmother. The one I danced the Moon Dance with. I think we're destined for one another."

The woman laughed. "And what god do you think sent that dream, Badru? Which god hates you so much they would send you a trumped up desert princess with a fake moon stone?" She shook her head. "If you've dreamt of this girl, it was the work of the Trickster. Little scheming brat that he is, I'm sure he's sitting somewhere right now laughing his fat little belly off."

K'lrsa flushed with anger, her hands balling into fists. "I am a first daughter."

"Are you? And that pretty little stone around your neck is a moon stone? And that feather in your hair, what is that? A secret tool for making your *Amalanee* horse fly?"

K'lrsa sat up as straight as she could, glaring across at the woman. "The feather is some ridiculous woman's idea of what a desert princess should wear. As is the dress. But I am a first daughter, and I did have a real moon stone until I gave it away."

"Pzah. No woman gives her moon stone away. And no Rider lets herself be taken captive."

K'lrsa clenched her teeth. "Sometimes we have no choice."

"There's always a choice." The woman looked her up and down once more. "Maybe you weren't a very good Rider."

K'lrsa ground her teeth together as she fought the urge to hit the woman. The old hag laughed and signaled to Badru that it was time to leave.

K'lrsa grabbed her reins. "Please. Help me. If I leave with these men, they'll kill me."

The woman slapped her hand away. "I doubt that." She glanced past K'lrsa and made eye contact with Harley as she raised her voice. "Harley's a smart man, most of the time. I'm sure he'll realize that he should sell you in Boradol for whatever he can. You're still pretty if nothing else."

Badru looked like he was about to say something, but the rest of his group arrived and stopped a short distance away.

A man in yellow rode forward. "Herin. We have a messenger from the palace..."

The man didn't have a chance to finish his sentence, because K'lrsa talked over him. "Herin? You're Herin?"

She glared at the man. "To some who forget themselves. Yes."

The man flinched away from her, bowing his head.

K'lrsa closed her eyes and took a deep breath. She had no choice. "Then, Herin dan G'la of the Summer Spring Tribe, I call on our blood tie and ask that you shelter me."

For one moment, K'lrsa thought the woman would kill her. The look in her eyes was certainly enough to kill.

But when she spoke, lazy and casual, the tone of her voice belied the cold, hard anger in her gaze. "You really know nothing of the tribes, do you? Just because I was once of them and your gadja father was, too, doesn't tie us by blood." She started to turn away.

"No. But the blood vow I took with your sister does."

The messenger startled, gaping at them. Badru's hands turned white where they gripped his reins. Barkley made a strangled sound and when K'lrsa turned to look at him his head was bowed as if he'd lost all hope.

Harley looked as if he'd fall right off his horse.

Herin ignored K'lrsa and turned her grel-like gaze on Harley instead. "I told you never to return."

Badru urged his horse forward. "Grandmother? What is this? What is she saying? Is Lodie still alive? How is that possible?"

"Silence." Herin glanced towards the other riders, but only the messenger was close enough to hear the conversation. The others clustered together in small groups, chatting amongst themselves. One man in green sat alone, off to the side.

Herin gestured him over. When he reached her side, she turned back to K'lrsa. "Explain yourself, girl. Now."

K'lrsa tried to hide her trembling. She felt like a hare caught in the sights of a desert hawk with nowhere to hide. "My moon stone. I told you I gave it away. I...I gave it to Lodie, L'dia, so she could escape and find shelter with my tribe. I...I owed her. Ask Harley. She escaped the night we reached Crossroads."

"Is this true, Harley?"

He licked his lips and tried to choke out the words, but failed. Barkley finally answered for him. "Lodie did escape with another slave. She took a horse with her. And K'lrsa did have a moon stone that was also missing the next day."

Herin's lips pressed so tight together that the wrinkles in her face seemed to multiply. She forced a shrug. "So you gave a slave named Lodie a moon stone. How does that make you and me blood?"

K'lrsa flinched at the look in the woman's eyes, but she had to continue. This was her only hope.

"We swore a blood oath before I gave it to her. I made her a sister of my blood so my tribe would take her in. Since hers is gone now."

Herin raised one eyebrow, but didn't say anything, so K'lrsa continued. "Before she left, Lodie told me to ask you for help if I needed to."

"Pzah. Now I know you're lying." Herin shook her head. "My sister, the one once known as Lodie, is dead. She died the same night she poisoned the last Daliph. You can ask any of the hundred men who watched it happen."

The man in green whispered in her ear, and Herin nodded, her eyes moving from K'lrsa to Harley to Barkley to Reginald. And then to the messenger. Harley and the messenger both looked ill.

The old woman continued, "Whoever you met, she wasn't who you think she was. But I can't let these lies spread, either." The man in green rode his horse over to the messenger's side and took his reins away from him.

Herin turned to the waiting riders and called out, "Guards. Take these individuals into custody. If any of them speak so much as a word, kill them. Badru. Come."

Four men in white rode forward to surround them as Herin and Badru rode away, whispering furiously to one another.

K'lrsa looked to Barkley, but he was staring at the space between his horse's ears, looking for all the world like a man who rode to his death.

Harley and Reginald didn't look any better.

What was happening? What had she said?

<u>46</u>

They crossed the bridge into Toreem and then immediately cut to the right, away from the main thoroughfare. The guards led them along a narrow path to the end of the city and guided them through a large set of doors—each one twice the height of a man on a horse—cut into the hillside. They left the horses at a large stable just inside the doors, the stalls carved directly into the rock.

When K'lrsa tried to stay behind with Fallion, one of the guards grabbed her arm and dragged her along. Fallion whinnied and bucked at the young slave girl who tried to take his reins.

K'lrsa couldn't speak, but she gave him the signal for calm and he settled down, allowing the girl to lead him away. At least he'd be well-fed—she could smell freshly-cut sweet grass on the cool air.

The guard dragged her down a cold stone corridor, easily wide enough for two wagons to fit abreast. She kept tripping on her long skirts, but the guard didn't slow in the slightest, just dragged her forward by her arm so they kept pace with the others.

She wanted to ask where they were taking her and what was going to happen to Fallion, but when she opened her mouth to speak he gave her such a deadly look she swallowed her questions and focused instead on walking without tripping.

The guards escorted them to the end of the corridor and then down a small narrow passageway, barely wide enough to fit two men abreast. Guttering torches lit the way, casting jumping shadows on the wall. Her escort shoved her forward and followed along behind; he was so large he blocked out all light from the bright, spacious cavern they'd left behind.

Barkley dropped back by her side and squeezed her hand briefly, but kept facing forward, his jaw clenched tight. She knew he meant it for encouragement, but he was shaking too badly to hide his evident fear.

The harsh scent of burning animal fat filled her nostrils. Underneath it she caught the scent of decaying flesh and excrement.

That scent grew stronger as they walked down the passageway.

The passage turned a corner and ended abruptly, opening into a small room. A group of rough-looking men in brown uniforms with red belts sat at a table in the center of the space, playing dice.

Behind them was another passageway, this one devoid of torches and even more narrow than the one they'd left. Faint moans echoed down the passage, but the men at the table didn't seem to hear them.

The room had the rancid smell of days-old sweat layered over the metallic bitterness of blood and the earthy stench of shit.

K'lrsa tried to back away, but bumped into her guard who shoved her back into the room.

"Well, well. What do we have here?" One of the men at the table leaned forward, eyeing her up and down as he spoke. He slowly licked his lips when he met her eyes.

K'lrsa shuddered.

Her guard stepped forward. "Herin wanted these four taken into custody. She said to kill them if they speak. She'll be down for them shortly. Leave 'em be until then."

Another man from the table stood up and came towards them, smiling through blackened teeth. "That so?" He paced back and forth, studying each of them. "Wonder what they have to say that the old bitch wants to hide?" He leaned close to K'lrsa and sniffed.

She stood her ground, glaring back at him.

She wasn't bound; if the man tried to touch her, she'd kill him. She could do that without speaking.

The first man picked up a coin from the table and flipped it in the air, gold catching the light as it spun. "Good question. Anyone willing to share what you know for a golden bevel?"

Reginald snorted. "Hell. I'll tell ya for free."

The man flipped him the coin. "Well, whatcha waitin' for. Out with it."

As Reginald reached for the coin, his escort stabbed him through the back without even a flicker of expression or grunt of effort. Reginald collapsed to his knees, spitting blood before he fell forward on his face, dead.

"Herin said any who talk die." The man wiped the blade off on Reginald's shirt.

The man at the table stood, his chair scraping against the cold stone floor. "I wasn't done talking to that man." He put his hand on his own knife, but didn't unsheathe it.

All around the room, men reached for their knives.

Herin swept into the room, the man in green trailing along behind her. "Seems he was done talking to you, though, doesn't it?"

The men in brown all bowed their heads and murmured something about Omala. All except the man who still had his hand on his knife. He just sneered at Herin. "You don't run this place old woman. The Daliph does. And I run this prison."

Herin grunted. She nodded her head, acknowledging his point, but then she looked to the man in green.

Before K'lrsa, or anyone else, could even realize what was happening, the man who'd spoken was dead, the man in green's knife buried in his eye.

"Well, now that that's settled. What to do with the rest of you?" Herin surveyed the room, pivoting slowly to look at each person.

She stopped on Harley, who immediately dropped to his knees, hands clasped before him. "I'm sorry, Herin. I am. I didn't tell anyone. It was..." He glanced around the room. "She told, not me."

Herin glared down at him, arms crossed across her chest. "I told you to go and not come back. I told you to go and keep going until you found the end of the world. Did you find the end of the world, Harley?"

He bit his lip. "No. I...we couldn't keep going. The northern lands are so cold and desolate and no one speaks trader's tongue, and...Men died, Herin. I had to. I had to come back." He bowed his head. "I'm sorry, Herin. I, I made a mistake. But it's over now. It won't happen again."

"You're right. It won't." She flicked her eyes at the guard behind Harley; the man stepped forward and slit Harley's throat.

K'lrsa gasped. She backed away, but there was nowhere to go. Herin's guards blocked the entrance.

The cold stone walls seemed to be collapsing in on her, moving closer and closer with each panicked breath.

Herin turned her attention to Barkley. He met her gaze and threw his shoulders back. K'lrsa was surprised that Herin was just as tall as Barkley—she had to be as tall as any woman K'lrsa had ever met. (Other than Lodie that was.)

Barkley held his own, but he had a resigned look like he knew what was coming.

Herin tilted her head to the side, studying him. "Heard enough to guess? Or already knew?"

Barkley took a deep breath. "Already knew. I joined Harley in Crossroads on the way out, but I'm from Toreem. I...I used to help my father with the brickwork around the palace when I was young." He met her eyes. "I saw...too much."

Herin nodded and turned her attention to K'lrsa. K'lrsa wanted to look anywhere but into Herin's black eyes, but she forced herself to meet the woman's gaze. If she was going to die, she'd do so as a Rider, not a sniveling coward.

Herin smirked.

"And you...foolish child who just destroyed the lives of four men because you don't know enough to keep your mouth shut."

She stepped forward, the spices on her breath overpowering the stink and decay K'lrsa had smelled before. "I should kill you." She smiled. "I want to kill you."

She pursed her lips together until her eyes almost disappeared behind her wrinkles. "Unfortunately, I have no idea what that fool of a boy would do if I did. Then again, he'll probably make just as many foolish mistakes if I let you live." She shook her head. "Men. Ridiculous how easily they let a pretty face ruin their lives."

K'lrsa glanced at Barkley, but he was staring down at the floor.

Herin fingered the hilt of the blade strapped at her waist for a long moment as everyone waited in tense silence.

"Pzah." She let the blade drop back into its sheath. "Some lines even I won't cross. Doesn't mean I have to do anything other than keep you alive, though."

She turned to the man in green. "Kill them all except the girl."

He nodded and the men in white stepped forward, knives flashing as they attacked the prison guards and the other prisoners.

Barkley didn't move as the man in green raised his sword to kill him.

"No." K'lrsa grabbed at his knife arm, but Herin pulled her away, her fingers like claws, her grip so strong K'lrsa felt as powerless as an infant. She shoved K'lrsa against the wall of the passageway. "Don't be a fool, girl. It's been a bloody enough day already."

K'lrsa tried to shove past Herin to go to Barkley's side—he was already down, there really wasn't a point—but the man in green stepped forward and rapped her on the temple with his knife hilt.

The last thing she saw as she collapsed to the cold stone floor and her world turned black, was Barkley's vacant-eyed stare. Her only friend was dead.

She was all alone again.

47

K'lrsa awoke in a large four-poster bed draped in blue and red gauzy fabric that blew in the breeze from a nearby open window. The scent of summer flowers floated on the air—unnatural with winter so close. Underneath the pleasantness of the flowers was the slightest hint of what K'lrsa had come to think of as "city stench"—the combined odor of garbage, people, and animals shoved together in too small a space.

She didn't move, unsure where she was or who might be nearby. She sent a small prayer of thanks to the Lady Moon that she was still alive and not chained in a darkened cell somewhere.

Badru's voice reached her from across the room. "It's done."

"Pzah, you foolish boy. You don't understand." Herin hissed the words, clearly wanting to shout. "She will ruin you. We have to get her away. Now."

"No."

"Badru."

"No. I dreamt of her. She was sent to me. I won't be parted from her now that I've found her."

K'lrsa tried to shift slightly to see them, but the bed creaked and she froze once more. Badru and Herin fell silent.

K'lrsa held her breath, waiting, hoping they wouldn't come to see if she was awake.

"Pzah. You'd risk it all for a dream? Nothing but a boy's fancy." Herin paused and K'lrsa could picture her scrunching her lips together in disgust. "Some days you're no better than him, taking what you want without any thought for the consequences."

Badru's voice was ice when he responded. "You forget yourself, *Omala*. Don't you ever compare me to him again."

The silence stretched for what seemed like forever, the room full of tension. Finally, Herin spoke again, softly. "Fine. She stays. But you can't just throw a girl of the tribes into the Daliph's court. She must be prepared."

"Then prepare her."

A door opened and a gust of wind blew the curtains up so K'lrsa could see Badru standing in the doorway, clothed in a rainbow of color—his vest a blue that matched his eyes perfectly, his pants striped in every color she could imagine, and a red belt tied around his waist.

Herin faced him in her loose black dress; the man in green leaned against the wall next to her, silent as always.

The curtain fell back, blocking her view once more.

"Badru. I'll do this. But you must promise me one thing."

"What?" He didn't sound like he wanted to promise anything.

"You won't attempt to see her again. Not until I tell you you can."

K'lrsa willed Badru to refuse. And for a moment, as the silence stretched, it seemed like he would. But then he said, "So be it. But make it soon. Now that I've found her, I won't take kindly to any lengthy delays."

K'lrsa heard the door close.

"Pzah. Foolish boy. He'll get us all killed. And for what? Love?" She barked a short laugh, the sound like grating rocks. "We have to stop this, Garzel. Save him from himself."

There was a small grunt of agreement. K'lrsa pushed the curtain aside to see them.

Herin stood in Garzel's embrace, her head leaning against his chest. She looked exhausted. Garzel stroked her hair softly. His shoulders were stooped and face just as weary as hers. They looked in that moment like they were propping each other up, both ready to collapse without the other's support.

K'lrsa was embarrassed to have witnessed such a personal moment, but before she could turn away, Herin saw her.

"I shoud've killed you when I had the chance."

She left the room and Garzel followed.

48

K'lrsa explored her room. It was large, larger than any room she'd ever been in, even the main rooms of the inns they'd stayed at on the way.

There were four windows, currently open to allow a breeze; a box of brightly colored flowers hanging just outside each one provided the scent of summer. The windows could be latched closed with wooden shutters—one pair each in red, blue, green, and yellow—that were currently fastened by hooks to the outside wall.

The room was three or four stories above a paved courtyard—high enough that K'lrsa felt dizzy when she looked down. There was nothing between her and the distant ground except empty air. Other windows were open in the rooms that surrounded the space, but there were no people visible.

A mountain rose above the rooms opposite her. Its shadow stretched across the courtyard like a grasping hand.

Harley and Barkley were dead because of her. Because of what she'd said. And Reginald, too.

She shivered at the chill breeze. She didn't really care about Reginald. He would've harmed her given the chance. And Harley was planning to sell her off to other men who would hurt her. But Barkley...Barkley had been her friend. He'd tried to help her.

And now he was gone and she didn't understand what was happening and the only person who seemed to care for her,

Badru, was banned from seeing her. And Herin, the woman who should've helped her, wanted her dead.

K'lrsa shook the thoughts away. She'd made it this far. She was in Toreem. And in the Daliph's own palace. All she had to do now was find him and kill him.

One moment, that's all she needed.

She tried the door, but it was locked, so she explored the rest of the room.

The far end of the room contained the four-poster bed wrapped in bright, light fabrics. It could easily fit four people abreast with room at the end for two or three more.

Opposite that was a large bathing area hidden behind a stone half-wall that contained a large tub, a basin for washing, and a floor-to-ceiling mirror.

K'lrsa stripped out of the loose blue dress they'd given her.

Naked, she stared at herself in the mirror for a long time. She'd never seen herself in more than a small handheld mirror her mother owned—a treasured possession her mother almost never allowed her to use—so she'd never seen more than a glimpse of part of her face before. Maybe just an eye or her lips.

She'd never seen it all together.

And she'd certainly never seen her entire body, never known what others saw when they looked at her.

She'd always known she was attractive, of course, just from the way men responded to her, even in the tribes. Their mouths would broadened into smiles when she approached or they'd stop to help her string her bow or give her special treats they'd bartered for from the traders.

There'd even been one trader who broke into a jaunty tune every time he saw her. But she'd never known what the men who eyed her so appreciatively were actually seeing.

Now she did.

She saw what they saw. Long legs, toned and muscular. The curve of hips leading to a narrow waist. Well-formed breasts— not as much as many women, but definitely a woman's curves, and enough to fill a man's hand. Black hair that fell loose in soft waves and was long enough to cover her breasts when pulled forward.

The high cheekbones, pointed chin, generous lips, and large brown eyes were a distant echo of her mother's.

Yes. She understood now what men saw in her. But it didn't matter. It didn't change who she was.

She was still just K'lrsa.

She turned away and threw the dress back on.

It didn't change anything and she had better things to do than stare at her reflection all day.

But she did catch herself glancing back at the mirror often, fascinated by her own expressions.

The rest of the room consisted of a large sitting area with cushions and low tables arranged in a circle atop a large carpet woven in a pattern of reds, blues, greens, yellows, and oranges with room for at least a dozen people to sit comfortably.

In the corner was another mirror, this one attached to a table with a chair in front of it. On the table were jars and brushes. K'lrsa opened a few of the jars, but they made her feel ill, the scents were so overpowering and bitter. She put them back and resolved to stay away from them.

Bored, she banged on the door and shouted, but no one came.

K'lrsa sat on a narrow stone bench under the central window and stared outside, listening to the sounds of Toreem. Even though she couldn't see the city, it was alive in the scents and sounds that found their way to her window.

She wished her room faced the plain and Boradol so she could catch a glimpse of home.

She longed to be back there, bickering with her mother about her latest unsuitable suitor or playing hoops with her sister.

She missed the feel of the sun baking her skin and the sight of baru stampeding across the plains. And the fresh smell that lingered in the air after a storm passed.

She buried her face against her knees, aching for what she'd lost.

She forced herself to think of her father, to remember why she was here. It was hard. The memory was so worn and used by now it seemed more like a bad dream than something that had really happened to her.

She wanted to be angry, to burn with that white-hot fire she'd felt the first day, but she just felt sad. And weary.

So much had happened since the day she'd sworn revenge. Events had overwhelmed her, swept her along like a spring flood, tugged and tossed her where they willed.

No more.

She had to take control.

The Daliph was here. Somewhere. Just down the hall or across the courtyard. The man whose actions had twisted her world into something she couldn't even recognize.

He was here, and she could finally achieve her goal. She could finally kill him.

And then this would all be over and she could join her father in the Promised Plains.

She could find peace and rest.

At last.

For a moment, she thought of Badru, his blue eyes shining with recognition and love when they first met. He wasn't a dream. He was real and alive and he wanted her.

She remembered the feel of his child in her arms, the boy's heavy weight as he nestled against her.

A little voice whispered that that could be real, too, if she just chose Badru instead.

She shook it away. "No."

She remembered lying in Badru's arms on the warm desert sands, the sky above them blanketed in stars, feeling safe and happy.

"No," she said, louder. "That's not why I'm here."

Herin had been right. The dreams were the work of the Trickster.

But the trick hadn't been on Badru. It was on her.

The Trickster was taunting her with a life and love she could never have.

For a moment, she wondered if she could kill the Daliph and still have Badru. Fulfill her vow and follow the call of her heart.

But no. The only way she'd kill the Daliph was if she was willing to give her life to do so. If she wanted him dead, she had to sacrifice everything. Even Badru.

K'lrsa rested her chin on her knees and rocked silently back and forth.

As twilight fell, she looked up at the sky, hoping to see the Lady Moon, but the sky was dark and barren, empty.

She nodded to herself. Of course it was. Her gods were long gone, left behind in the desert. She was alone now.

She stood and walked to the mirror. She stared into her own eyes and saw the fear there, but she pushed it away until only determination remained. "I swore a vow to the Great Father to kill the man who killed my father and destroy the Daliphate. And I will. I K'lrsa dan V'na of the White Horse Tribe swear this. To the Great Father. And to myself."

She said the words, but they didn't make her feel any better.

49

Later, Herin returned to the room with Garzel trailing along behind her—ever-silent in his green robes. Four servants entered behind them, bearing trays laden with more types of food than K'lrsa had ever seen at one time, the smells staggering in their complexity.

Her stomach growled. She hadn't eaten since breakfast in Boradol what seemed like a lifetime ago.

She opened her mouth to speak, but Herin gestured her to silence using the closed fist of the Riders. K'lrsa studied the woman's maimed hand, wondering once again what the woman had done to be deliberately harmed in such a way.

They stood on opposite ends of the seating area, glaring at one another until the servants finished arranging the trays of food and closing the windows. Only after they'd left, leaving K'lrsa alone with Herin and Garzel, did Herin lower her fist.

With Garzel's assistance, Herin sat on the cushions and gestured for K'lrsa to join her as Garzel lowered himself to the cushion on Herin's left.

K'lrsa stared at the selection of food. There were soft white cheeses and flat discs of bread so fresh they were still steaming. And olives and dates and nuts. And meats swimming in sauces of all colors. She leaned close to smell the dishes, curious about what they contained. Some burned her nose, others smelled cool and fresh.

She held back even though her stomach demanded food. She'd long ago learned to ignore her hunger; in the desert she'd often gone an entire day without eating. It was hard to, though, with so much food spread before her.

"Eat. We have much to discuss," Herin said.

Garzel loaded a piece of bread with one of the soft white cheeses and held it to Herin's mouth. She took a bite, chewing slowly, and then another bite. K'lrsa looked away, unable to hide her disgust. No one in the tribes would ever allow another to feed them like a baby. Especially not a Rider.

Herin saw the look and shook her head. "Such a simple world you live in. All black and white and easy choices." She took another bite as K'lrsa dunked a piece of bread in one of the bowls near her that had green sauce and some sort of white meat floating in it. "Tell me. If you had a choice to die or to continue, scarred, changed forever from what you were, what would you choose? Would you quit? Just lay down and die? Or would you fight on for as long as you could?"

K'lrsa took a bite of food, refusing to answer. She thought she'd want to continue. But it would go against everything she'd ever known to be a burden on others.

She dipped a piece of bread into a bowl with dark meat in a bright red sauce and took a bite. Immediately, her mouth started to burn and her eyes poured tears. She spat the food out in her palm, gasping as the fire from the food consumed her mouth.

Herin laughed.

Her mouth was still full so it made her choke. Served the old crow right. K'lrsa hoped she choked and died.

Garzel pounded on her back until she spit out whatever it was that had made her choke.

He poured a glass of white fluid from a metal pitcher beaded with water and held it towards K'lrsa, signaling that she should drink it.

"Cow's milk." Herin coughed one last time. "It'll calm the heat."

189

K'lrsa swallowed the whole glass in three gulps. It tasted awful, but Herin was right. It did take away the burning sensation in her mouth. "Thank you." She nodded towards Garzel. "Why doesn't he speak?"

"Can't. He has no tongue."

Garzel opened his mouth to reveal a small stub of flesh. K'lrsa flinched as he wagged it back and forth. Garzel laughed and sat back once more.

"A gift from the former Daliph, may he burn in eternal fire." Herin took another bite of food offered by Garzel—this one a small roll wrapped in green leaves.

"Why does he feed you? Can't you feed yourself?"

The woman should be able to manage, even with her maimed fingers.

Herin shrugged. "Habit after thirty years. Garzel has fed me since the day I arrived here. Women at court aren't allowed to feed themselves. Easier than using these."

She waved her mangled fingers in front of K'lrsa's eyes.

"What happened?"

Herin smiled, the expression reminding K'lrsa of a hawk about to strike. "Another gift from the Daliph."

"That's horrible. What did you do that he would do that to you?"

Herin glared at her until K'lrsa chose to look away.

At last, Herin answered, "Do you think a woman could do *anything* that would justify this? That any person could do anything that would justify this?"

"No." K'lrsa spoke softly, shamed. "I just…this world is so different from the tribes. I thought maybe…it was part of the law here or something. I wanted to know if there was something I might do that would lead to the same punishment."

Herin shook her head. "No. It won't happen. The new Daliph isn't like the old one."

After they ate for a long time in silence, Herin continued speaking. "My fingers and thumbs. In the olden days, this was how a Daliph marked his dorana. Dorana are the Daliph's chosen companions. By cutting the fingers and thumbs of his dorana a Daliph in the old times showed how powerful he was because each dorana he kept required many slaves and poradoma to tend her every need."

She took another bite of food, chewing slowly. "This practice was replaced with the *meza*—a symbol of the dorana's dependence on her Daliph but something she didn't have to carry with her for the rest of her life."

"So why did the former Daliph do that to you?"

"Because he was a sadistic bastard who enjoyed inflicting pain on as many people as he could."

K'lrsa choked on the olive she'd been eating.

Herin shrugged. "He was."

"So you were one of his dorana?"

Herin laughed—a harsh, grating sound like metal on stone. "Me? No. He was a cruel, evil man, but not even he was that arrogant. Or foolish. No. I was just something he kept close for amusement."

Herin had clearly been beautiful once—her eyes still were when she relaxed—but now her body was all bones and sinew, her face covered with the wrinkles of anger and unhappiness.

K'lrsa shivered. "Did the Daliph like you that much? That he kept you so close?"

Herin spat out an olive seed, reminding K'lrsa for a moment of Lodie. "No. He hated me that much. Now, enough of the past."

Herin leaned forward. "You are trouble. More trouble than you're worth. If I had a say in the matter, you'd be on your way back to your tribe already, tied up in the back of a wagon, never to be seen again until you were out of the Daliphate. Better yet, I'd just have you killed."

"So why am I still here? You seem very powerful."

Herin snorted. "Not powerful enough." She shook her head. "The Daliph does what he will. And he decided to make you one of his dorana, the blasted fool."

"The Daliph? When did he see me? Where?"

Had she missed a chance to kill him? When? And did this mean that Herin had crossed Badru, giving her to the Daliph to get her away from him?

Herin studied her, eyes narrowed, lips pressed tight together so the wrinkles blossomed on her cheeks. "Tell me something, girl. Why are you here? Why didn't you escape with Lodie when you had the chance?"

"It didn't occur to me." K'lrsa shoved a bite of food into her mouth and avoided Herin's intense gaze.

"That's a lie. I will find out the truth."

Yes, she would. When the Daliph was dead at K'lrsa's feet.

"Can I see Badru again before I'm made a dorana?"

She knew there was no future for them, but she wanted for just one moment to feel his lips against hers here, in the real world.

Herin grabbed her by the throat, the movement so fast, that K'lrsa was choking before she even knew what had happened. "Never speak that name again. Ever."

"I don't understand..." K'lrsa barely managed to gasp out the words.

"You're right. You don't. You're a silly little girl who has no idea what events she's set in motion." She shoved K'lrsa away. "As far as you're concerned, Badru is dead. The boy you saw in your dreams is just that, a dream. You are now a dorana of the Daliph of the Toreem Daliphate. Act like it."

K'lrsa rubbed at her throat. "And how do I do that when I don't know the rules?"

"You'll learn them. And until you do, you won't leave this room."

K'lrsa poked at the olives on the plate in front of her. "I'm sorry I upset you, Herin. But...I love him, you know." She didn't dare say Badru's name again, but she knew the older woman understood who she was talking about.

"Is that so?"

"I do. I've been dreaming of him for weeks. He's all that sustained me through...through everything I saw."

Herin laughed. "A dream. You fell in love with a dream. What do you know of him? Truly?"

K'lrsa leaned forward. "You don't understand. It was instant. Our connection. The Lady Moon brought us together. We've danced the Moon Dance in the Great Desert. Night after night, our bodies moving together so perfectly…"

Garzel grunted and Herin nodded agreement. "Pzah. A dream. Put it aside. Real life is nothing like that little fancy of yours." She leaned forward. "And if I hear you speak of your dreams again or say that boy's name to anyone other than me or Garzel, I will kill you myself, blood bond or no. Do you understand?"

"Yes."

She ate another olive, waiting for Herin to say more, but she didn't. "When will I meet him? The Daliph?"

Herin gave her a long look, her eyes hooded. "When you're ready to behave like a true dorana."

"When will that be? A few days? A few weeks?"

Herin snorted. "Perhaps never. I won't have you shame him, or me, or your poradoma." She stood with Garzel's assistance. "Rest well, girl. Tomorrow your life changes in ways you never expected."

K'lrsa watched them walk towards the door, all the questions she wanted to ask dying on her tongue.

Herin opened the door and waited as the servants cleared away all the dishes of food, most still heaped high as if they hadn't been touched.

After they'd gone, Herin turned to K'lrsa once more. "You should've stayed home. And if you did wish this for yourself? You'll soon learn what a fool you were."

After Herin closed the door, K'lrsa heard the sound of a large bar slamming into place, locking her inside.

<u>50</u>

K'lrsa felt restless, agitated. The room she was in was spacious and beautiful, the fabrics nicer than anything she'd ever known before. But she was caged, trapped, stuck for who knew how long. Maybe forever.

She stripped off the loose silk robe and kicked the pillows backwards until she had a cleared area large enough to practice the hundred and five attacks.

As she worked through them, flowing from Crouching Cricket to Striking Hawk, from Slithering Snake to Pouncing Cat, she tried to puzzle through all that had happened since she'd met Badru and Herin.

Why couldn't K'lrsa speak Badru's name? Was he a secret? He hadn't seemed it. And the stablehands had taken his horse just like they'd taken anyone else's.

His clothes were very fine even though they'd been all black like Herin's. So he wasn't some poor relation snuck into the palace.

She longed for Barkley. He'd know the answers. He'd help her understand.

She jumped high, kicking at an imaginary opponent's jaw, snapping his neck. Her muscles were tight after so many days of riding without the opportunity to practice. It had been weeks since she'd been able to move through the full attack forms and her body felt the difference.

She was like a child, starting over, unbalanced, unsure.

And Lodie. Why had the mere mention of her name caused Herin to kill everyone who heard it? What was so secret about selling your sister into slavery?

And why was the Daliph making her a dorana? She'd thought it was an honor reserved for daughters of the best families in the Daliphate—a political alliance as much as anything else. So why choose a girl of the tribes as dorana? It made no sense. Even Herin had said it was a foolish thing to do.

So why do it? And when had he seen her?

K'lrsa stopped, breathing hard, her skin sheened with sweat. She'd only made it through the first sixty attacks. She'd need to work her way up to the final attacks, the leaping, diving, spinning ones. She was too stiff to try them now.

Each night she'd work at it until she once again flowed through the forms as easily as breathing.

And in the morning, in the morning she'd devote every ounce of energy to becoming the perfect dorana. It was the only way she'd ever leave this room. The only way she'd finally have her chance to kill the Daliph.

She grabbed a soft cloth from the bathing area and wiped her body down.

The cloth turned black with the grime of travel. It was nice to really sweat and have the chance to scrape away the dirt of the road and feel clean once more.

She turned to the bed. It was too exposed. Too large. And too soft. She'd never be able to sleep in it.

She pulled off a blanket, grabbed a handful of pillows, and made herself a small sleeping area in the space between the wall and the bed. It was a narrow space, barely enough for her to lie in, but it at least felt safe and familiar.

She blew out the lights scattered around the perimeter of the room and snuggled into the small, dark place she'd made for herself.

There was so much she didn't know, so many questions running through her mind. She knew she'd be awake most of the night trying to answer them.

She was wrong. She fell asleep almost as soon as her head touched the pillows.

She dreamt.

The sky was as black as spilled ink; the stars so plentiful it was as bright as midday. Badru sat before her, his hair tied back in the braid of a Rider; a sun stone around his neck gently pulsed to the beat of his heart. It quickened when he saw her.

He smiled, gesturing her closer.

She didn't join him. Her heart filled with the music of the Moon Dance and she began to move. She was one with the night as she danced across the sands, her hips swaying to the gentle rhythm of the world pulsing around her.

Badru came to his feet, joining her, their bodies moving in perfect unity, the heat of his skin calling to hers, his mouth like honey as they kissed.

The whole universe opened before them, the stars surrounding them as they danced on and on and on, lost in time and one another. The moment seemed to last an instant and forever as they held one another, their souls merging into one.

51

K'lrsa was jolted awake by a foot kicking hers.

"Up. Time to meet your poradoma and see if there's any hope of turning you into a dorana before I die." Herin stood at her feet, arms crossed.

K'lrsa stood; the cool of the morning air from the open windows made her skin prickle. She couldn't believe she'd slept so soundly that anyone, let alone the small entourage standing in the middle of the room, had entered without waking her.

Garzel leaned against the far wall, arms crossed. He was no longer the only one in a green robe. Three more men in green stood in the sitting area. One was probably K'lrsa's age—young and fiery with an edgy energy to him like he'd burst into motion at any moment. The others were older, closer to her father's age.

The leftmost one had skin so dark it seemed to suck up the light. K'lrsa tried not to stare at him, but it was hard. He was large, too, towering over everyone and wider than any man she'd ever seen.

He wasn't fat, no. Just, large. Powerful.

The third man was forgettable. Average coloring, average build. Her eyes slid right past him to the two servants busy arranging trays of food on the low tables.

K'lrsa walked forward, still nude. She saw no point in covering herself—the morning breeze felt refreshing, and she'd often walked through camp with no clothing or partially clothed when the mood suited her. Until, that is, she noticed the way the youngest man's eyes roved over her flesh like hands and the way the third man shook his head in dismay.

She quickly grabbed the silken dress from the half-wall and threw it on.

Herin smirked. "These men are your personal poradoma. They will do everything for you from here on out—clothe you, bathe you, feed you. Welcome to true royalty, *Princess*."

She made a mock bow in K'lrsa's direction. K'lrsa glared at her. She was really starting to hate the woman.

"Sayel. Step forward."

At Herin's command, the large black-skinned man stepped forward, the loose robe that covered his body straining with each movement as muscles rippled below the fabric. He smiled and his teeth shone white against his skin.

"K'lrsa dan V'na of the White Horse Tribe, this is Sayel Abadaro. He is your head poradom, the one in charge of your other poradoma. He is also in charge of you. Whatever he tells you to do, you must do." Sayel mopped at his brow and bowed slightly to her and to Herin.

"Sayel is a third-generation poradom. Understand that it is a great honor to be a poradom. One entrusted to men the Daliph trusts above all others because they protect his most treasured possessions."

The way she spoke, it was clear she was reminding Sayel and the other poradoma as much as she was explaining the poradoma to K'lrsa.

"An honor to serve the Daliph and to guard you for his pleasure." Sayel bowed to K'lrsa and then introduced the other two poradoma as Tarum and Morlen. Tarum was the young one who'd leered at her. Morlen was the middle-aged man who was forgettable in every way.

K'lrsa's stomach growled. The delicious smells of the food made her realize how hungry she was. "Very nice to meet you." She plucked a handful of grapes from a nearby tray.

Herin slapped them out of her hand—the blow hard enough to sting.

"Ow. What was that for?"

"You're a dorana now."

"I know. And?"

Herin grabbed the grapes from the floor and shook them at her. "Doranas don't feed themselves. Their poradoma feed them."

"It's just a handful of grapes."

"It doesn't matter."

K'lrsa glanced at the men who were silently watching them. "You mean I have to eat the same way you did last night? With someone shoving food into my mouth?"

Sayel bit his lip, his eyebrows drawn tight in concern. "Herin…"

She waved him aside. "She'll learn, Sayel. She has to if she ever wants to leave this room." She directed the last sentence at K'lrsa, her eyes like bottomless pits.

K'lrsa bit back the hundred different things she wanted to say. "Fine." She looked at the three men in green. "Can someone please feed me some grapes?"

Obviously that wasn't what she was supposed to say, because the poradoma looked shocked and the two servants who had just finished destroying the bed she'd made for herself, laughed, whispering quietly back and forth until a glance from Herin silenced them.

"You must be prepared first."

K'lrsa looked at Herin. "What does that mean?"

Sayel snapped his fingers and Morlen and Tarum left, returning quickly with an armful of clothing each. They started to lay out the articles of clothing on the bed; there were so many different items K'lrsa couldn't imagine what they were all for. And in such a riot of colors it was almost painful on the eyes.

"Is this my new wardrobe?" K'lrsa asked.

Sayel chuckled like a doting uncle asked a silly question by a young child. "Oh no, my dorana. This is what you'll wear today."

"All of this?" She'd never thought she'd long for Mistress Hawthorne's ridiculous outfits, but they looked simple by comparison. "Why?"

"Because you're a dorana. And this is what a dorana wears."

"To eat breakfast?"

"Always."

She stepped towards the windows and gazed out at the clear sky. The sun shone weakly above her. "No. No, I won't do it. Tell the Daliph thank you very much, but I don't want to be one of his dorana."

Sayel spoke slowly, like that would somehow make her understand. "It is a special honor to be declared a dorana. No one would refuse such an honor from their Daliph, even, especially, one such as yourself."

"One such as myself?" K'lrsa turned on him, arms crossed tight against her chest to keep from striking him.

"Yes. One who has come from nowhere and never worn fine silks nor eaten delectable meals. Look how many colors he gave you. Even blue. You can't refuse."

"Yes, I can."

The servants had stopped even pretending to work. They stared at her like she was some disfigured animal they'd never seen before, their expressions equal parts fascination and horror.

Sayel stared at her, his mouth hanging open. Morlen and Tarum were equally stunned.

Herin just rolled her eyes and shook her head. K'lrsa could almost hear her thinking how stupid the Daliph had been for selecting her.

Sayel tried again. "To be a dorana is the highest honor a woman can receive."

K'lrsa laughed. "The highest honor a woman can receive is to be smothered in clothing and not allowed to feed herself?"

Sayel blinked and stepped backward slightly.

"Leave." Herin shooed everyone from the room. "Give me a moment with her. Tribeswoman to tribeswoman."

As everyone left, Herin grabbed Sayel. "I don't have to tell you that discretion in this matter would be best?"

His eyes widened in alarm as the two servants left, muttering to one another. "Yes, Omala. Of course." He raced from the room, calling after them.

K'lrsa was sure he was already too late. By dinner, the story of her refusal would be all over the palace.

And what would that mean for her chance to kill the Daliph?

<u>52</u>

Herin slammed the door and turned on her. "Are you a fool?"

"No." K'lrsa sat on the stone bench under the windows, arms crossed against her chest.

"Do you want to die?"

"No. Of course not." K'lrsa answered without thinking, but it was true. She didn't *want* to die anymore. She would, if it meant killing the Daliph, but she didn't want it. Not now that she'd found Badru.

Herin stepped closer. "Do you want Badru to die?"

"No." What did he have to do with it?

Herin glared down at her. "Then obey your poradoma and keep your mouth shut. Wear what they tell you to wear. Do what they tell you to do. Don't show yourself to be the ignorant tribal savage you are."

"Tribal savage? What does that make you?" K'lrsa stood, trying to loom over the woman, but Herin was at least half a head taller than her.

"Someone who learned the rules of the game I was forced to play." Her eyes were flinty as she added, "I suggest you do the same."

K'lrsa stepped around her and grabbed another handful of grapes, munching on them as she paced the room. "I don't understand. What have I done that's so wrong?"

Herin rolled her neck and grimaced in pain. She lowered herself to a cushion and Garzel joined her. He loaded a flat disk of bread with spiced meat and greens and held it for Herin to take a bite. K'lrsa decided that if Herin could eat so could she and used bread to scoop a mouthful of eggs—so soft and creamy she sighed in bliss.

"Where to begin?" Herin took another bite of food. "Dorana belong to the Daliph."

"Yes, I understand that."

Herin frowned at her, reminding K'lrsa of her own mother when she was disappointed.

"No. You don't. They *belong* to him. They're his possessions. Their bodies are his. They can't do anything without his permission."

"Anything?"

"Anything."

K'lrsa peeled a nectarine, trying to think what that meant. She took a bite, relishing the juicy sweetness.

"The poradoma are a gift from the Daliph to his dorana. His way of giving her permission to eat and dress herself."

"Really?" K'lrsa laughed.

Herin nodded. "Dorana are a symbol of the Daliph's power and mastery over his world. They must only act as he wills them to."

"Then I don't want to be one."

"You have no choice. You were already a slave. As a slave, you have no say in who owns you or what they ask you to do. Now the Daliph has made you his dorana. You have no say in that either."

"How can that be?"

Garzel grunted at Herin, his words unintelligible. Herin nodded, pinching the bridge of her nose. "Let me start over. You were a woman of the tribes. A Rider?"

"Yes."

"Did you notice as you came here that women dress differently than the tribes? That they're treated differently?"

"Yes. How could I not notice?"

Herin nodded. "You saw, but did you understand what you saw?"

K'lrsa shoved another bite of food into her mouth. She'd never liked learning through discussion. She learned better through action, by doing. Hand her a bow and point to a target and she'd work all day every day until she hit it every time. But talk to her about ideas and concepts and she grew bored. Especially when she didn't understand.

"Women in the Daliphate are always covered. They're never allowed outside the home alone. They never ride horses."

"You rode a horse."

Herin waved the comment away. "Pzah. Listen, child. We don't have time for this. Those men are out in the hallway right now talking about you like a pack of magpies. Women here, unless they are slaves or whores, so far beneath notice that they aren't even considered women, don't ride, don't walk alone, don't display their skin, don't speak their minds, and don't have opinions or thoughts or ideas of their own."

K'lrsa opened her mouth to speak, but Herin gestured her to silence with the closed fist of the Riders.

"And dorana, dorana are the most elite of all women. They do nothing for themselves. They say nothing. They think nothing. Nothing that the Daliph doesn't command them to do or think."

K'lrsa spit a grape seed into her hand. "That's ridiculous."

"That's the Daliphate." Herin leaned back, studying her. "If you'd prefer I can always sell you off to the Gilded Lily like Harley intended…"

Herin raised an eyebrow and waited for K'lrsa to respond.

For a moment, K'lrsa wondered if that life would be better than this one. Free to speak and move, to think. Yes, her body would be sold to any man willing to pay the coin. But her spirit would be free. Her mind would still be hers.

Wouldn't that be better than this life where she couldn't dress herself, feed herself, or, it seemed, speak for herself?

Herin rolled her eyes. "You would actually think about it, wouldn't you? I told you, child. It's too late. He's already chosen you." She stood. "You are a dorana. You can either learn how to be a proper one and someday leave this room. Or you can fight against your fate and slowly die here. Which do you choose?"

K'lrsa stood as well, glancing back at the pile of brightly covered fabrics piled on the bed. She had no choice if she wanted to succeed in killing the Daliph. "I'll learn. Show me what I need to do."

Herin nodded. "First, you must let the poradoma dress and feed you. And that," she sighed, "requires you to wear the *meza*."

"What are those?" K'lrsa didn't actually want to know, but she felt compelled to ask.

"The *meza* are the Daliph's symbol of his power over you. They show that you are subject to his will in all things. The *meza*, and the golden *tiral*, which you only have to wear for court appearances, mark you as a dorana."

K'lrsa crossed her arms. "Yes, but what *are* they?"

"You'll see. Just remember, you have no choice but to wear them." Herin glanced at the breakfast dishes and grimaced. There was no hiding that they'd eaten.

She walked to the door, opened it and gestured the poradoma back inside.

"Thank you, Omala." Sayel bowed to her before entering the room, Tarum and Morlen trailed along behind him.

Herin gestured to the center of the room. "K'lrsa, stand here. Sayel, let's begin with the *meza*."

Sayel bowed low before K'lrsa. "May I have your hand, my dorana?"

K'lrsa extended her hand to him and watched as Tarum opened a carved wooden box for Sayel's inspection. Inside were five woven silk tubes of different sizes. Sayel studied her hand, holding two of the tubes up to her fingers before choosing the second largest tube.

He fit one end of the tube over her thumb, the silk snug against her skin; he fit the other end of the tube over the first finger of her hand. When he was done her first finger and thumb formed a small circle joined together by the tube.

Holding her fingers like that was slightly uncomfortable after a time. K'lrsa flexed her thumb and finger, trying to straighten them.

The silk pulled taut, refusing to slide off her fingers, and cold metal pressed against the first joint of her thumb and finger. She gasped and started to pull harder.

"What is this? Get it off me."

"Stop it." Herin gripped her wrist, the bony ends of her fingers digging into K'lrsa's skin. "The *meza* will do you no harm as long as you remain calm. But the harder you pull, the deeper the blades will cut into your skin." She let go of K'lrsa's wrist and wiggled her fingers before K'lrsa's eyes. "Pull hard enough, they'll slice clean through."

K'lrsa trembled, shaking uncontrollably. What kind of place was this?

As Sayel bound her other hand she fought back the tears, knowing she wouldn't even be allowed to wipe them away herself.

"And I wear these every day?"

"Every day, all day. From the moment your poradoma wake you to the moment they leave you for the night."

K'lrsa flexed her fingers slightly and felt the blades touch her skin once more. "Why do this? A woman can do nothing with these on."

"That's the point, girl. A dorana isn't meant to do anything. She's an ornament, there to look pretty and nothing else."

K'lrsa stared down at her bound hands and then over at the piles and piles of brightly-colored clothes on the bed.

She closed her eyes.

It didn't matter. None of it mattered as long as it took her closer to her goal. They could bind her how they wanted as long as she was eventually able to reach the Daliph and wrap her hands around his ugly, fat neck and watch his froggy eyes bulge out of his head until he died.

She flexed her fingers and felt the blades of the *meza* kiss her flesh.

A reminder.

A reminder that the Daliphate must be destroyed. Not just for her father, but for all the women it bound, the women hidden behind long black robes, forbidden to speak or act for themselves.

If she failed, a woman of the tribes might one day find herself bound like this, glad to be honored by the Daliph's attention. Or the corruption might spread to the tribes until women were considered lesser, unequal, their bodies something to be hidden, their voices silenced.

K'lrsa shuddered at the thought.

She wouldn't let that happen. No matter what, she would destroy the Daliphate and everything it represented.

53

After they'd fastened the *meza* to each of her hands, they dressed her.

First came a full-length bright yellow silken dress. It was softer than anything she'd ever touched and had twenty small pearl buttons on each arm, running between her wrist and elbow. Morlen carefully buttoned each one as Sayel pulled the ties on the back of the dress tight.

K'lrsa wanted to comment on how ridiculous it was to design an outfit that required three grown men to put on, but one look at Herin's stony face silenced her.

Next came the first overdress; red with half-sleeves and a split skirt that showed glimpses of the yellow dress beneath. Tarum fastened the series of tiny hooks in the front, his hands drifting towards where they weren't needed and didn't belong.

K'lrsa glared at him, but he never met her eyes, his head bowed as his hands wandered—as if she wouldn't notice what he was doing as long as he didn't look at her.

She didn't like him. Didn't trust him. Something in the way he looked at her and touched her was different from Morlen and Sayel. A perversion of the role of a poradom.

On top of the red dress they placed a blue top with cap sleeves and eyelets all over that allowed glimpses of the red dress beneath. This one fastened in the back with fifty small golden buttons so delicate that it took a special tool to fasten them.

K'lrsa wanted to laugh it was all so ridiculous, but she kept her expression neutral; Herin's presence in the corner reminded her what was at stake.

If she could survive this farce, she could see the Daliph and kill him.

This was just a distraction. An obstacle to be overcome. A diversion sent by the Trickster.

It was nothing.

What they made her wear didn't change who she was.

Finally, they wrapped her waist ten times with a brilliant green sash woven through with thread of gold.

Sayel stepped back with a soft smile and nodded to himself.

"Now for your hair and makeup." He led her over to the small table with the mirror and the foul-smelling jars. It was only ten paces away, but K'lrsa almost tripped three times on the way there.

She wondered how she'd manage to kill the Daliph when she couldn't even walk. (Or smooth back the stray piece of hair tickling her nose.)

"Allow me." Sayel smoothed the hair away from her face, his touch gentle, like a father tending his small child.

K'lrsa wanted to flinch away, but she reminded herself that this was his duty. His role was to tend her. It wasn't his fault that the whole thing was twisted and wrong.

As she stood in front of the mirror, Morlen braided her hair into an ornate headpiece that wrapped around her head like a crown, strips of colored cloth woven through.

Sayel opened the various jars on the small table, humming to himself as he worked. He painted her cheeks, lips, and eyes with the contents of the various jars, occasionally stopping to exclaim in surprise things like, "Oh, wonderful. Look at how the ochre emphasizes her eyes."

The odors made her nauseous, but she fought against the urge to turn away and run to the open window for a quick breath of air.

She closed her eyes and entered a light version of the warrior's Core. Anything to not experience what they were doing to her.

When he was done, Sayel led her over to the large mirror in the bathing area. He stood behind her, resting his hands on her shoulders and smiled at their reflection in the mirror.

"You are the most beautiful dorana the Daliph has ever chosen."

K'lrsa didn't even recognize herself in the painted doll in the mirror. Her eyes looked twice the size they normally did, highlighted in bright colors. Her lips were bright red and wet like red meat.

She couldn't stop staring at herself, horrified and mesmerized.

They'd obliterated her. Hidden who she was under layers of fabric and face paints.

She flexed her fingers, feeling the kiss of the *meza* against her flesh, reminding herself that somewhere beneath all those layers she was still there.

She was still K'lrsa dan V'na of the White Horse Tribe and she was still here to kill the Daliph.

That woman? The one in the mirror that she didn't even recognize?

She was an illusion.

K'lrsa struggled to cling to what she knew was real, but it was hard when what she saw was so different from the truth.

<u>54</u>

It was a long, exhausting day. Sayel made her walk around the room over and over again. He wanted her to glide with every step, as if she were floating on air, but all she managed to do was trip and fall so many times that she suspected Tarum purposefully failed to catch her on the last attempt.

Sayel helped her to her feet. "It's okay, my dorana. You had no training, no way to know that one day you'd rise to such glory. The other dorana, they practice from the time they can walk, preparing for that day when the Daliph takes them as his own. You have much to learn."

She tried to picture an entire childhood spent learning how to walk as if she weren't touching the ground and failed.

When lunch arrived, she wasn't even capable of sitting on her own. Tarum and Morlen had to lower her to the cushions.

K'lrsa bit back a comment about how just a little bit of extra space here or there would make the outfit so much more practical. And she swallowed her disgust at having to eat from Tarum's fingers.

The food was delicious. More plentiful and diverse than anything she'd ever eaten on the plains. She had her choice of five kinds of cold meat and four types of cheese and nuts and olives and bread spiced with cloves and coriander. (She was quickly learning the words for all the various spices.)

It was a bounty unlike anything she'd known.

But all she really wanted was to sit at her mother's fire eating yet another bowl of hare and sour greens boiled over the fire. And to use her own cursed hands. That was far preferable to nibbling a delicious soft cheese from Tarum's fingers as he watched her intently.

Herin and Sayel spent the afternoon lecturing her on the proper way for a dorana to interact with strangers. They paused often to argue back and forth, adding more and more to the lecture as they realized how little she knew. A woman who grew up in the Daliphate would at least know the basics. Like how a woman must avoid all eye contact with a strange man by casting her eyes to the floor. The floor, not the ceiling, not straight ahead. The floor.

And how a woman must never initiate conversation with a man she didn't know.

And must never respond to a comment made by a man she didn't know unless he was an honored guest of the Daliph's. Even then, there were another ten rules about which men she could respond to with more than a demure comment about the Daliph and his glory.

By the time dinner arrived—a selection of meats floating in sauces, some sweet, some spicy—she could barely stand. She tried to refuse the spicy dishes, but Sayel insisted that she must learn to eat them. What if the Daliph wanted to feed her with his own hand? She couldn't refuse what he offered her, could she?

She also couldn't eat it and then make gasping noises and demand milk, either. That would look like she was rejecting his gifts and that was not acceptable.

(K'lrsa held back a comment about how maybe the Daliph should give his dorana gifts they actually wanted instead of torturing them with spicy foods and ridiculous amounts of clothing.)

Over and over she was told how she must learn proper decorum. Modesty.

She must be unassuming in all things, even choking down food she couldn't stand and didn't want to eat.

Over and over, K'lrsa reminded herself that she was doing this for a purpose.

Over and over she wondered what she'd been thinking on the day she ignored her father and set off to avenge him.

Finally, after what seemed like days, they undressed her and left her alone in her room, free of the *meza* and the many-layered costume of the dorana.

She'd promised herself she'd work through the hundred and five attacks, but she was too tired. Instead she curled up on the floor, wrapped in the blanket from the bed, not even bothering with the pillows, and fell asleep.

She found herself in the desert. Badru waited for her. He smiled when he saw her, and stood to throw his arms wide.

She ran to him, buried her face against his neck, and cried.

He flinched backward for a moment, surprised, but then he gathered her close in his arms and held her as she wept herself dry.

When she was done, she sank to the sands, exhausted.

She was in the Lady's land, but she didn't hear the music of the Moon Dance. Not tonight.

She just wanted to go home. To the real desert. To her mother and sister and, yes, even her brother.

55

K'lrsa's days fell into a long, grueling routine.

Each morning as the sun rose, the poradoma arrived to dress her. First, Sayel would fasten the *meza* to her fingers and then they'd smother her under layer after layer of beautiful fabric, each one fastened with its intricate ties or hooks, the fabric soft and silky against her skin, finer than anything she'd ever felt.

Next, one of the poradoma would help her sit and feed her a breakfast of fresh fruit, nuts, and bread. She was eating more than she ever had in her life and it showed in the way her hips and thighs were broadening. Just a bit. Just enough to notice.

She'd never cared about her figure before. Her body served her purpose and if it didn't serve her purpose then she trained until it did. She'd been strong and lean when she was captured, her body honed to what she needed to survive in the desert.

But the poradoma didn't want that. They had lengthy discussions about whether they should allow her to gain a small amount of weight or whether they should start restricting her meals to keep her looking like she had when she first arrived.

Which would her Daliph prefer? Did he like her exotic slender form? Or would he prefer a woman more like the others, curvy and fleshy? And what to do with her muscles? A woman so muscular was unseemly.

She tried not to listen, but each night as she studied herself in the mirror, the things they said about her body crept back

214

into her mind.

After breakfast they made her practice walking. Then Sayel would lecture her on the history of the Daliphate or drill her on proper behavior.

Through it all, Herin sat in the corner, watching them like a grel waiting for its prey to die. K'lrsa kept silent, knowing the woman wanted her to fail.

And then? Then she'd be sold off like the property she was. Where and for what, she didn't know.

After a brief stop for a meal at midday, they would spend the time until dinner drilling her on more history and etiquette. Finally, after Morlen or Sayel or Tarum had shoved her dinner into her mouth, they left her alone to collapse in exhaustion.

Herin, Garzel, the poradoma, and the occasional slave were the only people K'lrsa saw. During the day she was absolutely, never, ever allowed close enough to the windows to see anyone or for anyone to see her, and the windows were fastened shut before she was left alone each night.

Badru never came to see her. And she didn't dare ask Herin about him.

She saw him in her dreams some nights, but the music of the Moon Dance was gone. More often than not if she arrived in the Lady Moon's land before him, she turned and walked away into the empty desert, alone. She craved silence and solitude.

She tried to learn what they wanted her to learn, but it was hard.

Everything they wanted her to do or say or not say was contrary to who she was. She'd never lowered her eyes for anyone. Would never think to stop herself from speaking her mind. Had always done for herself, never looking to anyone else for help.

She reminded herself, every morning, why she was doing this. To kill the Daliph. To avenge her father and herself.

But holding to her purpose, keeping her anger alive enough to make it through each day, was almost impossible.

When she thought of her father, which she did each night before she went to sleep and each morning when she awoke, she was more often sad than angry. Even picturing how he'd looked at the end wasn't enough to drive her hatred anymore.

Lodie had been right.

Revenge in the moment was easy. A cold revenge was not.

She forced herself to practice the hundred and five attacks each night, relishing the feel of movement, of kicking and slashing and cutting her enemies. She pushed herself until sweat shone on her skin, imagining over and over again the sound the Daliph would make as he gasped out his last breath and died at her feet.

After enough days, even those images weren't enough to drive her forward.

She just wanted it to be over.

<u>56</u>

K'lrsa lost count of how many days passed. More than ten. Less than sixty. They were all the same, blending into a never-ending blur where she felt herself slipping away more and more with each day. It was almost habit now to look to the floor and silence herself.

She couldn't sleep. She didn't want to dream of Badru or wander through her hazy memories, searching for the reason she'd come here.

It was the middle of the night when she rose, her only clothes the two thin strips of cloth she'd taken to wearing at all times to protect her modesty. Tarum still leered at her a bit too much and his hands still lingered a little longer than they should when he helped to dress her, but it helped a bit. And she'd take every bit she could.

She lit a lamp—just enough to see by—and started working through the hundred and five attacks. She was exhausted and tired and heart-sore, unable to find the balance she needed to truly flow from one to another.

She knew she should stop before she hurt herself, but she didn't care.

She didn't care about anything anymore.

She was just starting the attack forms for a fourth time when her door opened and a man snuck inside, closing the door quietly behind him. He wore a heavy cloak that covered him from head to toe, the hood pulled over his face.

K'lrsa landed softly, resting on the balls of her feet, ready to attack.

"K'lrsa." The man threw back his hood. It was Badru.

So beautiful, so golden and blue-eyed and smiling at her with such warmth.

"Badru!" She ran forward and hugged him, forgetting that she was covered in sweat and not much else and that this was the Daliphate and not the tribes.

He flinched away from her and she pulled back, staring down at the floor. "I'm sorry. I forgot myself." She felt blood rush to her cheeks and quickly threw her night robe on, covering herself. "I'm...I'm still learning your ways."

That was part of it. But the other part of it was that touching him reminded her of bodies entwined under the desert sky, his hands moving along her body like fire.

"Don't be. I, I liked it. I just didn't expect to find you so..." It was his turn to blush and look away. "Not like we haven't touched in our dreams."

She forced herself to meet his eyes. The act felt bold and reckless after so many days spent staring at the floor in silence. But this was Badru, not the Daliph or his men. He wouldn't force her to look at the floor and remain silent. He loved her. Her. K'lrsa. A Rider. A warrior.

"Dreams aren't reality, Badru."

He took her hand. "But they can be." He ran his fingers down the side of her face and leaned in to kiss her.

She knew she should pull away, but she didn't. She was so lonely, so scared. All she wanted was to find comfort in him. She kissed him back, fierce and desperate, pressing her body against his.

Once more she felt him draw back with surprise but then he answered her need with his own, pulling her against him, devouring her mouth with his own, his hands roaming along her body. He'd touched her like this before in the moon dream, but somehow, here, now, it felt so much more powerful and intense.

His hands grasped her robe, pulling the fabric upward. She pushed him away and backed up so there was plenty of space between them.

"No, Badru, we can't."

He shook his head. "You've been listening to my grandmother. Just because she says we can't be together doesn't mean anything."

He reached for her and she backed away. "No, Badru. I'm a dorana now."

"I know." He smiled at her, continuing to advance.

"We can't be together."

He laughed. "Why do you think that?"

"Once I'm trained, I'll be given to the Daliph."

"I know." He smiled at her, still confused, still reaching for her.

K'lrsa took his hands in hers and held his gaze. "I know dorana are eventually released to marry another, but that won't happen for me, Badru. I won't survive that long."

He jerked his hands from hers. "What do you mean?"

K'lrsa knew she should keep her plan to herself. She still didn't know how Badru fit into things. She still didn't understand the significance of his and Herin's wearing black while others wore brown or single colors.

But Badru was the mate of her soul, the one sent to her by the Lady Moon. If she couldn't trust him, who could she trust?

"I'm going to kill him, Badru. The Daliph. That's why I'm here. When they present me for the first time, I'll attack." She turned away. "I don't expect to survive it."

Badru was silent behind her. She turned back to him. "You won't betray me, will you? You won't tell anyone?"

Badru started to laugh and then stopped. "You're serious."

"Yes."

"You came her to kill the Daliph." He was half-smiling as he looked at her.

"Yes. And I'm sorry he made me his dorana so that we couldn't be together, but it gives me my chance."

Badru sat on the stone bench by the window, his legs stretched wide before him. "You can't."

K'lrsa crossed her arms. "Yes, I can. And I will. You grew up in this vile place so you don't understand what women are capable of, but I can do this."

"I wasn't saying that you weren't capable, K'lrsa. You have met my grandmother, haven't you? But you can't...you can't do this. And why would you want to?"

K'lrsa paced back and forth as she told him the story of the Daliph's raiding party and finding her father. She cried as she remembered the horror of seeing her father staked to the ant hill—the act of having to describe that moment in words somehow reawakened her emotions in all their original intensity.

Badru came to her and held her in his arms as she cried, rocking her back and forth and murmuring in her hair that she was safe now, she had him, he'd protect her.

After she'd cried herself out, K'lrsa raised her head from Badru's shoulder and looked into his eyes. "I swore to my gods that I'd avenge him. That I'd kill the man responsible for my father's death and destroy the Toreem Daliphate."

He smoothed her hair back from her face. "But the Daliph didn't kill your father. The men in that raiding party did."

She pulled away from Badru to pace the room once more. "It was his men. If I kill them, he'll just send more. And more." She took his hand in hers, begging him to understand. "The Daliphate is destroying my people, Badru. They give us liquor and smokeweed and silk to betray our secrets. They make us forget our sacred trust. The Black Horse Tribe has led slavers across the desert. Slavers!"

He frowned. "And for this you'd kill the Daliph?"

"You have to cut off the head of the snake to kill it."

Badru shook his head. "No. This is wrong. No."

She stepped back, crossing her arms over her chest.

"What if it wasn't the Daliph's men? Did you ever think of that?"

"It was."

"How do you know?"

"They had swords and one wore the Daliph's colors. Plus, when he came to summon my father, L'ral said so."

Badru tried to grab her hands, but K'lrsa backed away.

"Maybe it was a trick, K'lrsa."

K'lrsa thought of her father, dying, muttering the words, "Not the Daliph..." But no. He just hadn't wanted her to avenge him. Hadn't wanted his daughter to risk her life that way. She shook her head.

Badru reached for her again, grabbing her hands. "I know the Daliph, K'lrsa. Very well. He didn't order this. His men didn't do this. He doesn't want to destroy your people. He wants trade, yes, and he's willing to pay for it in whatever goods the tribes want, but he doesn't want to destroy the tribes. He needs them."

She pulled free and turned away from him. "No. You're wrong." She paced around the room again. "He still deserves to die. If not for what he did to my father, then for what he's done to me."

"To you? He made you his dorana. Against the advice of everyone."

She stared at him, realizing in that moment how different they were from one another. "You would think that's an honor, wouldn't you? Because you're one of them. You don't understand me at all."

He shook his head. "What do you mean?"

"It's not an honor, Badru. To be bound. To be kept from feeding myself. To be told I can't speak to anyone. That I have to stare at the ground lest I meet the eyes of some strange man. It's a curse, Badru. It's torture. He didn't ask if I wanted this, he just acted. He took away my life and I've never even met him."

He stared at her, his mouth slightly open. "You don't understand, K'lrsa."

"No, you don't." She shook her head. "Just go."

"K'lrsa..."

"Go. Get out. Now."

When he hesitated, she said, "I'll scream until someone comes, Badru. Go. Now."

He hesitated a heartbeat longer and then turned towards the door. "As you wish. But I swear to you on all my gods and my love for you, that you're wrong about this. About all of it."

57

K'lrsa stripped off the robe so she'd be ready to fight when the guards came for her, certain that Badru would go straight to the Daliph with news of her plans. The Daliph was his ruler and friend. He'd have to tell him.

And when he did, the Daliph would order her taken. Sold maybe. Killed even.

She might've lost her chance to avenge her father, but if this was the end, she'd die fighting.

But as night slowly passed and darkness was replaced by the first rays of the sun leaking through the window blinds, she realized that Badru hadn't betrayed her.

He'd loved her enough to protect her.

(Or thought her so incapable it wasn't even worth mentioning.)

She dwelled on that thought as she waited for her poradoma to arrive for yet another stultifying day of practicing how to walk and talk as if she didn't exist.

But instead of her poradoma, Herin stormed into the room, alone except for Garzel. "I should give you to the poradoma. You know that's possible don't you?"

K'lrsa shook her head, exhausted from a night of wondering when they'd come from her. "What are you talking about Herin?"

"Failed dorana. Ones who the Daliph rejects. Every generation or so it happens. And when it does the dorana is given to a poradom as a reward for him and punishment for her. She's stripped of all titles, all belongings."

"Good thing I don't have any of those then."

Herin slapped her, the blow so sudden and shocking that K'lrsa just stared at her.

"You're a threat and a fool and I wish I'd killed you the day I met you."

K'lrsa collapsed onto the stone bench. "So do I."

Herin shook her head, pacing the room. "I knew you had a reason for coming here. I knew it." She glared at K'lrsa, eyes narrowed to little black points. "I just figured you'd followed the cursed dreams here, never even realizing you were walking into danger because you were so blinded by love.

"It never occurred to me you were stupid enough to think you could kill the Daliph." She shook her head once more, clenching and unclenching her fists. "You and my sister...arrogant, foolish...I should kill you now."

"So do it then."

Herin glared at her and K'lrsa flinched.

"Pzah. Must I be surrounded by fools? First the boy and now you."

Garzel grunted at Herin. She nodded in reply. "I think you're right. It's the only way now. The only way forward if there is one." She gestured towards the door. "Summon her poradoma."

Garzel left.

"What are you planning, Herin?"

She would not be given to Tarum like some sort of twisted prize. She'd kill him first. Or herself.

Too bad the windows were still barred for the night. She'd heard that a fall from a height could kill a person. She didn't know what height, but she had to assume she was high enough.

She tried to care about never having her chance to kill the Daliph, but she honestly didn't.

Somewhere along the way she'd lost that spark that had kept her anger burning. Now she was just numb, like banked coals—the spark still buried somewhere deep inside, but the fire itself gone.

She'd only continued in this direction because there was no other path to take.

Herin picked at something in her teeth as she watched the doors.

"Herin. What are you going to do?"

Herin glanced back at her, a half-smile on her lips. "I'm going to present you to the Daliph just like you wanted."

"What? Why?"

Herin snorted. "Don't smile, girl. I'm not doing you a favor."

58

When the poradoma entered the room, their arms were draped with even more clothing than usual.

Sayel smiled at her as he hummed a jaunty little tune. "I was starting to worry we'd never be able to present our dorana," he confided to Herin where she sat in the corner, her mouth fixed into a flat line.

She quirked an eyebrow, but didn't say anything.

He came to K'lrsa, placing his hands on both sides of her face. "Ooh. We'll need extra makeup to hide those dark circles, but you're so beautiful, he won't even notice. He's bound to love you at first sight."

Herin snorted her opinion, but Sayel wouldn't be deterred.

As Morlen and Tarum laid out her garments, he said, "You'll see, Herin. We've turned this fierce desert cat into a proper young lady."

No they hadn't. They'd almost broken her—a few more weeks and she would have lost all sense of who she'd once been—but she was still a Rider. And now that she was finally going to have a chance to kill the Daliph she felt the flames of her anger stirring.

K'lrsa allowed them to dress her, standing still as they placed layer after layer of brightly covered cloth on her body. She rehearsed the hundred and five attacks as they fastened the buttons and tied the ties that bound her tight, trying to figure out which ones would be possible given her ridiculous garb.

After they'd finished with all the normal layers plus a few extra, Sayel reverently held up a full-length jacket of gold wire.

The metal was crocheted in a fillet pattern—more open spaces than metal—that allowed the colors of her outfit to peek through.

"This is the *tiral*. It's crocheted from spun gold. Isn't it beautiful?"

It was something alright. K'lrsa smiled and nodded. "Very much so."

"This is the formal court garment of the dorana."

He carefully helped her place each of her arms through the long sleeves that extended past each wrist and ended in a fabric loop that Sayel placed over the middle finger of each hand.

It weighed on her shoulders, heavier than it looked.

Sayel had saved the *meza* for last. He opened a delicate white box to reveal a set of *meza* woven of gold inside. "Aren't they amazing?"

K'lrsa's stomach clenched at the thought of wearing them, but she managed to nod.

"They were made especially for you. See the blue sapphires? None of the other dorana's *meza* have these. The Daliph truly favors you." He smiled at her like a proud, doting father.

K'lrsa forced herself to smile back as he bound her fingers, but the whole time she was wondering how she'd be able to attack the Daliph when she finally met him. Between the *tiral*, the *meza*, and all the layers of clothing, she could barely walk let alone strike a man hard enough to kill him.

After they finished with her hair and makeup, Sayel stepped forward with a small bottle. "One last touch to make you as beautiful as you can possibly be."

He had her lean her head back and dropped something into her eyes. She blinked at the sudden brightness of the room.

"Don't worry, my dorana, we'll help you. But look how beautiful."

He gestured to the mirror and she saw that her pupils were so large they almost obliterated the brown of her eyes. She looked like a newborn baru—weak and vulnerable.

She shuddered.

Sayel finished by affixing a small golden cuff to the top of her right ear. "You'll receive one for each year you're a dorana. It's your dowry."

She flexed her fingers, feeling the kiss of the *meza* against her skin, and reminded herself once more why she'd allowed them to do this to her.

All these days of preparation and it was finally time.

She was going to kill the Daliph.

Or die trying.

59

K'lrsa walked through the hallways of the palace with Sayel and Morlen on each side, their hands on her elbows to assist her. Herin and Garzel were ahead of them and Tarum behind, but she could barely make out their shapes. The drops had made everything so bright that she kept her eyes almost completely closed.

The *tiral* surrounded her like a cage.

When she tripped on it for the fourth time, Herin whirled around. "Pzah, child. Just take smaller steps, would you?"

K'lrsa didn't answer, but she did shorten her steps and found that it did help. She hated taking such mincing little steps, but no denying that it worked.

The people they passed were a blur of colors—most brown or tan, with the occasional pop of a single color—a blue belt or red scarf—but never more than that.

No black like Herin wore. Or Badru.

She never had been able to get an explanation for the colors. Sayel had started to tell her once, but Herin had signaled him to silence.

They made their way down a twisting maze of corridors, the beige stone of the walls offset by colored tiles along the top and the bottom—just a blur of red, blue, orange, yellow, green, black, and white to K'lrsa's eyes.

As they turned a corner and saw two giant doors ahead of them, K'lrsa stopped, too dizzy to continue. Sayel had tied the underdress so tight she couldn't manage more than shallow breaths. She tried to pull air into her lungs, but she couldn't get enough. Panicked, she breathed faster, sucking air in and out of her lungs as fast as she could.

The room started to spin.

She swayed and only Sayel and Morlen's grips on her arms kept her upright.

"It's an exciting moment, isn't it? To finally meet your Daliph?" Sayel's bright smile against dark skin filled her vision.

K'lrsa nodded, struggling to breathe.

"We're almost there. Just ahead. See the doors?"

K'lrsa glanced at the double-doors ahead, three times as tall as any man, and patterned with interlacing colors of red, blue, green, yellow, orange, black, and white. People entered through a small side door—all men from what she could tell.

K'lrsa closed her eyes and focused on the Pattern to calm herself, desperately seeking the Core. She repeated the standard phrases until the world finally stopped spinning.

"My Daliph," Sayel cried. The air moved as her poradoma bowed.

At last, she was going to meet her enemy. This was it. The moment she'd dreamt of for months now.

Before K'lrsa could open her eyes, he spoke. "Sayel. Grandmother. What's the meaning of this?"

Badru.

It was Badru's voice.

Badru was the Daliph?

Her eyes flew open. Badru stood before her, his shape hazy, but recognizable. He was dressed in clothing as colorful as hers—reds, blues, oranges, greens, yellows. On each side stood a woman, also dressed in colorful clothing—one mostly in green with yellow woven throughout her accessories, the other mostly in red with orange accents. Both wore the *tiral* over their clothing.

Behind him four guards in white waited.

K'lrsa swayed, her mouth opening and closing.

No.

No, it couldn't be.

Herin's hand clamped across her mouth before she could speak. "Silence," she hissed.

K'lrsa almost laughed.

What would she say?

Badru, the man she thought she loved, was the Daliph, the man she'd sworn to kill.

<u>60</u>

"*Omala*, what is she doing here?" His voice cut the air like shards of glass.

K'lrsa's poradoma stepped back, leaving K'lrsa, Herin, and Garzel to face Badru and his entourage.

Herin bowed to him. "I decided it was time you met your newest dorana, most honored leader."

"Without consulting me first?"

"Yes." Herin bit the word off, not even flinching back from Badru's anger.

K'lrsa desperately wanted to be able to see his eyes, to read his expression, because his voice sounded so cold, so cruel. But the drops in her eyes had blinded her so all she could do was listen.

She should've known. All those riders outside the city. The way Barkley and Harley had reacted when they saw him. Herin and Lodie and the fact that she'd been made a dorana. How had she missed it?

"Take her back to her rooms. Now. I don't want her here."

Sayel choked back a gasp.

"As you wish." Herin didn't even bow this time.

One of the women at Badru's side giggled and snuggled against him.

K'lrsa pushed past Herin, desperate for a glimpse of Badru's face. "You're the Daliph?" she asked as she finally

232

came close enough to see him, those beautiful blue eyes now flat and cold, more cold than even Herin had ever looked.

For a moment, she thought his gaze softened, but then he looked past her, his jaw clenched. "I said, take her back to her rooms. Now," he roared.

Sayel and Morlen stepped forward to grab her, but K'lrsa twisted away. The movement sent her sprawling to the ground at Badru's feet.

He glanced down at her, his face completely blank, before stepping over her and proceeding to the large double doors.

The dorana who'd giggled before, did so again, her green eyes twinkling with evident amusement before she too stepped over K'lrsa's arm.

The doors opened to a rush of sound from the vast crowd inside the room. Badru stepped into the doorway and the sound ceased, hundreds of men falling silent at the sight of him.

Of their Daliph.

She lay on the floor, watching, as he stepped inside and the doors closed behind him. Her stomach clenched so tight she was surprised she didn't throw up.

And then she laughed.

She laughed and she laughed and she laughed until the tears were running down her face, smearing her makeup and washing the blinding drops away.

"Stop it, child. There's no time for that. Morlen, Sayel, get her up. Now."

After they helped her stand, K'lrsa turned to Herin. "Don't you see? It was all a big joke, wasn't it? You were right. It was just the Trickster having his fun. The dreams, the Moon Dance, my father...it was all just one giant prank. The little bastard must be lurking in a corner somewhere laughing his fat little belly off." She raised her voice, "Where are you, you little brat? Show yourself."

Herin closed her eyes for a moment and took a deep breath. "I wish that were true, child." She took K'lrsa's arm in hers and led her back towards her rooms. "Come."

K'lrsa held her chin high as she walked away from the throne room. She turned her back on Badru the way he'd turned his on her.

Sayel walked on her other side, quietly wiping away the one last tear that managed to escape her control.

Badru was the Daliph, but it didn't change things.

She'd sworn a vow.

The Daliph still must die.

Which meant Badru must die.

61

As soon as they reached K'lrsa's rooms, she turned on Herin. "You knew."

"Of course I did. And it was about time you did, too."

K'lrsa felt the tears welling up once more. The man she loved…the man she loved was the man responsible for killing the only person who'd ever supported her and encouraged her to be who she wanted to be. The only person who'd ever loved her unconditionally.

She'd spent days trapped in this room, being broken at *Badru's* orders.

"Oh, stop that." Herin shook her head in disgust. "You're a Rider. Act like one."

K'lrsa sniffed, forcing the tears back. Herin was right. She was a Rider and she needed to start thinking like one instead of like some lovesick fool pining after a man who had never been what she thought he was.

What did she know of Badru? That he had pretty eyes? And soft skin that glowed like the sun? That his mouth was like honey and his hands like fire?

So what.

That was nothing. She thought of her father—of his patience, his kindness, his intelligence. That's what she wanted in a partner and equal.

She'd let a pretty face turn her head. Fool.

"Get this off me." She twitched her shoulders, trying to dislodge the *tiral*, but it clung to her clothes, refusing to budge.

She flexed her fingers but stopped when the *meza* cut into her thumb.

"I said, get this off me."

No one moved to obey her.

"What?" She squirmed against the confines of her golden cage, more desperate now.

Sayel looked to Herin; so did K'lrsa.

Herin's lips pressed tight together until they disappeared into her wrinkled old face. "We can't. He may want to see you."

"Who?"

"The Daliph. He may want to see you so you need to stay dressed to receive him."

K'lrsa laughed. "After his reaction today, I don't think Badru wants to see me ever again. And I don't want to see him. I'm done being a dorana. Take it back. Take it all back."

Sayel stepped back in surprise. Morlen muttered to Tarum who just glared daggers at her.

Herin shook her head, looking ten years older than she had moments before. "Don't be a fool, girl."

"I don't want this. I don't want any of it. I just want…"

"To go home?" Herin asked into the silence.

"To end this."

She held Herin's gaze. They both knew what she meant.

But Herin continued as if she didn't. "Good. Because you can't go home. You're a dorana of the Daliph of the Toreem Daliphate and will be until *he* decides otherwise. Best get used to it."

Herin signaled the poradoma to follow and they left, slamming the door behind them.

K'lrsa went to the far window and stared at the courtyard far below, yearning for an end to it all, but unable to act with the weight of the *tiral* holding her back.

62

She spent the rest of the day at the window, gazing up at the mountain. She missed the desert and the way she could see forever in any direction. She longed for the clean, crisp air of dawn and the way the heat hazed her vision at midday.

She longed to lie with her head in her mother's lap and hear how everything was going to be all right, to know that she was loved and protected.

But she wasn't.

And nothing would ever be all right again.

By the time Herin and the poradoma returned, she was too exhausted physically and mentally to fight them. She stood still in the middle of the room as they removed the *tiral*. Sayel looked like he'd been crying, his eyes red and puffy.

"What of the Daliph?" she asked, quietly.

Sayel glanced at her and then away, apologetic. "He sent word. He won't see you."

"Good."

Herin paced the room. "Pzah. You fool. You know so little."

Sayel cleared his throat. "Omala, we've listened to your directions on how to train this dorana, but we've failed. He won't have her now. Unless we act to fix her."

K'lrsa flinched at the way Tarum studied her, his eyes caressing her body, not even trying to hide his lust.

Had it come to this?

Herin waved Sayel away. "Oh, he wants her still. Be assured of that."

Tarum looked away, clearly disappointed. K'lrsa felt a rush of relief, quickly followed by a hot surge of anger.

Since when had her life become subject to the lusts of men? Badru or Tarum, what gave them the right to dictate her life because they did or didn't want her?

She clenched her fists. She needed to stop letting everyone push and pull her where they would. The *meza* bit into her skin, reminding her just how much of a prisoner she was.

Trapped in the Daliph's palace. In this room. Bound and constrained. Her every movement watched. Her every action dictated by someone else.

"So what now, Herin?" she asked.

Herin sat on the stone bench, her shoulders slumped. "I don't know. The Daliph will decide."

"Decide what?"

"Whether to keep you."

Sayel flinched even though he'd just said the same a moment before.

"And if he chooses not to?" K'lrsa tried to hide her trembling, but her hands betrayed her, vibrating with fear.

Herin met her eyes, but didn't answer.

Slaves entered the room, carrying trays of food; two closed the windows, locking K'lrsa back in her cage.

As Tarum helped her to the cushions, his hands lingered a little more than before. K'lrsa wondered what Badru would do.

Would he reject her now? Send her away?

The boy of her dreams wouldn't. The boy who'd held her close as she cried, the one whose body matched hers so perfectly, who danced with her on the desert sands—that boy would never hurt her.

But the Daliph? The man who'd stared at her with dead eyes and stepped over her as if she was nothing—that man was capable of anything.

So, which was he? The young man she loved? Or the leader she hated?

63

K'lrsa thought Badru would come to her that night. That he'd apologize for his coldness, tell her it was all an illusion, remind her how much he loved her and cared for her.

But he didn't.

She stayed up all night, watching the shadows under the door, waiting for his steps to block out the light, but he never came.

As the sun snuck his rays through the window blinds to cast the room in soft gray light, she realized the truth.

That boy she'd met—the one who filled her dreams, the one she'd thought was her soul mate, so perfect and wonderful. He didn't exist. He was just a trick sent to distract her.

All that passion, those moments they'd spent together, they weren't real. They were dreams. Illusions. Her own longing for a true equal had blinded her to the truth. Badru was a beautiful but callous man who didn't actually care about her.

Sure, he'd held her as she cried for her father. But maybe the whole time he'd been holding her, he'd been laughing inside, knowing that his men had been the ones to bring her those tears. Maybe he'd listened, secretly amused by her trusting innocence.

And now that she knew the truth, the game was over. He'd just move on to his next victim and charm that girl the same way he'd charmed K'lrsa.

She collapsed to the floor, exhausted, bone weary after two nights without sleep and too many days of being beaten down, her sense of self destroyed.

She sat like that for a long time, pitying herself, hating herself for being so blinded, so foolish. Her mother had been right about her. She *was* just a foolish girl who didn't know anything and couldn't do anything special.

She certainly couldn't avenge her father by killing one of the most powerful men in the world.

As her thoughts spiraled downward, ever more negative, a small part of her fought back.

What was this? Was she her father's daughter or not?

Because her father's daughter would never quit so easily. That girl would never believe herself incapable of anything

Her father's daughter had spent days hunting the baru, days practicing with Fallion and her bow, until she accomplished what no one else had ever accomplished.

Her father's daughter was a Rider. A woman who would fight until she won.

She stood, chin held high.

She knew Father Sun and Lady Moon were far away, left behind in the desert.

She knew she was alone.

But it didn't matter.

She didn't need anyone except herself.

She took every girlish dream, every swooning thought of Badru and his beautiful eyes, and crushed them until nothing was left.

Badru was dead to her now. He was nothing. No one.

But the Daliph, the Daliph was still very much alive.

And he still needed to die for what he'd done to her father.

And her tribe.

And her.

64

When the poradoma came to dress her, K'lrsa refused. "I'm a Rider of the White Horse Tribe, not some little doll to be dressed for a man's amusement."

"Pzah. Don't be a fool." Herin sank onto the stool by the dressing mirror. Her skin looked dry and ashen, the bags under her eyes almost black. "Just because you had your heart broken."

K'lrsa crossed her arms. "I didn't have my heart broken."

"No?"

"No."

Herin grunted. "Well, whatever caused this snit, get over it. Let your poradoma dress you."

"No."

"You need them, child."

K'lrsa shook her head. "No, I don't. Leave. I'll be fine."

Herin closed her eyes and pinched the bridge of her nose. "Yes. You do. Displease your poradoma and your whole life will be a misery."

K'lrsa laughed. "How? They won't bind my fingers? They won't shadow my every step? They won't force me to wear so much clothing I can't even walk?"

Herin came to stand in front of her, so close their noses almost touched. Her breath smelled of cinnamon. And decay. The stench of the crypt. "How you ask? Displease your poradoma and they can wait too long to take you to the toilet.

Or forget to feed you. Or to give you water. They can dress you in too much. Or not enough." She turned away. "You need them, girl. Remember that."

K'lrsa glanced to where Sayel, Morlen, and Tarum watched them. Sayel was studying the floor, looking for all the world like a father who didn't want to see what had become of his once-promising daughter. Morlen kept looking to Sayel for guidance and fidgeting as if he wanted to be anywhere but there.

Tarum leered at her, smiling that nasty smile of his.

"You're wrong." K'lrsa turned away from them all. "Leave."

She heard Herin and Sayel muttering to one another, arguing fiercely but too quietly for her to make out the individual words.

A hand stroked her back as someone pressed his body close to hers. She could smell his—because it had to be Tarum, didn't it?—garlicky breath as he leaned close.

Without thinking, K'lrsa struck him, the back of her fist connecting with his nose.

She turned to see blood gushing through his hands. He stared at her, his eyes wide with shock, as if he'd never imagined that she might defend herself.

Fool.

Everyone stared at them.

"You struck him," Sayel finally managed to gasp. He turned to Herin. "She struck a poradom."

"I see that."

K'lrsa expected Herin to defend her. Everyone had seen what he did, hadn't they? He'd touched her. Why was it K'lrsa's fault that she'd reacted?

Sayel licked his lips, clearly agitated. "They told me it was impossible. That she was nothing more than a desert savage. They told me, but I told them they were wrong. That my dorana was special, that she could be trained. I was wrong."

"I'm sorry." K'lrsa met his eyes, begging him to understand that she'd had to act. But she wasn't sorry and it showed in her words.

"She must be whipped." Morlen came towards her, suddenly menacing. She'd never noticed before how strong he was. She shivered, watching him approach, knowing she couldn't defend herself again.

"No." Sayel called him back. "There's still a chance the Daliph wants her. We can't harm her. Not like that." He glared at her, clearly agreeing that the only real solution would be to whip her.

K'lrsa bit back her response. Sayel had been her ally, the one who'd made this experience tolerable. And now he'd turned on her, too.

Sayel stepped to the door. "Herin's right. She needs to understand how much she needs us." Sayel called in the servants. "Remove all food. All blankets. All clothing. And the chamber pot." As they scrambled to obey, glancing at each other with wide-eyed looks, he turned to Morlen. "And remove the robe, whatever it takes."

Herin nodded slightly, as if satisfied with how Sayel had chosen to handle the situation.

When Tarum approached to take her robe, K'lrsa tore it off and flung it at him. She was not going to let him near her again.

Sayel came to stand before her, his expression part sad, part stern, ever the disappointed father. "This is for your own good, my dorana. The sooner you learn your place, the better for all of us."

She didn't respond, so he continued. "The glory of a dorana reflects on her poradoma. You are willful and stubborn and, as you are now, unfit as a dorana. If the Daliph rejects you, it will ruin not only you, but us. We need you to succeed. Today I hope you'll learn that you need us as much as we need you."

He led everyone out the door.

As the door closed behind them, K'lrsa turned away with a shrug.

She didn't want to be fit to be a dorana. If that day ever came, she hoped she'd still have enough of herself left to slit her wrists. Better that than turn into some mewling fool who never spoke her mind, never asserted herself, and whose sole purpose was to be beautiful so other men could admire the Daliph and his power.

<u>65</u>

K'lrsa cleared a space in the middle of the room and worked her way through the hundred and five attacks, relishing the feel of the cool air against her skin as she leapt and kicked and slashed, reminding herself with each attack who she was.

She was a Rider.

She was K'lrsa dan V'na of the White Horse Tribe.

She was the equal of anyone. Man or woman.

She was strong and capable and could do anything if she set her mind to it.

And no one could break her.

She didn't care that she was naked—she was used to that from her time in the tribes. It was only in the Daliphate where men eyed her like a dead pig, roasted for the feast, that she'd learned to feel shame in her nakedness.

And after so many days of being surrounded at all times, the silence was a balm on her soul. At last she was alone with her own thoughts and feelings. Free to be herself. No one to tell her how to sit or stand. Where to look. What to say or not say. No one to judge her.

She could just be herself.

But as the day progressed, the air turned chill and the sky darkened, clouds boiling in the sky. The breeze through the windows turned from refreshing to chill.

She tried to close the windows, but the shutters were latched to the outside wall and she couldn't reach the fasteners. She'd need the special stick the servants used.

She rubbed her arms as she paced the room, the sweat of her exertions cold against her skin.

There were no blankets, no clothes. The only fabric came from the thin curtains that covered the bed frame—so thin and diaphanous she could see through them as if they didn't exist. She unwound the fabric from the end post and tugged to pull it free, but it held, surprising sturdy.

She kept unwinding the fabric until it was completely free of the bed, but there wasn't enough to provide much warmth.

She grabbed all the pillows from the sitting area and added them to her small sleeping space, burrowing in amongst them and throwing the fabric from the bed over top. It was sparse comfort, but enough.

She shivered and burrowed deeper, reminding herself that she'd spent far worse nights in the desert before she came here.

She'd become soft and forgotten who she was, lulled into complacency by the food and comfort of the palace.

She fell into a deep sleep, exhausted after the last few days. Her dreams were odd, gray and shifting. She saw Badru reaching for her, but turned her back on him. And her father, watching her from a distance, his eyes sad. She called to him, but he disappeared, lost in the fog, replaced with strangers riding in the distance, men she didn't know who wore the Daliph's colors and carried his swords, but with the skin coloring and attire of the tribes.

She awoke well past midday. The storm had passed, the room now warm as the sun shared what warmth he could.

Her stomach growled; she'd never eaten breakfast and barely eaten dinner the night before. Her bladder demanded attention, bursting with desperate need.

She tried the door, but it was locked. She shouted, but no one responded. She didn't even hear anyone outside in the hallway.

Her mouth watered at the thought of a sweet bun full of walnuts and drizzled with honey. Or tangy olives stuffed with bitter cheese. Or chicken swimming in that yellow sauce she loved so much...

She flushed with shame—when had she become so weak? She'd set out to kill the Daliph and he'd turned her into this? Couldn't she go a day without food? Couldn't she spend one day without others around.

She shook her head and shoved her hunger away. Her bladder, however, wasn't so easily dismissed.

She considered peeing in the corner, but she wouldn't give them the satisfaction of showing herself to be the savage they said she was.

She'd just have to resist her body's urges until they came back. It wouldn't be long, she was sure of it.

K'lrsa knelt in the middle of the room, her feet and legs pressed tight together, and bowed forward until her forehead was touching the ground. She started the Pattern, deepening her breaths as she repeated the dawn litany over and over again.

It took her five tries to set aside the needs of her body and two more to banish thoughts of Badru and Herin and her father, before she found the Core.

She floated there outside of time and sensation, at peace for the first time in days, and waited.

66

"Up girl." Herin kicked K'lrsa's foot.

The need to pee and find warmth and food rushed back to K'lrsa like sharp knives.

"You, help her to relieve herself. You, set that food on the table."

Strong hands lifted K'lrsa and carried her to the bathing area where a chamber pot once more stood in the corner.

She sighed as she relieved herself, reveling in the feel of emptying her bladder after so many hours denied. When she tried to stand, her legs cramped. She leaned heavily on the arm of the strange poradom who led her back to the seating area.

Garzel closed the windows, using a long stick to pull each shutter closed. It was well past the middle of the night, the sky inky and black with just a few stars remaining and the hint of dawn coloring the blackness.

Why had they left her for so long?

The poradom wrapped her in a heavy silken robe; she pulled it tighter, feeling warmth return to her stiff limbs.

"Do you understand now, girl? You need them." Herin sat next to a large tray of food—morsels of meat floating in creamy gravy, fresh baked bread that steamed in the cool air, olives stuffed with tangy cheese. Her favorites.

K'lrsa didn't answer. She seated herself on the other side of the tray and stared at the food, but refused to reach for it. She glanced at the poradoma, both standing silent now.

Were they here to feed her?

No. She shook her head. She wasn't that hungry yet.

She might never be again.

She pondered her choice for a moment, knowing what it might mean. More hours locked in here alone. No food or blankets. Helpless.

But only because they'd made her that way. She could easily feed and protect herself on the plains or in the desert.

She refused to surrender. She wouldn't let them punish her until she was grateful to them for no longer punishing her.

Herin rolled her eyes as she took a bite of an olive held for her by Garzel. "Leave us." Herin waved to the two poradoma.

They hesitated, but left at a nod from Garzel.

K'lrsa's stomach grumbled, loud enough for all to hear.

"Eat, child."

K'lrsa shook her head and Herin glared at her. "Pzah. Child, do you never think? Food keeps you strong, doesn't it?"

K'lrsa nodded.

"In the desert, would you ever turn away from food?"

"No."

"Why?"

"Because you never know when your next meal might be. You eat when you can, whatever you can."

Herin nodded. "Exactly. Even if it doesn't seem so, this world is just as harsh as the desert. So eat while you can. Keep your strength."

When K'lrsa hesitated, she added. "Forgotten how to feed yourself? Want me to call one of the poradoma back to feed you?"

K'lrsa shook her head and reached for a piece of bread. She closed her eyes, relishing the feel of its warmth against her skin. She dipped the bread in the creamy gravy, sighing softly as she took a bite of chicken steeped in coriander and curry and cumin, delighting in the way the flavors mixed with the soft yeastiness of the bread and the onions cooked inside it.

Once she started, she couldn't stop. She shoved bite after bite of food into her mouth, barely finishing one mouthful before she started on the next. She knew she looked like a glutton, but she didn't care. She'd never realized what a pleasure it was to feed herself, to feel the food she ate, to use her own hands to bring food to her mouth.

"Thank you," she whispered, when she'd finally eaten every last crumb and drop of food.

"Oh, so you are capable of gratitude. How nice."

Herin leaned back, smoking from a long pipe Garzel held for her, the gray smoke spiraling into the air, the smell almost sickly sweet, but appealing in some strange way. "Did you know...?" She took another long pull on the pipe and blew the smoke out in a long stream. "Some women's sole ambition in life is to have a daughter chosen as one of the Daliph's dorana."

K'lrsa laughed, a short bark of sound.

Herin nodded. "It's true. Young girls are raised to believe that to be a dorana is the greatest honor a woman can achieve. To be so beautiful and talented that the most powerful man in their world wants them? Cared for her entire life? Never having to lift a finger? It's a dream for many girls."

K'lrsa didn't want to believe that anyone could be so foolish as to want this, but Herin stared her down until she smoothed the expression of disbelief from her face.

Herin leaned forward as Garzel took the pipe away. "Don't fault them, child. This is the only life they've ever known. They've never ridden across the plains, hair streaming behind them in the wind. They've never slept alone in the desert with only the moon for company.

"They were born into this and they make the best of it. You, who have tasted true freedom, see the bars they don't. You see the *tiral* as the cage it is." She shrugged. "They see it as a bounty of wealth gifted to them by the most powerful man in their world."

"Then let them have it. If they want it so much, let Badru choose one of them instead."

Herin looked almost sad. "I would if I could, but it doesn't work that way. He made his choice and now you both must live with it. This is your life now. You have to accept that."

"Who says, you old hag? If he's so powerful, tell him to set me free. Tell him to change his mind and let me go."

Herin quirked an eyebrow at her. "He doesn't want to let you go. He loves you."

"If he loved me, he'd free me."

Herin laughed, the sound like grating glass. "Oh, yes. Right. And then what? You just ride home through the Daliphate?" She shook her head. "This is your life now, child. Make the best of it. You think I didn't want to go home? You think I didn't want to escape? You think I enjoyed this?" She waggled her fingers at K'lrsa.

K'lrsa didn't answer.

"This wasn't my choice either. But I made the best of it." She leaned closer, holding K'lrsa's gaze. "I survived. And thrived."

"You gave in."

Herin spat to the side. "I never gave in. I just learned the rules of their game so I could win it. Will you?"

"I don't want to win this game. I don't want to be what they'd make me."

"So you fail." Herin sat back shaking her head. "And you call yourself a Rider."

"I do. What about you? Look at yourself. The old Daliph is dead and yet you chose to stay. You know how they treat women here and yet you let them do it. Not only that, you support the man responsible for it."

"It's not that simple."

"No? You have power, *Omala*. You could change things. But you don't. They broke you."

Herin glared at her. "I do what I can. But you can't move a mountain in a day."

"You don't do enough."

"Easy to say I haven't done enough when you know nothing about this world. I've risked everything to keep you alive. And to protect Badru even though neither one of you has made it easy."

K'lrsa looked away and played with a patch of loose strings in the carpet.

Garzel helped Herin stand, both showing their age in the time it took for them to rise and walk to the door.

Herin paused and turned back to her. She licked her lips, hesitating a moment before she spoke. "The former Daliph was a smart man. Not known for his subtlety..."

She watched K'lrsa carefully as she spoke. "After I'd been here a few moons, and lost a couple fingertips, he gave me two gifts. One was a desert falcon—a beautiful bird in the prime of its life, strong and fierce. The other was a pretty little songbird, no bigger than the size of a baby's fist."

"And. So?" K'lrsa willed the woman to leave.

"Both were in cages I couldn't open. I could feed them and care for them, but I couldn't free them."

K'lrsa waited.

"Do you know what happened?"

"You killed them?"

Herin pressed her lips together but continued as if K'lrsa hadn't answered. "I did everything I could to care for those birds.

"The songbird thrived. It loved its life, hanging in the bright sunlight, eating pomegranate seeds, and singing. It sang morning, noon, and night.

"The falcon...the falcon knew what it was to be free. It longed for its desert home. It flew against the bars of the cage day and night trying to escape. I fed it, I talked to it, I did everything I could for it, except the one thing it wanted. I couldn't free it.

"Day after day, night after night, it banged against the walls of its cage." She met K'lrsa's eyes. "Until one morning I found it dead."

K'lrsa flinched. "That's a terrible story."

"Yes. It is."

Garzel held the door open and Herin walked through. "Get some rest. We start again in the morning."

"What of the songbird?" K'lrsa called after her.

"I still have it and it still sings morning, day, and night, happy as can be."

67

K'lrsa dreamt of Badru that night. She didn't want to, but she couldn't stay awake another night.

He was waiting for her when she entered the moon dream.

He stood and held his hand out to her, begging her with his eyes to take it.

She turned away, but he came after her, not touching her, but circling around in front of her, once more begging her to take his hand.

She turned away again and saw the Lady Moon standing there watching them.

"Why do you turn away from the one I chose for you, my daughter?"

K'lrsa glared at her. "Do you know who he is?"

"Badru, son of Jania, grandson of the one now called Herin."

"And Daliph of the Toreem Daliphate."

The Lady Moon approached, her face that of a young mother, all soft compassion and confusion. "Yes."

"I swore to kill him."

The Lady Moon laughed, the sound so joyous and pure that it made K'lrsa's heart ache with longing to feel that way herself.

"Did you? Are you sure?"

Before K'lrsa could ask more, the Lady Moon faded away. K'lrsa turned, but Badru was gone, too.

She sat on the desert sands, watching the Hidden City in the distance, and tried to think.

But all she could remember was the way she'd danced the Moon Dance with Badru, how perfect it had been, how their bodies had fit together as if made for one another.

She awoke to the memory of his body pressed against hers, his hands stroking her skin.

She wanted to hate him.

She even told herself she did.

But her dreams told the truth. Despite everything, her soul still yearned for him. He was still the only man she'd ever wanted.

When the poradoma came to dress her, she let them, staring at a spot on the floor like she'd been taught. It did her no good to fight them. If she did, they'd just leave her alone in this room until she died.

When they placed the golden *tiral* on her shoulders, K'lrsa met Herin's gaze and saw her nod slightly. They were taking her to see Badru.

Why?

"Come." Herin led the way to the audience chamber.

As they walked, K'lrsa thought of her dream of the night before. Had the Lady Moon truly chosen Badru for her?

And what had she meant about K'lrsa's vow?

Was this all the work of the Trickster?

She felt so turned around, she didn't know what to do.

This time no one stopped them from entering the audience chamber. And K'lrsa could actually see because Herin had told Sayel not to use the eyedrops.

The room they led her to was a large circular space with a domed ceiling at least three or four stories above them. Tiles covered the ceiling in a mesmerizing pattern of colors—reds and yellows, greens and blues, whites and blacks and oranges—all winding together yet somehow sharp and distinct.

Light streamed through large windows spaced evenly around the room just below the tiles—each one the size of a tall horse.

Hundreds of men sat on low cushions at a series of long curved tables that radiated out from a central dais that dominated the far wall of the room. The men mostly wore shades of muted brown. Here or there a man wore a single-colored headband or belt, but most wore no color at all except for those directly in front of the dais. There, a few men sat in robes of one color—red or yellow—or a man wore multiple colors but never more than two.

The men spoke in low murmurs but the combined weight of their voices was almost deafening.

Along the walls, guards dressed in white with multi-colored belts striped yellow, blue, green, and red watched the crowd with intense eyes, hands resting on their swords.

The dais had three levels. On the lowest level were the men in the solid-colored robes of yellow and red. On the level above them sat four dorana—each a bright spot of color in the otherwise drab room. The one on the far left had dusky skin and pouty lips. She wore mostly green and yellow and had one golden cuff on her ear. She was young and beautiful and K'lrsa hated her on sight.

She must be the one who had laughed that day.

Beside her was an older woman, her skin more yellow than brown, but somehow exotic instead of sickly. She wore mostly green and had two cuffs on her ear. She was more attractive than any woman K'lrsa had ever seen. She carried herself with assurance as if she owned the room even though she carefully kept her gaze averted.

Before K'lrsa could look to the other two dorana, her gaze was drawn upward to the highest tier.

Badru sat alone on a large chair that shone golden under the noonday sun.

He wore a blue vest, his arms bare to show leanly-muscled arms. His pants were striped in every color, his narrow waist bound with a green belt that matched her own. He stared at her, his piercing blue eyes holding hers, but his expression as cold as stone.

"Psst." Herin hissed at her and K'lrsa dropped her gaze, reminding herself that she must be the ever-dutiful dorana if she wanted to go any farther.

Twenty steps. That's all that separated her from Badru.

And when she closed that gap?

What would she do?

Attack? Finally have her revenge and be done with it all.

Or should she listen to the Lady Moon, and her heart? Should she wait until she knew for sure?

She had twenty steps to decide.

Sayel placed his hand on her back and gently guided her towards the dais, the eyes of every man in the room on her as she stepped forward. They whispered softly to one another, a low susurrus of sound spreading through each section of the room as she passed.

She forced herself to keep her gaze focused on the floor, but it was hard not to look.

When she was almost to the dais, just five steps from making her fateful decision, a man at the table next to her said to his neighbor, just loud enough so she could hear, "I'd heard he'd taken a desert whore as his dorana, but I didn't believe it until now."

"I know," the other replied just as softly. "Good thing she has the poradoma to feed her or she'd probably dunk her face right in the serving bowl and slurp it up like a horse at trough."

The men laughed.

K'lrsa turned on the man who'd made the joke; she tried to strike him but was unable to raise her hand enough to do so. He choked on his food, staring bug-eyed at her.

Sayel pulled her back. "Look down. Now. You are a dorana of the Toreem Daliphate, not some unschooled savage that would stare down a strange man. Remember yourself." His fingers dug into the back of her neck, forcing her head down.

K'lrsa cried out.

"What is this?" Badru called. She looked up to see him standing, his fists clenched in anger as he watched them.

He strode down the dais, his personal guard rushing to keep pace with him.

"Pzah," Herin muttered, before shutting her mouth on the rest of what she wanted to say.

"What is this?" Badru demanded, standing in front of them.

Sayel bowed low. "Nothing, most honored leader. Your dorana just forgot herself for a moment."

"K'lrsa, did he harm you?" Badru lifted her chin, searching her eyes.

"Sayel? No. He's right. I forgot myself."

"You cried out like he'd hurt you."

She shook her head. "It's fine. Nothing really. Sayel was just reminding me of my proper duties as a dorana. These men made a comment about my being a desert whore and eating my food like a horse at trough. I reacted before I could stop myself. I...I looked at them. I'm sorry."

She bowed her head, ashamed at her actions.

And then angry as she realized what she'd just done. She'd apologized!

Apologized because two men had called her a whore and compared her to a horse and she'd dared to react.

She shook with anger. And fear. The role of the dorana was so easy to assume now.

Badru turned to the table. "Is this true? Which of you said this of my dorana?" His voice was eerily calm. Every man at the table sat up straighter; the closest two men shifted away from him.

Herin stepped forward. "Most honored leader, men will jest. I'm sure they meant nothing of it."

Badru shook his head. "I am the Daliph. She is my dorana. An insult to her is an insult to me."

Herin looked as if she wanted to say more, but stepped back, exchanging a quick glance with Sayel.

"Which of you said it?"

"I did, most honored leader." The first man met Badru's eyes, defiant, chin held high.

"And I laughed, most honored leader." The other man also met Badru's gaze without flinching.

K'lrsa noted that they each wore two colors.

Badru looked back and forth between the men, his expression flat but his eyes blazing with anger. "Eight lashes each."

A gasp ran through the room, building into a roar of argument. Badru strode back to his seat, ignoring it all.

"Enough," he roared down at them.

Silence fell immediately.

Guards in white escorted the two men to the base of the dais, firm but respectful. Whoever these men were, they were powerful.

And Badru was going to have them whipped? For her sake? Or his own pride?

She didn't know and couldn't ask.

The first man shook off his guard's grip and stepped forward. "Most honored leader. Please reconsider. It was just harmless talk. I've always been one of your most loyal supporters, you know this."

"Do I, Pavel? You insulted my choice of dorana, which means you insulted me." Badru's face was as dark as a spring thunderstorm.

"I never meant to. And you must admit, it is a unique choice you've made." The man knelt in front of the dais, his head bowed.

Badru's lips pressed even tighter together before he looked away from the man and addressed the crowd. "An insult to my dorana is an insult to me. Let all know it. Prepare them while my dorana takes her place."

The man at the base of the dais stared up at Badru, his mouth open as if this was the last thing he'd expected.

"Should I make it ten, Pavel?"

"No. No, most honored leader."

Sayel led K'lrsa to a blue cushion on the far end of the level below Badru and helped her remove her *tiral* so she could sit. She didn't look at Badru or the crowd even though she knew they were all watching her.

When she was seated, Badru spoke to the room yet again. "My dorana will watch. Let none speak ill of them for doing so."

K'lrsa dutifully raised her gaze to watch the guards lead a now bare-chested Pavel to a post off to the side of the dais. The man was older, his skin sagging from what had once been a muscular frame. He wiped sweat from his brow as he glanced towards Badru, waiting for a reprieve.

None came.

A man dressed in red bound Pavel's hands to the post. "You are sentenced to eight lashes for insult to the person of the Daliph. Have you aught to say?"

Pavel shook his head.

"Very well. Grab the post."

Pavel gripped the post and closed his eyes.

The entire room held its breath as the man in red raised the whip and brought it down, the crack as it met Pavel's flesh reverberating around and around the space which suddenly seemed small.

Pavel screamed, keening in agony.

K'lrsa wanted to close her eyes, but she didn't. She forced herself to watch every blow and to listen to every scream.

Badru didn't flinch, but others did, muttering quietly to one another as they glanced at the scene before them. Some nodded in satisfaction, but far more looked scared, upset that their Daliph would beat a man over such a minor thing.

By the eighth blow, Pavel was weeping, his back crisscrossed with livid red marks. K'lrsa felt ill, swaying in her seat. Sayel stroked her arm and murmured his support.

As the guard motioned the second man forward, K'lrsa sent a silent prayer for strength to Father Sun.

She willed herself to watch as that man, too, was whipped, crying and screaming with each blow, the blood flowing freely down his back.

When it was done, Badru nodded and sat on his throne once more. "I trust everyone has learned now? Good. Nesbit, call the first supplicant."

<u>68</u>

K'lrsa sat through a series of supplicants asking judgement or favors from Badru. She didn't listen to what they had to say, too upset after watching the men whipped to pay any attention.

They shouldn't have said that about her. In the tribes she would've slapped the man who'd insulted her and been done with. But they hadn't deserved to be whipped, their backs cut open and bleeding.

She was close enough to Badru to attack him, but she didn't, too numb to even think of doing so.

Had he really been defending her? Or just himself?

When they returned to her rooms, Morlen and Tarum undressed her while Sayel paced back and forth, clearly agitated.

He finally stopped and turned to Herin. "I think we should give her training over to Antoon."

Garzel stepped between Sayel and K'lrsa, but Herin signaled him back.

"No."

"With all due respect, Omala, this is a matter for the poradoma to decide. You have no power here."

Herin grunted. "I'm a woman, I have no power anywhere in the Daliphate. And yet you'll listen to me anyway. Giving her over to Antoon would be a mistake."

Sayel rubbed at his face. "I can't do more than I already have. And yet she still fails. Antoon will fix her."

261

"Antoon will break her."

Herin and Sayel faced off, neither one backing down. The room suddenly felt too small for so many people.

Herin took a deep breath. "Sayel, you can't do this. If Antoon trains her he will destroy everything that makes her appealing to the Daliph."

"She'll be a proper dorana."

"He doesn't want a proper dorana. Don't you understand that?"

K'lrsa glanced at the other two poradoma. Morlen looked worried, running K'lrsa's belt through his hands over and over again. Tarum glared at Herin's back as if he might attack her at any moment.

Sayel shook his head. "It is the duty of the poradoma to train the dorana to her tasks. When she fails, we fail."

"Don't do this, Sayel."

They squared off until Sayel finally turned away. "One more chance, Herin. If she fails, I give her to Antoon to train."

Herin nodded. "Fair enough."

As everyone milled around, unsure what to do next, Herin shooed them towards the door. "Go. We'll begin again tomorrow, but for tonight she needs a break."

Sayel hesitated. "What if he comes to see her?"

"He won't."

"But what if he does? If he were to come and find her without her poradom and without her *meza*...The shame of it..."

"Oh, pzah. There's no shame in it. You men and your honor. If he comes he'll want to be alone with her anyway. Leave. Now."

Sayel's shoulders stiffened, but he ordered the poradoma to leave, removing the *meza* from K'lrsa's fingers before he followed them.

After they were gone, a long silence filled the room. K'lrsa stood by the window staring up at the sky as the sun set behind the mountain, washing the clouds in a brilliance of color—red, orange, yellow. For a moment it looked as if the sky was on fire. And then the sun disappeared and twilight fell.

She fingered the beautiful purple flowers in the box outside the window, amazed that they still bloomed even with the chill in the air. She'd seen the servants bring new flowers each morning to replace the ones that died each night. Sayel said they grew them year-round just for the dorana.

The strong aroma of the flowers filled the air as she crushed a petal under her fingers. She missed the simplicity of the desert where everything had its season.

Herin and Garzel argued quietly in the corner by the door, their gestures occasionally intense as they discussed something K'lrsa couldn't and didn't care to hear.

She sighed, wondering what she wanted to do now. She'd had the chance to kill Badru, but she hadn't taken it.

And why?

Because he'd lashed out at those men? Defended her?

She thought of her father who was always so gentle, reasoned, and calm. Would he have ever ordered a man whipped, even if he could?

No.

And yet Badru hasn't hesitated to do so.

And maybe it wasn't for K'lrsa's sake but his own. To protect his pride in front of so many men. How many times had Sayel lectured her on how a dorana was merely a reflection of her Daliph?

She needed to make a decision.

If she wasn't going to kill Badru, then she needed to go home.

If she was, then she needed to act the next time she had the opportunity.

Neither prospect appealed to her in that moment. Nothing appealed to her.

She stared up at the sky, longing to see the Lady Moon.

She turned back to Herin and Garzel, shivering as the night turned colder. "So what now, Herin? Sayel's right. I'll never be a proper dorana. We can spend days drilling me on what I should do, but you and I both know it's not who I am."

Herin pursed her lips. "I know." She glanced over at Garzel and he nodded slightly. "Which is why I'm going to help you escape before that fool boy destroys the entire Daliphate over you."

K'lrsa choked on her surprise. "Why?"

"You saw what he did today. He had one of the most powerful men in the Daliphate whipped. And for what? Because he said what everyone else was thinking?"

"The man called me a whore and said I'd eat out of a horse trough if given the chance."

Herin nodded. "Exactly."

"If I hadn't been wearing all those ridiculous layers, I would've hit him."

"He would've been perfectly within his rights to beat you to death if you'd so much as touched him."

K'lrsa waited for Herin to say she'd been exaggerating, but of course she hadn't.

What kind of world allowed a man to beat a woman to death because she defended herself against him?

"That's awful."

"That's the world you live in now. You are a slave, K'lrsa. Property. Badru can call you whatever he wants to and dress you up as pretty as he pleases, but everyone knows that you are nothing more than a tribal trash slave dressed up as a dorana. And you always will be."

"I'm a Rider of the White Horse Tribe."

"No. You are a slave. Nothing more." She shook her head as she paced the room. "No one cared when they thought this was just a whim of Badru's, elevating a slave to the level of dorana. They weren't happy, but it wasn't worth risking their positions. But now that he had one of his closest advisors whipped for insulting you?" She shook her head. "Badru made many enemies today. You need to go before he makes more."

"I don't understand."

"Of course you don't."

"What will Badru do when he finds me gone? He loves me."

Herin spat. "And that's the problem. He can't love you, he's the Daliph. He has to lead those men; he needs their respect.

He can't put a slave above them and expect them to follow him."

"How then? How will you get me out of not only the palace, but the Daliphate?"

Herin glanced at her and away again.

"You're not going to, are you? You're just going to take me somewhere quiet where you can kill me without witnesses."

Herin pinched the bridge of her nose. "Don't be ridiculous. If I wanted to kill you, I'd just have Garzel throw you out the window."

K'lrsa moved away from the windows, watching Herin and Garzel the whole time. "I'm not going. I don't trust you."

"You don't have a choice."

"Yes, I do. I can scream until someone comes."

"And then what?"

There was a knock at the door and it immediately swung open. Badru strode into the room in full court dress.

K'lrsa's heart flipped at the sight of him. She turned away so he wouldn't see it.

Herin jerked her back around. "You do not turn your back on your Daliph. Ever."

Two guards flanked Badru, their eyes flat black as they watched the scene. The one on the left's knuckles were white where he grasped his sword, the metal of the blade visible where he'd started to draw it.

"I would speak with my dorana." Badru stared at K'lrsa, ignoring everyone else in the room. "Alone."

"No. I can't let you do that, Badru." Herin stepped between them.

The guard on the left drew his sword and stepped forward, pointing it at Herin.

Herin eyed the blade and laughed.

Badru gestured the guard to step back. "Who is the Daliph here, old woman? You? Or me?"

Herin dropped into a low bow, her forehead almost touching the ground. "Apologies, most honored leader. Forgive this one for forgetting her place." She said the words, but the rebuke was clear in her words.

Badru stared down at Herin for a long moment before he finally stepped forward and helped her to rise. "You are forgiven, grandmother." He kissed her on the cheek. "But you grow old and I worry for you. Perhaps you should take some time to rest."

Herin's back stiffened and K'lrsa expected her to make one of her normal biting comments, but Herin simply said, "As you wish. Will you keep the guards with you?"

"No. I will speak with my dorana alone, just the two of us. Or do you think that one woman can defeat a Daliph?"

Herin raised an eyebrow.

It wouldn't be the first time. She didn't speak the words, but K'lrsa heard them as if she had. So did Badru.

He shrugged away Herin's concern, gesturing for Herin, Garzel, and the guards to leave.

K'lrsa flexed her fingers. She was still wearing the day clothes of a dorana, but her fingers were free of the *meza* and she didn't have the *tiral* restricting her movements.

This was her chance. If she wanted to kill Badru, she had to act now.

Badru walked everyone to the door. "Do not enter for at least a candlemark, no matter what you hear."

He closed the door firmly behind them and turned back to K'lrsa, smiling. "At last we're alone, my love."

69

"This is for my father," K'lrsa screamed, and launched herself at him.

Badru countered her attack with ease, a slight smile on his face. She'd underestimated how much even the few layers she still wore would restrict her movements, the skirts tangling her legs, the sleeves holding her back from delivering a full blow.

She'd also expected Badru to be only partially trained, if that, but he flowed easily into a fighting stance unfamiliar to her, balanced lightly on the balls of his feet as he waited for her next attack.

He raised one eyebrow as she circled him, looking for an opening. "This is hardly how I expected to be greeted by my dorana after I saved her today."

"You didn't save me." She struck at his neck, but he easily blocked her.

"No? I defended you. In front of all my senior advisors."

She shook her head and kicked low, aiming for his legs. He jumped high, easily avoiding the strike.

"You weren't defending me. You were defending your honor."

He smiled and shook his head, dancing backward as she tried a three-blow attack. "No. It was for you that I did that, K'lrsa. No one should ever speak of you that way. Ever."

"I can defend myself." She managed a glancing blow to his chest and smiled to see him wince.

"I see that. But not at court, K'lrsa. It's not allowed."

"Because I'm a slave?" She struck him again, this time on the shoulder. "Because I'm your property?" She kicked him in the shins.

He danced away from her, the smile now gone. "Yes. And because you're my dorana. And a woman."

She screamed and lunged at him, her hands outstretched to claw out his eyes. He pushed her aside, tripping her as he did so she fell onto a pile of cushions.

"I don't make the rules, K'lrsa."

"Yes, you do. You're the Daliph. You make all the rules. You enforce the rules."

He shook his head. "It's not that easy."

She struggled back to her feet. "It is."

And in that moment she knew that she'd been right all along. That Badru had to die. That the Toreem Daliphate must fall. It was evil and corrupt and the only option was to end it before it destroyed her people and their way of life.

She attacked him again, but he grabbed her wrists and pulled her close until their noses were almost touching. "Stop this, K'lrsa. I love you. You know that."

She twisted free of his grip and aimed an elbow at his nose, but he ducked back before she could connect.

"Your men killed my father."

"No they didn't."

They circled each other once more.

"I know what I saw, Badru."

"Your father staked on top of an ant hill, his belly sliced open." Badru held his hands out before him as if ready to catch her again.

K'lrsa kicked at him, but he stepped backward before she could connect with his knee. "And his eyes gouged out and his..." She shook her head, trying to banish the image of her father's last moments.

"Exactly."

K'lrsa closed on Badru, landing a few blows against his chest before he grabbed her wrists once again. She blinked to clear the tears from her eyes as she struggled to free herself.

Badru looped his leg through hers and they both fell onto the cushions of the seating area. Badru landed on top of her, pinning her body with his.

K'lrsa struggled, but he was bigger than her and had positioned his arms and legs so she couldn't get in a blow to free herself.

"Listen to me, K'lrsa. Think. Why would my men do that to him? What do I gain by that?"

"What they did to him is one of the greatest insults a man can receive. A man bound like that won't go to the Promised Plains; he won't be able to find his way to the Lady Moon's side."

K'lrsa bucked again, trying to throw him off, but he pushed down against her, breathing heavily. "And why would my men do that? What would they care about your father's journey to the afterlife. Think, K'lrsa. What do I gain from that?"

K'lrsa finally succeeded in pushing him off; Badru sprang to his feet and stood nearby, watching her carefully as he tried to recover his breath.

She sat up but didn't try to stand. "You tell me. What did you gain?"

"Nothing. It wasn't my men, K'lrsa. Here." He pulled a folded piece of parchment out of his pocket and held it out to her. "A report from my men on the border. None have raided your lands. Ever. Read it for yourself."

K'lrsa bit her lip and looked away, flushed with shame. "I can't read."

"Then have my grandmother read it for you. Or Sayel." He crouched down far enough away that she couldn't reach him. "It wasn't my men, K'lrsa."

"How do I know you're telling me the truth?"

He sighed. "Because I'd never lie to you. Or do anything to harm you."

"You didn't even know me then."

He met her eyes with his brilliant blue ones and she felt herself drawn in by his gaze, a part of her melting and flowing towards him. "I love you, K'lrsa dan V'na of the White Horse

Tribe. You are more important to me than anything else. Anything."

She wanted to believe him so much. She wanted to be wrong about him, to believe that he was the man of her dreams and not the cruel leader she'd seen hints of in the past few weeks.

She forced herself to look away. "Words are easy to say, Badru. I'm still your slave and always will be."

Badru sat back on his heels, not moving. "I can't change that, K'lrsa."

"You're the Daliph."

He laughed softly. "That doesn't make me all-powerful."

She met his eyes, forcing herself to hold back from losing herself in him. "In the tribes a man and a woman come together as equals. They each choose to be with the other. One isn't forced or coerced to mate. It's a choice, freely made." She looked away. "If you love me as you say you do, then you'll free me and give me the chance to choose to be with you."

K'lrsa waited. She watched as Badru stared down at the carpet, chewing on his bottom lip.

She knew she could attack him while he was distracted, but she held back still wanting him to be the man she hoped he was.

"I love you, K'lrsa. But I don't think I can do as you ask." He looked so sad she ached to comfort him. Instead she stood and turned away from him.

"Go then. As long as I'm your slave, I want nothing to do with you."

She trembled, waiting to see what he'd do.

At last, he walked to the mirror and straightened his vest, smoothing any sign of emotion from his face as he smoothed all signs of their fight from his clothing.

When he was done, he walked to the door, stopping for one last longing glance before he opened it and left her alone.

She stared out the window, refusing to cry, refusing to regret the demand she'd made of him. She loved him, too, but she refused to be with a man she couldn't freely choose to be with.

70

After Badru left, K'lrsa paced the room, thinking about what he'd said about her father's attack.

If his men hadn't killed her father, then who had? Who else was capable of doing that to him? Who would think to punish him in that way?

She remembered G'van and his talk about the times changing. Was he capable of something like that? Was someone else in the Black Horse Tribe?

She shook her head, refusing to believe that anyone in the tribes would attack another like that. Life was too fragile, too tenuous to turn on your own. They had a sacred trust to protect, they couldn't afford to fight with one another.

But G'van had turned away from the ways of the tribes. He'd led slavers across the desert.

Maybe the Black Horse Tribe was behind the attack on her father.

And if that was true, if the Black Horse Tribe *was* responsible for her father's death…

Then her family was in danger. None would suspect the truth until it was too late. They would ride to the annual gathering and demand expulsion of the Black Horse Tribe, expecting them to surrender to their banishment without conflict. But what if they fought back? What if they killed her tribe the way Lodie's tribe had been killed all those years ago?

She'd left her family and tribe behind to kill the Daliph when the real enemy had been right there at home, free to visit her camp whenever they wanted.

It made sense. But could she really trust Badru?

She wished her father were there to help her see the correct path. She needed him so desperately—his calm, his intelligence, his quiet strength. He'd tell her the right path to take.

But maybe he had.

He'd told her not to seek revenge against the Daliph.

And so had the Lady Moon.

What if her father hadn't been trying to protect her? What if he'd known who was really responsible for the attack?

She clutched her arms to her chest, shivering.

What had she done?

She'd let her pride and arrogance blind her to the truth.

She needed to go home.

Now.

When Herin came the next morning, K'lrsa grabbed her arm and pulled her aside. "I'll do it. I'll run away."

Herin snorted. "Too late."

"What do you mean? Why?"

Herin glanced in the direction of the slaves as they set out the breakfast dishes and opened the windows. "Badru was quite distressed to find you unattended by your poradoma last night. He reminded me and Sayel that they are not just responsible for tending to your needs but are also there to protect you against all threats."

"But you and Garzel were with me."

"Exactly." Herin turned away as Sayel entered the room, Morlen and Tarum trailing along behind him.

Morlen carried a new outfit unlike anything K'lrsa had yet seen. It consisted of a simple top, vest, and split skirt.

"Is this what I'm going to wear today?"

Sayel frowned. "Yes. The Daliph has requested your presence outside the palace." He glanced at Herin, shaking his head.

She shrugged.

K'lrsa looked back and forth between them. "What?"

Sayel wrung his hands. "I worry that you're not yet ready for such an outing, my dorana."

Herin laughed. "If you'd trained her as a true dorana, she'd never be ready for such an outing." She turned to K'lrsa. "Badru has asked that you go riding with him."

"On Fallion?" Her heart soared at the thought. She'd missed him so much, but hadn't dared ask about him, afraid what she'd hear.

"Yes. On Fallion." Herin held her gaze. "Recall, of course, that no women of the Daliphate ride horses."

Before K'lrsa could mention that Herin did, Herin continued. "I'm not considered a woman when I'm riding."

"What? How is that possible?"

Herin gestured to her black clothing. "This sets me apart. When I wear black, or when Badru wears black, we are indicating that we have stepped outside of the normal rules. Badru can walk the halls without everyone prostrating themselves across his path and I can ride a horse."

"But you always wear black."

"I do."

"And people defer to you."

"They do."

"What would happen if you didn't wear black?"

Herin smirked. "I'd have to wear some ridiculous outfit like you do, and, because I am the honored grandmother of the Daliph, the Omala, I wouldn't even be allowed to walk for myself. I'd be carried around by four bearers, surrounded by a bevy of servants at all times, each one trying to anticipate my every want and need before I even thought to form the words."

Herin shook her head. "No. Not for me. And everyone knows," she glanced around the room as if to emphasize the point, "that it is far better to listen to what I say even when I wear the black than to make me don the formal attire of the Omala."

She held K'lrsa's gaze. "Remember yourself today. You may be on Fallion, but you are still a dorana. Do not speak to anyone except the Daliph. Do not make eye contact with any of the men. And do not argue with the Daliph. Just because you're riding a horse, it doesn't change the rules you must live by."

71

As they made their way down the long series of corridors to the base of the palace where Fallion was stabled, K'lrsa wondered if she could flee while she was outside. Fallion was so fast, no other horse could match him.

Except Badru's horse, of course. Perhaps. It, too, was an *Amalanee* horse, but could any horse truly compare to Fallion?

She forgot herself when she saw Fallion standing in front of the stalls and ran forward to throw her arms around his neck. "Fallion." He nickered and rubbed her face with his nose. "Oh, *micora*, how I've missed you."

"And he's missed you." Badru stepped out of a nearby stall, dressed head to toe in black, his words laced with affection as he watched her. "The grooms have tended him as well as they can, but he clearly pines for you."

He watched her, his expression cautiously hopeful; she looked away, not sure what to feel. She was so powerfully drawn to him every time she saw him, but that didn't change who he was or that she was his property, subject to his every whim.

Near the entrance, a dozen courtiers milled around, waiting for them. Most wore dull brown with bits of color, but one was dressed in solid yellow and another in solid red. Six guards in white flanked them, ever vigilant, even though the great space was otherwise empty.

"And I've pined for him." K'lrsa scratched Fallion's nose and the soft spot behind his ears, smiling at his contented chuff.

Badru came to stand beside her, stroking Fallion's mane. "He won't let anyone else ride him. They exercise him in the yard, but he needs a good run."

"He needs to go home." She held his gaze for a long moment. "So do I."

Badru winced and glanced away. "Don't say that. I don't want to lose you now that I've found you."

K'lrsa rested her face against Fallion's, breathing in the horsey smell of him. She hadn't realized how much she missed him until now. She longed for the days they'd spent riding together across the plains, the heat baking their skin, the tang of sage grass in the air.

"My family needs me, Badru. If what you said was true, that it wasn't your men, then I need to go back and find out who it was."

He turned back to her, his eyes sad but determined. "You can't be the only one who can protect your people."

"No." Chances were she'd go back and her mother would keep her so firmly under control that she wouldn't be able to do anything. But she had to try.

"But you *are* the only one I love. The only one I'd have at my side." He reached for her hands.

She shook her head and stepped away. "I'm chained to your side, Badru. If you love me like you say you do, free me and let me go home."

She wanted to turn and walk away, but she remembered Herin's caution about turning her back on the Daliph.

Badru shook his head, his nostrils flaring, his lips pressed tight in anger. "Fine. I free you." He practically spat the words at her.

"What?"

"I free you. You're not a slave anymore." Badru turned to the crowd of courtiers. "Nesbit, come here. I need your assistance. I want to free this dorana from slavery. I need you to prepare the writ."

At Badru's words, a young man cried out in shock, stumbling backward. The rest of the crowd of courtiers started whispering amongst themselves, some gesturing urgently and shaking their heads. One sent a young runner off towards the palace.

An old man, the one in yellow robes, made his slow way towards Badru, his face carefully neutral.

Herin darted killing looks at K'lrsa as she stepped forward. "Most honored leader, is that wise? Perhaps you should take time to consider this."

"No." Badru barely even glanced at her as he waited for Nesbit to reach them. "You know how I've always felt about slavery, grandmother. It's time I did something about it."

Herin pressed her lips tightly together, swallowing a barrage of words. She glanced towards the courtiers, and finally hissed, "Think, Badru. I can't protect you from yourself."

"I never asked you to, *Omala*. Remember, I'm the Daliph not you."

Herin licked her lips, preparing to argue, but Garzel stepped forward and rested a hand on her shoulder. She backed away, glaring back and forth between K'lrsa and Badru.

The stooped old man in the yellow robe finally reached them.

"Nesbit. You will see that the proper documents are drawn up to free this slave."

The man coughed—a loud, wet, phlegmy sound that made K'lrsa's skin crawl. "Most honored leader, I beg your pardon, but that's not possible."

"Not possible? I'm the Daliph."

"Yes, but the law states that any man, woman, or child once made a slave can never be freed." He bowed his head. "It is believed that any person who has sunk to that level can never again rise above it." He darted a glance at K'lrsa and then back at the ground.

"I know the law, Nesbit. Change it."

"Most honored leader, each slave has been made so through poor thought or poor action. If you free even one, chaos will follow."

Badru laughed. "I doubt that very much. As a matter of fact, now that I think of it, I don't want to just free K'lrsa."

The old man's eyes bulged as he stared at Badru. Garzel physically restrained Herin from stepping forward once more.

Badru continued as if he didn't notice. "I think that any slave owner who wishes to free their slaves, should be able to do so. It's their property, let them dispense with it as they will. What do you think? A written proclamation signed by the owner and witnessed by two free witnesses? That should suffice." He waved a hand at Nesbit. "Amend the law accordingly."

The old man braced himself against Fallion, not even realizing what he was doing as he swallowed heavily. "What of the other Daliphana, most honored leader? Perhaps you should consult them first?"

Badru glared at him and Nesbit flinched backward. "No. The Toreem Daliphate is mine to rule as I see fit. If they want slaves, let them keep them. I do not."

Nesbit bowed low, but K'lrsa could see the uneasiness in his eyes as he did so. "As you wish." He was shaking so hard he could barely stand. He glanced towards Herin, but she shook her head slightly.

As Nesbit turned to leave, Badru called him back. "I'm not done, Nesbit."

K'lrsa stepped forward and rested her hand on Badru's arm. "Don't you think that's enough for one day, most honored leader? I believe your people will need time to adjust to this new law of yours."

She was grateful for what he'd done. He'd freed her! He'd really freed her. But watching Herin and Nesbit's reactions, and seeing how the courtiers had reacted, she realized that freeing her wasn't as simple as she'd thought it would be. There were undercurrents here she didn't understand and she didn't want Badru to ruin himself for her.

She'd just wanted to be free.

Badru shook off her touch. "No. This change will mean nothing unless another change is made as well."

Nesbit eyed him warily. "And what change would that be, most honored leader?"

"I want you to also draft language for the return of property to each freed slave."

Nesbit choked, coughing until his eyes watered; he bent over in half, hacking up what seemed like a lung.

Herin stepped forward. "Most honored leader…"

Badru silenced her with a look. "As I said, there is no point in freeing a slave only to leave them destitute and without means. For every slave that is freed, I want the property that was seized at the time they were taken returned to them."

Herin and Nesbit exchanged horrified looks as K'lrsa tried to think through what that might mean. Who owned that property now? What would that mean to them to suddenly lose what they'd purchased or acquired? Could someone now buy a slave and free them in order to harm an enemy who owned that slave's property?

She opened her mouth to speak, but shut it again at the look in Badru's eyes.

"As my first act under this new law, I give back to K'lrsa dan V'na of the White Horse Tribe her horse, Fallion. She is free to ride him whenever and wherever she wishes." He bowed his head towards her. "As much as an *Amalanee* horse can belong to anyone, he is yours once more, my love."

She stared at him. Whenever and wherever she wished? So she could just ride Fallion through the gates and never come back?

She could go home.

He'd well and truly freed her.

But when she thought of traveling alone on Fallion back through the Daliphate, she realized how impossible that really was.

Her freedom was still an illusion.

At least it was a start, though. K'lrsa threw her arms around Badru. "Thank you!"

72

Herin pulled K'lrsa away and hissed, "You are still a dorana. Act like it."

She then turned to Nesbit who had finally started to recover from his coughing fit. "Nesbit, there are obviously many complex matters to consider in drafting such an important law as this one. Allow me to assist you in this while the Daliph and his dorana go for their ride."

Nesbit nodded, letting Herin guide him away towards the group of courtiers. Herin glanced back at them once, her expression pure venom.

"Badru, was this wise?" K'lrsa asked, stepping close to him so only he could hear her.

He shrugged. "Probably not. But you were right. I am the Daliph and it is in my power to change things." He shook his head. "I've always hated slavery. Ever since the day I learned that Lodie was my great aunt. I watched how she was treated and…" He shook his head. "No. It wasn't wise, but it was the right thing to do. Now, come. Let's find out whose horse is the fastest—your Fallion or my Midnight."

They left K'lrsa's poradoma in the stables. Sayel tried to object, but Badru didn't even pretend to listen.

He led K'lrsa and a party of six soldiers and five courtiers along the narrow path by the city wall and over the bridge. Everyone in the streets stared; they whispered and pointed, but none attempted to bow or call out.

She realized how useful it was for Badru to be able to shed his identity as Daliph simply by dressing in black.

She shuddered at the thought of how restricting it would be to have people bowing to you everywhere you went, demanding attention or favors or just watching what you did every moment of every day.

As they rode onto the large grassy area outside the city wall, K'lrsa's tension eased. No more people. No more walls. No more city stench. Just unending grassland and open skies.

She took a deep breath, inhaling the smell of freshly cut grass.

They were only a short distance from Toreem, but if she closed her eyes she could pretend that she was back home, alone, surrounded by nothing except the sky and the land as far as she could see.

A breeze blew against her face and without even thinking about it, she reached up to unbind her hair, letting it fall down her back and dance in the breeze, relishing the feel as it tugged her hair first one direction and then another.

As they rode forward, she sighed. "I miss my home."

"What's it like?" Badru rode beside her as the rest of the group fell back to give them privacy. "Grandmother never speaks of it. Lodie used to tell me stories of the great desert storms and sands that never ended."

"You knew Lodie when she was in the palace?"

Badru glanced back to make sure no one could hear them. "Yes."

"Did you know she was Herin's sister?"

"Everyone knew. The old Daliph reveled in the fact."

K'lrsa tilted her head to the side, catching something dark in the way he'd answered. "How so?"

Badru shook his head. "It isn't really my story to tell."

"Please, Badru. I need to understand. Why were you all so upset the day I arrived? What happened here between Herin and Lodie and the old Daliph?"

"And Garzel." He pressed his lips into a tight frown.

"And Garzel."

Badru stared ahead, thinking. Finally, he nodded to himself. "Very well. But remember, this isn't my story. It's theirs."

"I understand."

He shook his head, but he continued. "When my grandmother was newly married, she accompanied her husband here to pay tribute to the then Daliph. She was very beautiful then, the type of woman that all men saw and immediately wanted."

K'lrsa tried to picture that, but he was right. At some point in her life Herin had been very beautiful before the ravages of time and anger replaced that beauty with something darker.

"Well, the Daliph saw her and he was no different. So he took her."

"Took her?" She stared at Badru.

His jaw clenched. "Took her. Dragged her from her husband's side and had his way with her." He shook his head, nostrils flared in anger. "Can you imagine? Coming to the court for the first time, excited and happy, a honeymoon with your new husband, and the Daliph drags you from your new husband's side to rape you?"

K'lrsa shivered, suddenly noticing the dark storm clouds on the far horizon and the chill in the air. "I'm so sorry."

"Don't apologize to me."

K'lrsa tried to imagine apologizing to Herin and knew she never would, that she'd never even mention what she'd learned.

Badru continued. "It gets worse. The Daliph took her husband as well."

"He wasn't killed when she was taken?"

Badru grimaced. "No. Herin was the Rider. Her husband was an artist, a gentle man, good with his hands, but not a fighter."

"What happened to him?" Watching Badru's face, K'lrsa knew she didn't want to hear it, but some part of her wanted to know every nasty, dark detail.

"They cut his tongue out and made him her poradom. He was forced to attend his own wife. To dress her and feed her. And to escort her to see the Daliph every time he wanted her. He was forced to watch as…" Badru shook his head. "I hated that man so much. I'm glad he's dead."

"Her husband?" K'lrsa stared at him, surprised.

"No, the Daliph. Garzel was, is, Herin's husband."

"Garzel?" She thought back to the way he was always with Herin, always by her side. She remembered that small moment they'd shared on the day she was captured. To think what they must have been through together…A lifetime of watching the one you love tortured…

"Why didn't they fight back? Why didn't they run?"

Badru shrugged. "Garzel would never leave without Herin. And Herin could never break free. The Daliph watched her too closely." He smiled weakly at her. "Now you understand why she doesn't care much for the notion of love."

"But Garzel stayed with her all those years. He saved her, supported her."

"Exactly." He nodded as he studied the clouds on the far horizon. "If he hadn't loved her, he could've saved himself. And she could've killed herself and been done with it. But because they loved one another, they both held on."

"A Rider would never kill herself."

He quirked an eyebrow at her. "No?"

They rode in silence for a long time before Badru continued. "They almost jumped one night."

"Jumped?"

"Out of the window of her room. The slaves forgot to latch the window tight and it was banging in the wind. They stood there, holding hands, staring down at the cobbles below, ready to die together."

"So why didn't they?"

"They weren't sure it would kill them."

"And Lodie? How was she a part of this?"

Badru glanced behind them once more, but the courtiers had fallen even farther behind. Two guards still rode close enough to reach them quickly, but not so close they'd be able to hear. "Lodie came to rescue them. She, too, was once a Rider. It was about five years later."

He smiled. "No one knows how she managed it, although there were plenty of rumors of murder or seduction, but she was eventually sold into the Daliph's household as a slave. She thought she'd pass unnoticed until she could rescue them, but the Daliph knew who she was immediately."

"What did he do?"

"Used her to torment Herin. And Herin to torment her." He glanced at her briefly before continuing, a bitter smile on his face. "Oh, he had great fun with it before they realized he knew. He'd have Lodie wash the floor of the great room naked in front of everyone while Herin sat next to him pretending not to notice. Or he'd rape Herin while Lodie was there."

K'lrsa shuddered, imagining how horrible that must've been. She almost wished the old Daliph were still alive just so she could kill him for what he'd done to Lodie. And to Herin. And to Garzel.

"How do you know all this? You weren't even born then."

Badru glared at the space between Midnight's ears. "Because he continued to toy with them like that until the day he died." He shook his head, lost in memory. "Herin and Lodie hated each other by then, or at least it seemed like they did."

He turned to her. "You really met her? She's really alive?"

K'lrsa nodded. "I think so. That's who she said she was. She has a birthmark on the base of her neck in the shape of a cactus flower and her left ear is cut like a slave's."

"That's her, alright." He shook his head. "I can't believe my grandmother hid that from me."

"Hid what?"

Badru took a deep breath and glanced behind them again. "Lodie is the slave who poisoned my grandfather. He'd made her his taster—I think because he suspected Herin had tried to poison him the year before and he thought she wouldn't poison Lodie no matter how much they seemed to hate each other."

He glanced at K'lrsa, a slight smile on his face. "Did you know, each finger joint Herin lost was for a time she tried to kill the Daliph?"

"Really?"

He nodded, smiling. "My grandmother is nothing if not persistent. Anyway. Lodie was his taster. And one night, in the great hall, in front of everyone, she tasted his food, told him it was fine, and handed it to him." He shrugged. "She coughed a bit as she did it, but that was the only sign that anything was wrong.

"It was his favorite—dates stuffed with goat's milk cheese drizzled in honey—so he immediately shoved one in his mouth. Meanwhile, Lodie was holding her arms across her stomach, trying not to cough.

"When the Daliph started to choke, she laughed at him. 'Did you really think my life mattered more to me than killing you you sick bastard?' she asked, and then she collapsed.

"Dead. Or so I thought. And then he collapsed. Dead."

K'lrsa stared at him, rapt. "But she lived?"

Badru shrugged. "I didn't think she had. No one thought she had. The room erupted into chaos; I had to act."

"Act?"

He glanced at her and away, biting on his lip. He was silent for a long time as they rode across the plain, watching lightning from the distant storm strike the ground. "By the time my grandfather died, there were only two potential successors— myself and his youngest son, Kalel.

"Fighting for the position had started a few years before when the Daliph had a fainting spell. He told everyone that the last man standing would be his heir. Unleashed a bloodbath. He loved it, the bastard, watching us kill one another."

Badru grimaced. "He'd tell us stories at dinner of the moves his various heirs had made towards one another, praising the winners, shaming the losers. Kalel, he was the worst. Or best, according to my grandfather.

"He didn't just eliminate his rivals, he tortured them and betrayed them in the worst possible way he could imagine. He killed more of his brothers, and later his nephews, than any other."

Badru laughed. "Kalel's actually the reason I was a potential heir. He killed so many of his brothers that my grandfather had to make all his grandson's eligible, too, or risk Kalel coming at him directly."

"So what did you do when your grandfather collapsed?" K'lrsa watched him, wanting to know but not wanting to know at the same time.

Badru squared his shoulders and met her eyes. "I killed Kalel. While everyone was swarming around my grandfather, I stuck my eating knife in Kalel's neck."

K'lrsa flinched. She'd know he was going to say it, but to picture the man she loved cold-bloodedly stabbing another was too much.

Badru held her gaze. "I don't regret it. He deserved to die. He was as bad as or worse than my grandfather."

K'lrsa tried to shake away her disgust. Murder was almost unheard of in the tribes—life was too precarious for men to kill one another for no reason. But in the Daliphate it seemed to be a common occurrence. "So what happened to Lodie?"

Badru shook his head. "I don't know. By the time I made it to my grandfather's side, he was dead. Lodie and Garzel were gone. My grandmother said she'd sent Garzel to throw the body on a trash heap somewhere. No one dared question her."

He smiled. "Seems she survived somehow after all. Maybe she had the antidote?"

K'lrsa frowned. From what Lodie had told her, she'd expected, even wanted, to die.

Badru continued, "I didn't know that Lodie was alive." He clenched his jaw tight and glared straight ahead. "My grandmother lied to me."

The thunder of the distant storm rolled across the sky, echoing his mood. "I thought I could trust her, but now I know I can't."

K'lrsa squeezed his arm. "I'm sure she did what she thought was best for you."

He gave K'lrsa a long look. "Are you? Because I'm not." He shook his head, dislodging his memories and anger. "Enough. Should we see whose horse is fastest?"

Before K'lrsa could say another word, he kicked Midnight into a run and Fallion leapt after him. They raced towards the dark storm clouds gathering on the horizon.

73

K'lrsa gave Fallion full rein. She leaned low over his neck, relishing the feel of the wind whipping at her hair and the way she and Fallion flowed together. She was out of riding shape and knew she'd feel it in her muscles later, but for now she lost herself in the perfect harmony of riding such a magnificent creature.

This. This was what was wonderful and amazing about being alive. This was what made all the suffering and pain of life worthwhile. These moments of pure bliss, flying across the plains, completely lost in the moment.

Badru slowed Midnight just enough for her to reach them and then both horses surged ahead, racing side by side, their hooves barely touching the ground as they streamed across the plains, leaving their escort far behind.

They dashed into the midst of the storm, never slowing as rain pelted their skin.

K'lrsa laughed, her joy spilling outward to encompass Badru and the horses and the storm raging above them.

She was free. After weeks of being held down, pulled back, twisted and constrained, she could finally just be herself.

Badru laughed, too, the joy on his face matching her own as they thundered onward under the dark sky. He looked as young as her when he smiled, the burden of leadership that had aged him beyond his years washed away for just those few moments.

They rode in a large circle that eventually took them away from the storm and back to their escort. The guards were furious, the tension around their eyes showing what they thought of their Daliph riding his horse into a thunderstorm with a strange woman and no one else by his side.

The courtiers just stared at them, mouths agape as if Badru and K'lrsa were deranged demons.

K'lrsa didn't care. Let them think what they would. She wasn't a proper dorana and she never would be.

She was a Rider. A free woman who made her own choices and to the fiery pit with anyone who dared have an opinion about it.

When they finally pulled to a stop, Badru let out a loud whooping yell. "That was fantastic."

He pulled her to him and kissed her, his breath cinnamon, his lips melting against hers like honey. She wrapped her hand around the back of his neck and pulled him deeper into the kiss, losing herself in the sensation of his mouth against hers, as if she'd been starving for him her entire life.

It was a perfect moment.

Until she heard the muttered comment from one of the courtiers about expecting no less from a desert whore.

Badru jerked back. "Who said that?"

Everyone froze.

Badru turned to one of the guards. "Rulen. Who said it?"

The guard pointed to a young man dressed mostly in brown but with a green belt and orange headscarf who cringed back from them.

"Yorel, did you just call my dorana a desert whore?"

The young man swallowed his fear and raised his chin. He rode his horse forward, glancing at K'lrsa before he met Badru's eyes. "Yes, most honored leader. I did. Because that's what she is."

Badru slapped him. "She's my dorana."

Yorel held his hand to his reddened cheek, his eyes tight with anger. "My sister is your dorana. A true dorana. A proper woman. An example for all of what is beautiful and precious."

He glared at K'lrsa. "This woman is nothing more than tribal trash dressed as a dorana. She shames all women with her wanton ways. Bad enough that she rides a horse. Worse yet that it's a stallion. But to go racing after you? With her hair down? And to kiss you like that for all to see?" He shook his head. "It's unacceptable."

The muscle in Badru's jaw twitched. "I'm sorry you feel that way, Yorel. It seems Toreem is no longer an appropriate place for you."

Yorel's eyes widened. "What?"

"Leave. You are no longer welcome in Toreem."

"You can't do that. My father is one of your most trusted advisors. My sister is your dorana." He looked around for support, but no one would meet his eyes. "You've given me two colors. I'm one of the most esteemed members of your court."

"Not anymore." Badru shrugged, the gesture overly casual. "I don't need you, Yorel. Or anyone else. Not if you won't support me."

The young man stared at him, mouth hanging open. "You can't mean it."

"I do. Just be glad K'lrsa has asked me not to whip those who offend her honor." Badru looked past the man, meeting the eyes of each courtier and guard. "Listen well. If I ever hear anyone else refer to K'lrsa as a whore or desert trash or a slave or insult her in any other way, I will have them killed. Is that understood?"

The courtiers nodded, each looking away quickly, some fidgeting with their reins as they watched out of the corner of their eyes to see how Yorel would react.

Yorel ignored everyone as he turned his horse towards Boradol. He held his head high as he rode away at a slow, steady pace. At a glance from Badru, two of the guards followed behind him.

K'lrsa was grateful Badru had defended her, but as she watched the courtiers look at each other, she couldn't help but think he'd made yet another mistake because of her.

How many more could he afford to make?

74

When they returned to the stables, Herin was waiting for Badru. She took him aside, whispering urgently. Without so much as a glance in her direction, Badru left, throwing his reins to the closest groom.

K'lrsa's poradoma weren't there. She didn't know how to return to her rooms and honestly didn't want to.

When a young slave girl, half her face covered in a bright red birthmark, came to take Fallion's reins, K'lrsa waved her away. "No. I'll take care of him. Thank you."

She led Fallion to his stall and started currying his coat, grateful for the old familiar rhythm and the comfort of his solid presence.

As she worked, two men arrived in the area outside of the stall, calling for their horses.

"I tell you, Fanel, no one will actually free any of their slaves. It doesn't matter."

"No? You don't think so? What about Tamil? The fool's childhood sweetheart is a slave. Her husband gambled everything away. Tamil bought her for twice what she was worth. And now that his wife is dead, you don't think he'll free her at the first chance he has?"

K'lrsa crept closer, trying to get a look at the two men without letting them see her.

"I don't." The first man was middle-aged, dressed in brown with a yellow belt.

The second man was shorter and fatter, but about the same age. He wore brown with a red headscarf. "And why's that?"

"Because the man owns over a thousand slaves. He can't free one without acknowledging that the others deserve more than to work his fields for the meager food and shelter he provides."

Tamil raised an eyebrow. "And what about you, Fanel? Will you free your slaves? I know you haven't bought a slave since your father died five years ago."

Fanel grimaced. "I don't like owning slaves. My father's brother was sold as a slave. I knew the man, so I can't pretend that there was some flaw in his character that made him deserving of slavery when my father wasn't. But I can't survive without slaves. Not when everyone else will keep theirs. And if I have to give them back the property that was taken from them, too? No. I won't free any."

"Then what the Daliph said means nothing." Tamil nodded in satisfaction.

Fanel shook his head. "It means everything. He played right into their hands."

Tamil frowned. "Do you really think so?"

Before Fanel could answer, the young slave girl walked up leading two beautiful gray horses. Not as beautiful as Fallion or Midnight, but nicer than any other horses she'd ever seen.

The men rode away without finishing their conversation.

As she worked on Fallion's coat, K'lrsa wondered what Fanel had meant. Whose hands had Badru played into? And what would happen now?

He'd freed her out of love, but what had it cost him?

She hadn't wanted to ruin him. All she'd wanted was to be able to choose to be with him. And to go home to protect her family.

But she might have handed Badru's enemies the tool to destroy him. Herin had certainly seemed to think so.

She shook her head.

It didn't matter. She'd be gone soon and everything would go back to the way it had been before she arrived.

Badru would be fine.

She spent the next candlemark with Fallion. He didn't need that much care—he'd been well taken care of, his coat shone and eyes and teeth looked good—but she needed his familiar presence and the comforting routine of tending to him.

She was just standing there, leaning her forehead against his neck, when she heard the sound of a horse arriving in a hurry.

"I need to see the Daliph. Immediately." The man who spoke had the accent of the tribes.

K'lrsa peeked around the corner to see who it was. He was middle-aged and dressed in baru-hide pants and vest, but he also wore a multi-colored headscarf marking him as one favored by the Daliph.

He looked tired, as if he'd been riding long hours for days. His horse didn't look much better. It wasn't a tribes horse, though. Clearly he'd switched out horses as he rode.

The man looked familiar, but she couldn't place him.

A courtier in a brown robe with a green belt came forward, smiling and bowing his head obsequiously. "I'm not sure that will be possible, honored sir."

He glared at the man. "Well make it possible. This is too important to wait."

Another man, this one in a brown robe with a yellow belt and yellow headscarf approached them. "K'var. A pleasure to see you once more." He bowed low.

The only K'var she knew was a leader from the Black Horse Tribe. What was he doing here?

"Faroon. I need to see the Daliph. Now."

Faroon shook his head and held his hands forward in a placating gesture. "I'm afraid that won't be possible, most honored guest."

K'var shook his head. "You don't understand. I *have* to see him now. The tribes are set to expel us. If they do that, we're ruined. The sands will turn against us and we won't be able to lead his traders across the deserts anymore."

Faroon frowned at him. "What can the Daliph do if your own people have turned against you?"

K'var's glare made Faroon step back three steps, holding his hands out in protection. K'var sneered at the man's cowardice. "Give us weapons. And men. So we can destroy any who oppose us before they vote. It's the only way for him to retain his trade route."

K'lrsa bit her lip to keep silent. He wanted to attack the other tribes? Her tribe?

Faroon bowed his head, clearly holding back from saying something cutting. "Very well. Follow me and I'll arrange an audience with the Daliph as soon as possible."

They disappeared into the palace, leaving K'lrsa alone once more.

She waited until she was sure they were gone and then snuck out to grab the slave girl. "Do you know that man that was just here?"

The girl nodded.

"Has he been here before?"

The girl nodded again.

"Tell me about him." K'lrsa glanced to the side, hoping no one would arrive to take her back until the girl could tell her what she knew.

The girl shook her head.

"Why? Why won't you tell me about him?"

The girl opened her mouth to show the stub of a tongue.

K'lrsa grimaced in distaste as well as frustration. "Who did that to you? Was it the current Daliph?"

The girl shook her head.

"The former Daliph?"

She nodded, staring down at the floor.

K'lrsa shook her head. "The world is definitely a better place now that that man's dead."

The slave girl flinched back, her eyes wide. She looked around, searching for anyone who might have heard K'lrsa's comment.

K'lrsa grabbed her arm and shook her. The girl trembled in her grasp. "It's okay. He's dead. No one's going to punish you because you heard me say something mean about a dead man."

The girl stared at K'lrsa like a hare caught in a hawk's claws before she jerked free and ran away down one of the nearby corridors.

Before K'lrsa could go after her, Sayel appeared. "There you are, my dorana." He smiled until he saw that she was alone. "Where's the Daliph? Or his guards?"

She shrugged. "He had to leave. Something urgent."

"And he left you unguarded? In the stables?" Sayel shook his head, clearly wanting to say more but refraining because it was the Daliph.

"He freed me, Sayel. He said I can have Fallion back and ride him whenever I want."

Sayel frowned. "He may have freed you from slavery, but you're still a dorana and should act as such." He grabbed her by the elbow. "Come along now. It's time for your evening meal. And…" He leaned closer with a delicate sniff. "A bath. No dorana should ever smell of horse."

K'lrsa grimaced, but she let him lead her away.

75

After dinner, K'lrsa waited for Sayel and Morlen to leave, but they didn't.

"What's this? Why are you still here?"

Sayel sighed, not even bothering with his normal raised eyebrow of rebuke. "The Daliph has ordered that you should have two poradoma with you at all times."

"All times?"

"Yes."

"Even when I'm sleeping."

Sayel nodded. "Especially when you're sleeping. He worries for your safety, my dorana."

She stood and paced the room. Badru had freed her from slavery and yet she was as trapped as ever. "I don't need protection, Sayel. Tell him I said no."

Sayel shook his head, looking more like a disappointed parent than her mother ever had. "You are a dorana."

"Yes. I'm well aware of that."

"It seems you are not or you would never make such a suggestion."

"What have I done now?"

"A dorana would never presume to tell the Daliph what he should or should not give her."

K'lrsa rolled her eyes and turned away. "This again."

"This always, my dorana."

297

She raised a hand before he could start the lecture on how all she was was a reflection of the Daliph and therefore subject to his will in all things and...

"Can I at least be alone in my room? Can you position yourselves outside?" She turned to see them both looking uncomfortable. "I want to practice the hundred and five attacks. And I generally wear a little less than this to do so."

Sayel shook his head. "We dress you every day, my dorana. There is nothing we haven't seen."

K'lrsa raised an eyebrow. "It's different, Sayel. Trust me? Please?"

He nodded his head and signaled for Morlen to accompany him. "Very well. We'll be just outside if you need us."

"Thank you."

K'lrsa worked on the hundred and five attacks until sweat was pouring down her skin and the stray wisps of hair that had escaped her braid were plastered to her face and neck. She was determined to get back into the shape she'd been in when she'd come to this place, to once more be the true Rider she'd once been.

She'd just finished Striking Snake when the door opened and Badru came inside. He was still dressed in the black he'd been wearing for their ride, his face streaked with dirt. He pulled her into an embrace and buried his face against her neck.

"What a day it's been," he sighed as he stepped back to smile at her. "All I've wanted since I returned to the palace was this." He pulled her into a long, deep kiss.

She lost herself in the sensation of his mouth on hers, fitting her body against his the way she had so many times in the Moon Dance.

And then she remembered what she'd heard in the stables and pulled away, pushing him backward.

"What?"

"I need to ask you something."

He settled himself on a cushion, burying his face in his hands. "Not now, please. It's been a long day and I just want to spend some time with you without thinking about anything except how beautiful you are and how much I love being with you."

He reached for her. "Come here. Help take my mind off everything."

K'lrsa didn't move, her arms crossed tight against her chest to keep from reaching for him. "No."

"K'lrsa. You're my dorana. I thought you would..."

"Oh, do finish that sentence please. You thought your dorana would, what? Bow at your feet? Kiss you and make it all better? Put aside her own needs and wants because you told her to?"

He slumped forward. "K'lrsa, please. I wasn't trying to start a fight with you. I've just had a long day and you were all I wanted at the end of it."

"Me? Or some perfect version of me that doesn't exist? This is me, Badru."

He rubbed at his face. "You know, we seem to do better when we don't have to actually speak to one another."

She laughed. "Convenient isn't it? When you don't have to listen to what I want? When you can just have your way?"

He stood and glared at her. "I never forced you to do anything in the moon dreams, K'lrsa. You wanted me as much as I wanted you. And before you were my dorana. Never say I forced that on you. I am not my grandfather."

She rested her hands against his chest, meeting his eyes. "I didn't, Badru. I'm sorry if that's how it sounded."

He grabbed her hands. "Please, can we just spend this time together without talking about all the rest of it?" He kissed her palm, sending shivers down her spine.

She wanted to give in, to let him touch and kiss her and make the world disappear. But she couldn't do that. Even now K'var might be racing back to the plains, an army at his back ready to slaughter everyone she loved.

She stepped back. "I'm sorry, Badru. But I have to know. What did you give K'var of the Black Horse Tribe today? Did you promise to help him destroy my tribe? Are you going to help him kill my mother and sister and brother?"

Badru frowned. "How do you know about K'var?"

"I heard him when he arrived. He said he was here to ask you for men and weapons to attack the tribes that oppose him. He wore your colors, Badru. The White Horse Tribe, my tribe, is the one that opposes him."

Badru turned away from her. "I haven't met with K'var yet. I spent the day with Herin and Nesbit working through the language on freeing slaves and returning their property. The entire palace is in an uproar over my announcement. The sooner we release the new language, the better."

"So you'll turn him away? Send K'var home to fight his own battles?"

Badru's shoulders tensed. "It's not that simple, K'lrsa."

"What do you mean?" She grabbed his shoulders and forced him to look at her.

"We need the trade they bring us."

"No, you don't. You were fine without it for centuries."

He shook his head. "We were the poorest of the Daliphana before we opened the trade route across the desert. We were the only Daliphate without access to the ocean, at the mercy of the others for everything. We were poor and backwards, our main export our own people to serve as slaves in the other Daliphana. We can't go back to that, K'lrsa. My people won't accept that."

"So you'd kill my people?"

He winced, closing his eyes. "I don't want to."

"But you will?"

He met her gaze. "Unless another tribe is willing to take us across the desert, I'll have no choice but to support K'var."

K'lrsa shook her head. "No. We have to stop trading with you. We have to go back to who we were before or you'll destroy us."

"It's too late to turn back now, K'lrsa. We won't give up on trading across the desert now that we're able to and the tribes won't give up all they've gained from that trade either."

"If you loved me…"

"It's not about loving you." His face darkened and he stepped away from her. "I'm Daliph of the Toreem Daliphate, K'lrsa. I have to do what's best for *my* people."

She'd thought they were past this, but here she was face-to-face with the Daliph not the young man she loved. "Go."

"K'lrsa..."

"No. Go. Get out." She grabbed a pillow and threw it at him. "Get out!"

Badru knocked the pillow aside, glaring at her. "I do love you, K'lrsa, but it's time you stopped acting like a spoiled child and saw how complicated the world really is."

K'lrsa screeched and launched herself at him, clawing at his eyes. She managed to gouge his cheek before he pushed her back.

He left, the heavy bar slamming into place, locking her inside.

She glared at the door, glad he was gone and hoping he'd never come back. Ever.

She threw herself into practicing the hundred and five attacks again, leaping and kicking as the anger churned inside her.

She tried to picture her enemies with each attack, but she didn't know who they were anymore.

Badru?

K'var?

Time?

Change?

Maybe Badru was right. Maybe it was already too late to save her people.

76

K'lrsa lay in her sleeping corner and stared at the ceiling. She didn't want to sleep, afraid her heart would betray her once more and she'd spend the night lost in Badru's arms.

Instead, she struggled not to remember the real kisses they'd shared, the softness of his lips, and the way his arms had wrapped around her, so strong and yet so tender.

She tried to banish those images with memories of her father, but it was no use. She kept coming back to Badru and the way being with him obliterated everything else.

She needed to go home. To get away from him before she lost herself so completely she could never leave.

He was going to help K'var destroy her tribe.

Not to save the lives of his people, but to make sure that they continued to prosper. Her people would die so his could choose from five platters of food at each meal instead of four.

And he knew it. He knew that if he helped K'var he'd be sentencing her family to death. He knew, and he didn't care.

How could she love a man like that?

K'lrsa heard the bar on her door slide away and the door open, slowly, quietly; if she'd been asleep she would've never heard it.

She crept to the edge of the bed, peering around the corner to see who it was. Maybe Badru had come back to apologize.

But no. Whoever it was moved too carefully. Badru would've entered with a lantern, striding into the space as if he owned it. (Which, she guessed, he did.)

This person crept across the room, familiar enough with its layout to avoid the sitting area. He tripped on the pillow K'lrsa had thrown at Badru and hissed a curse as he stumbled into the wall.

Tarum.

Tarum was sneaking into her room in the middle of the night. She shivered and crept from the edge of the bed to the bathing area, keeping to the darkest shadow along the wall.

As Tarum passed through a shaft of moonlight coming in through the slats of the left-most window, the knife he held caught the light.

He'd not only come to her room in the middle of the night, he'd come armed. K'lrsa suddenly felt calm, all the uncertainty and fear of the last few weeks melting away into hard-edged certainty.

He was here to kill her.

But she was going to kill him first.

As he reached the edge of the bed, looming over her little sleeping space, she launched her attack.

He stepped aside at the last moment; the kick she'd aimed to shatter his kneecap turned into a glancing blow. He stumbled away from her, holding the knife between them.

As she approached, he slashed at her but missed. K'lrsa stepped forward as the knife whizzed through the air and delivered a blow to his arm, forcing him to drop the blade.

It clattered to the floor, the sound sharp and distinct.

Before K'lrsa could grab it, Tarum rushed her, pinning her arms to her sides as he drove her backward into the wall.

"What are you doing here?" She stepped on the inside of his foot and then tripped him while he was off balance.

He kept his hold on her so they both crashed to the ground, the breath he expelled as she landed on him heavy with the scent of onions and garlic.

Tarum flipped over on top of her, pinning her body with his as he grabbed her wrists and forced her arms above her head. He grinned as he ran his eyes down her body, his leering smile on full display.

K'lrsa kneed him in the groin and pushed him off.

She sprang back to her feet as Tarum stumbled to his, the knife once more in his hand.

He sneered at her as he waved it in her direction. "Shut up, whore."

"I am so tired of being called that." K'lrsa aimed a kick at his gut.

Tarum staggered under the blow, but managed to keep the knife. He shrugged, breathing heavily. "A mule is a mule, and a whore is a whore."

He slashed at her again, managing a shallow cut along her arm.

"So, what? You figured you'd come in here and have your way with me? Then what? Run away? Because the Daliph will kill you for touching me."

"You're no dorana." He slashed at her once more.

She laughed. "Yes, I am. But you always were a fool. You didn't think it through, did you? Didn't plan this out at all."

He slashed at her again and managed a deeper cut along her thigh. "I have a plan. You're going to die. And then they'll reward me."

She jumped back, avoiding another attack. "Who? Who wants me dead?"

"Everyone. You've ruined everything." He grunted as he lunged again. He was tiring, his breath now coming in ragged gasps.

She circled him, wondering if she could reach the door before he caught her again.

"And did they, whoever they are, tell you to rape me first?" She stumbled a bit as he lunged for her once more.

"No. But might as well get a little payment now." He ran his eyes down her body, his gaze groping at her exposed flesh.

Rage surged through her veins and she jumped forward, her heel driving his knee backward until it made a sickening crunch. He fell heavily to the ground, screaming.

K'lrsa glanced towards the door, wondering if anyone had heard him. And, if so, who would come? Tarum's accomplices? Or a rescuer?

She circled him warily. He was still on the ground, but the knife was sharp and his reach long. "Why did they want me dead?"

She stumbled again, feeling dizzy.

"Feeling it aren't you?" He grinned at her, completely confident even though he couldn't stand.

"What?"

"The poison."

As K'lrsa struggled to stay standing, Tarum laughed softly. "They didn't want to take any chances."

K'lrsa forced herself to focus on Tarum and ignore the way the poison dragged at her limbs and her mind. She launched into Crouching Cricket, her body speeding through the air as she leapt at him.

Bones crunched as her heel connected with his face.

He collapsed, dead.

She stared down at him, her vision unfocused as she struggled to stay standing.

"Help," she cried, but the word was no more than a whisper.

K'lrsa fainted.

77

She awoke in her bed, the flimsy curtains blowing against her face in the cool breeze from the open windows.

One of the Daliph's guards stood next to the bed, his face as still as stone. When he saw that she was awake, he signaled to another guard stationed by the door.

Herin sat next to the bed on a small stool; Garzel behind her. They both looked tired; the wrinkles on their faces had multiplied overnight.

Herin gestured the guard to leave. He stepped far enough away that he wouldn't hear their conversation, but stayed close enough he could react if Herin or Garzel tried something.

K'lrsa wanted to laugh at the absurdity of it, but then she remembered that her own poradom had tried to kill her.

"What happened last night?" Herin asked, demanding and belligerent.

"Isn't it obvious? Tarum tried to kill me. I killed him first." K'lrsa tried to sit up, but fell back into the pillows, closing her eyes against a wave of dizziness.

Herin pursed her lips like she was sucking on a lemon. "That's not what Balor says happened."

"Who is Balor? I'm telling you, Tarum came here last night and attacked me with a poisoned knife." She rubbed at her forehead, willing the headache that had just appeared to go away.

It didn't work.

"Balor is a well-known and well-respected poradom. He says he found Tarum in your rooms. That the two of you were together, naked. He killed Tarum and subdued you for proper judgement."

"Together? Me and Tarum?"

Herin raised an eyebrow but didn't speak.

"Oh, honestly, Herin. Do you think I would ever be with Tarum? I hate him." K'lrsa tried to sit up again and fell backward.

"He was very handsome."

"He wasn't my type."

"We didn't find a knife."

"Where do you think this came from?" K'lrsa pulled her sleeve back to show the wound on her arm.

All that remained was a faint white line, as if the wound had healed long ago.

K'lrsa stared at her arm. "That's impossible. He cut me here last night."

Herin didn't say anything, but her expression showed exactly what she thought of K'lrsa's tale.

K'lrsa forced herself to sit up and pulled the covers back from her thigh. That wound also looked long-healed.

"What is this? What happened?" She grabbed Herin's arm. "Herin, I don't know what happened last night, but I swear to you on the Great Father and the Lady Moon that I was attacked and poisoned. Look at Tarum. I killed him with Crouching Cricket."

Herin pulled K'lrsa's hand from her arm.

"Herin?"

"No one will believe you. Balor is a senior poradom. Your supposed wounds are long-healed. There is no knife. And Tarum's throat was slit." She shook her head.

"So what's going to happen to me?"

Herin met her eyes. "The punishment for a dorana caught with another man is death."

"But I wasn't with him."

Herin shrugged, not even looking the least bit upset. "Balor says you were. Zenel was stationed at the door with Tarum and he says Tarum begged him to leave for a candlemark so you two could be alone together. He says he knew how wrong it was, but he knew how much you cared for each other."

"Zenel? Who is Zenel? He's a liar, too."

Herin nodded in mockery. "Lots of liars in the poradoma."

"Herin, you saw how Tarum was with me. He was always touching me more than he should've. Always looking at me."

"He was your poradom. They have to touch and look at you."

She shook her head. "You know Tarum was different. What about Sayel? Does he know? He doesn't believe this does he?"

"No, he doesn't."

"Well, that's good, isn't it?"

"No."

"Why not?"

"Because Sayel was your head poradom. He was responsible for guarding your honor. If he says it's a lie, everyone will think it's only to protect himself."

K'lrsa lay back, trying to clear the final dregs of poison from her mind. She needed to see Badru. He'd save her. He'd know the truth. "What happens now?"

"Badru will see you this afternoon."

K'lrsa felt a small surge of hope.

"He'll deliver his judgement in front of the full court."

The full court? K'lrsa glanced at her. "What aren't you telling me, Herin?"

"Two senior poradoma have accused a dorana of consorting with a man other than the Daliph." Garzel touched her shoulder and Herin rested her hand on his, squeezing gently. "By the laws of the Daliphate you will be beheaded."

"Beheaded?"

Herin nodded. "By the Daliph's own hand."

"No. It won't happen. He won't do it."

Herin once more looked like she was sucking on a lemon. "He must. Or risk losing everything."

"No." She stared at Herin, noting how nervous she was. "You don't think he'll do it either, do you?"

"Pzah. He's a boy in love. Who knows what he'll do?" She leaned forward, spitting her words. "But if I have any say in it, he will swing that sword without a single moment's hesitation."

K'lrsa stared at her, too surprised to speak. Herin had never been her friend, but to think that she'd encourage Badru in this...

Herin stood slowly, Garzel supporting her with a hand under her elbow.

Desperate to keep them by her side, K'lrsa said, "Tarum was ordered to kill me."

"By whom?"

"I don't know. He didn't say."

Herin stared towards the door.

"Do you believe me, Herin?"

Herin took a deep breath and turned back to her, her face completely blank. Now K'lrsa knew where Badru had learned that particular trick. "It doesn't matter if you're innocent. What matters is what everyone else believes."

"What?"

"The truth is irrelevant. If they think you're guilty, they'll want you punished. If Badru doesn't punish you, he'll fail even if he's right."

K'lrsa closed her eyes against a wave of dizziness. "That doesn't make sense."

"Of course it does. The only thing that matters is how people perceive their leader."

K'lrsa grabbed at Herin. "But you'll tell Badru, won't you? You won't let him kill me thinking I've betrayed him, will you?"

Herin stepped away. "No."

"Why not?"

"Because he doesn't need the temptation. He needs to believe you've betrayed him so he can do what he must."

Herin turned away.

"Herin!"

She turned back to K'lrsa. "Make your peace, child. And spare a thought for the others who are going to die today, too."

"Others? Who?"

"Your poradoma. Morlen and Sayel."

"No."

Herin nodded.

"Why?"

"Because they failed to protect your honor."

K'lrsa threw herself back against the pillows. "My honor is just fine. Herin, if you let this happen, whoever tried this will go after Badru again."

She nodded. "I know. But with you gone, it won't be so easy to strike him down."

As Herin walked away, K'lrsa called out after her. "He'll find out eventually, Herin."

She shrugged.

"You can't do this, Herin. It'll break his heart."

She paused with her hand on the door and turned to look at K'lrsa. "I'd rather see him with a broken heart than a broken neck. And you? What would you rather see? Do you love him enough to let this happen? Or will you ruin him completely?"

Before K'lrsa could respond, Herin left.

78

K'lrsa struggled out of the bed and stumbled around the room, working the last vestiges of poison from her body. She still felt a little weak, but nothing like when she'd awoken.

"I need to see Badru." She faced off against the guard nearest the bed, but he ignored her as if she didn't even exist.

"I need to see Badru." The guard by the door glanced to the other guard and then he, too, ignored her.

She paced the room from wall to wall to wall to wall, desperate for escape.

The door opened and Sayel stepped inside, his eyes cast downward.

"Sayel. Am I glad to see you." She hugged him, but he was stiff and awkward in her embrace. "Sayel? What's wrong? You believe me, don't you? You know Tarum tried to attack me. You know I'd never be with him like that."

He met her eyes briefly and then looked away. "Herin said you confessed."

"What?" She turned away and paced the room, her hands clenched and unclenched. "That meddlesome, loathsome hag. That dried up old bag of horse shit."

She turned back to Sayel. "I said no such thing. Tarum tried to kill me last night; I killed him before he could."

Sayel glanced at her and then away again. "I want to believe you, my dorana. But Balor said..."

"Forget what Balor said."

He forced himself to look at her. "Balor said he found you together. He was poradom with my father. I've known him my entire life. Who am I to believe?"

"Me, Sayel. You know me. After all these days can you honestly believe that I would be with Tarum like that?"

He shook his head. "I don't know what to believe, my dorana. Balor is a friend and mentor. He says he killed Tarum and subdued you."

"How? How did he subdue me, Sayel? Do you see any marks on my body? Did he have any marks on his body? I'm a trained warrior, Sayel. I wouldn't be taken without a fight."

When he looked skeptical, she said, "Did you know that I've fought the Daliph? That I'm his equal?"

He swallowed, stepping back. "You fought the Daliph?" For a moment he was once more the disapproving father figure, shaking his head in shame. "Oh, my dorana. What am I to do with you?"

His eyes narrowed as he studied her. "You fought the Daliph?"

"Yes."

"And you were able to match him?"

"I landed a few blows even wearing the dress of a dorana."

Sayel's eyebrows drew together. He paced the room, tilting his head first to one side then to another, before finally turning back to her. "The Daliph is one of the best fighters I've ever seen. But if Balor lied, what did happen and why won't Herin believe you?"

K'lrsa shook her head. She'd never understand Herin if she lived an eternity. "Herin said she doesn't care about the truth, she cares about perception."

She shrugged. "There's something else I don't understand, Sayel. Tarum cut me twice last night, but my wounds are completely healed."

"What?" Sayel grabbed her arms, his fingers leaving bruises in her flesh.

She showed him the two long-healed scars. "See?"

Sayel gasped as he ran a trembling finger along the scar on her arm. "Those weren't there yesterday."

"No. I told you."

Sayel stumbled away from her, shaking his head, clutching at his chest.

"What?"

He shook his head again and stared into the distance. "Rumors. There were always rumors. But..."

"Sayel! What is it?"

He met her eyes; it was the first time she'd seen him scared. "Death walkers."

"What are death walkers?" She grabbed his arms and shook him. "Sayel? What are they?"

He glanced at the two guards who continued to stand as still as statues and whispered, "Those who worship the death god. It's said they can heal any wound." He traced her scar once more. "It's even whispered that some can bring the dead back to life."

K'lrsa shivered. "And you think they're the ones who healed me?"

He nodded.

"But why? Why not just let me die?"

Sayel shook his head. "I don't know."

K'lrsa paced the room, trying to figure out what to do next. Sayel watched her, alternating between wide-eyed fear and hand-wringing uncertainty.

The door swung open and Herin strode into the room, Garzel at her heels as always. Herin glared at her. "Time for your trial. Sayel, help her get dressed."

Garzel handed Sayel two small pieces of pale brown baru hide, but before K'lrsa could ask what they were, Sayel turned on Herin. "You lied to me."

Herin barely spared him a glance.

"Herin. Death walkers healed her," he hissed.

Herin snapped at the guards, "Leave us. Now."

They hesitated, but at a nod from Garzel, both stepped into the hallway.

313

She turned on Sayel as soon as they were gone. "Of course I lied to you, you fool. You're as bad as the boy when it comes to *your dorana*."

Sayel glared at Herin. "What about the death walkers?"

She waved her hand, shooing away his concern. "Dealt with."

"How?"

Herin studied him for a long moment until the silence in the room was almost painful. "Tell me something, Sayel. Would you do anything you could for your Daliph?"

"Of course."

"Would you give your life for him?"

"Yes." He stood straighter, holding his chin high. "It's part of the vow I made as a poradom."

"Then stop asking questions and serve your Daliph. Shut up and die like the good little soldier you are."

Sayel shook his head. "I don't understand."

Herin pinched the bridge of her nose and glared back and forth between K'lrsa and Sayel. "Must I always explain myself? Fine. K'lrsa must die. And she must die at the hands of the Daliph. If she doesn't, the court will turn on him."

When K'lrsa stepped forward to protest, Herin held up a hand to silence her. "Hear me out. The rumor of K'lrsa's infidelity has spread throughout the palace. Everyone believes it." Again Herin held up a hand to silence K'lrsa. "It doesn't matter if you weren't, girl. What matters is what people believe.

"And the people believe that you are tribal trash that would open your legs for any man. Not only that, they believe you did so."

K'lrsa clenched her hands, wanting to punch each and every one of them, but let Herin continue.

"It doesn't help that just yesterday the Daliph sent the whole palace into chaos by freeing you from slavery. You, the lying, cheating whore."

She turned back to Sayel. "What do you think happens if Badru believes her story? If he spares her and ignores the word of one of his senior poradoma?"

She looked back and forth between them. "What will people think of their Daliph if he takes the word of some plains savage over the words of an honored member of his court? Do you think people will believe he knew better than them?

"Or do you think they'll see a weak, love-blind fool willing to sacrifice his entire Daliphate for what's between a woman's legs?"

K'lrsa gasped at the crude description.

Sayel rubbed at his chin as he thought about what Herin had said.

Herin continued, "The only way to save Badru now is to let him be seen as a strong leader that hasn't been seduced by a pretty face. He must do this. "

Sayel sighed. "Is there no other way?"

"No."

K'lrsa stared back and forth between them. Were they really going to do this to her? To Badru?

"Enough." Herin nodded at the baru hide in Sayel's arms. "We need to dress K'lrsa for her audience."

Sayel held up a small piece of baru hide, barely bigger than his hand, an eyebrow raised.

"What's that?" K'lrsa asked.

"Your top."

She stared at Herin. "I can't wear that. That's…there's nothing to it."

Herin smiled, the expression so uncharacteristic and strange it was more frightening than anything K'lrsa had ever seen before. "I know."

K'lrsa held the baru hide against her chest. "No tribe member would wear this, Herin. It's impractical. I'd be better off naked."

"If you'd rather, that's fine, too. But if you intend to wear clothing, this is the clothing you'll wear."

K'lrsa met the old woman's gaze for a long, long moment.

She wanted to refuse, but what did it really matter? Too much clothing, too little. It was all the same. Just someone trying to play tricks on her mind, but it didn't change who she was at her core.

She sniffed. "Alright. Give it to me."

<u>79</u>

As K'lrsa walked down the hallways of the palace towards the audience chamber, Herin and Sayel ahead of her, two of the Daliph's guards behind her, she finally understood the difference between the atrocious garb of a dorana and what she was wearing now. She might hate the layers and layers of clothing that dorana were required to wear, but it told others a story. That she was special, important, deserving of care.

What she wore now told them that she was a savage. Beneath them. Other.

Men didn't even try to hide their leers as she passed, making suggestive comments about what they'd like to do with her body. Women turned away in disgust or made biting comments about where a piece of trash like her actually belonged.

K'lrsa held her head high and stared straight ahead. She refused to let these people shame her. She would not bow her head before them, she would not blush in shame.

Her hands twitched as she walked, longing to tug the top that barely covered her breasts a little bit higher or to pull the skirt that barely covered her butt down just a little more. She didn't do it, though, because doing so would be a sign of weakness. It would let the men and women who mocked her know that they heard their comments and that they mattered to her.

They didn't.

She was a Rider and that was something inside her, something that had nothing to do with what she wore or how she looked or what anyone else thought of her. That was at the core of who she was and something no one could ever touch.

(Or so she told herself as her hands once more itched to adjust her top.)

There was one advantage to Herin's choice of costume. For the first time in weeks, K'lrsa could walk down the hallway at a normal pace, her feet no longer tangling in her skirts at each step. And, fortunately, the outfit fit amazingly well. If she did have to fight, she thought it would actually stay in place.

They reached the doors to the audience chamber and K'lrsa took a deep breath, knowing that as bad as the walk there had been, it would be a hundred times worse inside. She stood tall, proud, staring towards the dais and Badru as the doors opened before her.

K'lrsa fought the urge to cover her ears and flinch away from the wall of men's voices that assaulted her.

She was a Rider. These men were nothing to her.

Only Badru mattered.

He sat on the central dais, his dorana arrayed one level below him in their cacophony of color. The blue pillow she'd once sat on was gone, her space filled in as if she'd never been there.

Poradoma in their green robes—some so old they looked ready to die at any moment, some so young they probably hadn't even reached their tenth summer—filled one entire section of the room.

Lawkeepers, their yellow robes as bright as the sun, filled a smaller area next to them, followed by the punishers in their robes as red as freshly-spilled blood.

Guards in white stood shoulder to shoulder around the entire perimeter of the room.

Men in brown with hints of color here or there filled every single space in the room, practically sitting on top of each other.

The only empty space was a small area in front of the dais and the narrow path between the doors and that space.

K'lrsa struggled to breathe as the walls closed in around her. She'd never been near this many people, this many men, all hostile. There wasn't a kind face in the entire room.

Not even Badru's.

Nesbit rose from his seat, shuffling forward as he coughed his skin-crawling phlegmy cough.

The room fell silent.

Herin and Sayel stepped aside and K'lrsa walked forward through the narrow pathway to the area of judgement before the dais. They'd added so many tables for the occasion, they'd barely remembered to leave enough space for her to reach it.

Sayel followed a step behind her. They were joined by Morlen as they reached the small area where Nesbit waited.

At least they'd left enough room for Badru to behead her without accidentally striking one of the witnesses at the same time.

Barely. Those in the front rows would receive more than just a close-up view.

She looked to Badru, ignoring the rest of the room.

He held her gaze, never looking away, never betraying a single emotion.

Nesbit cleared his throat and spoke so all could hear him. "Most honored leader, before you stands the one formerly known as K'lrsa dan V'na of the White Horse Tribe, now a dorana of the Toreem Daliphate."

He cleared his throat; K'lrsa winced at the thought of what he spit into his handkerchief before continuing, "This one is accused of consorting with a man other than her Daliph. Namely, her poradom, Tarum Alavane. They were discovered together in her chambers by senior poradom, Balor Lenivano."

He nodded towards an older man whose muscular frame had long since gone to fat. Where Sayel was large but clearly strong, this man was simply large, his neck full of fleshy folds that gathered under his chin.

"Tarum Alavane was killed on sight. This one was held for your judgement as is proper."

Badru's jaw twitched as he glanced at Balor, but that was the only emotion he showed as Nesbit read the charges. She wished he'd give her a sign, any sign, that he believed her. She stared at him, willing with every bit of her being for him to realize that this was a lie and a travesty.

But she wasn't blind to the hatred in the eyes of the men behind her. Their anger was like a palpable thing prowling the edges of the room.

Herin was right, these men believed her guilty. Even if Badru knew she wasn't, what could he do?

"Balor, stand." Badru leaned forward, watching the man like a desert cat studying its prey.

"Most honored leader." He bowed as he stepped forward, wheezing slightly from the effort of walking the five steps from where he'd been seated.

This was the man who was supposed to have subdued her? She wanted to laugh, but didn't.

"Tell me, how did you discover the two?"

K'lrsa held Badru's gaze as Balor described coming to her door in the middle of the night to check that the Daliph's orders, that K'lrsa be protected at all times, were being followed. He played to the crowd as he described how shocked he was when no one was there outside her door and how he heard noises coming from inside the room.

"Animal noises," he said, looking out at the crowd with a meaningful glance at K'lrsa in her barely-there clothing. "The savage screams of a wanton woman. I entered immediately and…" He widened his eyes, licking his fat little lips as he paused for effect. The crowd hung on his every word, eager to hear what he'd found.

"Stop."

Balor turned back to Badru, his open jaw nestled into his fat little neck.

"Did you knock or in any other way announce your presence before you barged into the room of my dorana?"

Balor choked at the look of fury on Badru's face. "N-no, most honored leader. There was no time. I entered immediately."

Badru frowned at him. "It didn't occur to you that she might be with me?"

"With you, most honored leader? Why would you have been there?"

Badru raised one elegant eyebrow as Balor mopped at his sweaty forehead. "She is my dorana."

The crowd whispered like a late spring storm wind.

"But...she's...you'd never..." Balor looked around the room, but whoever he was looking for either wasn't there or refused to meet his eyes.

Badru leaned back in his chair, but no one was fooled by his casual pose. He was as relaxed as a desert cat on the prowl. "K'lrsa, my love, have I ever visited you in your rooms?"

Herin hissed under her breath, but K'lrsa kept her gaze focused on Badru. "Yes. More than once."

The whisper of the crowd grew to a raging gale that swirled around them.

Badru raised his hand and they were once more silent. "At night?"

"Yes."

He glanced towards Balor who looked on the point of fainting. "Did I ever tell you or anyone else when these visits might be?"

"No." She didn't dare hope, but she felt a small fluttering in her stomach. He believed her and he was going to show everyone, show them that she'd never betray him, that Balor was lying.

Badru stood and glared down at Balor, his voice as soft and bright as a dagger. "And yet I'm to believe that Balor found you consorting with one of your poradoma in the middle of your rooms for anyone to see?"

He slowly looked around the room, stopping here or there for an extra moment. K'lrsa didn't recognize most of the people he looked at, but he finished with a long, angry glare at Herin.

She glared right back at him, their eyes meeting like locked swords.

"Interesting." Badru once more lounged in his chair. "Please continue your *tale*, Balor."

Balor trembled, barely able to force the first few words out and then continued in a mad rush as he described leaping into the room and finding them naked in the middle of the room. He said he grabbed Tarum's hair and slit his throat before the man could react and then hit K'lrsa, knocking her out as she cried over her lover's dead body.

He tried to play to the crowd, but no one was willing to anger Badru by responding and he ended up rushing through to the end and standing before Badru, head down, sides heaving as he breathed heavily.

Badru nodded slowly. "So she was easy to subdue then?"

"Oh very easy, most honored leader. She is a woman after all. Barely more than a girl."

Badru almost smiled at that, but caught himself in time to smooth the expression from his face again. "And you say she was naked when you found her?"

"Yes, most honored leader. Naked and entwined with..."

Badru waved him to silence and glared at the crowd who were once more whispering among one another like scandalized grandmothers.

Badru pursed his lips. "And you subdued her?"

"I did, most honored leader."

"Easily?"

"Yes, most honored leader." Balor mopped at his forehead again, the underarms of his robe now stained a darker green from his sweat.

Badru shook his head. "Are you sure it was K'lrsa you found?"

Balor stared at him, confused.

"I've seen K'lrsa fight. And I've seen you walk five steps to the middle of this room." He leaned forward. "And if I were a betting man, my money would be on her."

Balor stood up straighter, puffing out his chest. "How dare you."

Badru waved him to silence. "Nesbit."

The old man shuffled forward with a slight bow. "Yes, most honored leader."

"What is the penalty for giving false witness to the Daliph?"

Balor sputtered and choked, but couldn't manage any words. Badru glared at him until he went silent once more.

"Nesbit?"

"Death, most honored leader."

Badru nodded slowly as the sound of the crowd whispering and arguing blew around the room like the first hints of a desert sandstorm.

"She confessed," Balor shouted, swaying on his feet.

"To whom?"

"To Herin." Balor turned to look at Herin.

She met his gaze and then looked up to Badru, her expression flat.

Badru shook his head. "Don't bother, grandmother. I'd rather not have to kill you today."

Herin made a slight choking sound, but otherwise didn't react to his comment.

Badru stood and paced the dais, his hands clasped behind his back.

He was too relaxed, too at ease. He'd already planned this out, all of it. He was just play-acting for the crowd.

A part of her was furious that he hadn't found a way to tell her beforehand, another part in awe that he could play everyone so well.

"We have a dilemma. The penalty for a dorana betraying her Daliph is death. And the penalty for providing false witness is death. Now, either K'lrsa has betrayed me or Balor is lying to me. One is innocent, one is guilty. But which?"

He turned to study them and then shrugged casually. "I guess I could just kill them both."

Balor stumbled backward.

Badru started pacing again. "No. That wouldn't be fair. And I can't pardon them both, because I'd pardon the guilty one if I did that..."

He paused once more, staring out across the room, but not making eye contact with anyone.

The silence in the room was like a heavy cloak, hot and smothering.

Badru pursed his lips and nodded to himself. He clapped his hands together, the sound echoing around the silent space. "That's it! Balor, you claim to have subdued this woman when you found her last night. You will do so again now. Or you will die."

Balor stared at him, confused. K'lrsa tried to hide the small seed of hope growing inside her.

"Most honored leader?"

"I propose a battle to the death."

The roar of the crowd grew and grew, whipping around the room until K'lrsa covered her ears against the cacophony of sound.

K'lrsa glanced at Herin. She was watching Badru, a slight smile on her lips. He nodded towards her before roaring for silence.

Nesbit cleared his throat and spoke into the quiet. "Most honored leader? How do you propose this be done?"

Badru barely spared him a glance, speaking to the crowd instead. "It is written in our laws that anyone accused of a crime that is punishable by death may, with the permission of the Daliph, defend himself in hand-to-hand combat. Is this correct, Nesbit?"

"Yes, most honored leader. But who would Balor fight?"

"K'lrsa, of course. She defends herself, he defends himself. The victor lives, the loser dies."

Nesbit shook his head. "The law specifically says he, not she."

Badru waved Nesbit's concern away. "A technicality. All of our laws say he, Nesbit." He raised his voice to address the crowd. "I declare that K'lrsa dan V'na of the White Horse

Tribe shall fight Balor Lenivano to the death and whosoever survives shall be pardoned of all charges against them. So be it."

As everyone stared at him in silence, Badru shouted. "Clear a space. The fight begins now."

Balor lurched forward, crawling up the steps of the dais. A guard blocked him from reaching Badru. "Please, most honored leader, I need at least a candlemark to prepare."

"Did you have a candlemark to prepare last night, Balor? Did you sit outside listening to the animal sounds for a candlemark as you *prepared* yourself?"

More than one man in the crowd chuckled at the way Badru asked the question.

Balor trembled. "No."

"Then you don't need one now. The fight will start immediately."

Balor collapsed.

<u>80</u>

Sayel and Morlen flanked K'lrsa as men shoved the four tables nearest the dais away to clear enough space for K'lrsa and Balor to fight. Even then it was only a space fifteen paces by fifteen paces wide, leaving barely enough room for her to use the hundred and five attacks.

Herin approached them, but Morlen stepped in her way.

"What's this?" She glared him down, arms crossed across her chest, but he held his ground.

Sayel answered, "You were going to testify against her." He swallowed heavily before adding, "You can't be trusted."

Herin laughed, the sound like a crypt door opening. She opened her mouth to say more but then turned her back on them instead and studied the crowd.

Men crowded forward like a swarm of locusts jostling for the best view, some even standing on tables. When they saw Herin, most turned aside, finding somewhere else to watch from so that K'lrsa stood in a clear space five paces wide.

She was glad—so many people in such a tight space made her palms sweat and heart race.

Once the space was ready, everyone settled into an expectant hum, waiting.

Nesbit stepped to the center of the cleared area. "Combatants, step forward."

K'lrsa moved to stand in front of him, Balor next to her. Sayel, Morlen, and Herin sat on the steps of the dais, the space they'd just vacated filling in with the grel-like observers—all avid interest, waiting for blood and death.

Nesbit cleared his throat and raised his hands toward the ceiling. "I call on the gods of land and sea to witness this combat. May they guide the hand of the man, or woman, who is innocent and give them victory this day."

He lowered his hands. "This is a battle to the death. May only he, or she, who is true of heart walk out of this circle alive. Shake hands."

K'lrsa didn't want to touch Balor, but he grabbed her hand before she could back away. He pulled her close, their clasped hands pressed between his ample belly and her slim frame.

His pupils were tiny dots, his skin sheened with sweat. As he whispered in her ear, she caught the scent of spoiled milk. "You lose either way."

K'lrsa pulled free, shaking. She didn't want to fight this man, she just wanted to leave. To go home and get away from all of this.

"Begin."

Balor rushed her, his arms held wide as he growled under his breath, his lips stretched tight in a pained smile.

K'lrsa scrambled away. She managed to avoid his initial charge, but he immediately came after her again, sucking air in and out of his lungs in loud, pained gasps. This time he managed to grab her and clutch her to his chest.

He squeezed, his massive, fat arms wrapping around her like one of those desert snakes that crush their prey before slowly consuming them.

K'lrsa struggled, frantic to escape as he pressed tighter and tighter. Breath fled her lungs as her bones ground together.

She frantically sought the warrior's version of the Core. And found it, barely.

She almost fell out of it again when she saw Balor through her spirit eye. Blackness laced his flesh, lending him strength as it slowly corrupted his body. Already the darkness wrapped around his heart, lungs, and brain.

Whatever it was, it was killing him, but until it did, he'd be as strong as ten men.

"Lady Moon and Father Sun, help me."

Dots danced in her vision, threatening to pull her back from the Core.

She fought back, knowing that if she lost her focus she was dead.

The blackness was everywhere, filling Balor's body. Not only did it strengthen him but it protected him from any pain as well.

It filled his entire body.

Except for one place—his toes. They still shone with the white of a normal spirit.

K'lrsa stomped her heel down hard on his right foot.

He shivered, but continued to tighten his grip. She stomped again. And again.

And again. Until he finally eased his grip and she was able to squirm away from him.

"What did you take?" she hissed, circling him.

His smile turned to a grimace as the poison started to burn like fire through his veins, turning from black to red in K'lrsa's vision.

"Herin." K'lrsa dodged to the side as Balor lunged for her. "He's taken something. Find the Core. See for yourself."

Balor came for her yet again, his steps now slowed by the poison burning its way through his body.

If she could just avoid him long enough, he'd die and she'd win.

"Attack him, you coward," someone shouted.

"Stop running."

"She can't. She knows she'll lose."

"She's scared."

"Balor told the truth."

The voices spiraled higher and higher—accusing and angry—buzzing around the room like a swarm of angry wasps.

K'lrsa came too close to the edge of the crowd and someone shoved her from behind, propelling her into Balor's grasp. He grabbed her forearm; his hands crushed her bones like soft cheese.

She screamed.

This was it. The end. He'd kill her now.

But Balor swayed, unable to move as the poison raged through his body, an inferno to her spirit vision.

The crowd shouted, blaming her, hating her.

She could wait, watch as Balor collapsed at her feet.

But they'd never accept that. They'd never believe she'd won.

Balor was right. She lost either way.

If she fought him, he'd crush her.

If she waited for him to die, the crowd would turn against her and she'd still lose

Balor's grip slackened just enough for her to pull free as he struggled to keep from screaming, the poison burning inside his skull.

Before he could collapse, she stepped back and swung her left leg high, aiming at his head.

Her foot connected and the sound of shattered bone echoed through the room.

Balor fell dead at her feet as K'lrsa swallowed the scream of agony that threatened to claw its way out of her throat.

The shattering sound hadn't been from Balor—it was her foot, the bones bursting into little bits as she impacted with a skull as solid as a brick wall.

K'lrsa collapsed to the ground, curled upon herself in pain. The Core disappeared. The roar of the crowd crashed down upon her like an early spring storm—violent and dangerous— and pounded her into the floor.

Balor lay before her, dead.

She'd won.

Or had she?

81

Garzel and Herin were by her side immediately. Garzel scooped her up and they headed for the door, Herin shoving everyone out of the way, not even waiting for them to see who she was and step aside.

"Wait. Where are you going?" Sayel followed, trying to stop them, but Herin and Garzel ignored him, continuing their relentless pace.

K'lrsa was in too much pain to care. She just wanted to be somewhere safe. And quiet. Away from all these men and their anger that threatened to turn on her at any moment.

She'd won, but their anger was like a living, breathing creature pacing the edges of the room with eyes like banked coals ready to burst into flame at the slightest provocation.

By some miracle, they reached the hallway without anyone stopping them. K'lrsa drew large gulps of air into her lungs and closed her eyes against the pain.

"This way." Herin led them to the left, away from K'lrsa's rooms.

"Where are you taking her?" Sayel demanded. He rushed ahead, blocking their path with his bulk.

"Somewhere safe." Herin spat the words, trying to go around Sayel.

"No. I won't let you. She's my dorana. Give her to me."

Sayel was right. She didn't know what Herin was capable of. The woman would've gladly watched her beheaded not a candlemark ago.

K'lrsa pushed against Garzel's chest with her good arm. "Let me down. Let me go with Sayel."

"We don't have time for this, you fools." Herin glanced back towards the audience chamber where men were starting to trickle out into the hallway. "Move. We'll talk as we go."

Sayel stepped aside and they started down the hallway once more, Herin and Garzel almost running as Sayel trailed along behind them.

"Where are you taking her?" he demanded.

"Somewhere private."

"Why?"

Herin whirled on him. "To heal her arm and foot before it's too late."

Sayel glanced at K'lrsa's injured arm, noting how the skin sagged downward where Balor had pulverized the bones. He glanced towards her foot.

And then he turned on Herin, shaking his head, unable to speak, the whites of his eyes bright against his dark skin. "No...How?...You're..."

"We don't have time for this, Sayel." Herin glanced down the hallway once more.

K'lrsa rested her head against Garzel's chest, in so much pain she could barely keep her eyes open. "What is it, Sayel? Just let her help me, please."

He stepped close, glancing around. "You don't understand, my dorana. Your wounds are beyond healing. If..." He licked his lips. "If Herin says she can heal you, it's because...because she's, they're...death walkers." He hissed the last two words.

K'lrsa's eyes flew open and she looked back and forth between Herin and Garzel. "Are you?"

Herin put her nose to K'lrsa's, her eyes vast pools of emptiness. "Listen to me, you foolish little girl. No one in that room realizes what just happened. They don't know that Balor took Lover's Bane before that match. They don't realize that you shattered your arm and your foot fighting him. Which means we can heal you before they do and you'll be whole once more.

"But if we stand out here in this hallway until enough witnesses see the truth, then you're struck with your injuries forever. Tell me, *Rider*, what good will you be with no arm and no foot?"

K'lrsa blinked for a moment, absorbing Herin's words. "None. I couldn't hunt, couldn't ride."

"Exactly. So can we go now, *Princess*?"

K'lrsa nodded.

"Wait." Sayel stepped forward, searching K'lrsa's face. "You can't let them do this to you, my dorana. You'll be tainted forever."

She smiled weakly, resting her head against Garzel's chest, as she struggled against the pain. "I already am, Sayel."

When he still wouldn't move, she forced herself to meet his gaze. "Don't you see? They already healed me once. Let them heal me again."

While Sayel was absorbing her words, Herin and Garzel took off, running down the hallways, no longer caring if anyone saw them.

Sayel followed, struggling to keep up.

———————————

Herin led them down a series of back staircases and dark hallways that seemed to never end, shoving silent slaves with fearful eyes out of the way.

At last, they emerged in a narrow hallway that led to the room where Barkley and Harley had died.

"Paren, get me the prisoner from yesterday," Herin demanded as they rushed into the room.

A large man with a dark goatee stood from the table where he'd been playing dice with two other guards. "Why? Gonna slice him up more?"

"What I do with him is no business of yours. Get him. Now."

The man spat to the side before lumbering down the dark hallway where the prisoners were kept. He returned a few moments later with a filthy man bound in chains at his wrists and ankles. "Need him back by mornin' so they can hang 'im."

"I know."

The prisoner tried to turn back, but Sayel grabbed him and pulled him along as Herin and Garzel led the way down another series of dark hallways and staircases.

At last, they reached a room carved from black rock, two guttering torches, one on each wall, the only source of light. It made K'lrsa long for sunshine and open spaces.

Two beds filled most of the room, one along each wall. Opposite the door sat a small table with two chairs—one with a broken leg that made it tilt at a dangerous angle. In the corner, a faded wooden cabinet stood, ready to collapse in on itself at any moment.

Garzel placed K'lrsa on the right-hand bed and gestured for Sayel to place the prisoner on the other. The prisoner curled in on himself, watching them all with angry brown eyes, but he didn't speak.

K'lrsa wondered if he was another who'd had his tongue removed.

He had two fresh white bandages on his dirty skin—one on his arm, one on his thigh.

Herin opened the cupboard and placed black candles and dark metal instruments on the table. They clanged together, the sound echoing off the ceiling. The tools were so old and dirty they seemed to absorb the light from the torches.

K'lrsa wanted to flee, but her wounds were too painful. And Herin was right. She needed her arm and her foot. No one survived in the tribes if they couldn't care for themselves.

And Badru...what would Badru want with her if she was maimed?

Sayel leaned against the closed door. "You're death walkers..." He shook his head. "I would've never believed..."

Herin glanced at him. "Oh, please, Sayel. Quit acting like I just killed your favorite puppy."

He frowned at her, but didn't say anything more.

"What are you going to do, Herin? How does it work? Why do you need this man?" K'lrsa spoke to distract herself from the throbbing, aching pain of her wounds.

"Must you always question?"

K'lrsa held her gaze.

"Fine. Sayel is right, this is death walker magic. And death walker magic requires balance. You can't just heal someone. Or raise them from the dead. You have to transfer the injury. Or the death."

"So you're going to give that man my injuries?"

"Yes."

She glanced at the man's fresh bandages once more. "Like you did last night."

Herin nodded as she arranged the candles around a dark black bowl.

K'lrsa shook her head. "No. I won't let you do it."

She didn't know how she'd survive without her arm or her foot, but she wasn't going to inflict those injuries on someone else just so she could be whole and healthy.

"Pzah, girl. Not like he's going to worry about it where he's going. He's sentenced to death. He'll hang tomorrow. So we can heal you and you can live your life without a shattered arm and foot and he'll be in pain for less than a day. Or you can sit there all noble and perfect and never walk again and this man will still die tomorrow."

K'lrsa glanced at the prisoner and back at Herin.

Herin added, "He killed a young boy. For sport."

Did that change things? Did that mean he deserved this?

She shook her head again. He might be dying tomorrow. He might be a horrible person who deserved to be punished. But she couldn't do it. She couldn't let another pay for her choices.

Herin looked to Garzel. He shrugged.

Before K'lrsa could react, Garzel hit her on the head with the hilt of his knife.

Her world went black.

82

K'lrsa awoke, expecting to have a headache, but she felt great. Famished, but otherwise fine.

"Eat." Herin shoved a plate of food into her hands and K'lrsa started eating.

She kept eating until the entire plate of food was empty and she was licking the crumbs from her fingers. "I'm sorry. Did any of you want any?" she asked, looking around the room at last.

"No. It was all for you. Healing is hungry work." Herin was seated at the table, Garzel stationed behind her as always.

Sayel sat on the floor, blocking the door. The prisoner slept on the other bed, his face flushed as he muttered and cried in his sleep, his arm now bound tight with wrappings.

"He'll be fine. I gave him milk of poppy."

"He isn't fine, Herin. He has four wounds that should be mine."

"Pzah, girl. Can't you just be grateful for once?"

K'lrsa sat forward. "Grateful? Should I thank you for last night? You healed me so I couldn't prove that Tarum had attacked me. You're the reason I was going to be put to death today. And you want me to be grateful?"

Herin let out a deep sigh. "I did it to protect Badru. See how well that worked. Foolish, love-sick boy. He ruined everything."

"No he didn't. He found a way to save me and not lose the support of his people."

"Did he?"

K'lrsa blinked, taken aback by Herin's question. "Yes?"

Herin shook her head. "When are you going to learn that men act from belief not facts you shove in their face? Those who believed Balor's story still do. Nothing you did or said in that room was ever going to change their minds."

"How can they think Balor subdued me? He could barely walk to the dais!"

"You're a woman."

"But I fought him. I…"

Herin pinched the bridge of her nose and closed her eyes as if she was in intense pain.

"So Badru's still in danger?"

Herin nodded. "As long as you're alive, yes."

"Then I need to leave. I wanted to go home anyway. Let me go, now. I'll saddle up Fallion and ride out the gates and never come back."

Herin shook her head. "Too late. You leave now, you're running because you're guilty. No. You have to stay right here by Badru's side, may the Lady help us all."

They sat for a long time in silence, Sayel studying a crack in the floor like it held all the answers to the universe, Herin and Garzel having a private conversation of glances and touches.

K'lrsa wondering how she was ever going to get home to save her people.

At last, K'lrsa asked, "How did you learn to do it, Herin?"

"What?"

"Death-walker magic."

Herin traced her finger through a pool of water, drawing the same shape over and over again. "The Daliph."

"Badru?"

Herin shook her head. "The former Daliph."

Sayel looked up. "Why would he do that? Why would he teach you that?"

She laughed. "He didn't mean to." She met Sayel's accusing glare. "But if you watch something done often enough, you figure it out for yourself."

"What do you mean?" K'lrsa frowned, remembering all the horrible stories she'd heard about the former Daliph. "Did he heal people?"

Garzel rested his hand on Herin's shoulder and she reached up to squeeze it. "No. Not exactly." She sighed deeply. "He killed people. Then brought them back so he could kill them again. And again."

Herin studied the table, not looking at either of them. "He liked to break people, hurt them until they lost themselves and would do anything he asked. He'd spend days on someone, finding that perfect spot where they'd do anything he wanted, but weren't so far gone as to be useless."

She shrugged. "Seems I wasn't so easy to break." She swallowed, still staring at the table, her finger frozen mid-way through the shape she'd been drawing. "He cut me. He burned me. He hit me. See?"

Herin raised the hem of her robe to reveal skin crisscrossed with faint scars. There wasn't a single spot that didn't have at least one mark.

She smiled, an ugly smile full of hurt. "It never worked. I was still as angry, as defiant as ever." She flexed her hands, studying the stumps of her fingers.

"He didn't want an ugly bed slave, so when he was done with his entertainment for the day he had his death walkers heal me. I watched. And I learned."

"But your fingers...he never healed those?"

Herin flexed her hand before her eyes. "Couldn't. If you remove something from the body, it stays removed. That's why Garzel still has no tongue. And why Daliphs behead their enemies."

Sayel spoke up. "You said he liked to kill people and bring them back."

Herin met his eyes and nodded.

"Do you know how to do that, too?" Sayel trembled.

Herin turned away from him and looked back to K'lrsa. "When the Daliph realized that he couldn't hurt me enough to break me, he turned his attentions to Garzel.

"At first he just tortured Garzel the way he'd tortured me."

Garzel quietly moved to sit in the broken chair, delicately balancing his weight so the broken leg didn't tip him onto the ground. He reached across the table and held Herin's hand.

She stared into his eyes as she continued. "When that didn't work, he slit his throat in a fit of anger."

A chill ran down K'lrsa's spine.

Herin continued, still staring at Garzel. "I still remember sobbing and holding him in my lap as the blood pumped out of his neck and he died in my arms. I cried the entire day. I wouldn't eat, I wouldn't speak."

Her jaw twitched as she clenched her teeth. "I tried to kill myself that night, but failed. The next morning they brought Garzel back to me. I was so happy, so overjoyed, I couldn't hide it."

She squeezed Garzel's hand and looked down at the table. "The next day, the Daliph killed him again.

"And again every day after."

Herin's voice was barely a whisper. Garzel wiped a tear away from her eye with his free hand.

K'lrsa shivered. "Didn't you…? At some point, didn't…?"

Herin glared at her. "Didn't I stop caring? Stop crying? Stop reacting?" She laughed. "I wish."

She reached her other hand across the table to hold both of Garzel's in her own. "Garzel was sent to me by the Lady Moon the same way Badru was sent to you. He's my one true mate. My center. So, no. It never stopped hurting to lose him. And never ceased to make me smile to get him back."

She stood, shaking away her memories. "See, child. Sometimes it can be the worst possible fate to find that one true love. Love can lead you to destruction just as easily at it leads you to salvation."

Herin checked on the prisoner as she continued, "It's why I didn't want you to stay. I knew what the bond between you and Badru could do and I didn't want that for him."

K'lrsa sat forward. "But what about the positives? What about having your equal at your side? Someone who will support and love you through anything? What about knowing that you've found your other half? That you're not alone in this world?"

Herin chuckled. "How's that worked for you both so far?"

K'lrsa frowned. "We're good for each other, Herin. I wouldn't have survived here this long without him."

"You've caused his downfall."

K'lrsa shook her head, trying to deny the truth of Herin's words. "No I haven't. He's still the Daliph."

"For how long? Because of you, his enemies felt strong enough to move against him last night."

K'lrsa shook her head in denial.

Herin raised an eyebrow. "They would've never dared something like that if they didn't think he was weak."

"You're wrong. And they failed today. That can only make him stronger."

She glanced around the room, but Sayel, Herin, and Garzel all looked skeptical. "Badru handled it well. He showed them that they couldn't force his hand. That he's smart and clever and knows more than they do."

Herin laughed. "You don't understand this world, child. These men."

"I'm not a fool."

Herin pinched the bridge of her nose. "No, you're not. You're just young and naïve. We've all been there at some point. Fortunately, time eventually heals that particular affliction. As long as you survive long enough.

"Until it does, I suggest you talk less and listen more. Sayel, take her back to her rooms."

K'lrsa wanted to say more, but Herin raised an eyebrow, daring K'lrsa to ignore her advice.

K'lrsa bowed her head and followed Sayel out of the room.

He led her back through the series of dark and twisty hallways, lost in his own thoughts, doubt and worry clouding his face.

K'lrsa walked next to him wondering if Herin was right. Had she caused Badru's downfall? And, if so, what did that mean?

For him.

And for her.

83

When they reached her rooms, Morlen was there waiting. He rushed forward, searching her face and her body for signs of injury. "You're well, my dorana?"

"I am, Morlen. Thank you."

She surprised herself with the small surge of affection she felt for the man. She glanced back and forth between Sayel and Morlen realizing that she actually liked these men assigned to turn her into something she'd never be. Somehow they'd become like uncles to her.

How bizarre.

Sayel pushed him towards the door. "I'll stay here. You go, get rest. I want either you or me by her side at all times from now on."

Morlen nodded and left, leaving K'lrsa alone with Sayel who proceeded to pace back and forth. He was such a big man he seemed to take up the entire room.

"Sayel, stop. What's wrong with you?"

He turned to her. "She's an abomination."

"Who?"

"Herin. And Garzel. Death walkers. They pervert the natural order." He glanced at her arm and then away.

"They didn't want to be."

He shook his head. "They had a choice. Maybe not in what the Daliph did to them. But they chose to use what they learned for themselves. They chose to..."

341

"To heal me. To save me from Badru's enemies."

He dropped onto the stone bench by the window. "I know. And that's what makes this so hard."

"Makes what so hard?"

He looked up at her, his eyes sad. "I have to tell the temple."

A chill ran down her spine. "What will they do when you tell them, Sayel?"

He looked away, biting his lip. "Kill them. Such knowledge is forbidden and the only way to eliminate it is to eliminate those who know."

He studied his hands, not meeting her eyes.

"Is that all they'll do?"

"No. They'll…they'll kill you, too. And me."

K'lrsa approached Sayel carefully, as if she was face-to-face with an adder snake coiled to strike at the slightest movement. "Is that best, Sayel? What will happen to Badru if they kill Herin, Garzel, me, and you? What will happen to the Daliphate?"

"I don't know, but I have to tell them." He buried his face in his hands.

K'lrsa sat down next to him and rested her hand on his back.

He looked at her, tears in his eyes. "I took vows, K'lrsa. Vows to protect the Daliphate. Vows to the temple."

She nodded, waiting.

Sayel stared down at his hands, his forehead a wrinkle of conflicting emotions.

She knew she couldn't let him tell, but she wasn't sure what she'd do to stop him.

Could she kill Sayel if it meant protecting herself? And Badru?

She didn't know.

———————

They were still sitting there side-by-side when Badru barged into the room without even knocking. He immediately ran to

K'lrsa, took her hands in his, and kissed them. "You're unharmed. I thought...watching you..."

She nodded slightly, glancing to the two guards behind him. Sayel had tensed at Badru's arrival, a thrum of energy racing through his body, his leg shuddering against K'lrsa's.

"Badru, can we speak in private?"

He glanced back at his guards. "Wait outside."

They hesitated—the first time she'd ever seen anyone hesitate to follow his orders—but they left.

"What is it, my love? What did you want to tell me?"

K'lrsa let Sayel speak. She knew how badly he wanted to tell his secret.

"Most honored leader, K'lrsa *was* injured in the fight."

Badru looked back and forth between them. "How? Where?"

"Balor crushed my arm. And when I kicked him, it broke the bones in my foot."

Badru half-smiled. He took her hands in his and made a point of examining each arm. "I don't see any injuries now. Surely you weren't miraculously healed."

K'lrsa and Sayel looked at one another.

Badru, noting the silence, tensed. "K'lrsa, how were you healed?"

He knew. Or suspected.

She met his eyes. "Herin. She's a..."

He stepped away from her, shaking his head slightly. "Don't. No. I don't want to know this."

K'lrsa stood and took his hands in hers. "You have to, Badru. Herin is a death walker. So is Garzel. They healed my wounds last night and again today after the fight."

His hands trembled in hers. He looked around the room, shaking his head. "Abominations. They're both abominations."

He pulled away and turned towards the wall, his shoulders shaking.

"There's more, Badru."

"More? What else could there possibly be? You tell me that my grandmother and her husband, the only two people I've known and loved my whole life, are death walkers. What more can there be?"

She took a deep breath and glanced back at Sayel before she spoke again. "I don't know for sure, but I think Herin used death walker magic to bring Lodie back to life."

Badru turned to stare at her, his eyes wide, his mouth hanging open. Sayel choked behind her, but she only had eyes for Badru.

"So Herin knows enough to bring someone back from the dead? It's not just healing, it's..." He clenched his fists. "It makes sense."

He paced the room. "Death walker magic requires balance. A life for a life." He turned on K'lrsa. "Who did she use to heal you?"

"A prisoner sentenced to death tomorrow." K'lrsa wanted to reach out to him, but she was scared by the look in his eyes and the way his hands kept clenching and unclenching as he walked back and forth, faster and faster.

He kept pacing the room as they all wondered the same thing. *Who had she killed to save Lodie?*

"What shall we do, most honored leader?" Sayel looked surprisingly small for such a large man.

Badru met Sayel's eyes. "You know as well as I do. They have to die."

As Sayel nodded, the door opened and Herin entered with Garzel.

Badru drew his sword and rushed her.

84

Herin danced to the side, more spry and limber than K'lrsa had thought possible. "Pzah, boy. Don't be a fool."

Garzel slammed the door before the guards could see. He drew his own sword and Badru charged him. The clash of their swords echoed throughout the room as Garzel threw Badru back.

Badru glared at Herin, his face twisted with pain. "You're an abomination."

Herin shrugged, moving carefully to keep Garzel between them. "I know some of what the death walkers know. It doesn't make me one. I'm not part of their order."

"But you know what they know. You have to die."

"If you kill me, you have to kill her, too."

A tremor ran through Badru's arm and he lowered the sword. "You healed K'lrsa."

"Yes. I saved the girl you love. You're welcome." She seated herself on the seat in front of the small mirror. "Without me some doctor somewhere would be cutting her arm off right now. And her foot. Would you rather I'd left her to that fate?"

He raised the sword slightly and Garzel stepped forward, his own sword held at the ready. "Whose life did you take to save Lodie's?"

Herin shook her head.

"Grandmother. Whose life did you take?"

She glared at him. "L'dia was my sister. She sacrificed everything to save me. Do you think I could just sit there and watch her die after all those years? After what he did to her because of me?"

"Whose life did you take?" Badru emphasized each word.

Herin waved her hand at him. "Put your sword away, boy. We don't have time for this."

Badru's fingers turned white where they gripped the sword hilt. "I'm the Daliph, woman."

"And I'm your grandmother. The only reason you stand where you are today is because of me. So put your cursed sword away."

"I would've managed without you." He said the words, but there was no conviction behind them.

Herin laughed, the sound filling the room like harsh sunlight and grel ready to feast. "Boy, you'd've never lasted long enough to become Daliph if it weren't for me, let alone stayed Daliph for more than a day. Now put that sword away so we can plan how you're going to live through the night."

Badru put the sword away, but he shook his head. "You go too far, old woman. You are my grandmother and for that I'll spare your life and protect you from the temple. But you've lied to me too many times for me to trust you now."

Herin frowned, her face a mass of wrinkles, but she didn't speak or act as he stepped to the door and called in his guards.

"Escort my grandmother and her poradom to her rooms. Station a guard. She's not to leave without my express permission."

Herin stood slowly. "Badru, don't be a fool."

He whirled on her like a desert windstorm. "I am your Daliph, woman. Treat me as such."

Herin smirked and bowed her head. Just a bit, but she did bow it. "Very well. You know where to find me when you need me."

"I won't."

Herin raised an eyebrow, but she didn't say anything more.

She strode from the room with Garzel trailing along behind, her head held high, never looking back.

Sayel followed them out with one final glance at K'lrsa. She hoped he'd accept Badru's decision in this.

85

K'lrsa shivered. She didn't like Herin and she didn't doubt that the woman would lie, cheat, and kill if she had to, but she suspected that Herin was probably the only one of them who saw the truth of their situation.

She took Badru's arm in hers. "Are you sure that was wise?"

"Yes. It's time I stepped out from under her shadow. My subjects have never liked that I accepted counsel from a woman. And a foreigner at that."

"Like me."

He glanced at her and away again. "It's different."

"Because you'd never accept my counsel?"

Badru frowned, but didn't answer.

K'lrsa let go of his arm and walked over to the window. "I need to leave, Badru. As long as I'm here, they'll use me against you."

"No."

"Badru."

"No. I can't lose you. Not right now. Please, K'lrsa. You're the only one I have left."

She crossed her arms tight against her chest. "I have to go back to my family, Badru."

"No." The muscle in his jaw twitched as he clenched his jaw. "I forbid it."

She laughed, a short, bitter laugh of disbelief. This again. "You forbid it? I'm a free woman, Badru. You freed me."

"You're still my dorana." He wouldn't look at her. He stared at a spot on the floor like a stubborn child.

"I see." Fury burned through her bones like fire. K'lrsa turned away and studied the beautiful purple flowers in the window sill—they too were where they didn't belong.

Badru grabbed her shoulders and pressed his body to hers. "It's not like that, K'lrsa. I need you. I love you."

She twisted away from him. "No. You don't love me. You don't know what it means to love someone. If you did, you'd let me make my own choices instead of trying to hold me here against my will."

His blue eyes pleaded with her to understand.

"I have to go, Badru. Someone tried to kill me last night. And most of the people in that room today think you should've finished the task. I don't belong here."

She grabbed his hands. "My family needs me."

"I need you." He pulled her close. "You belong at my side. Can't you see that? Don't you love me?"

"Of course I do."

"Then stay."

She shook her head. "No."

They stood there, staring at each other, neither one willing to give in. It was one of the hardest things K'lrsa had ever done to resist the pull she felt towards him. He was her true mate, sent to her by the Lady Moon. But she knew. She knew this is what had to happen.

She tried once more. "I swore a vow, Badru, to kill the man responsible for my father's death. I can't keep that vow if I stay here."

His face lit up with a smile. "That might not be true."

At her surprise, he raised a hand and continued, "I don't know yet, but I suspect…give me three days."

"Three days?"

He nodded. "Yes. Three days. And then you can leave with my blessing. I'll send men to escort you home. Three days. That's all I ask. Please?"

He took her hands and kissed the knuckles of each finger, staring into her eyes. She felt herself melting, her will weakening at his touch. "Three days. But then I leave no matter what."

"No matter what." Badru kissed her on the cheek and left, almost running from the room.

She didn't know what he thought would happen in three days. She didn't care.

She just knew that, finally, she was going home.

It was time.

86

The next morning, Morlen brought the *tiral* and her court attire when he came to dress her. She looked back and forth between Sayel and Morlen. She knew she couldn't wear the outfit Herin had forced on her the day before, but she didn't want to be bound by the *tiral* and *meza* either.

She'd had a small taste of freedom and she didn't want to lose it. "Must I?" she asked.

Sayel nodded. "I think it would be best, my dorana. The court is still on edge this morning. It would be best if you…"

"Acted proper?"

He nodded.

"Very well."

She let them dress her, not pleased, but resigned to three more days of suffering before she was once again free. Somehow knowing that it would end soon made it easier to bear.

When the doors to the audience chamber opened and the volume of conversation in the room hit her like a physical blow, K'lrsa was glad she'd listened to Sayel and Morlen. Her outfit was like armor; it deflected anger and judgement, letting the men see her in a role they understood.

The room was packed—there wasn't a single empty seat and men were pressed hip-to-hip at each table.

Badru stood, smiling down at her, the blue of his vest matching the blue of her topmost layer. She didn't believe for a moment that it was a coincidence. "K'lrsa, my love. Here, sit beside me."

The chair that had dominated the top of the dais was gone, replaced with a large lounging couch with room enough for two.

As she walked through the now-silent room, she ignored everyone except Badru. She focused on gliding along in the way Sayel had taught her, her steps shorter by half than her natural stride.

She heard whispered comments as she passed; the words "whore", "cheater", and "murderer" ghosted along in her steps, but she ignored them, refusing to let these little men bait her once more. As she ascended the steps to Badru's side, she caught the look on the youngest dorana's face—her ebony skin and bright green eyes twisted in hate.

It didn't matter. None of it did. All K'lrsa had to do was play her part for another three days and she could ride away from this place and never look back. She'd miss Badru, yes, but the rest of it? No.

As Badru leaned in to kiss her cheek, she whispered, "Is this wise?"

He nodded. "I have to show everyone that I believe you."

Sayel removed the *tiral* and K'lrsa took her place by Badru's side. She scanned the room without actually looking at anyone. So many men, packed so close together, their anger throbbing beneath the surface...

She closed her eyes, forcing herself into a light version of the hunter's Core, trying to block out how the ceiling pressed down upon her. The air was so thick it was hard to breath, the sound of so many voices like physical blows. She floated there, trance-like, outside of time, until Nesbit stepped forward and cleared his phlegmy throat.

"Most honored leader. Are you ready to begin today's audience?"

"I am, Nesbit. Call the first supplicant."

As Nesbit turned to the room, Badru leaned close and whispered, "Whatever happens next, you must remain silent."

K'lrsa frowned.

"Promise me, K'lrsa. This is important. Remember where we are."

She nodded, not happy, but resigned to act the proper dorana. For his sake.

And her own.

"I call forth K'var of the Black Horse Tribe."

K'lrsa tensed as K'var rose from a far table and strode to the base of the dais. He looked around the room as if he owned it, his multi-colored cloth on full display, worn as a belt.

"Daliph Badru." He bowed low, a slight smirk on his face. "A public meeting? You honor me."

The tone of his words said the exact opposite. A small stir ran through the room.

"K'var. I trust your journey here was a good one."

K'var raised an eyebrow. "Of course, Your Excellency. A true pleasure."

Once again there was a subtle rebuke in how he spoke even though each word was proper.

K'lrsa glared at the man and Badru dug his fingers into her wrist. She took a deep breath and focused her gaze on the stitching on the hem of her skirt, reminding herself that she mustn't speak, mustn't react.

"What brings you here today, K'var?"

He bowed low. "I ask for the assistance of the Toreem Daliphate to protect our mutual trade interests."

"What kind of assistance?"

K'var licked his lips and looked pointedly at K'lrsa before he responded. "It's a delicate matter, Your Excellency. Perhaps one we could discuss in private."

Badru shook his head. "No. If you want something from me, ask for it now. Or leave."

K'var raised an eyebrow as a murmur ran through the crowd. "We are allies, Your Excellency. Would you set that aside?"

"No. But I won't deal with you in secrecy either. Ask what you will, K'var, but do it here in front of witnesses or leave."

K'var's face flushed red before he controlled himself once more. He bowed low. "As you wish, Your Excellency." He turned to address the crowd, ignoring Badru as he raised his voice for all to hear. "The Black Horse Tribe has worked with the Toreem Daliphate for many years now. We have led your trading caravans across the Great Desert, where none can pass with safety unless escorted by one of the tribes. And through our efforts, and yours, we have brought prosperity to the Daliphate."

"And yourselves," Badru added.

K'var nodded to him. "Yes, we have been well-rewarded for our efforts. We, too, prosper."

He turned back to the room, making sure that every eye was on him. "The food on your tables, the clothes on your back. All of this is because of us, the Black Horse Tribe."

Badru tensed, but didn't interrupt.

"But the other tribes grow jealous. They see how we prosper and they envy us our wealth."

K'lrsa wanted to attack him for uttering such ridiculous lies. Like she or her tribe had ever wanted the silks and salts that K'var and his type valued so highly.

Badru gripped her wrist so tightly she knew she'd have a bruise.

"These tribes want to end our trading with the Daliphate." Men muttered to one another around the room, the buzz of their voices like a swarm of angry bees. "They would expel us from the tribes and take away our access to the desert. This would destroy us."

He turned back to Badru. "And you."

The buzz of anger grew, weaving its way around the room until the walls were practically vibrating with the tension.

Badru raised a hand and the room grew quiet once more, but the anger stayed, hanging heavy on the air. "Why is this our battle, K'var? You are responsible for your relationship with the other tribes, not us."

"If they attack us, they attack you."

Badru tilted his head to the side, but he didn't respond; the tension in the air increased with each word he spoke against K'var.

"What would you have us do, K'var?"

"Help us defeat them."

"How?"

K'var stepped forward, resting one foot on the bottom step of the dais. Everyone stiffened at the gesture and he quickly stepped back once more. "Give me five hundred troops and another two hundred swords."

K'lrsa gasped. Fortunately, Badru laughed at the same moment, hiding the sound. "And what could you possibly need five hundred troops and two hundreds swords for? Do you even have two hundred men to wield the swords you ask for?"

"We will kill them. Every man, woman, and child of the tribes that oppose us."

K'lrsa swayed in her seat. Badru glanced at her and away just as quickly. "And what of the fifty swords my grandfather already gave you?"

K'lrsa stared at him. Badru's grandfather had given the Black Horse Tribe swords? Why hadn't Badru told her about it before?

K'var bowed his head. "They've been invaluable, Your Excellency. They've allowed us to triumph in the small skirmishes that naturally arise between jealous tribes."

K'lrsa stared at him. What was he talking about? The tribes hadn't fought amongst one another for hundreds of years. What skirmishes?

And then she finally understood.

It hadn't been the Daliph's men who'd raided her tribe. It was the Black Horse Tribe, attacking their own, unprovoked.

Sayel grabbed her shoulders, holding her down in her seat. She bit the inside of her cheek to keep from speaking.

This wasn't the time. Or the place. She couldn't attack him, not in the full court garb of a dorana.

But as she stared down at K'var with his smug grin and arrogant posture, she realized something.

This man. This man of the tribes.

He was her enemy.

He and those like him were the source of the corruption. *He* was the reason her father was dead.

K'var continued talking, "If we want to win this battle, Your Excellency, we have to attack our enemies with overwhelming force. The tribes will gather on the next full moon. Without your help, we'll be banished. With your help, we'll eliminate our enemies and we can both continue to prosper."

"What of diplomacy, K'var? Can't you talk to or bargain with these tribes?"

There was an angry murmur around the room at Badru's suggestion.

"No." He stood taller. "They'd have us turn away from all trade. They'd rather scrape and scrabble, barely living, than trade with you or any other of the Daliphana."

"But surely you could reach a peace? Let them continue as they want and you continue as you have?"

K'var shook his head in an emphatic no. "They would never agree to that, Your Excellency. They believe that we have a sacred trust, that we must protect the desert from all foreigners." He met K'lrsa's eyes. "They are wrong, misguided fools, that believe in long-dead myths and gods."

K'lrsa glared at him, unable to respond in front of Badru's subjects. She knew she should look away, too, but she couldn't.

K'var's eyes narrowed as he studied her.

"Thank you, K'var. We'll consider your petition. Next supplicant."

K'var flinched at the casual dismissal. He turned towards the back of the room as if expecting someone to intervene on his behalf, but no one did.

"K'var. Back to your seat."

K'var glared at Badru, the look openly hostile, and turned away.

He didn't go back to his seat, though; he stormed out of the room, a handful of men at the table closest to the door following him out, each cloaked so that his face was hidden.

Badru tensed as he watched them leave, but he allowed Nesbit to call the next supplicant.

This man walked to the front of the dais, shaking but resolute.

"Pavel? What is it?"

The man looked at Badru and then away again.

"Most honored leader. I...I am here on behalf of a number of your poradoma. We...we believe Balor was poisoned yesterday. We accuse the one once known as K'lrsa dan V'na of the White Horse Tribe of cheating and we demand her life as forfeit."

The room erupted in a roar of noise in support of Pavel.

87

Badru raised his hand, demanding silence. It was a long time in coming, and when it did many of the men glared at Badru with sullen expressions.

"Nesbit?"

Nesbit shuffled forward. "Yes, most honored leader?"

"What are the rules of combat to the death?"

"My Daliph?"

Badru leaned forward. "The rules, Nesbit. Do they state what type of weapon the combatants are allowed?"

A small wave of sound raced through the room.

"No, my Daliph. The rules simply state that he who survives is the victor."

Badru looked back to Pavel. "There you go, Pavel. If K'lrsa did poison him, it was allowed and she won within the rules."

K'lrsa stared at Badru.

"Next supplicant."

Pavel stood at the base of the dais and stared up at Badru, his mouth slightly open. He'd obviously expected Badru to defend her or deny it. Not this.

Pavel returned to his seat, shoulders slumped, shaking his head slightly.

Others were equally stunned, muttering to one another.

K'lrsa looked around the room, noting how many men shifted in their seats, glaring at Badru and then away before he saw them.

He might think he'd ended this, but he hadn't.

She wished Herin were there. She'd know what to do.

88

K'lrsa spent two more candlemarks sitting at Badru's side as he listened to supplicants. None of the others were near as interesting as the first two and she spent most of the time lost in the hunter's version of the Core, trying to keep from screaming from the lack of air in the room and the feel of everyone's eyes on her while she wasn't allowed to look at any of them.

Badru left immediately after the last supplicant, with a slight squeeze of her hand but no look or kiss. As he walked through the double doors, a dozen men followed, each with at least two colors accenting their brown clothing, whispering urgently at his heels like dogs after a treat.

Sayel escorted K'lrsa back to her rooms and there she paced, wondering what Badru would decide about K'var's petition.

"He won't do it, will he, Sayel?" she pleaded.

Sayel turned back from staring out the window. "Do what, my dorana?"

"He won't give K'var the troops he requested, will he?"

Sayel chewed on his lip, his eyes sad. "Why wouldn't he, my dorana?"

"Because...it means the death of my tribe. If he helps K'var he'll sentence my people to die."

Sayel shrugged slightly. "And if he doesn't he'll sentence his own people to poverty and suffering."

"But he loves me."

Sayel frowned. "Yes."

"Then..."

She stopped at the expression on Sayel's face. "You don't think that matters? You don't think his love for me will change his decision?"

Sayel sat on the bench by the window, resting his hands on his belly. "I don't think it can, my dorana. Especially not now when Pavel has accused you of poisoning Balor. Badru has to make the decision that's right for his people not himself."

K'lrsa buried her face in her hands. "I should've killed him when I had the chance."

"K'var?"

"No, Badru."

Sayel flinched. "The Daliph? You would kill the Daliph?"

K'lrsa raised a hand to calm him, but then dropped it again. "That's why I came here, Sayel. To kill him because I believed he was responsible for the death of my father."

Sayel clutched at his chest as if he couldn't breathe. "Oh, my dorana. No. You..."

"I didn't do it, though, did I? I fell in love with him instead and convinced myself he wasn't responsible." She came to stand by his side, staring up at the mountain behind the palace, marveling once more at how strange this world was compared to her home. "I was wrong."

Sayel shook his head. "Wrong?"

She took a deep breath. "If I'd been strong enough to kill Badru, he wouldn't be here now to help K'var, and my people would be safe."

Sayel stood and paced the room, waving his hands in agitation. "No, no. Any Daliph would assist K'var. Those trade routes, my dorana. We must have them. They're all that we have. If the Black Horse Tribe is the only tribe that will trade with us, then we must protect them at all costs. Any Daliph would know this and do it."

He stopped. "If you had killed Badru, the troops would already be on their way. Any other Daliph would've met with K'var the day he arrived and sent him away by the next morning leading five hundred men ready to kill every member of the tribes if they had to. No, Badru is your only hope."

"But you just said that he has no choice in this."

Sayel chewed on his lip. "I don't think he does. But if there's any way to avoid this action, Badru will find it. As you said, he loves you. But you must trust him, my dorana. You must."

She nodded, but she wasn't sure she agreed.

89

Badru came to see her in the middle of the night, clearly exhausted, his shoulders slumped, dark circles under his eyes. She was just as tired. She'd worked herself into a frenzy wondering what she'd do if he couldn't save her people, practicing the hundred and five attacks until she could barely move.

"What did you decide?" she demanded as he pulled her close, burying his face against her neck.

He shook his head. "Can't we just forget that for now? Forget I'm the Daliph. Forget you're from the tribes. Can't we just be the man and woman I see in my dreams at night, dancing on the desert sands?"

He kissed her before she could answer and she lost herself in the sensation of his mouth against hers, the feel of his hands as they moved along the curves of her body. She ran her hand along the line at the base of his spine, shivering at the intensity of his touch.

But when he moved his kisses to her neck, she shoved him away, once more remembering who she was and what was at stake.

"I can't do this, Badru."

He stared at her, confused, angry.

"I need to know what you've decided."

He rubbed his face and turned away from her.

"Badru?"

"We need the trade, K'lrsa."

She came around in front of him, demanding that he look at her, but he turned away again. "What are you saying?"

He shook his head. "We can't go back. We can't...We need the trade."

It felt as if he'd ripped the heart from her chest. "You're going to do it? You'll let him slaughter everyone I know and love?"

He finally met her eyes. "I have no choice, K'lrsa."

"You always have a choice, Badru. You're just not willing to pay the price to do what's right."

"What's right? For whom? Your tribe or my people? Life isn't simple, K'lrsa. It isn't all right choices and wrong choices."

She clutched her arms against her chest, wondering how she could've been foolish enough to love him. "It is to me. You can deny K'var and save my family and friends. Or you can help him slaughter every single person that matters to me. Pretty simple choice. But I guess you'd rather have your silks and salt than protect the lives of my people. Do you honestly think that all of this is worth more than a single life?"

He clenched his fists. "Do you know what will happen if I deny K'var? They'll kill me. And you. And Herin. And Sayel. And anyone else they can think of.

"Because if the Black Horse Tribe stops trading with us, we're done. It's the end. We go back to begging for scraps from the other Daliphana. Without that trade route, we're nothing."

She stared at him for a long time, wishing he'd change his mind, but she knew he wouldn't no matter how much she cried or pleaded with him to do so. And she'd be damned if she was going to weep and wail at his feet.

She turned away. "Fine. Then let me leave. Tonight. Let me ride Fallion back home as fast as I can and warn my people. Give them a chance to defend themselves."

"You said you'd give me three days."

He tried to pull her close, but she jerked away from him. "That was before I knew you were a murderer."

"I'm not..." He shook his head, his face twisted with grief. "I love you, K'lrsa. I thought what we shared meant something, but I guess those dreams were more real to me than they were to you."

His words were like a dagger in her gut. "I could say the same of you, Badru."

He left, slamming the door behind him.

She collapsed to the floor and curled into a ball, angry as much as she was sad. She had to leave. She had to warn her people.

But how?

90

When Sayel came for her the next morning, she shook her head and crossed her arms. "No. I'm not playing these games anymore. Badru freed me, he gave me Fallion back. I want to go home. Now."

Sayel glanced at Morlen, but Morlen just shrugged. Sayel walked towards her, hands held out to calm her like she was a skittish colt that had never been ridden. "My dorana..."

"Don't my dorana me."

When Sayel flinched, she relented, uncrossing her arms and taking his hands in hers. "Sayel, I need to help my people. I need to warn them."

He chewed on his lip, not quite meeting her eye.

"What?"

Sayel opened and closed his mouth with a small sigh. "My dorana. Think. If Badru does this, if he helps them, then he does so expecting to triumph. He can't let you warn your people. It will cost him troops and, if your tribe wins, trade."

She shook her head, denying his words even though they rang true.

A knock at the door pulled her attention away from Sayel; a young slave girl entered the room, a pile of soft baru hide in her arms, so creamy and rich it must've been worked by a master tanner.

The girl held the clothes away from her body, eyes focused on the ground. K'lrsa shook as she watched her.

This is what the Daliphate was. This is what it did to people—enslaved them, beat them down. This young girl should be running, laughing loudly as she chased her friends. Instead, she cowered in the doorway, ready to run away at the slightest harsh word.

This is what Badru wanted to protect.

She turned away, bile burning the back of her throat.

This is what the man she loved thought mattered more than the lives of her sister and her mother and her brother.

"What is this?" Sayel demanded.

The girl whispered, "From the Daliph, honored poradom."

When K'lrsa turned back, the girl was gone and Sayel and Morlen were inspecting the clothes. "What are these?" Sayel asked.

K'lrsa took the pants and admired the fine stitching along the inside of each leg. She ran her hand over the smooth baru hide. They were finer than anything she'd ever owned. This, at last, was a true Rider's outfit.

Did Badru really want her to wear it? Or was this some trick played by his enemies?

K'lrsa stripped off her robe and put on the pants and vest, running her hands along her thighs, lost in memories of riding Fallion, her hair streaming behind her in the breeze, and the pure joy of freedom.

"My dorana...I..."

She ignored him as she stepped to the mirror and braided her hair into a single, simple plait down her back.

Before her stood a Rider, not a life-sized doll or some man's lustful fantasy of a Rider or even some seamstress's idea of a Desert Princess.

It was just her. K'lrsa dan V'na of the White Horse Tribe. Rider. Hunter. Protector.

This was who she was.

She smiled, finally comfortable with what she saw.

The woman who smiled back at her was different from the girl who'd arrived in the palace. That girl hadn't known who she was or what she really wanted. She was beautiful, but generic, a piece of clay to be molded by whosoever cared to do so.

But this woman, this woman knew herself. She knew what she wanted and what mattered to her. She was willing to sacrifice her dream of personal happiness to help those she loved. She was strong enough to stand up for what was right.

This woman had a fire inside that had nothing to do with anyone's perceptions of her. She knew that they could call her whatever they wanted and dress her in whatever they wanted, but she'd always be true to herself.

She wasn't trying to prove herself to her mother or please a man—not even the man of her dreams. She was herself, flawed but powerful, weak but strong enough to succeed.

There was another knock at the door. It opened as she turned around.

Badru stood there, resplendent in his court attire, the blue of his vest matching the blue of his eyes.

She longed to touch him, kiss him, lose herself in him.

But she couldn't.

She met his gaze, her chin held high, not caring what the four guards behind him thought.

She wasn't some possession to be ordered about. Not anymore.

He stepped into the room, smiling. "I'm glad to see they fit. I had them made especially for you. The seamstresses worked all night."

She forced herself not to match his smile. "So you're going to let me go."

He nodded.

When the smile broke across her face, he held up his hand. "On one condition."

K'lrsa closed her eyes. She was tired of conditions and constraints. She just wanted to be free, to go home.

"K'lrsa...Please?"

She looked at him again, sighing deeply. "What condition?"

"You spend one more day by my side." He held his hand out to her, clearly expecting her to take it.

She didn't. "Why?"

He met her eyes, secretly begging her, but she wasn't going to do that again. She wasn't going to let his pretty blue eyes and sweet smiles turn her aside.

"I want you there when I speak to K'var again."

She crossed her arms. "Are you going to deny him?"

He glanced at the guards and Sayel and Morlen. "I don't know yet. But if you're going back to your people, don't you want to be able to tell them as much as you can about the threat they face?"

The threat they faced. Him. He was the threat.

She should kill him, but she knew she wouldn't. She loved him.

She wanted to refuse—she didn't want to spend another moment of her life surrounded by men who hated her just for who she was—but then she'd just be locked in this room for who knows how long, wondering what was happening.

"Fine. I'll come with you." She took his hand.

91

As they walked down the halls to the audience chamber, everyone stopped what they were doing and stared, whispering to one another in hushed tones after they'd passed.

K'lrsa walked side-by-side with Badru—his equal. He ignored everyone; so did she. This was how it should've been all along, not her dressed and bound, escorted like a prisoner to sit one step below him. But her, there, walking next to him, her hand in his.

When they reached the audience chamber and the giant double doors opened, the room fell silent as always. But there was a note to the silence, a hidden vibration that threatened to shatter the windows and break the walls. It was the sound of hundreds of men who wanted to speak, but didn't dare breathe.

Badru placed K'lrsa's hand on his arm—her fingers clearly free of the *meza*—and led her to the top of the dais where she sat on the couch while he stood before everyone, turning slowly so they could all see him.

"I, Badru Palero, Daliph of the Toreem Daliphate, call on all of you to witness that this woman, K'lrsa dan V'na of the White Horse Tribe, who was brought to me as a slave and who I chose as my dorana, is a slave no more. Nor is she my dorana."

The sound in the room exploded, so powerful it shook loose a small tile from the ceiling that shattered into dust as it hit the floor at Badru's feet.

Badru held up a hand and the room settled once more into silence, but it was a restive thing, like a horse ready to spook. "K'lrsa dan V'na comes to us as a Rider, hunter and protector of her tribe. She is under my protection while here or in any part of the Toreem Daliphate. Any who harm her while she is under my protection will die."

A whisper of rage passed around the room and was gone.

Badru turned to Nesbit as if he hadn't just made an earth-shattering announcement. "Nesbit. Call forth the supplicant."

"Yes, most honored leader." Nesbit cleared his throat while Badru seated himself. "I call forth K'var of the Black Horse Tribe."

K'var walked forward from the back of the room, his expression stony, his eyes darting back and forth between Badru and K'lrsa. K'lrsa met his gaze and he flinched. She smiled.

She noted that he wasn't wearing the multi-colored cloth of the Daliph's favor today, but didn't dare ask what that meant.

"K'var."

K'var bowed, tilting his head just enough that the gesture was almost mocking. "Your Excellency."

"Before I tell you my decision, I'd like to ask you a few more questions."

K'var almost laughed, but stopped himself with just a slight snort. He glanced around the room as if looking for the men to witness the weakness of their Daliph.

K'lrsa tilted her head to the side as she imagined what it would feel like to poke his eyes out with Cutting Cat. He flinched away from her, focusing his attention on Badru instead.

"Of course, Your Excellency. What would you like to know?"

Badru leaned back, appearing to lounge in his chair, but he sat with the deadly calm of a desert cat ready to attack. "You mentioned yesterday small skirmishes with the other tribes."

"I did."

"Who started these conflicts?"

"Your Excellency?"

"Who attacked first, K'var?"

K'var shrugged. "It's hard to tell, Your Excellency."

Badru leaned forward, all lithe grace and danger. "I don't think so, K'var. See, I've been researching a certain *skirmish* for some time now."

K'var straightened up, his eyes darting towards K'lrsa.

"Before K'lrsa came to us, her tribe was attacked." Badru stood and paced, looking at the men in the room as he continued. "She, and others, believed that the attack was by *my* men. At *my* order."

K'var watched Badru closely, but he didn't speak. Badru continued to address the room, ignoring K'var. "It seems the men who attacked and killed her father wore my colors. And carried swords.

"But I didn't order my men to attack the tribes."

He turned to K'var at last, glaring down at him, his face a mask of controlled fury. "As a matter of fact, K'var, I discovered just last night that *you* led that attack."

K'lrsa clenched her hands into fists, her fingernails digging into the palms of her hands in half-moons of agony.

She struggled to breathe. That meant K'var was the one responsible for her father's death. Her father's killer was just ten steps away from her.

"What say you, K'var?"

K'var shrugged and addressed his answer to the crowd. "I told you, the other tribes are jealous. They want what we have. Most are harmless. They want but they don't act. But one man—B'nin of the White Horse Tribe—spoke against us. He wanted us expelled. He would have taken everything from us. So we killed him."

Sayel grabbed K'lrsa to keep her from running down the steps and attacking K'var right then and there. Badru continued to watch K'var, not looking back at her. "How?"

K'var glared past Badru and met K'lrsa's eyes with a slight sneer. "He was an arrogant, trusting fool. We had an ally in the tribe. He led him into an ambush and we killed him."

An ally?

"What became of this ally?"

K'var glared at K'lrsa once more. "He had a change of heart. He tried to save the man. So we killed him, too."

L'ral? L'ral had betrayed her father? She gasped, the pain in her chest squeezing all the air out of her lungs.

"So you killed this man, your enemy, and you made it look like my men were responsible. That should've ended it."

K'var sneered. "The man's son has rallied the tribes against us."

Badru nodded. "I see. So you need my help because you failed to control your enemy and then botched killing him and, as a result, turned all of the tribes against you?"

K'var glared up at him, but didn't respond.

Badru paced back and forth, every eye in the room on him. "It's true that we need the trade across the desert. But I'm not so sure that we need *you*, K'var."

Badru glanced back at K'lrsa.

She stiffened.

No. She would not lead men from the Daliphate across the desert. She would not participate in the ruin of everything she knew and loved.

But it didn't matter whether she would or not, it just mattered what people thought. Isn't that what Herin had told her before?

An excited murmur ran through the crowd as men whispered to their neighbors.

K'var shook his head. "No. You need us. You have no choice. No other tribes will agree to what we have."

Badru smiled. "Oh, there's always a choice, K'var. A very wise woman told me that just yesterday." He glanced back at K'lrsa once more and she felt a rush of affection for him. "Tell me something else, K'var. Did you approach any of the other Daliphana for assistance?"

K'var shifted his weight back and forth as a surge of anger ran through the room.

"Answer me."

K'var held his chin high and glared at Badru. "Yes, Your

Excellency. I did."

He met Badru's eyes, defiant, but with glimmers of fear flashing in his eyes.

"What did you offer them in exchange for their help?"

K'var's lips twitched. "We don't have an exclusive agreement to trade with you."

"No?" Badru let that question hang in the air before he continued. "That isn't what I asked you. What did you offer them?"

K'var shifted his weight again, glancing towards the back of the room. "We had to protect ourselves. We couldn't leave the fate of the tribe to…"

"To me? To an untried, young Daliph? A weak man? One who might act based on love or conscience instead of greed?" Badru's lips quirked upward into a half-smile.

K'lrsa glanced around the room—too many men were agreeing with that assessment. Not in obvious ways, but in slight glances at their neighbors or the slightest nodding of a head here or there.

Badru should stop. He didn't realize how thin the earth under his feet really was. One misstep and K'var would win this confrontation.

Badru stepped down one level. "What did you promise the other Daliphana, K'var?" His voice hardened as he continued. "Better yet, what did you promise my enemies here in the Toreem Daliphate?"

K'var swallowed and forced himself to look only at Badru. A small bead of sweat made its way down the side of his face, but he didn't stop it. "Your Excellency?"

"What did you promise my enemies if you helped overthrow me?"

K'var backed away, shaking his head. "Your Excellency…I would never…" He smiled, but the smile faltered as Badru took another step towards him.

"No?"

Pavel and the man next to him whispered intently back and forth, almost ignoring the conversation. Around the room, small pockets of conversation erupted as Badru continued to stare at K'var.

Badru raised his voice so all could hear him. "K'var of the Black Horse Tribe, I Badru Palero, Daliph of the Toreem Daliphate, say that you are guilty of conspiring with the other Daliphana and with my enemies to overthrow me."

The room buzzed with conversation. Badru held up a hand, demanding silence. The men around him fell silent, but the room pulsed with the words they wanted to speak.

"K'var of the Black Horse Tribe, I sentence you to death. Now." Badru held his hand out. "Someone bring me a sword."

The room erupted like a pot boiling over, men jumping to their feet and shouting as K'var turned and ran towards the back of the room.

92

A man stood on the table at the far end of the room, next to the doors. "Oh, enough," he roared, his voice like rocks banging together.

He threw back his hood and the room collapsed into silence as everyone turned to stare at his squat toad-like face. He stepped forward a few steps, graceful and deadly as a giant sand serpent.

K'lrsa tried to breath, but she couldn't.

She knew this man. She'd seen his face on a coin once.

It was the former Daliph.

But he was dead. Lodie had poisoned him. She'd killed herself in order to kill him.

Except, Lodie wasn't dead. And, it seemed, neither was the former Daliph.

Badru trembled where he stood half-way down the dais stairs.

The man continued, "I am so tired of watching you play at Daliph, you foolish little boy. Step aside and let a real man run things."

Badru pointed his sword at the man. "We all saw you die you vile old man." He screamed, "He's a death walker. Kill him."

No one moved, too stunned to react.

The former Daliph laughed, the sound like rusted metal. "Kill me?" He spat to the side. "I'd like to see that."

He drew the sword at his waist and pointed it at Badru. "I want my throne back, boy. Now."

<u>93</u>

No one moved for a breath of time and then the room erupted into chaos, men moving in all directions, turning on one another, fleeing, fighting, some moving toward Badru, some moving towards the former Daliph.

K'lrsa stood on the top of the dais and watched it all.

Badru dove into the crowd, intent on reaching his grandfather. K'lrsa screamed for him to come back, but her voice was lost in the tumult of sound as men fought and died all around the room.

K'var slit the throat of a guard too stunned to react and took his sword, turning back towards Badru. But he was too late to lead the charge. Two of Badru's own guards turned on him, one driving a sword into Badru's back as Pavel cut down the other.

K'lrsa cried out as she watched Badru fall. She lost sight of his body as two more guards turned towards her, weapons bared.

Sayel stepped in front of her, blocking their attack with his considerable bulk, flowing through the sword forms with such ease and grace she wondered how she could've ever thought him fat.

She tried to dodge around Sayel to reach Badru, but there wasn't room, so she had to stand back and watch, helpless as more and more men rushed to the position where she'd last seen him.

It was impossible to tell enemy from foe. She watched two guards fight side-by-side through the crowd, saving each other's lives at least a dozen times before they finally reached the dais and the first turned on the second, stabbing him through the heart.

Badru's grandfather stood across the room and watched the carnage. He laughed and clapped his hands in delight as yet another man died at his feet.

K'lrsa swore to herself in that moment that someday she'd make him pay for this.

Someday. But not today. Today she needed to save Badru.

Sayel grabbed her hand and started to drag her towards the back wall. "Come."

She pulled away. "No. I won't go without Badru."

He glanced back at the swirling mass of fighting men. "It's too late, my dorana. Badru is dead. Let me save you."

She grabbed his robe. "It's not too late. Herin can save him."

Sayel flinched backward. "No. No, my dorana…"

"We have to, Sayel. Or else evil wins. And what then? My people die and who knows who else. We have to save Badru, Sayel, no matter the cost."

Sayel glanced at the crowd and back at her. "It may cost us our lives."

"I don't care. Let's go."

K'lrsa charged past him, lashing out with a chop of her hand at the first man who tried to stop her.

94

They made quick progress as they raced down from the top of the dais. Not only were they coming from above everyone else, so had the advantage of height, but the men, even those that should've known better, didn't pay any attention to K'lrsa. She was past most of them before they could even think to react, leaving a trail of dead or broken fighters behind her.

Those she didn't get, Sayel did, slicing to each side like death himself.

They pushed, shoved, and fought their way to where K'lrsa had last seen Badru.

"Find him, Sayel," she screamed, fighting to look for Badru as she defended herself from a new attacker—this one an older man in brown robes with a red sash.

Sayel cut the man down and threw his body into a crowd of approaching men, clearing a small space for them.

"There!" K'lrsa dashed forward, shoving a pair of fighting men aside. Badru was on the floor, his clothes torn, his body covered in footprints from the men who fought and died above him.

Sayel pulled her back and shoved the sword into her hand. "Protect me."

As K'lrsa slashed to every side, trying to manage the heavy weapon, Sayel used a small knife to cut Badru's clothes from his body.

"What are you doing? We have to go." K'lrsa side-stepped a sword thrust from a former guard, kicking out at the man as he stepped past her and shattering his kneecap.

"The colors. He'd be too recognizable." He threw Badru's headpiece into the melee.

K'lrsa drove her elbow into another guard's face and turned away as his nose shattered.

Sayel flung Badru's body over his shoulder and shoved her towards the dais. "Go."

She tried to turn back towards the entrance, but he pushed her forward again. "We can't go that way. Go."

K'lrsa scrambled back up the stairs of the dais. She glanced backward. Sayel was right, a group of at least a dozen guards were fighting their way forward from the main doors in a tight, organized group, slowly but surely cutting their way through the intervening crowd.

And behind them, smiling in triumph, the former Daliph stood.

K'lrsa's heart sank. They had Badru, but they were trapped.

She slashed at a man in red robes who grabbed at Sayel.

"What are we going to do?"

95

"Follow me." Sayel led her to the far end of the dais. Badru hung limp from his shoulder, the blood of his wound dripping onto the ground with each step.

"What are you doing, Sayel?"

They worked their way down a small flight of stairs hidden behind the dais. The roar of the fighting suddenly died, leaving her ears ringing with the memory of the sound.

"Those stones, there. Press them all at once." He pointed to three large black stones arranged in a triangle at eye-level.

K'lrsa pressed on the stones, putting all her strength into pushing them inward. Finally, they gave with a click and a section of the wall slid to the side, revealing a dark passageway.

"Go." Sayel shoved her through the opening.

K'lrsa stumbled, her hands fumbling for the wall on the other side of the passage. When she found it, she stepped to the side to make way for Sayel to follow, unsure what she'd find in the dark enclosed space.

Sayel pushed her farther into the passage, shoving her aside as he pulled a lever to close the panel once more and plunged them into a darkness so deep K'lrsa couldn't see her own hand.

She took deep breaths and struggled not to scream as she felt the walls pressing in on every side.

Sayel reached out and found her hand in the darkness. "Calm, my dorana. Calm."

She held onto him, desperate to know she wasn't alone. He gave her hand a final squeeze and reached past her to pull on another lever. A small section of the outer wall shifted downward. Not much, but enough for the daylight outside to illuminate the passageway in each direction.

It was just wide enough for two men abreast, but the ceiling was low, almost touching Sayel's head. Once more K'lrsa struggled against the feeling that the walls were closing in on her. She tried to find the hunter's version of the Core as Sayel turned back to the first lever and pulled it to the side, grunting as it twisted and bent under his hands. "There. That should slow them a bit."

He pushed her gently towards the right. "Move, my dorana. I'm not the only one who knows of these passages. They can't follow through this entrance, but they'll find another. Go."

K'lrsa obeyed, stumbling forward.

The passages were built into the outer wall of the palace, so there weren't many choices to make as they ran. It was either continue forward, exit into another room, or go down a level when the opportunity presented itself.

Sayel had her go down at every opportunity. They moved through darkness after they left that first section of passageway. K'lrsa desperately wanted light as she struggled with every step to keep from screaming as the walls pressed close around her, but Sayel said no.

"We do that, we might as well surrender. They'll know exactly where to find us."

So K'lrsa continued in the blackness, her fingers trailing along the rough stone of the passageway. She could smell the freshness of water and the occasional stench of rot and decay as they made their way down and down and down.

"Shouldn't we exit? Find somewhere to hide?" K'lrsa asked as they descended yet another level; Sayel's heavy breathing filled the space behind her.

She tried not to think about Badru, draped over Sayel's shoulder, limp, unmoving.

Dead.

"One more level, my dorana. We're almost at the servants' quarters. There we can change."

He directed her to exit into a storage room, the shelves stacked high with coarse servants' robes. K'lrsa quickly threw one over her Rider's clothing and turned to see Sayel donning one as well.

He'd dropped Badru at his feet in a tumbled pile.

K'lrsa knelt by Badru's side and took his hand in hers. It was cold, too cold, and slightly stiff. She'd known it would be, but still the feel of his slack, lifeless hand caught at her throat, choking her.

Badru was dead.

He was really dead.

She curled in on herself, unable to control her shaking.

"Come, my dorana. We must dress him."

She shook her head. "What's the point? He's dead, Sayel."

He pushed her gently to the side and propped Badru up against his knee, forcing a robe over his head, and moving his arms into each hole, struggling with his stiff limbs. "Yes, he's dead." He met her eyes. "But, as you told me, Herin may be able to save him. If we can find her in time."

K'lrsa fought back the tears, shaking her head at the hopelessness of it all. Sayel brushed his thumb along her cheekbone. "Later, my dorana. Now we must go."

"Where?"

"To Herin. We have to reach her before the Daliph's men do."

K'lrsa struggled to her feet as Sayel once more threw Badru's body over his shoulder. "Badru is the Daliph," she mumbled.

Sayel glanced at her and away again. "Not anymore, my dorana. Come. We must hurry."

He grabbed two more robes and led her out into the hallway, glancing in both directions as he dashed down the hall to her right.

96

Sayel led her through a series of dusty hallways to another set of hidden passages—these ones ran along the other side of the palace. He'd grabbed a torch as they passed through the final hallway, so at least this time they didn't have to navigate the cramped spaces in the dark.

They went down two more levels and along a section slimy with mold before exiting into a dank, dark hallway with only one sputtering torch to light it.

"Where are we, Sayel?" K'lrsa whispered, scared to speak in such a dead space.

"Herin's rooms."

K'lrsa stared around her at the damp floor and shadows clustered in the corners of the hallway. "Really? Why would she choose to have rooms here?"

"Safety."

He led her around a corner and came to such an abrupt stop that she ran into his back. Two guards stood in front of a door halfway down the hall. At the sight of Sayel, they placed their hands on their swords and advanced forward.

"Move aside. I need to see the Omala. Now." Sayel's voice had a slight tremor to it as he shouted at the men.

K'lrsa peered past him, trying to decide if the men were Badru's or had already been replaced with the former Daliph's men.

"No visitors." The one on the left drew his sword and took another step forward, trying to see who Sayel had behind him.

"Herin," K'lrsa shouted.

The guard turned his attention from Sayel to her, squinting to see her in the gloom. Sayel shoved the end of his torch into the wall, stubbing it out so the man wouldn't be able to see her.

The second guard pulled his sword as the door to Herin's rooms opened and she stepped forward. She looked tired, her hair hung loose around her shoulders and stuck out in different directions. It was matted, like she hadn't bothered to brush it.

Garzel stood behind her.

"What?" she demanded. The two guards flinched away from her.

K'lrsa glanced at the two guards and Sayel. She didn't know what to say. How do you tell a woman that her grandson is dead and you're hoping she can resurrect him?

But she didn't have to say anything, because Herin's gaze focused on the body slung over Sayel's shoulder and she clutched at the doorframe, shaking. She turned back, her eyes meeting Garzel's as she choked out Badru's name.

The guard closest to Sayel finally came close enough to catch a glimpse of K'lrsa. His eyes darted to Sayel and he tightened his grip on the sword. Before he could attack, Garzel pushed past Herin, a long knife in his hand, and attacked the guard closest to him, slitting the man's throat without hesitation.

As the first guard turned to stare at Garzel, too surprised to understand what had happened, Herin threw a knife, striking him in the eye. The man dropped to the floor, dead.

"Get inside." Herin stepped aside to let Sayel past her.

K'lrsa didn't move. She stared back and forth between the two dead guards.

"Princess, care to get in here before someone else comes along?"

K'lrsa stumbled past the bodies into Herin's rooms. "You didn't have to kill them."

"No?" Herin turned to Sayel. "He's back isn't he? Aran? How much time do we have?"

"You knew? You knew he was alive?" K'lrsa screeched, her voice spiraling out of control. She wanted to rip the woman into tiny pieces, and would have if she wasn't the only person capable of saving Badru.

Herin barely glanced at her. "I suspected." She moved around the room, pushing furniture aside and grabbing various boxes and bags she'd hidden which she handed to Garzel to pack.

"And you never told Badru?"

"And how was I supposed to do that? Tell him I was a death walker? That I'd learned from Aran so I thought maybe he too was still alive?" She shook her head. "Pzah, girl. You saw how he reacted when he finally found out about me. The only reason he spared my life is because I'd saved you and he didn't know how to be grateful for that and still kill me."

Garzel moved a large wooden chest away from the wall while Herin bound her hair back into a messy bun at the nape of her neck. Sayel thrust the servants' robes at them and they both threw them on.

Herin looked around the dark, closed space one last time. "Can't say I'll miss it." She smiled at Garzel and he smiled back.

K'lrsa stared at them, horrified that they could smile at a time like this.

Herin saw the look and just laughed. "Wait until you've seen as much as we have, child." She walked to the wall and pressed four tiles set in a square pattern until the wall slid open to reveal another passageway.

She stepped into the darkness, not even bothering with a torch. "Follow me. We don't have much time."

97

They raced down another series of passageways, Herin leading with K'lrsa right behind her followed by Sayel and Garzel behind him. K'lrsa focused on keeping Herin's back in sight and tried not to think about getting trapped in the passages, forever lost, doomed to stumble through the blackness until they finally collapsed and died.

Eventually, they came out in the room that Herin had used to heal K'lrsa. The secret entrance was located behind the table.

"Quick. Lay him down on the bed." Herin rushed to the cabinet while Sayel obeyed her orders.

Garzel opened the door to the hallway, but immediately shut it again. He barred the door shut and they all stood there in tense silence as they heard the sound of shouting voices and running feet. Someone tried the door but passed by when it wouldn't open.

Herin worked on Badru's body, her jaw clenched tight as she smoothed back the hair from his forehead and straightened his limbs. She started washing his wounds, slowly and methodically, ignoring everyone else as they heard yet another set of men race by outside the door.

Herin and Garzel exchanged a worried look, but Herin kept working.

K'lrsa stood to the side, biting her lip, wanting to help, but not knowing what she could do.

"Herin…?"

"Just stay out of my way. We don't have much longer."

K'lrsa bit her lip and backed into the corner, watching Herin work. Sayel stood next to her, holding her hand in his as they both watched and waited.

There were so many injuries—cuts on his arms and legs, the deep wound in his back that had likely killed him—and yet he looked so peaceful lying there. So young. And innocent.

Just a boy, not the leader of an entire Daliphate.

She wondered how scared he'd been, standing on top of that dais day after day ordering men to obey him and wondering if they would.

"Can you save him, Herin?" K'lrsa finally asked, unable to stay silent any longer. "You saved Lodie, right? So you can save him?"

Herin glanced at Garzel again, but didn't answer. He was still standing at the main door, his ear pressed to the wood, listening to the men running up and down the hall.

"How long ago was he killed, Sayel?"

Sayel shook his head. "Around midday. We tried to get him to you as fast as possible, but…"

Herin signaled him to stop talking and turned back to Badru's body, moving his arms, noting the stiffness that had started to form.

Garzel grunted something and Herin flinched. "No." She shook her head violently side-to-side.

He grunted again, louder, more forceful.

"No. I won't do it." She stared up at him, stricken. "I can't…"

"What? What's wrong?" K'lrsa stepped forward, looking back and forth between them.

They all flinched as another group of soldiers ran down the hallway outside and someone paused to try their door once more.

Garzel knelt in front of Herin, taking her hands in his. He grunted at her again, staring into her eyes.

Herin looked like she might cry, the expression so wholly unexpected that K'lrsa stumbled away from them. What was he saying?

Sayel gently pushed K'lrsa aside and stepped forward. "I'll do it."

"Do what? What are you talking about? Sayel?" K'lrsa clutched at his arm.

He glanced back at her with a sad smile, stroking the side of her face with his fingers. "Ah, my dorana. Don't you see? To save Badru, someone must take his place. A life for a life."

K'lrsa stared at Sayel, trying to understand what he was telling her. She looked past him to Herin who was watching her quietly, waiting. She looked back at Sayel.

"You? You're going to...? No." She looked at all three of them, backing away. "No."

Another group of soldiers ran by, shouting to one another. Sayel looked towards the door and back at her. "We're out of time, my dorana."

She looked towards the passageway. "Can't we go through the passages? Can't we find someone and..."

"Just kill them?" Herin asked, watching her closely. "A prisoner maybe? Or a slave? Some young girl you find cleaning the floor?"

K'lrsa opened her mouth and closed it again. She wanted to say yes, anything to save Badru. But, no, that wasn't true. It wasn't fair to save him at the cost of some child's life.

Herin turned to her. "If you want Badru to live, someone must die."

K'lrsa glanced frantically between Sayel, Herin, and Garzel. "Isn't there another choice?"

Herin shook her head. "No. We only have about half a candlemark more to complete the ritual."

Sayel stepped forward, blocking her view of the rest of the room. He took her shoulders in his hands and stared down at her. "I am a poradom. I swore to give my life for my Daliph."

"Not like this you didn't. And I, I need you."

He shook his head. "No, you don't, my dorana. You are strong and fierce and intelligent. You don't need me or anyone else. And Badru can do what I cannot. He can overthrow his grandfather. I? I am just a poradom."

She fought back her tears. "You're not *just* anything, Sayel. You're my friend."

He smiled, his teeth shining against his dark skin as he leaned down to kiss her gently on the forehead. "Thank you for that, my dorana."

He turned away from her. "Let us begin."

98

K'lrsa sat next to Sayel and held his hand as Herin finished her preparations. He was calm as he stared at the ceiling and breathed softly.

K'lrsa watched him, tears streaming down her face, wondering why it was that death followed her. First her father, then Barkley, and Badru. And now Sayel. Every man she cared for died.

On the table, Herin arranged two shallow black bowls, a knife made of some sort of dark black stone that seemed to suck up the light in the room, some odd carved stones, and three black candles.

She nicked Sayel's wrist and collected his blood in the first bowl, and then did the same with Badru's blood in the second bowl even though it barely flowed enough for her to fill it. When she had enough, she marked Badru's eyes, mouth, and heart with Sayel's blood and then marked Sayel with Badru's blood.

She lit the candles, muttering under her breath as she lit each one. They smelled like a decaying corpse—damp and putrid. K'lrsa covered her mouth and struggled to ignore the stench.

Herin dipped the stones in the blood and placed them on Badru's and Sayel's chests in an elongated diamond pattern, one end pointed towards their heads, one towards their feet.

K'lrsa wanted to ask Herin to explain what she was doing, but one look at Herin's face and she kept silent.

"Go stand by Garzel."

K'lrsa kissed Sayel on the forehead and wiped away the tear that trailed down his cheek. "I'll miss you, Sayel."

"And I you, my dorana."

"Pzah, girl. We don't have all day." Herin shooed her towards the corner of the room where Garzel grabbed her and pulled her against his chest.

K'lrsa turned around just in time to watch Herin plunge a knife into Sayel's heart. She struggled to rush back to his side, but Garzel held her tight murmuring something unintelligible but kind in her ear.

She kicked and fought as Sayel's body convulsed under the blow.

Badru sat up, gasping for air, his body perfect once more, his wounds gone.

"Where am I? What happened?" His voice was hoarse, like he had a cold. He coughed to clear his throat.

He watched Herin clean the knife she'd used and set it back on the table. "Grandmother? What have you done?"

"Pzah. What do you think I've done, you fool? I saved your worthless, ungrateful life."

Badru turned on K'lrsa. "And you let her do this?"

"Let her? I begged her to."

He buried his face in his hands, shaking his head. "I didn't want anyone to die just so I could live."

"Oh, enough." Herin threw a bag of food at him. "You're a Daliph. Men die for you every day. Every slave who dies working the fields dies so you can eat. Every soldier who dies, dies fighting to protect your interests. Just because you don't stab them through the heart yourself doesn't make them any less dead. Get over it."

Badru dug around in the sack, shoving food into his mouth as he glared at Herin. She didn't flinch, just stood in front of him, hands on hips, staring him down.

Finally, Badru stood and walked over to the other bed. "Sayel."

K'lrsa stepped forward and rested her hand on his arm. "He wanted to, Badru."

"Why?"

"Because he swore to give his life for you. And because you can do what he can't. You can defeat your grandfather."

Badru shook his head.

"Pzah. Quit pouting and start thinking. Your grandfather has control of the Daliphate. And if he finds you here, he'll kill you. Again. And I can assure you, if that happens, I won't be able to save you. So stop worrying about how you got here and start thinking about how you're going to get out of here. How we all are."

They froze as a group of men passed by, one trying the door yet again. This time he didn't quit, pushing and shoving against the door over and over again.

"I heard voices. Someone get an axe," he called. "I want to know what or who is on the other side of this door. Now."

99

They fled back into the dark passageways. K'lrsa held Badru's hand as Herin led them upward three levels and down another series of passageways to a small storeroom, the shelves along each wall crammed with sacks of grain, dried meats, and glass jugs full of pickled vegetables.

"We should be safe here. For now. But he won't quit until he finds you, Badru."

Badru paced the small space as the rest of them huddled against the shelves. "We need to rally support as soon as possible. The sooner he's defeated, the better."

Herin shook her head. "Think, boy. Who are your allies? Tell me, Badru, who do you *know* will stand with you?"

"Pavel. And..."

K'lrsa bit her lip. "Pavel's dead. He was killed protecting you."

"Who else?" Herin demanded.

"I...most of my council would probably stand with me, except maybe..."

Herin waved a hand at him, dismissing what he was about to say. She turned to K'lrsa. "Why did Aran act now? What happened today to force him to show himself?"

K'lrsa glanced at Badru, but he was glaring at the door, lost in thought.

She told Herin what had happened with K'var, how Badru had called for his sword to kill the man and the former Daliph had declared himself.

Herin turned on Badru, contempt clear on her face. "Did you learn nothing from me, you foolish boy?"

"I am your Daliph, woman. Speak to me with respect."

"Ha. Not anymore. You *were* my Daliph. Now you're just a spoiled and foolish boy who lost his throne. And for what? Love?"

"He was conspiring against me."

"Boy, if you killed everyone who'd ever conspired against you, you wouldn't have any subjects left."

Badru stared at her, stunned.

Herin glanced to Garzel and he shrugged. She nodded. "We can't stay here."

K'lrsa stepped forward. "Then we go to my tribe. We warn them of what's happened here."

Badru shook his head. "No. We have to regain my throne."

K'lrsa glanced at him, but shook her head. "No. Herin's right. You don't know who to trust and we can't allow the tribes to be destroyed." She focused her attention on Herin and Garzel. "He killed everyone in the Summer Spring Tribe, Herin. He'll kill the rest, too, if given a chance. We can't let that happen. The tribes need to survive. We have to protect…it."

"Protect what?"

They all ignored Badru. Herin met K'lrsa's eyes and nodded. "You're right. We have to get to the tribes before Aran does."

"No. I'm not leaving." Badru blocked the door to the hallway, his arms crossed.

K'lrsa sighed. "Badru, you can come back later."

"No."

"Badru, listen to me. We have to go before he finds you. And we have to warn my people. You can fight him another day when you're strong and have allies behind you."

"No. I have to fight him now."

"Why?"

"This is who I am. This is my birthright. I am the Daliph. He had no right to take that from me."

K'lrsa sighed. She glanced to Herin, but the woman was in a deep conversation with Garzel.

"Let it go, Badru."

"This is who I am, K'lrsa. Without this, I'm nothing."

"You're still the man I love."

He laughed—a short, bitter sound and turned away from her.

K'lrsa tried not to feel hurt, but she was.

<u>100</u>

"Time to go." Herin reached for the stones that would open the secret panel.

"I'm not going. I'm not giving up." Badru leaned against the door to the hallway, arms crossed tight against his chest.

"Pzah, boy. There's nothing for you here now. You can leave now and start anew. Or you can stay here like a whiny child and admit defeat."

"I can fight."

Herin pinched the bridge of her nose. "No. You can't. Too many people saw you die today, Badru. If you go back now, they'll know you were raised by a death walker and they'll kill you."

His jaw clenched as he glared at Herin.

K'lrsa turned away. She just wanted to leave. She wanted to grab Fallion and ride and ride and ride until Toreem and the Toreem Daliphate were far behind her. She was done with men and their power plays.

She closed her eyes.

But she couldn't just leave the man she loved behind to die again. Not after the sacrifice Sayel had made to save him.

She turned toward him and forced a smile, softening her voice. "Badru, we're going to the tribes. You'll be with me."

"And what will I be there? A foreigner? A stranger?"

She grabbed his arms and looked deep into his angry eyes. "You'll be my mate. The man I've determined is worthy to stand by my side." His gaze softened slightly. "It's true, we don't have Daliphs or Kings, but I'm a first daughter of a first daughter of a first daughter going back as long as tribal memory. You'd have standing, Badru. People would respect you."

He looked away, chewing the inside of his cheek. "What if I didn't want that? What if I wanted to prove myself without you?"

K'lrsa stepped back, crossing her arms against the pain in her chest. She shook her head, turning away from him.

"K'lrsa, wait. I didn't mean it like that." He grabbed her shoulders and pulled her back to him, whispering in her ear. "I love you. You know that. But I have to prove myself. I have to earn my own place. I've never relied on anyone else before and I don't want to start now."

She pulled away from him. "No? Your being the Daliph had nothing to do with your grandfather? Or the actions of your grandmother?" She grabbed a bag from the floor and threw it over her shoulder. "Fine. You want to prove yourself, then prove yourself. You can be just another young warrior, one of hundreds. Just like I would've been just another young slave girl if you hadn't made me your dorana."

"It's not the same, K'lrsa."

She glared at him. "It is. I only had status here because of you. Without that, I was nothing. If you come to the tribes, you can come as my mate—a man I've judged to be my equal, a man sent to me by the gods to help rescue my people—or you can come as Badru, a trained warrior willing to lend his sword to help protect the tribes. Your choice."

She turned to Herin. "Can we go now? I need to get out of here."

Herin nodded to Garzel. "The stables. We need the horses."

He opened the panel and ducked into the passage. K'lrsa started to follow.

"K'lrsa, wait." Badru grabbed her arm, but she shook him off.

As she followed Garzel, she cursed herself for being such a fool. She should've known Badru had never seen her as an equal.

He didn't want to be with her no matter what. He only wanted to be with her if he could be the all-powerful Daliph and she could be the pretty little songbird in a golden cage sitting by his side.

He didn't understand that she was the desert hawk, as much a warrior and leader as he was.

Maybe more so.

Garzel grunted something at her. She still didn't understand his words, but she knew he was urging her to give Badru time.

She shook her head, dismissing his comment.

He gave her a light shove and grunted again.

"Okay. Fine."

She sighed.

He was right. Badru had lost everything today. She needed to give him time to grow and accept that his life had changed forever just like hers had on the day her father died.

She laughed at herself.

What had she expected? That their love story would be like all those tales she'd grown up on? The girl meets her hero and he's perfect and she's perfect and they live happily ever after in a perfect world together?

She'd known better than that.

But it was one thing to know that's not how life was and another to live it.

She shoved those concerns aside for another day. Right now she needed to escape this place before the former Daliph found them and killed them all.

<u>101</u>

It was the middle of the night by the time they finally crept their way down a small hallway near the stables. They'd managed to avoid Aran's men, but just barely.

They huddled together in the hallway, looking out at the stables. No one was around—it was absolutely silent, the horses asleep in their stalls.

Except for Fallion who raised his head and nickered in their direction. K'lrsa glanced around once more and then darted forward. "Shh, *micora*." She scratched his nose, closing her eyes as he nuzzled at her ear in happy affection.

K'var stepped out of the neighboring stall, sword drawn. "I knew you wouldn't be able to resist taking your precious horse with you."

K'lrsa backed away from Fallion and dropped into a fighting stance, circling away from him until his back was to Herin, Garzel, and Badru. She saw Badru moving forward and shook her head sharply.

This was her fight, not his.

Badru took another step towards her and Garzel grabbed him and pulled him back into the darkness of the hallway.

"Alone?" She asked. She glanced around, careful to keep an eye on K'var as she did so. "That doesn't seem like you."

He shrugged, waving the blade in a lazy circle near his leg. "I figured one girl and her horse were no match for a trained Rider with a sword."

K'lrsa smiled, channeling the flare of rage she felt at his dismissal of her status as a Rider. "Good. Because you and I have a matter to settle."

"Do we?" He circled to her right, waving the sword to distract her, but she focused on his hips, ready for any sign that he was about to attack.

"You killed my father."

He laughed. "Oh that. Miserable waste of air, that man."

She suppressed the anger that burned through her veins and threatened to blind her.

Now wasn't the time to let her emotions rule her. If she did that, she'd lose.

And she wasn't going to lose.

"I swore a vow to Father Sun that I'd kill the man responsible for his death."

"Did you now?" He lashed at her with the blade, barely even trying, the swipe a lazy flicker of movement.

She easily danced out of his way.

"Pity you made a promise you can't keep, but I'd expect nothing less from B'nin's daughter."

K'lrsa danced aside as he slashed at her knee, this time a fast strike, aiming to injure. While he was overextended from the blow, she leapt and kicked him in the chest. He stumbled backward.

He recovered quickly, raising an eyebrow as he reassessed her. "He begged for mercy, you know. Cried like a little baby for me to spare his life."

K'lrsa felt white-hot rage fill her and fought to push it back.

K'var laughed. "Your father was a sniveling coward."

He slashed at her again, this time aiming for her head. K'lrsa ducked under the blow and caught him with a strike to the jaw as she came back up.

"No, he didn't." She danced backward. "I found him, you know. *Before* he died. I freed him."

K'var's eyes widened in surprise.

"You failed, K'var. In everything." She smiled at him, smirking, daring him to attack her again.

He did, rushing at her with the sword held high over his head in a double grip, slashing down at her. "Not everything."

K'lrsa rolled to the side, kicking his legs out from under him as he passed. "How so?"

She danced backward, waiting for him to stand, knowing she should end this now, but desperate to hear what more he had to say.

"The Daliph—the true one, not your little upstart lover—is sending an entire army against the tribes. Not just five hundred troops like I asked for, but five thousand. The White Horse Tribe and all the others that stand against me will be destroyed."

She shivered, glancing towards the darkened hallway where Herin, Garzel, and Badru waited.

"When?"

K'var laughed. "Like you can do anything to save them now."

He slashed at her again. "I should let you go. Let you run home to cry in your mother's lap until they come for you. But you'd never arrive in time. The word goes out in the morning. Every soldier within three days' ride of the border will descend on your tribe. Meanwhile, you'd never make it past Boradol before someone stopped you. A woman. Alone. On a horse?"

He smirked. "Too bad you won't be there to see it."

K'lrsa circled him, holding her rage close to her chest, refusing to lash out at him now.

She waited.

And waited.

K'var shrugged and launched another slashing attack, this one aimed at her thigh. She dodged the blow and slammed her elbow into the back of his neck and then, before he could react, she spun around, driving her knife—the same knife she'd used to kill her father—into his back and through his kidney.

She twisted the knife and yanked it free.

K'var dropped to the ground at her feet. "Too bad *you* won't be there to see it, K'var."

She started to shake as she stared down at his body, feeling colder than she ever had before.

She'd thought that when she finally killed the man who'd killed her father it would all be better. She'd feel some sense of joy or relief. She'd be happy again.

But she wasn't.

She didn't feel anything.

102

Badru ran to her side and pulled her into an embrace. She leaned into him, closing her eyes, grateful for the comfort and warmth.

"Enough you two." Herin opened Midnight's stall. "We can't stand here all night."

K'lrsa reluctantly pulled away from Badru, her hands running down his arms until just their fingertips were touching. She stared into his bright blue eyes.

"Pzah, fools in love. Get on with it, girl. There are saddles in the back of the tack room. One gold, one silver. They're on a table against the far wall. Bring them."

K'lrsa hurried to fetch the saddles. They were small, not much more than a padded bit of fabric with a few thin strips to secure them to the horses, but finely made. The stitching shone in the faint light of the torch that lit the space.

As she picked them up, something rustled behind her.

K'lrsa whirled around, knife in hand, to see the young slave girl with the birthmark, cowering in the corner by the door.

"Don't worry. I won't hurt you."

The girl huddled in on herself, her eyes rolling back in her head like a skittish horse.

K'lrsa looked out at the stables, but Herin was talking with Garzel again.

She knelt down in front of the girl. "You knew, didn't you? That the former Daliph was alive?"

The girl nodded. She pointed at her mouth.

"That's why they cut out your tongue?"

The girl nodded again.

K'lrsa shook her head. "That man has so much to answer for…"

Herin came to the doorway. "What's wrong? What's taking so long?"

"Nothing."

K'lrsa stood, blocking Herin's view of the girl, but Herin pushed past her and glared down at the child who scrambled away from her, knocking over a stand of horseshoes with a loud clanging noise.

"Give me your knife." Herin held out her hand, her gaze fixed on the girl.

"No."

"She can't live. She's seen us."

K'lrsa stepped between the girl and Herin. "No. Leave her be. She can't speak. The old Daliph took her tongue."

"So?" She glanced back towards Garzel. "There are other ways to communicate."

"I won't let you, Herin. There's been enough death for one night."

Herin looked at her with a slight smirk. "She's just a slave. Expendable."

K'lrsa looked away, ashamed that she'd thought even for one moment of sacrificing a slave to save Badru. "No one is expendable, Herin."

Herin nodded. "Fine. But you're making a mistake. Now let's go."

K'lrsa waited until she was sure Herin wasn't going to come back for the girl and then followed.

It might be a mistake to let the girl live, but it was a mistake she was willing to make.

As they saddled up Fallion and Midnight, the young girl darted away down a nearby hallway.

Herin raised an eyebrow as she watched her go, but didn't say anything else.

103

K'lrsa listened for the sound of running steps that would signal soldiers coming to arrest them as she finished saddling Fallion.

She didn't think the girl would betray them, but what did she really know about her?

At last, they had the horses saddled and the carry bags that Herin had packed slung across their shoulders, the heavy weight of whatever she'd brought resting against each of their hips. K'lrsa wondered why they didn't use saddlebags, but Herin was in no mood for questions.

"Ready?" K'lrsa reached for Fallion's reins.

"Wait." Herin rustled through the bag at her hip. "Here."

She shoved something at K'lrsa, not meeting her eyes.

K'lrsa took the object and held it up. It was a moon stone, strung on a blue silk cord.

"Where did you get this?" She rubbed the stone between her thumb and forefinger, relishing its welcoming warmth.

"It was L'dia's." Herin wouldn't meet her eyes. "You gave her yours. It seems fair you should have hers."

"You've had it all this time?"

Herin glared at her. "It took some time to find it, but yes. Couldn't exactly walk around wearing it now, could I?"

And hadn't exactly given it back to her sister when she sold her to Harley, had she?

K'lrsa felt a gentle prod from the stone, a rebuke at her judgement of Herin. She closed her eyes and took a deep breath.

The stone was right. This was a special gesture. Herin could've kept it for herself, but she hadn't.

"Thank you, Herin." She pulled Herin into a quick hug.

Herin stiffened in surprise. "We don't have time for that."

K'lrsa smiled and gave Herin a kiss on her wrinkled, angry cheek.

She studied the stone for a moment and then ripped off the servant's robes she'd been wearing. If she was going to die, she'd die a Rider not hiding and cringing like a servant.

She tied the stone around her neck, grateful to once more feel the comforting presence of a moon stone against her skin.

It felt different from her own somehow, but familiar nonetheless.

Now she was truly a Rider once more.

She grabbed Fallion's reins and looked to Herin, Garzel, and Badru. "Let's go home."

104

The moon was full, dominating the sky above them, as they finally led their horses through the entrance K'lrsa had entered what seemed like a lifetime ago.

Garzel walked in front of them, a sun stone at his neck. She didn't know how he did it, but somehow he used the stone to cloak their movements. Not many people were out, but none looked at them. A man even almost walked into them until turning aside at the last moment as if he'd suddenly remembered something he needed to do down a dark, empty alley on their right.

They walked through the gates of Toreem without anyone stopping them; the guards didn't even look up from the game of dice they were playing.

K'lrsa had known the stones were capable of far more than just finding the occasional shelter in the desert, but she'd never known they could do this. So much knowledge had been lost when the Summer Spring Tribe was destroyed.

Once across the bridge, K'lrsa and Herin mounted Fallion, and Badru and Garzel mounted Midnight. They rode towards Boradol as the moon made its slow way across the sky.

K'lrsa stared at the distant walls of the town, despairing.

They had so far to go to reach the tribes and they'd have to travel by night, sneaking and hiding their way across the entire Daliphate while the Daliph's messengers rode at high speed, changing horses as they went, carrying her tribe's death with them.

Herin tapped her shoulder. "This is good enough. Stop here."

She nodded to Garzel who dropped down from behind Badru and walked around in front of Midnight.

K'lrsa looked to Badru for an explanation, but he seemed just as confused as she was.

Garzel pulled his sun stone off and held it to the small white teardrop mark between Midnight's eyes.

He grunted softly, the sounds he made a gentle chant. The stone in his hand started to glow, a brilliant yellow like the midday sun on a hot summer's day.

K'lrsa looked away, the echo of the stone's brilliance lingering against her eyelids.

Someone shouted from the direction of Toreem and she glanced back to see guards standing on the wall, pointing in their direction.

"We have to go." K'lrsa started to urge Fallion forward, but Herin stopped her.

"Patience, child. Either this works or we die here. Or at sunrise, or in a few days, or in a few weeks. This is our only hope. It's our only chance to escape Aran and save your tribe."

K'lrsa watched men ride out from the gates of Toreem, galloping towards them, swords drawn.

They had to go.

Now.

The blinding light faded and Garzel stepped away from Midnight. He stared up at Herin and shook his head.

Whatever he'd tried, it hadn't worked.

K'lrsa looked back towards Toreem. The men were gaining on them, whipping their horses to full speed. They'd never catch Fallion or Midnight on the run, but the horses were just standing there. Waiting.

For what?

Midnight shook himself and his coat shimmered like a thousand stars were hiding just beneath the surface.

And then…

And then wings appeared, sprouting from the space just behind where Badru sat. They were large, magnificent.

K'lrsa reached out a hand to touch them. They were real, but at the same time not. Solid under her fingers, but ephemeral, shimmering in and out of her vision.

Herin laughed, a sound like sunshine on a fresh spring. "It worked. Ah, thank the Lady, it worked."

Hooves thundered on the road behind them and K'lrsa glanced back to see a dozen guards racing towards them, close enough that she could see each one.

"Hurry, my love." Herin called.

Garzel grinned up at Herin as he stepped in front of Fallion and rested his sun stone against the small white tear drop on Fallion's forehead and murmured his chant.

Once more K'lrsa had to avert her gaze as the stone shone a brilliant white.

After he was done, Garzel mounted up behind Badru once more—there was just enough room for both of them to sit with their legs in front of Midnight's wings.

K'lrsa held her breath and waited for Fallion's transformation as the guards from Toreem came closer and closer. She glanced back, none had bows, at least.

Just when she was wondering if it had worked, Fallion shivered and the light of a thousand suns shimmered under his coat.

And then, he, too, sprouted wings. Beautiful, strong, wings.

K'lrsa laughed, the sound bubbling out of her.

"Later, girl. We have to get out of here now."

The guards were almost upon them, swords drawn. They'd slowed their horses at the sight of Midnight and Fallion, but they were still coming.

"Ready to see our horses fly?" K'lrsa asked Badru.

"Absolutely." His smile answered her own.

Fallion and Midnight raced across the grasslands, side-by-side.

The wind whipped K'lrsa's hair as she crouched low over Fallion's neck, Herin clinging close behind her.

"Faster, Fallion, faster." The words were lost in the wind of their passage as Fallion thundered across the plains, brilliant like the sun, full of grace and beauty, Midnight by his side, an embodiment of the evening sky over the Great Desert on a clear night.

Fallion leapt, his powerful legs launching him high into the sky. His wings beat downward, flattening the grass beneath him with each powerful stroke as he rose higher and higher.

All of K'lrsa's fears and worries and sorrows fell away behind her with each beat of his powerful wings.

She looked to Badru and saw the same carefree joy on his face.

They were free.

For this one moment, they were completely free.

GLOSSARY OF TERMS

Daliph: Leader of a Daliphate. Usually a hereditary position. The current Daliph can designate any of his sons or grandsons as his successor using any criteria he chooses.

Daliphate: One of seven territories ruled by a Daliph. (plural: Daliphana) Male-dominated society that engages in slavery and is heavily reliant on trade.

Dorana: One of a Daliph's chosen consorts. Considered the highest honor a woman can receive. The more dorana a Daliph has, the more powerful he is. A dorana can be released from her service. She is given an golden ear cuff for each year she serves as dorana that serves as part of her dowry.

Meza: Worn by the dorana as a symbol of the Daliph's power over her actions. Fastens to the thumb and index finger of each hand so that they form a circle.

Poradom: Guardian of the Daliph's dorana. A position of high regard in the Daliphana. Responsible for the training and care of the dorana. Trained warrior. (plural: poradoma)

Tiral: A long garment worn by the dorana to attend formal court appearances. Crocheted from gold in a fillet pattern. Has long sleeves that fasten to the middle finger of each hand with a fabric loop.

ALESSANDRA CLARKE

Alessandra Clarke has been losing herself in the worlds of fantasy novels since she was old enough to borrow her first book from the library.

She loves the worlds of Darkover, Valdemar, and Pern and wishes she could live a hundred lives just so she could read all the books on her to-be-read shelves while still having time to write, take her pup to the dog park, and see her friends and family.

You can reach her at aclarkewriter@gmail.com or online at www.alessandraclarke.com.